TAKE ME UNDER

TRUSTFALL
BOOK 1

DAKOTA WILLINK

This book is an original publication of Dakota Willink, LLC
Copyright © 2025 by Dakota Willink

All Rights Reserved.
In ordinance with the United States Copyright Act of 1976, no part of this book may be reproduced, scanned, or distributed in any printed or electronic form without permission of the publisher. Please do not participate in or encourage unlawful piracy of copyrighted materials in violation of the author's intellectual property.

Take Me Under | Copyright © 2025 by Dakota Willink

This is a work of fiction. Names, characters, places, and incidents either are the product of the author's imagination or are used fictitiously, and any resemblance to actual persons, living or dead, business establishments, events, or locales is entirely coincidental.

Cover art by Dragonfly Ink Publishing Copyright © 2025

ALSO BY DAKOTA WILLINK

SHAMELESS BILLIONAIRE CLUB

(Billionaire Dark Romance)

THE STONE SAGA

Heart of Stone

Stepping Stone

Set In Stone

Wishing Stone

Breaking Stone

TRUSTFALL TRILOGY

Take Me Under

Take Me Darkly

Take Me Forever

FADE INO YOU SERIES

Untouched (New Adult Romance)

Defined (Second Chance Romance)

Endurance (Sports Romance)

STAND ALONE BOOKS

The Sound of Silence (Dark Romantic Thriller)

"You may be deceived if you trust too much, but you will live in torment if you don't trust enough."

FRANK CRANE

To the Ellicottville OGs…

Cassidy London, Patricia D. Eddy, Gina Azzi, S.B. Alexander, Brooke Montgomery, Diana A Hicks, Kat Mizera, Melissa Ivers, and Echo Grayce.

For giving me the courage to trust again.

CHAPTER ONE

Anton

Bass vibrated through the underground club, the lighting pulsing in time with the music. Flashes of purple, green, and red sliced through the crowd, transforming the dance floor into something electric. Club members moved with a grace that bespoke privilege, and the air was thick with a heady mix of expensive cologne, sex, and secrets. Inside the building, it was impossible to tell day from night, but the rising and setting of the sun didn't matter when desires were at play. Club O was always open for business.

I stood just inside the entrance to the main gathering area, a silent spectator to the clandestine world before me. I watched a leggy blonde emerge from a set of steps leading up from The Dungeon, a space reserved for those exploring less than traditional sexual fantasies. She sauntered next to an attractive dark-haired woman I recognized immediately. Having no interest in the blonde, I settled my attention on the brunette. I had a thing for them. Always have and always will.

This one was clad in a short, barely there, black leather skirt. It gripped her hips, emphasizing the curves that would make the throat of any man turn dry. Her emerald silk tank left little to the imagination, the flowy fabric brushing against taut nipples. She met my gaze and winked.

The woman's name was Amber Hawthorne, heiress to a popular fashion clothing line and a regular at Club O. She'd been trying to get me into bed for the better part of a year. But play with her was never going to happen. Not that Amber wasn't tempting. On the contrary, her hourglass figure would look perfect sliding up and down the length of my cock.

But I had boundaries, and my number one rule was to never do anything that could jeopardize the club. Having sexual relations with a club member was a risk. Should any of them want more than one night from me, they'd find themselves disappointed. That disappointment could lead to scorn and vengeance. And what did they say about a woman scorned? It just wasn't a chance I was willing to take. Not when I'd worked so hard to get where I was. She, along with every other member of Club O, would have to look elsewhere to satisfy their desires.

Amber sashayed past me and headed toward the main vestibule near the exit. She paused at the statue of Venus, the goddess of sexuality, and glanced in my direction once more. I took note of the green silicone band around her wrist. It signaled that she was open to anyone interested, and a coveted unicorn to members of the club, there to make someone's dreams come true.

I looked away, not wanting to encourage her, and entered the posh main area on the ground floor.

Several silhouettes moved on the dance floor to the DJ's bewitching mix of *The Elephant* by Lxandra. The lighting in the club was deliberate, casting everything in seductive shadows.

Business was slow this early in the day, but I was pleased to see members lingering about. If they were still here at nine in the morning, it meant their night had gone exactly as planned. And as long as the members stayed happy, the referrals would follow.

Membership to Club O was granted solely through exclusive referrals. I wouldn't have it any other way. Word of mouth was how I maintained anonymity. To the outside world, the historic building that housed Club O was nothing but gated private property. It was just steps away from the chaos of the city that never sleeps, but New Yorkers barely gave it a second glance.

It took me years to reinvent the abandoned 150-year-old French Evangelical Church, which was only the last of many transformations it had undergone in its lifetime. The irony of what this building had become wasn't lost on me. Once occupied by the Catholic Church, French Evangelical immigrant settlers took it over in the late 1800s. Their pastors emphasized personal salvation and virtue more than ritual and tradition, believing in sexual abstinence and promoting a virginity pledge. Masturbation was forbidden, as it was thought to bring on impure sexual thoughts. It bemused me to think about what these holier-than-thou church folk would say about what had become of their place of worship.

The building had changed hands many times over the century, going from one religious organization to another. After a fire in 1962, the church was abandoned and sold for auction to a man named Jerry Arnold, one of the vilest humans to ever walk the earth. He had turned the marble basilica into what could only be described as a brothel. It was home to prostitutes and their pimps, the walls seeing more abuse than pleasure.

My fists clenched as memories tried to resurface. It was as if a branding iron had seared the images of what once was into my soul. I pushed them back, refusing to give my nightmares any room in my consciousness. Jerry was dead, and the seedy whore house laden with the stench of despair had ceased to exist over a decade ago—thanks to me.

I'd given the old building new life. It was now Club O, the name inspired by *Story of O*, an erotic novel written by French author Anne Desclos. Like the book, one might consider it a secret society. A person needed a referral to be considered, and only the wealthy elite were permitted access for a hefty fee. The sex was consensual—never bought and sold—and the scents of wealth and power were everywhere, intoxicating and dangerous. Discretion was everything. And always lingering in the charged atmosphere was a silent understanding that this was a space where secrets were traded as freely as the expensive champagne that flowed like liquid gold.

As I made my way to a seating section in the corner of the room, I glanced over at the bouncer standing near the bar. His eyes swept the room for any would-be concerns before settling on me. Rowan, the military veteran who was added to the payroll six months ago, gave me a silent nod before resuming his surveillance.

I sat down at a plush corner booth with my laptop. The stock market would open in a matter of minutes, its bell signaling the official start of my workday. Being the owner of a sex club kept things interesting, but that was only a fraction of my identity. Smart maneuvers in the crypto market was how I'd amassed the majority of my wealth. The digital currency had pulled me out of the gutter, allowing me to invest in more traditional stocks, and making me one of the wealthiest people in the country practically overnight.

"There you are," said a man whose voice I'd recognize anywhere.

I glanced up at Zeke Kristof, a friend and confidant I'd hired as my personal bodyguard. Our relationship dated back to some of my earliest memories, and he knew every secret there was to know about me. Hiring someone with his background and training wasn't cheap, but he was the only person I trusted with my life.

"Morning, Zeke." I nodded a thanks as he set a freshly brewed mug of black coffee in front of me.

"It's Monday. I went to your office in Cornerstone Tower first. I expected you to be there."

"I didn't feel like working there today."

"I don't suppose that has anything to do with a certain empty glass case in your office at Cornerstone," Zeke said with a knowing look.

I pressed my lips together, frowning from irritation. The case Zeke referred to should have had a Brutus Denarius secured within the glass walls. It was a rare ancient coin that had become my obsession for the better part of a year, but my recent attempt to obtain it had been a bust. I may have made my fortune on the currency of the future, but my passion was for the ancient. I was fascinated by it.

"Don't get me started," I snarled, turning to look at the stock tickers on my computer screen. I shifted my attention from traditional Wall Street and tabbed over to view today's cryptocurrency prices by market cap. Only a little after nine, and my eyes were already beginning to burn with fatigue. It was my own fault. I'd stayed up too late, restless and bored with everything around me.

I frowned again, reminded of the prior evening, and how that boredom had resulted in a night with Lisa Wells, a high-ranking staff member to the Governor. I'd gone to dinner at Krystina's Place, a local Italian restaurant renowned for catering to the rich and famous. I could eat there in peace, knowing that any meddling member of the press would be stopped at the door. Lisa and I had struck up a conversation at the bar after having both ordered a boulevardier as our pre-dinner drink. That one bourbon mixer quickly turned into two, then to dinner and wine, before we ended up at a nearby hotel.

The conversation had been easy, and the sex was great. Finding both was a rarity in my world. Lisa was one of the better lays I'd had in a while—perky, tight breasts and content to let me dominate her in bed. I considered myself an attentive lover, acutely aware of a woman's physical needs as well as my own. But it ended there. I wasn't the type to engage in flirtatious phone calls, and I'd never once sent a woman flowers. Bringing a date back to my penthouse was out of the question, and sexual encounters were limited to a single evening for my own protection. I trusted nobody—especially women who only had my wallet in mind.

This was why last night shouldn't have happened. Lisa was young—too young to understand that I had no desire to be tied down. I kept a tight lid on my past and personal interests, and only a select few knew who I really was or where I'd come from. I was an enigma among the elite social circles. All anyone knew was that I was a wealthy bachelor whose status had rapidly advanced with the rise of crypto. I liked being single and had no intention of committing to anyone, let alone a mid-twenty-something with dollar signs in her eyes. As easy as things had been between us, she'd inevitably wanted more beyond last night. They always wanted more.

"So that's it then? You're just going to let it go?" Zeke asked, bringing my attention back to the Brutus Denarius.

I blinked, pushing Lisa from my mind and refocusing on the conversation.

"Of course not. I'm just going to give the coin chasing a break for a bit."

"What if I told you there was another opportunity to get it?" he pushed.

"I'm not going halfway around the world again, Zeke. Unless you have a local connection—"

"I do."

My curiosity piqued, I closed the laptop and leveled my eyes with his.

"You have my attention. Go on."

Rather than answering, he slid a piece of paper across the table to me. It was a computer printout of a news article. It was dated five years ago, but the top was cut off and I couldn't tell the name of the publication. Picking it up, I began to read.

"Excavations are always ongoing around the Forum. However, for Dr. Martinelli, this particular dig is personal. The Oxford grad was candid when we visited the site, reminding us how heated the debate is about the burial place for Cleopatra and Mark Antony. Martinelli believes their ashes were buried in the Forum, a point of great contention amongst historians, and he was no stranger to receiving ridicule and harsh judgments from his peers. In 1988, the distinguished archeologist was rumored to have found a collection of Roman coins inside an ancient jug in Greece. The Brutus Denarius is said to have been among them. Experts would normally study such findings before sending the rare coins to a museum for historical preservation, but those familiar with the situation say they were never turned over."

"Other than the mention of the Brutus Denarius, I'm not sure why this is relevant. The article is over five years old."

"The article also mentions a person of interest, Dr. Martinelli, an Italian archeologist. If the rumors are true, and he actually has a collection of rare coins, it might be easy to find out. He's supposed to attend this year's Met Gala."

"And when is that?"

"Today."

"Fuck, Zeke. Today? I might be on the Forbes Top 100, but even *I'm* not that good. It'll be hard to gain entrance at this late hour."

"As it so happens, I already made a few calls to do exactly that. Alexander Stone had the connection I needed. Consider yourself on the guest list."

I raised an eyebrow. Alexander was a high-profile club member. He and his wife were darlings of social media, influencers, and tabloids. He was one of the richest men in the country and was heavily involved in real-estate investments. He had offered me advice on ways to diversify my money and, over time, I'd begun to consider him a friend.

"You've been a busy guy this morning, haven't you?"

"It was nothing," Zeke said mildly.

"Are you going to put on a tux and come with me?"

"No can do, boss. I was only able to secure a single reservation. Besides, I have background checks to run if we hope to increase the security staff as planned."

I shook my head, annoyed that more hiring was necessary. Rumors about the club's existence had begun traveling within circles I didn't like. That was all thanks to a nosy reporter, Mac Owens, who was obsessed with finding every bit of dirt he could on Alexander Stone. So far, the rumors were only whispers. Thankfully, we'd managed to feed Owens false information that led him away from the trail. But the damage had been done. It didn't matter that Owens had no proof of the club's existence. He'd insinuated enough in his reporting to perk the ears of anyone familiar with the lifestyle. Increased attempts at falsifying membership credentials had forced us to beef up security for the safety of our existing members.

"I wouldn't be caught dead at the Met Gala if it weren't for this coin. You know that, right? Too many fucking cameras." I paused and shook my head. "God, I hate paparazzi."

"Don't I know it," he said with a hint of arrogance that had me raising a brow. "That's why I also arranged it so you can skip the red carpet. A service door will be left open for you. You can slip in and avoid the worst of the pomp and circumstance."

With a sardonic smile, I leaned back in the booth and crossed my arms.

"I suppose you'll be asking for a raise soon."

Zeke tossed me a lopsided grin. "Only if you're offering."

CHAPTER TWO

Serena

The sun dipped low on the horizon, bathing the sky in hues of pink and orange, casting a warm glow over the streets of New York. The city was alive with people, cars honking, and the occasional dog bark. It was a living force—loud, unapologetic, and always in motion. The concerto of humanity pulsed through my veins.

The twenty-first-century city was a far cry from anything I could see back home in Lucca, Italy. The modernness was just one of the many things I loved about New York, and it made me wish I'd visited more often.

On this particular evening, the streets were bustling with people dressed in their finest. Some were on their way to dinners, Broadway shows, or other forms of entertainment. For me, the Met Gala was my destination. I never imagined myself attending such an event. It was too prestigious, catering to those who lived much differently than I did. They would arrive at the red carpet in expensive cars, while I took a cab until I was close enough to walk.

A cool breeze kissed my skin. The early May air was warmer than usual, but I still felt a chill on my naked arms. I rubbed them vigorously, hoping to warm a bit as I approached the Metropolitan Museum of Art. I strolled past the long line of trees and benches. When I got closer to the wide granite staircase, I hesitated. I'd walked up the famous steps plenty of times in the past, and normally would have enjoyed seeing people playing instruments, reading books, or simply lounging while contemplating life.

But tonight was different.

Tonight, I wanted to avoid the steps at all costs. The casual variety of people who usually occupied them would no longer be there, replaced by an electric atmosphere of cameras and flashbulbs. I couldn't help but feel a sense of anticipation for the possibilities ahead. Only the rich and famous would ascend the grand steps this evening—which was precisely why I needed to avoid them. I was far from being worthy of the elite.

The fact was, I had never been as financially strapped as I was at that moment. It was why imposter syndrome invaded my psyche. I knew I didn't belong here, despite my cultured façade.

I recalled the care and attention I'd put into my appearance earlier that evening. The expense of having my hair styled and my face made up was worth it. My eyes were smoldering, almost seductive, and my dark locks coiffed into a sophisticated updo. I'd hardly recognized myself in the mirror at my hotel room. A luxury salon visit was a rarity, but I knew my limitations. I seldom required fancy hair and makeup in my line of work, making my experience with so much fuss practically non-existent. Calling in professional help for tonight had been a must if I wanted to make the best possible impression.

My hand drifted up to smooth a strand of hair, now curled and pinned elegantly with a few loose tendrils cascading down the center of my neck and upper back. They ended just above the blood-red corset, intricately laced with a spill of scarlet chiffon that flowed dramatically over my legs to brush the ground. The lavish gown and heart-shaped ruby necklace were donations from the renowned French designer, Madeleine Toussaint.

Madeleine was my mother's childhood friend who had worked tirelessly to make her way in the fashion industry. She'd had a deep appreciation for my father's archaeological work before his passing, and it was by her invitation that I was here tonight. I had a need, and she had design skills to show off.

She understood the severity of my situation and what was at stake. The bedside promise I'd made to my father just days before his death required money—and lots of it. Archeological excavations didn't come cheap, and Madeleine had assured me that the guest list for the Met Gala would open the doors to the funding I desperately needed to keep the Rome project going.

Still, I couldn't shake my nagging doubts. As beautiful as the hand-sewn dress was, I had half a mind to ball up the cumbersome train—which, for all intents and purposes, was ridiculous—hail a cab to the JFK airport and return to Italy. The red carpet and glare of the cameras were not for an introvert like me. Being in the company of celebrities, musicians, fashion designers, and models would never be my forte, but I had little choice but to endure it. Only the ultra-wealthy had the resources to support my father's work, and bumping elbows with them was far more important than my discomfort or awkwardness. I had to pretend to fit in and act as if I knew what I was doing.

Focusing on putting one foot in front of the other, I forced myself to continue toward the grand staircase. However, the closer I got, the more my heart began to race. Anxious jitters threatened to overwhelm me, and I began to sweat to the point of feeling feverish.

Maybe if I just take a minute to sit down and collect myself...

I glanced over my shoulder at the bench I'd just passed. I

could sit for a moment. But before I did, I paused, realizing the dress would make it quite a challenge. It wasn't just the train that was an issue—the voluminous layers of chiffon were bulky and cumbersome.

I pressed my lips together tightly and started the awkward attempt at gathering the skirt's layers. I tried to move them to one side so I could sit, but the corset was so snug, I could barely bend to collect the chiffon. My stomach pitched, and I absently wondered if it was something I ate or because the dress was pulled too tight.

I released an impatient breath but suddenly stopped when I realized I was being watched. I glanced up to meet the observing eyes of a man in a bespoke tuxedo. He stood under the shade of a tree less than twenty feet away, staring with rapt curiosity.

Fabulous. Just what I need right now. An audience.

I tried to act indifferent to his attention, but something made me pause and take a second glance.

The man was anything but ordinary. He was striking in the most captivating way. I judged him to be close to my age or slightly older, perhaps around thirty-five. He was tall, standing well over six feet, impressive in his black tuxedo jacket, crisp white shirt, and solid black bowtie.

His dark brown hair was longer, but not too long, with natural waves curling at his collar. It was styled haphazardly, framing a tanned, chiseled face and sculpted square jawline. It gave him an air of refined elegance, yet there was something raw around the edges of all that masculine perfection. A hint of danger that made him even more alluring, reminding me of Henry Cavill circa 2012.

I'd encountered many attractive men throughout my life, but none had ever compared to the one standing before me. He was as intimidating as he was tempting, and I couldn't help but wonder what he'd look like without all that expensive clothing. I envisioned what it would be like to unfasten the buttons of his shirt and explore the span of his chest, over his shoulders, and...

I felt a sudden stirring deep in my belly, and my face flushed with heat.

What the hell was that?

The guy was gorgeous, but my physical reaction to him was a bit much—even if it had been a while since I'd last felt a man's touch. Ten months to be exact. But who was counting? I scolded myself for being so ridiculous.

I changed focus, intent on maintaining a modicum of grace as I resumed my attempt at sitting on the city bench. However, the pretense at poise was wishful thinking. To my horror, when I lifted the train, the pointed heel of my shoe caught one of the many hems, and I lost my balance.

"Oh!" I gasped, suppressing a curse as my flailing arms searched for something to hold onto. My current dilemma should have been predictable. The idea that I could ever be graceful in high heels and gown like this was laughable.

I braced myself for impact as the ground rushed to meet me.

But instead of falling onto hard concrete, I landed against the solid chest of my dark and mysterious observer. It was an embarrassing moment and incredibly cliché. Pretty woman falling into the arms of a handsome stranger. Only my life could resemble a Hollywood romcom.

However, my embarrassment was short lived, instantly replaced by the precipitous awareness of his firm grip—of one hand bracing my lower back and the other curling around my upper arm.

I inhaled sharply, the sudden intake of breath introducing me to his tantalizing scent. He smelled almost as good as he looked. It was an intoxicating, fresh combination of sexy male and decadent sin. A flush warmed my cheeks as our eyes met. His gaze was reserved and assessing, making me feel as if he could see through to my most intimate secrets.

I returned his stare, mesmerized by his incredible eyes. They were as dark as onyx with chocolate flecks that one could only discern if they were close enough—and boy, was I ever close. The intensity of his dark gaze sent a shiver down my spine, raising the hairs on the nape of my neck.

My pulse thrummed from his proximity. A perfect stranger should not arouse these feelings from me. I was oddly turned on in all the best ways, yet I couldn't recall a time in my life when I'd felt more humiliated. I wasn't sure how I was able to feel both at the same time.

"Are you alright?" he asked. His voice was as smooth as his appearance.

Unease etched across his flawlessly chiseled features, and I realized I was gawking at him like a smitten schoolgirl. He was devastatingly gorgeous—of that there was no doubt. But it was the potent sexual energy radiating from him that rendered me irrationally speechless.

I blinked twice and shifted slightly back, forcing myself to focus. Clearing my throat, I gave him a quick nod.

"I'm fine, thank you. It seems poofy layers are in vogue this season. I should have informed the dress designer about my terrible rapport with poof. We had a bad break up some years ago, and I swore I'd never go back."

A hint of a smile played at the corners of his mouth, almost as if he were holding back a chuckle. He glided his hand down the length of my arm, stopping near my elbow.

"Are you sure you're okay?"

"Yes, of course. Why?" I asked, biting down on my lower lip.

"Your pulse. It's racing."

"Is it?" I practically squeaked. I moved to pull my arm away, but he caught me and held firm to my hand.

Something dark smoldered in the depths of those ruthless eyes, and he seemed closer than he had been a few moments before. Our heads were only a foot apart, and I wondered if he would kiss me. Surely, I had to be mistaken. After all, we'd only just met, and I didn't even know his name.

Still, I couldn't stop myself from breathing in, needing to indulge in his scent once more. The tempting blend of pine and fresh water with his natural masculinity was a heady combination. It reminded me of that alluring smell of rain in the air just before a wicked storm.

Much to my disappointment, he stepped back until we were a respectable distance apart, but he continued to hold my hand in his. His fingers grazed my palm until I remembered I didn't have soft, feminine hands like most other women he probably interacted with. Mine were calloused from years of working in the dirt. Feeling self-conscious, I pulled my hand away.

His onyx eyes flashed, and his brows pushed together. If I wasn't mistaken, my action seemed to displease him.

"What's your name?" he asked.

"Serena."

"A name fit for a princess. I'm Anton."

Adonis. Apollo. Ares. Anton. Of course, his name would sound like it belonged to a mythical God. Why wouldn't it? Was Anton even the name of a God?

Someone in my line of work should know that answer, but the minute I'd laid eyes on this alluring man, my brain had turned to mush. I was utterly captivated by him. It was as if he had cast a hypnotic spell over me.

I bit my lower lip to stop swooning even more, then gave him a small smile.

"It's a pleasure to meet you, Anton."

"I can assure you—the pleasure is mine," he drawled.

Holy hell.

I fought the threatening blush and tried to ignore how his comment made me feel. The effort was in vain. Despite my best efforts, embarrassing heat flooded my cheeks. Between his affluent attire and ruthlessly handsome features, this man was way too sexy for his own good.

His eyes shifted to linger on the ruby around my neck before falling to the swell of my breasts. His gaze stayed there only briefly, but long enough for me to notice. I felt my flush deepen, but I didn't mind his slow appraisal. It didn't feel like inappropriate ogling but more like a show of appreciation.

"I'm on my way to the Met Gala. I assume that's where you're headed as well?" he questioned, looking pointedly at my dress.

"If I can muster up the courage to climb those steps, then yes. I'm here by invitation from a friend, the designer of my dress."

"Ah, I see. And your escort? Where is he, princess?" he prodded.

Escort? As in, my date?

I didn't think people used such formal terms anymore.

"Oh. Um...no escort. This is just business." My reply came out stilted and unsure. I couldn't quite understand why he was asking or calling me "princess," but it made my stomach flutter.

My father had used that term of endearment for me when I was a little girl. But with him, it was a fatherly thing said to his only daughter. With Anton, it took on a different meaning. Like I was the damsel locked in a tower and he was the rogue warrior sent to rescue me. After all, he had just saved me from a fall. What was he if not my knight in shining armor? I kind of liked the idea.

No. I *really* liked it—even though I knew I shouldn't. I was too busy to entertain fairytales.

My eyes focused on his, and I was instantly ensnared in his gaze once again. It caused my heart to do the sort of flip I hadn't felt since high school.

"All business and no play? Such a shame," he mused with a tsk-tsk.

"Not really. These things aren't my cup of tea."

"Oh?" he questioned with a raised brow.

"I don't fit in here. I mean, just look at me."

His eyes darkened.

"I am."

Jesus, Mary, and Joseph… So much seemed to be packed into those two little words, and I found myself blushing again.

"I just meant that these events are…" I fought a sigh of frustration as my foolish blathering continued. "I guess I don't… I don't know how to explain how I feel."

"Try me," he coaxed, as if it were so easy.

I looked away. I had a PhD, and I'd given countless lectures to hundreds of people, yet I could barely string more than four words together in front of this one man.

I bit down on my lower lip and contemplated how to describe my irrational fear of attending such a high-profile event, where I would be forced to interact with some of the world's most famous, influential, and wealthiest people. I was terrified of experiencing a monumental failure—a bitter defeat of everything I'd ever worked for. But worse, failure would mean I'd never follow through on my promise to my father.

Sweat began to bead on my brow, and my stomach lurched. For the second time in ten minutes, I thought I'd be sick. However, I wasn't so sure if it was from the tight dress or from my nerves. Perhaps it was neither. The feverish feeling had returned, and I was starting to think I was coming down with something. If I was going to be sick, I didn't want it to happen in front of him.

I brought my gaze back to meet his. The sexy stranger waited patiently for an answer I didn't feel comfortable giving.

"It's complicated." I tried to shrug off his question, suddenly overcome with the need to escape.

"Most things in life are, Serena." His gaze was heavy and

warm. It was like a blanket on the coldest winter day, making me want to get lost in all the comforts he could offer.

Still, I didn't want to admit my insecurities about not belonging—especially to someone who looked as confident as he did. This event was for the elite. For all I knew, he was among them, hailing from a prestigious lineage that I'd never measure up to. But at the same time, he didn't come across as an arrogant snob like one would expect from someone who appeared beyond approach. He seemed genuinely interested in hearing what I had to say.

"A lot is at stake," I said honestly. "There are investors here I need to connect with to keep the lights on. I know what to do and say, but I'm..."

Not good enough. Out of their league.

But I didn't say those words out loud. Instead, I paused and pushed my brows together in consternation. Something about this man made me want to divulge more about myself than I should.

"Go on," he encouraged.

"I guess I'm just not in a hurry to walk the red carpet. It's intimidating, and I'm awkward at these sorts of events," I admitted, pointing toward the museum.

"Is this your first time attending the Met Gala?" Anton asked, cocking his head to the side curiously.

"Yes, and surely it will be the last. You?"

"First time. This isn't really my scene either," he said. His eyes narrowed, and the set of his jaw tightened. "It's a bunch of rich people carrying little plates of food that will never get eaten, pretending to care about a cause while wearing ten-thousand-dollar suits and priceless designer dresses. It's become more about political statements and gaudy displays of wealth than anything else. Like you, I'm only here because I have a need. Otherwise, I'd find better things to do with my money. These celebrity events are all the same. Once you've been to one, you've been to them all."

I raised a brow at his cynicism, but I couldn't disagree.

"You're right about that. This isn't really all that dissimilar to other events I've attended, although none of them have been quite this grand. They were smaller scale with less media attention, but the pretenses and shows of wealth are all the same. You'd think attending things like this would get easier over time, but they don't. If anything, they've gotten harder for me." I looked down, focusing on an old, flattened wad of gum on the sidewalk. I wasn't sure why I was divulging so much, but I found myself continuing. "I guess you could say my insecurities rule me, even when I know the emotions are irrational."

"Emotions don't have to make sense, Serena. They just have to make themselves known," he stated as if it were that obvious. "You're a beautiful woman. You belong here as much as the next."

I slowly blinked twice, looking back up to meet his gaze as I processed his words. He was clearly flirting with me, yet there was something else to it as well. I'd lived in Italy long enough to see through smooth-talking Italian men, but this came across different. The heat of his stare stirred deep-rooted emotions, making me feel astoundingly exposed. It was as if he could see beyond my borrowed designer dress and ruby necklace, and lay bare every secret I'd ever held dear.

I looked down again, then gave him a brief sideways glance. I wasn't sure what game he was playing, but I wasn't here for it. I had no time for meaningless flirtation—if that's what this was. I needed to stay focused on what I set out to do tonight.

Reaching up, he placed his forefinger under my chin and tilted my head until all I could see were his endless onyx eyes.

"Do you know what a trustfall is?" he asked. His head tilted to the side as he carefully assessed me. His expression made me feel like a puzzle he was determined to solve.

My brow furrowed. I could deduce what it meant, but I wasn't sure how it would apply here.

"I'm sorry?"

"A trustfall. It's the ability to fall without questioning whether everything will be alright in the end. It means blindly jumping into uncomfortable situations and irrevocably trusting someone or something to catch you if you fall."

"Are you saying that I should just go in there and trust everything will be fine?"

"That's exactly what I'm saying. Although we only just met, you don't strike me as a delicate wallflower." He took my hand again and grazed his fingers along my calloused palm. "Sometimes pure grit is the thing that helps you fall when you least expect it. Trust yourself."

I pressed my lips together in a tight line. There may have been a time when I could do exactly as he suggested, but not now. Not anymore. Too much had changed, and too much was at stake.

"I don't think I can do that—at least not with the confidence you're suggesting."

Something dark flashed across his face before it was quickly masked. He seemed upset—perhaps even slightly angry. But then he pressed his lips together and nodded, seeming to come to a decision.

"Do you trust me, Serena?"

It was such an odd request from someone I'd just met.

"I don't know you, Anton" I replied hesitantly.

"I think we should remedy that," he stated. The corners of his mouth lifted slightly, his eyes showing just a hint of mischief before darkening with words unspoken. "Trustfall, princess. Let go and trust me to be your escort tonight."

I didn't know how I could wholly trust someone I barely knew—yet, strangely, I found myself wanting to do exactly that. Still, something told me that I wasn't just accepting his offer to escort me to the gala. He regarded me with curiosity and desire, a look that seemed to convey something deeper. It was as if he were demanding that I submit to unforeseen forces lingering just below the surface.

Trustfall.

The idea made me feel vulnerable and exposed, yet something in his unwavering gaze made me want to give in. The obsidian depths held a mesmerizing allure, and I found myself spellbound.

I wanted to do as he suggested even though my subconscious warned me to be cautious. I wanted to walk away from him and focus on what I came here to do, yet I also wanted to forget my obligations and give in to the feelings he provoked. He drew me in like a moth to a flame, making me both fascinated and wary. The internal tug of war was real. I was the epitome of opposites —a jumble of contradictions.

I took a deep breath, allowing my chest to expand as much as the tight bodice of my dress would allow, and tried to calm my hammering heart. Ignoring the warning voice in my head that said I couldn't afford this distraction, I accepted his outstretched hand.

Anton's eyes crashed into mine, and I allowed myself to give in—to trustfall.

"Okay, Anton. I'll trust you."

CHAPTER THREE

Serena

Anton smiled as if he'd just won a game a chess, and it made me wonder if this was a huge mistake.

"You should never do anything you don't want to do, princess. If a red carpet walk makes you uncomfortable, find another way."

"Once again, you make it sound so simple."

"That's because it is. Let me show you."

With my hand still in his, he turned away from the direction of the giant granite staircase and we began to walk.

"Where are we going?" I asked.

"We're eliminating hurdles one at a time until you begin to feel comfortable."

I had no idea where he was leading me, but I'd go along as long as it saved me from the scrutiny of harsh flashbulbs and the press.

A few moments later, we approached the ground-level entrance at 81st and 5th Avenue.

"This door is typically reserved for those requiring a step-free way to get into the building, whether it be for a handicap or otherwise," he explained. "But it's also used as a service entrance for large events."

Anton let go of my hand and tugged on the door handle. Considering the high-profile guests within the walls of the art museum, I expected it to be locked. When the door pulled open, I smiled.

"Today is our lucky day," I murmured.

Surprising me, he leaned in close. The brush of his jaw against my ear made my heart race. I could feel the whisper from his lips when he said, "There's no such thing as luck, princess. Only fortunate circumstances."

I angled away from him, flustered by his sudden close proximity, and released a small laugh. "Isn't that the same thing?"

He shrugged. "It's not luck if I knew the outcome. Like you, I want to avoid the press, so I arranged it so that the door would remain unlocked even after the caterers and organizers were finished with their preparations."

"You arranged it?" I questioned in surprise.

"I have friends in high places who can appreciate my need to enter unnoticed. I wanted to just walk across the street and slip in, leaving the press unawares. They have been ..." He paused, considering his words. "Well, let's just say the media has taken an interest in me recently. Inside the building is another matter entirely. The worst of the excess is on the steps—or so I've been told."

He casually motioned me inside. I tried to calm the pitter-patter of my heart as we made our way down a narrow corridor toward the main vestibule.

He dressed and acted the part of someone who belonged here. But if that were truly the case, he shouldn't have to sneak in through the back door. I took note of the mention that he'd walked here. No limos or fancy rides for him. That should have made him a little less intimidating, but it only seemed to make me more uneasy about my decision to blindly follow a strange man.

"Do you live nearby?"

"I live in a penthouse across the street."

A penthouse. On 5th Avenue. Of course, that's where he'd live. Where else would someone who looked like him take up residence?

"That's convenient," I said.

"It has its perks. What about you? You don't seem like you're from around here."

"That obvious, huh?"

He chuckled, the sound low and throaty as we continued to walk. It stole my breath away, causing a flutter in my belly. Everything about him was truly devastating, making it a struggle to feign the confidence I needed to continue speaking.

"That wasn't meant as an insult. New Yorkers just tend to stand out," he clarified.

"I was born in the States, but we moved around a lot for my father's work. If I can call any place my home, it would be Lucca, Italy. It's where my mother is."

"Is that where you live now?"

"Not full time, but I frequent there. Work requires me to spend most my time in Rome."

We passed through the Great Hall, under the three saucer-shaped domes. My shoes clicked over the marble mosaic floor as we walked under one of eight dramatic arches that sprung from giant limestone piers. I marveled at the design, wishing I had the time to study it further.

We continued on through a display of Egyptian artifacts toward the north side of the museum where the gala was to be held. When we reached the entrance, Anton stepped aside and ushered me ahead of him.

"After you, princess."

I hesitated before advancing, my nervousness rushing back. I hated to show weakness, but the truth was, schmoozing with donors always made me uneasy. Here it was even worse. This whole charade would highlight my shortcomings, which would surely lead to ultimate failure.

As if sensing my nerves, Anton squeezed my hand. I shifted my eyes to meet his intense gaze. My nerves didn't abate but seemed to shift focus. The heat in his stare made me restless in ways I wasn't sure I wanted to be, and I flushed.

"Trustfall," he reminded me quietly.

I smiled when he released my hand and moved his to the small of my back. It had been so long since anyone had touched me that way. I'd nearly forgotten how much I loved and appreciated the intimate gesture. I'd only just met him, but somehow, this stranger stirred a part of me that I'd long considered dead.

Asserting just a slight amount of pressure, he gave me an encouraging nudge. I walked through the entrance to the Costume Institute, and an otherworldly spectacle opened up before me. A gasp escaped my lips as I scanned the room. I felt as if I were Alice venturing through a looking glass into an extraordinary wonderland.

Floor lamps with shades crafted from enormous palm leaves were strategically placed around the periphery. A stunning centerpiece of four majestic elephants striped with rosy hues stood at the center of the room. They reared on their hind legs, gracefully perched atop a brilliant yellow base with their trunks raised high in perfect alignment. The elephants were constructed from tens of thousands of vibrant blooms arranged in a kaleidoscope of colors towering at least twenty-five feet high.

At the far end of the room, a triangle stage decorated with more lavish flowers hosted a band of musicians. The lead singer swayed with the microphone, a popular Billie Eilish song falling from her lips. Her voice was low and honeyed, the kind that wraps around you and makes the world fade away. The smooth and steady rhythm only seemed to amplify the lush atmosphere.

The scene was a bit outlandish yet truly breathtaking. It was the very definition of luxury, and unlike anything I had ever seen.

"Wow," I breathed quietly, and then turned to express my amazement to Anton.

However, before I could comment further, I was interrupted by a squeal followed by a familiar French accent.

"Ahhh! There you are, Serena!"

Startled, I turned toward the voice as Madeleine Toussaint approached me. I smiled, happy to see her.

"Hello, Madeleine," I said. She didn't have a train of chiffon trailing behind her. Instead, she wore a black rhinestone studded pantsuit. It was stylish yet practical, and more importantly, easy to maneuver in. While I was beyond grateful for everything Madeleine had done to get me here tonight, it would have been nice if I could have worn a less restrictive outfit. "Why have you dressed me up like a red cupcake, but you get to wear a sensible pantsuit?"

"Because tonight is not about me, *ma chérie*. It's about you," she declared in a matter-of-fact tone. She reached out to delicately lift the ruby heart pendant at my neck. She examined it for a moment before nodding her approval. Then, glancing toward Anton, she seemed to notice him for the first time. She gave him an appreciative once over. "Are you going to introduce me to your handsome date?"

"This is Anton," I said, suddenly realizing that I'd never

caught his last name. "Anton, this is Madeleine Toussaint, my dress designer and a family friend."

He extended a hand to her. "I'm delighted to meet you, Ms. Toussaint."

She raised a perfectly shaped brow. "Oh, I can assure you, *monsieur*. The joy is all mine."

When she batted her eyes, I nearly rolled mine but smiled with amusement instead. Even at the age of fifty-nine, she was a constant flirt. My mother would say it wasn't flirting, but just her French coming out—whatever that meant.

"Anton isn't my date. He and I just met on my way here."

"Ah, I see," Madeleine said with a nod. "I was waiting for you near the main staircase. I do not know how you managed to evade me!"

"I wanted to avoid the cameras, so I entered through a side door," I explained. She clucked her tongue at me in response.

"Pish posh. You are absolutely stunning. You were made to be captured on camera, and it does nothing for me if you aren't seen. I don't want you avoiding them all night."

My stomach tightened nervously at the reminder that she needed pictures of me wearing her esteemed dress. I hated having my picture taken. I must have had a mental lapse when I promised to pose tonight, but offered my assurance, nonetheless.

"I won't, Madeleine."

"Good girl. Now, turn for me so I can see all of you."

I playfully rolled my eyes and indulged her with a quick spin. Or at least, I attempted to. The train of my dress made it difficult to move with any haste. A sigh of frustration escaped my lips as I wondered if this was how Cinderella felt—all dressed up yet feeling more at ease in tattered rags. All I knew was that I couldn't wait for the moment when I could shed my glass slippers.

I attempted to flex my toes in the restrictive five-inch heels. My feet weren't actually encased in glass, but they sure felt like it. I seriously wondered how much longer I would be able to remain upright in the accursed shoes.

"Oh, Serena Martinelli, you are a vision," Madeleine said wistfully.

"I decided to splurge on hair and makeup at the last minute, and—"

"I'm sorry, but did you say Martinelli?" Anton interrupted.

I stopped the awkward twirl and glanced his way.

Not waiting for Madeleine to reply, I said, "Yes, that's me. Serena Martinelli."

"*Dr.* Serena Martinelli," Madeleine proudly corrected with an emphasis on my formal title.

Anton's eyes widened briefly before quickly recovering. They never strayed from my face, keeping focus on only me. Then his jaw hardened into a line of unmistakable irritation.

"Why do you ask?" I wondered, somewhat bewildered by his expression.

"No reason," he said curtly. "It was nice meeting you, Madeleine. And Serena, thank you for allowing me to escort you inside. Enjoy your night."

And with that, he turned and walked away. My brow raised over the abrupt departure.

Did I do something wrong?

"He's so lovely to look at. It's a shame to see him go, even if I do enjoy the view," Madeleine murmured. "Just met him, you say?"

"Yes, right outside. He..." I hesitated, not wanting to explain my near fall and all the subsequent events. I didn't know why, but my brief encounter with Anton felt special in some way, and I wanted to keep the details about our meeting private.

"He's a good friend to keep around, Serena. The minute you said his name, I knew who he was. He might try to hide from the press, but that handsome face can be recognized anywhere. Especially after he was included in the list of sexiest men alive by…" She pressed a finger to her chin. "Oh, I can't remember the name of the magazine, but it's a popular U.S. publication."

I blinked in confusion.

"He's really that well known?"

"My dear, are you going to tell me that you do not know who he is?" Her incredulous stare was nothing short of comical.

"I'm afraid I don't have a clue," I said with a laugh. Only select U.S. magazines made it into Italian circulation, but even if the magazine featuring Anton had been on the shelves in Rome, it was unlikely I would have paid much attention.

"That was Anton Romano. The magazine referred to him as a newly minted billionaire. All things considered, I assumed your meeting him was deliberate on your part. If you're looking for financial backers, he might be an interested party. The man was an overnight success. He made a fortune in cryptocurrency a few years back."

"Crypto?"

"That's right. Virtual money. It's changing the world—or so I'm told. I don't understand the concept. To me, money is a physical thing that you can hold. But I suppose it's all spent the same way no matter its form."

The sudden sound of loud voices caused me to look past Madeleine toward a crowd of people filtering in. Their chatter echoed throughout the room.

"Looks like the red carpet parade is over," I remarked.

"*Oui, oui.* Time to get this party going!" she said with an exaggerated clap of her hands. "I'll let you get to work. I spoke with Raul, the event organizer. He assured me he would seat you with people who might be interested in your cause. I looked over the seating chart when I arrived, and I approve. Your table is along the left wall, third row, second one in."

I followed where her finger pointed, and quickly noted how she said it was *my* table—not ours.

"Aren't you sitting with me?" I asked.

"Of course not!" She laughed as if the thought were preposterous. "Some designers like to sit with their muses, but that is not my style. You are my star here tonight, and you should be seated in a place of honor. I will be in my designated area mingling with my fellow designers. If all goes well, this evening will be a triumph for us both. We will catch up later. I know you will have the time of your life, my dear! Trust me."

With that, she swept away, leaving me alone as the room gradually filled with guests.

Damn her!

I had been relying on her to guide me through the evening. I was completely out of my depth and had no idea how to navigate a celebrity scene of this magnitude. I had hoped she would help ease me into the crowd.

Guests made their way to the tables, and the room filled quickly. I followed suit and headed in the direction Madeleine had indicated. I eyed the place settings on my approach, taking note of the bamboo utensils, floral-patterned china, and gold-rimmed champagne flutes atop a cerulean tablecloth. The stunning arrangement complimented the rest of the extravagant décor, reminding me once again how much I didn't fit in with such luxury.

I was the first to arrive at my table. I located the place card bearing my name, picked it up, and traced my finger over the gilded lettering before slipping the card into my red clutch purse as a keepsake to take home.

Glancing around the room one more time, I silently hoped I'd be able to locate Anton. I sighed to myself when I realized finding him now would be hopeless in the crowd that had filtered in.

"You're on your own tonight, Serena," I muttered to myself.

Anton's words from earlier filtered into my mind.

Trustfall.

Pulling out my chair, I shifted the layers of my dress to the side and sat as gracefully as I could while wearing a chiffon monstrosity. Using the back of my hand, I wiped the slight bead of sweat from my brow. The nauseous feeling was back, and if the body aches I was starting to feel were any indication, I was definitely coming down with something. I hoped to be able to keep whatever it was at bay for a little while longer, and prayed the evening would be a success.

CHAPTER FOUR

Anton

The sun had almost set, painting the sky a kaleidoscope of colors as I navigated the crowd and hurried down the museum stairs toward the street. Several people still lingered on the red carpet, all vying to get photos taken in their ostentatious clothing. I suppressed an eye roll as I breezed past a woman wearing a dress made of peacock feathers and leafy vines. Three men followed in her wake, each one balancing a section of ivy embellishments that made up her long train. The entire scene was ridiculous.

To help manage security at the gala, the surrounding area had been cordoned off for blocks. Disappearing into a crowd of pedestrians wasn't an immediate option, and it wasn't long before I was recognized. Camera flashes went off and reporters shouted questions at me, but I ignored them until they eventually fell back out of earshot. Their attention was precisely why I'd used a back entrance when I first arrived. I hadn't wanted the hassle, but I wasn't thinking about that in my haste to leave. I just had to get the hell out of there. Discovering who Serena was had left me disoriented and agitated.

Martinelli—Dr. Serena Martinelli.

I'd anticipated a meeting with an older gentleman, a seasoned archeologist as the article had implied, who I needed to convince to sell me the Brutus Denarius. Instead, I found myself face-to-face with a woman of mesmerizing beauty. With her flawless skin, deep blue eyes, and slender yet shapely figure wrapped in crimson, she didn't look like an archeologist. As hard as I tried, I couldn't picture her spending her days covered in dirt and searching for old bones. Yet, at the same time, she also didn't seem like the rest of the polished guests in attendance at the gala.

I thought back to the moment I'd first laid eyes on her. I had been unexpectedly stupefied, rendered speechless by a strange woman in red. I recalled the way the bodice of her gown clung to her slim body, the sparkling corset seeming more like a like a second skin. It cinched tight at the waist to accentuate her breasts and outline her every curve. Layers upon layers of fabric spilled from her hips, coming to a pool around her feet. I'd noted the toned muscular lines of her tanned shoulders and arms, and envisioned strong, lithe legs to match—legs that I wanted wrapped around me before we'd exchanged a word. I began to fantasize about sliding my hands under the layers of her ruby dress, roaming up her leg, pulling the fabric of her panties aside, and exposing her to my mercy.

Much to my annoyance, my cock twitched. There was something about her that affected me in the most inexplicable ways. She was both authentic and vulnerable—and I wanted her far more than I should considering I barely knew her.

I was a man who needed to have control of all things around me. Perhaps it was my background that made me that way. I supposed years of having no control over anything would do that to a person, but I never philosophized about it.

From the way I ran my business to the women I took to my bed, control was all I craved. I needed it like the air I breathed. It was that instinct that drove me to succeed in everything I touched. I researched and spotted trends, and I could anticipate things before they happened. That foresight was how I'd made my fortune.

For all the hype the media gave it, the Met Gala wasn't all that different from so many other events I'd been to. There were the handshakes, the top-shelf liquor, and the fake smiles. Everyone was sizing up the competition around them purely as a means to a selfish end. Everyone—and I mean everyone—wanted something. Including me. These events were as predictable as they were pretentious.

But I hadn't anticipated Serena Martinelli.

Despite her outward reservations, she managed to command the space around her. She had an elegance only seen in seasoned royalty yet maintained the innocence of a princess. She sounded American but there was a hint of an untraceable accent that signaled worldliness. She had mentioned Italy and years of moving around a lot, but her appearance was a true testament to the Mediterranean. Smooth shoulders that were made for kissing had been left temptingly bare, exposing tanned olive skin. Her nearly black hair had been fashioned up, leaving only a few ringlets to fall onto her back and cascade around her face.

Then there was her mouth—red and full. When I'd held her in my arms after her near fall, all I could think about was leaning in and biting her lower lip.

While she looked and dressed the part of a great Italian beauty, the callouses on her hands told a different story. I wanted to know how and why they'd gotten there. I wanted the story behind that just as much as I wanted to know why she needed investors. She was a mystery—a riddle that I was suddenly obsessed with solving.

She had unknowingly disarmed me, her every movement arousing deep, carnal desires. She'd upended every expectation I'd had for the evening. And the second I'd discovered her full name and title, my sole purpose for being at the gala had become uncertain. All I could think to do was make a quiet exit until I could clear my head and get my thoughts in order.

It shouldn't have mattered who I'd expected the archeologist to be. Man or woman, pivoting should have been easy. But I'd been caught off guard, and that wasn't something I was used to. She wasn't who I'd anticipated, and it bothered me more than I cared to admit.

I knew that once she found out I wanted something from her, the fragile trust we'd established could vanish in an instant if I didn't play my cards right. I needed a new plan that separated my physical attraction to the woman from the object of my desire—the Brutus Denarius.

I continued walking with no destination in mind, happy to be away from the buzz surrounding the Met. I gazed across the bustling street, not focused on anything in particular, and replayed the unexpected encounter with Serena over again in my mind. Her voice echoed through my thoughts as I tried to get a grip on why she had affected me so much. Taking a deep breath, I shook off the lingering unease.

In the fading light, I found myself at the edge of Central Park. The soft rustle of the trees provided a rhythmic counterpoint to the chaos of my thoughts. Perhaps the city had a way of revealing the unexpected, much like the woman who had left an unforgettable mark on my evening. My frustration grew, not at her, but at my own uncertainty. It was out of character for me.

Glancing at my Rolex, I frowned. I'd been gone from the

gala for close to an hour. I was wasting time. If Serena was *the* Dr. Martinelli who I'd been hoping to meet, and if she did, in fact, have the Brutus Denarius, meandering without purpose wasn't going to get me any closer to obtaining it.

"Fuck this. I'm going back," I muttered.

Turning around, I began to head for the museum. A few people who passed by slowed and pointed in my direction. Ever since my name had been listed in *Forbes*, that had been happening more and more. Add in the stupid gossip rag that had listed me amongst their sexiest men, and it was risky for me to wander the streets without Zeke nearby. He'd surely school me for it if or when he ever found out.

As I crossed East 84th Street, I noticed a familiar red dress slightly down the block. Serena's tight body wrapped in crimson wasn't an image I'd soon forget. She was a vision of beauty, sitting on the stone bench at the very spot we'd first met. My brow furrowed with concern, wondering why she wasn't inside. When she hunched over to rest her head on crossed forearms, my concern grew.

Was she…crying?

I never doubted my instincts. They'd served me well over the years, and right now, they told me something was wrong. Without thinking, I hurried my pace. The sound of my footsteps across the concrete sidewalk increased with the rhythm of my heart. An odd sense of worry gripped me as I approached her.

"Serena," I said once I reached her.

She looked up, her eyes reflecting a mixture of helplessness and surprise.

"Anton," she said warily.

"What's wrong?" I asked, crouching down to her level.

"Nothing. I just think…I think I'm coming down with something."

Her voice sounded strained, a stark contrast to the woman I'd left inside at the gala. Absent was the natural blush in her cheeks, now replaced with an ashen pallor.

"You look pale."

"Probably the flu combined with jetlag. I just need to get back to my room so I can sleep. I'll be fine," she insisted. She attempted to wave me off, but her arm fell limp to her side.

Christ. She's so weak.

I didn't know how illness had struck her so quickly, but there wasn't time to debate it. She belonged in a bed—not on a dirty stone city bench.

"Where are you staying?"

"I'm at…" Her brow pushed together to form a V as if it hurt just to talk. Reaching down into her red satin purse, she pulled out a keycard. "That's it. Midtown Motel. I couldn't remember the name. It's about twenty or so blocks that way."

She angled her head to signal the direction.

"The Midtown?" I stated, although it came out sounding more like a question born from disbelief. I was familiar with the building. The motel wasn't known for cleanliness or hospitality. In fact, it was just the opposite. I tried to imagine her inside the seedy urban motel wearing a formal gown and the sparkling ruby at her neck, and it was at complete odds. Not to mention, the contrast was nothing short of dangerous. She belonged in a palace fit for royalty. "Why in God's name are you staying at a place like that?"

"The presidential suite at the Four Seasons was sold out," she remarked, managing a weak, yet sarcastic smile. It was another reminder of how frail she looked.

I cringed at the idea of her having to walk or ride twenty or more blocks. She'd never make it five in her state.

"Let me help you."

"I'm fine. I just sat down to rest for a minute. I can call a cab—"

"You seem to think this is up for debate, princess," I stated and pulled my phone from my pocket. Going to the recent contact list, I located Zeke's number and pressed send. He picked up on the second ring. "Zeke, I need you to bring a car as close as you can to East 84th and 5th. Roads are blocked and I'm not sure how close they'll let you get The Met."

"I can get to you. Right now?"

"Yes. I've got a…" I glanced down at Serena, trying to think of a way to phrase my relationship with her. "I have a sick friend here who needs a ride."

I gave him a quick rundown, explaining where Serena's motel was. Luckily, he'd still been at Club O going through applications. Assuming traffic wouldn't be a huge issue, he estimated he could be here in less than fifteen minutes.

After ending the call, I looked down at Serena. She was leaning to one side, her head resting on the arm stretched across the back of the bench. Whatever argument she may have wanted to make moments earlier seemed to have died. Her eyes were closed, and her once radiant face bore the flush of fever.

I pressed my hand to her forehead.

Dammit.

She was burning up. I'd just been with her an hour earlier, and she hadn't shown any sign of sickness. Whatever she had seemed to be sucking the life out of her.

I began to pace, assessing the situation. She lived in Italy. Other than the gala, I had no idea what other business she had in New York—if any. If she had friends or family in the city, she'd most likely be staying with them over that sordid motel.

That led me to believe she was here alone. And sick.

New York would eat her alive if given the opportunity. Hell, that ruby necklace may as well have been a bullseye for street urchins and panhandlers. I wasn't entirely comfortable with the idea of leaving her alone right now—especially when I thought about where she was staying.

I cringed again at the mere thought of her being there. I

didn't know how she could attend the Met Gala, an event that cost over fifty grand a ticket, yet could only afford one of the cheapest hotels in Manhattan. Something didn't add up.

Less than fifteen minutes later, Zeke pulled up in my newly acquired Volvo XC90. It was a recent purchase, made only at Zeke's insistence for its ballistic protection. I looked down at Serena. She appeared to be sleeping.

"Princess," I said, nudging her awake. "Let's get you to a bed."

I held out my hand. She hesitated before accepting, but resignation came fast, and she allowed me to help her to her feet.

"Thanks," she murmured as I snaked an arm around her lower back.

Guiding her inside, the soft leather seats in the SUV offered a stark contrast to the hard bench she'd just been sitting on. As we settled into the comfort of the vehicle, her fatigue became even more evident. She rested her head against the door and closed her eyes again.

Zeke muscled the car through the clogged streets as I relayed orders on where to take Serena. Once we exited the secure perimeter around the Met, the roads filled with stop and go traffic, and people rushed in every direction. Bags of trash were piled several feet high in some places, waiting for the city waste management to haul them away. Some found it off-putting. To me, it was just another part of Manhattan.

When we reached the Midtown, I glanced out the window. A homeless woman lay huddled against the front of the building to the left of the hotel's main entrance. To the right, two men stood close to one another. One man was casually smoking a cigarette, discreetly holding out his free hand to accept whatever the second man was offering.

A drug deal.

I glanced down at Serena once more, and a nagging sense of responsibility needled at me.

Fuck.

I couldn't leave her here. I knew I was going to regret the choice I was about to make, but I went with it anyway.

"Zeke, change of plan. To the penthouse instead."

CHAPTER FIVE

Serena

I woke up with my cheek resting on a soft pillow. My head hurt, the throbbing ache settling just over my left eye, and my ears were plugged. But worse was the heaviness of my body, as if it would take every ounce of strength I had just to lift my head.

Slowly, I focused my gaze on the room. I didn't recognize the palette of rich colors—midnight blues, velvety purples, and muted golds. Elegant furnishing and décor surrounded a four-poster king-sized bed draped in satin. Lavish details extended to every corner, none of which were an extravagance afforded at the hotel I was supposed to be staying at.

This has to be a dream.

I blinked and tried to get my bearings. Tall, floor to ceiling windows revealed that it was nighttime. A flash of lightning in the distance transcended the barrier of the glass walls, blurring the lines between the room and the open sky beyond, leaving me suspended in air.

I looked around for a clock, or anything that would show me the time. I glanced at the nightstand, hoping to find my phone. Unfortunately, it held only a glass of water, a bottle of ibuprofen, and a cloth in a small ceramic basin.

I spotted my purse tossed haphazardly on a chaise lounge across the room along with a red gown.

The gown. The gala. The mysterious man with onyx eyes.

All at once, everything came flooding back. I pressed my fingers to my temples, recalling the events.

I'd struggled through the evening with what I'd suspected to be the onset of a flu. My mind had been anything but clear, and I'd found myself in the middle of too many pointless discussions. I hadn't been able to zero in on my priorities at all, and the entire evening had been a bust. I'd left without having made a single meaningful connection—which also meant I'd failed to get the funding I needed to continue the excavation in Rome.

The idea that I might not be able to continue my father's work brought on mixed emotions. I should be devastated, yet all I felt was an odd mix of disappointment and relief. I'd have to evaluate the conflicting reactions once I was feeling more like myself.

I thought about Anton, the stranger who made me foolishly believe that I could actually get a leg up at an event as prestigious as the Met Gala.

Trustfall my ass.

He'd made me drop my guard, and then abandoned me to the wolves.

Why did he leave so abruptly?

More images from the gala flashed in my mind. Across from me had sat a stunning man with ice-blue eyes and silver streaks at his temples. I'd recognized him instantly as Jace LeMont, an

Academy Award-winning actor who had starred in last year's highest-grossing film.

Then there was the woman who'd sat beside him. She was beautiful, dressed in a revealing blue gown with drastic pointed shoulders and a plunging neckline. I hadn't recognized her but assumed she must have been someone important to be on the arm of such a high-profile celebrity. They'd oozed elegance and poise, their movements graceful as they casually sipped their drinks served in the crystal, gold-rimmed glasses, completely at ease with themselves and their surroundings while I'd struggled just to keep down the hors d'oeuvre I'd consumed.

But then there was the older gentleman with a thick southern accent sitting next to me. His name was Allister Graham, a collector of ancient artifacts and an interested investor who could have possibly provided the funding I needed. The conversation I'd struck with him had potential—until his hand found his way to my leg under the table.

If I hadn't already felt the urge to vomit, he had pushed me to the edge. I'd excused myself from the table before I really did get sick all over the guests and made my way to the bathroom. When I lost what little had been in my stomach, I knew I had to leave. My body ached with fever. I recalled going outside to call for a cab. That's when Anton had come upon me.

From that point on, things started to get fuzzy. I'd been so tired. I remembered getting into his car…and then, nothing.

My eyes darted once again to the dress tossed over the chaise. Raising the comforter to get a view of myself, I found that I was dressed in a white T-shirt—a man's T-shirt. I lifted the collar of the shirt to find I was naked, save my cotton panties and the ruby necklace.

"What the hell?" I didn't remember undressing.

The last thing I recalled was Anton leading me to the backseat of an SUV. He'd climbed in next to me, so someone else had to have been driving. I'd fallen asleep, and I had no memory of how I'd come to be in this room—in this bed.

"Bad things happen to women who travel alone, Serena."

I could hear my mother's words as clear as day. She didn't like the idea of me coming to New York on my own, but I'd had little choice. We didn't have the money for her to accompany me, and my best friend, Caterina, hadn't been able to get off from work.

Now here I was in a strange bed, having no idea how I'd gotten here. I mentally checked my lady parts. Everything felt okay, but that didn't mean this wasn't a horror movie in the making. I had to get out of here before something really bad happened.

Before I could consider an escape, nature called. There was a door on the other side of the room cracked open enough for me to see it was a bathroom. Using what little energy I had, I swung my legs over the side of the bed. I stood, but my body swayed so much, I had to sit back down.

"Mother Mary," I muttered. I was sicker than I'd realized. In fact, I couldn't recall a time in my life when I'd felt this terrible.

I attempted to stand again, then slowly put one foot in front of the other until I reached the bathroom door. Once inside, I fumbled for the switch. I didn't find one, but my movements alone seemed to trigger the lights. I glanced around, trying to get my bearings. The bathroom was beautiful, boasting sophistication and functional class. Any other day, I would have paused to take in every meticulously curated detail, but right then, my fevered body could only focus on getting to the toilet.

After using the facilities, I went to the sink to wash my hands. A minimalist pendant light hung just above the mirror, highlighting the dark circles under my eyes. I looked like hell, and as much as I knew I needed to leave this strange place, my body longed to crawl back into the soft embrace of the bed.

When I exited the bathroom, I stopped short at the silhouette of a man outlined against one of the wide glass windows. Startled, I gasped.

This is it. This is how I die.

He slowly turned, and I held my breath. When Anton's beautiful face came into view in the dim light, I breathed a momentary sigh of relief before panic rushed right back in. After all, he was a stranger. Albeit, a very sexy stranger who made me weak in the knees, but that was beside the point. I was in an unfamiliar place wearing only a T-shirt that barely covered my underwear.

"Good. You're awake. You had me worried for a while there," he said, appraising me up and down.

"Where am I?" I demanded.

"My penthouse. How are you feeling?"

"I'm fine," I lied. The reality was that I felt ready to collapse. Everything hurt and I just wanted to sleep.

He moved over to the bedside lamp and turned it on. His head tipped to the side curiously as he studied my face. "You don't look fine."

"Gee, thanks," I replied.

His lips curved slightly to form an amused grin before he took a step toward me. Instinctively, I backed away and tried to ignore how good he looked in a snug black T-shirt and blue jeans. It was a drastic shift from the polished man I'd met outside of the museum. This version of him was darker. Edgier.

"Princess, you should go back to bed."

There was that word.

Princess.

It had stirred something in me when he'd first called me that, and even though I felt like death, hearing it again awakened that arousal once more. Not wanting to entertain why that was, I changed the subject.

"How did I get here?"

"You fell asleep in the car on the way to your…motel," he

replied, not bothering to hide his disgust over the last word. "I tried to wake you, but you wouldn't budge. I also didn't like the idea of leaving you alone in that place when you clearly weren't well. So, I brought you back here."

I pinched the bridge of my nose, trying to ward off the pounding in my head as I attempted to make sense of what he was saying.

"I don't remember coming here, let alone climbing into this bed."

"Like I said, you didn't wake up. I carried you from the car to the bed."

He carried me?

I blinked. Once, then twice, not understanding how I hadn't been aware for any of it.

"You put me to bed?" The phrase came out more like a question as my eyes darted to the red dress in the corner. Reaching up, I tugged at the collar of the T-shirt I wore. "Did you put this shirt on me?"

The corner of his mouth twitched, almost as if he were holding back a smirk, before he admitted, "Yeah. I did."

My eyes widened in shock, appalled to know that a perfect stranger had undressed me without my consent. The dress had a built-in bra, which meant I was braless once he'd removed it. My underwear was still in place—only a slight consolation—but my breasts had been exposed to him.

Completely exposed.

To my horror, I felt my nipples harden beneath the T-shirt—as if I were actually turned on by the idea.

I quickly crossed my arms to hide my traitorous body, equally furious at my physical reactions as I was by his audacity.

"You had no right to undress me."

"Your breathing sounded a bit shallow, and the bodice of that gown was very tight. I made a judgement call."

"You had no right," I repeated through gritted teeth.

"It was the best choice. I'm not going to debate my decision to remove it. You aren't the first woman I've seen naked, and you won't be the last. Calm down."

"Calm down?" I practically squeaked. I could feel my temper elevate with each passing second. He clearly didn't know that telling a woman to calm down worked about as well as baptizing a cat. "You are presuming, arrogant—"

"Yes, I'm all of the above, princess. And as appealing as you are to look at, I promise I didn't stare or touch you in an inappropriate way. I don't get off on taking advantage of incapacitated women," Anton stated flatly. "Now get back to bed. You look like you're about to pass out."

I straightened, feeling indignant. "You don't know what I look like when I'm about to pass out. This could be how I look when I'm tired."

"Right. I don't buy that for a minute. Bed. Now," he ordered, moving to take hold of my arm to guide me toward the bed.

I wanted to fight him but knew any physical resistance would be futile. He was right. I barely had the energy to stay upright. Nevertheless, I didn't have the luxury to sleep.

"I can't stay here, Anton. I have a flight to Italy to catch."

"When?"

I pressed my hand to my forehead and willed myself to remember the itinerary.

"Tuesday evening. It leaves around five."

"I hate to break it to you, but that flight left hours ago. It's Tuesday, just after ten."

"Wait, what? No." I shook my head in disbelief. There was no way I'd been here since last night.

"Anyone who sleeps for over twenty-four hours clearly needs it. Now, I want you to lie down."

I was weak and in no position to argue. Every time one of us spoke, the words banged around in my skull until I thought I might get sick. Perhaps he was right. If Anton were a psychopath intent on harming me, he would have done so by now. But still. There was no reason for me to stay here. I could easily sleep off this flu in the privacy of my own hotel room, whether he approved of my lodging choice or not.

Which reminded me—my room. Not only did I miss my flight, but I was supposed to check out earlier that day. I wasn't sure what would become of my personal belongings without notice of an extended stay.

"Anton, I can't stay here. I need to go back to the Midtown. My things are there. I was supposed to check out this morning and—"

"Not happening, princess," he insisted, and then turned my body so that my back was to the bed. Pressing my shoulders ever so slightly, he forced me to sit on the edge. Within seconds, I found myself tucked back under the plush satin comforter.

"I really need to go," I murmured faintly.

He brought his hand to my head. With a frown that seemed to express both concern and annoyance, he reached for the cloth in the basin and wrung out the excess water. With surprising gentleness, he ran the damp material over my brow.

"You're still burning with fever." Setting the cloth aside, he opened the bottle of ibuprofen, then handed me two pills and the glass of water from the nightstand. "Take this. It should help."

"I'm fine."

"Would you stop saying that?"

I looked dubiously at the pills. "I don't need—"

"It's Advil. Not poison." His interruption was flat with a hint of annoyance. "Now, here. Take these."

He pushed the pills toward me. I stared at them for a moment before giving in.

"I really need to go," I insisted again after I'd swallowed two caplets.

Ignoring me, he continued. "I'll go to the Midtown and collect your things for you. Just rest."

Then, without another word, he ambled out of the room. I didn't have the energy to chase him, never mind the idea of getting back out of bed. I wanted to, though. I wasn't only worried about my personal belongings left behind at the motel. I had so many other things I needed to take care of, too. For starters, the expensive plane ticket that was nonrefundable.

But my eyes hurt too much.

Perhaps if I closed them for a bit, I'd be able to find the energy I needed to fix the mess I was in. Succumbing to the heaviness in my lids, I surrendered to the darkness and was back to sleep within seconds.

CHAPTER SIX

Anton

I sat in the front passenger seat of the Volvo as Zeke navigated the city streets toward the Midtown Motel. Leaving Serena alone in the penthouse bedroom had left me on edge, even if it was only for a short time. Keeping a low public profile was becoming harder and harder, and having her there was a risk. For all I knew, she was a tabloid plant looking to get an inside scoop. Vultures were everywhere. While she wouldn't find anything incriminating about me lying around, I didn't like having strangers in my personal space.

I wasn't sure why I'd felt compelled to bring her to the penthouse in the first place. I was the moth, and she was the flame. I was drawn to her despite the danger. The sight of her so vulnerable had stirred a protective instinct I hadn't felt since my mother was alive, and it was unsettling.

However, when she'd emerged from the bathroom looking pale and gaunt, I knew I'd made the right choice. Her steps had been slow and deliberate and so weak that she reminded me of a fragile flower that might wilt at the slightest touch. Nobody could have faked that.

"Are you going to tell me what's going on?" Zeke asked, breaking the silence in the car.

"What do you mean?"

"This woman. You've been quiet ever since you brought her to the penthouse—near lifeless I might add. Not to mention, I don't think I've ever seen a woman inside your place before."

"That's because there hasn't been one. Ever. At least not while I was the owner."

"Exactly. And now we're going to get this woman's things from her hotel. Who you're sleeping with isn't any of my business, but I need to know if I should do a background check on her."

"It's not like that. She's the person of interest from the Met Gala—Dr. Martinelli."

"*She's* Dr. Martinelli? The archeologist?" Zeke asked, incredulous.

"Yes."

The very sexy archeologist.

I kept that opinion to myself. I wasn't used to being caught unawares, yet Serena had hit me like a sucker punch. Until I could figure out why this woman unnerved me so much, it was best to keep my thoughts private.

"The phrasing of the article had me picturing—"

"Someone different?" I finished for him. "I did, too. I don't know if there's any connection to the Dr. Martinelli that was mentioned in the article you showed me. I didn't have the chance to ask before she fell ill. It was all so unexpected, and it threw me off my game. I wasn't sure what to think when I learned her name, so I went for a walk. I came back and found her barely conscious on a bench. That's when I called you to come get us."

"You went for a walk? Where?" Zeke asked, not bothering to hide the accusation in his voice.

Shit.

I shook my head, regretting the slip up immediately.

"No need to get jumpy. I didn't go that far," I said. "I turned around near Central Park."

"That's well outside the security perimeter set up for the Met Gala, and too far for you to go alone. You're playing Russian roulette with your life, boss. I think it's time we revisit around-the-clock protection. I can only split my time between you and the club so much. I want to bring someone else in."

I pressed my lips together in a tight line, annoyed that he was pushing the issue again. I wasn't naïve. I knew my rapid rise in status meant increased threats. I'd hired Zeke because he was the only person I could trust with my personal security and sensitive club details. He had all the training, skills, and expertise necessary. I wasn't ready to bring someone else into the fold—even though I knew he was right. I was going to have to expand my circle sooner rather than later.

"We can start the vetting process for potential candidates next week," I replied.

It was the only concession I would make for now. If there was one thing I was good at, it was self-preservation. I didn't believe I'd ever trust anyone as much as I did Zeke, but knew it was in my best interest to heed his warning.

The motel loomed ahead, a grim picture against the more modern structures flanking the six-story building. Zeke pulled up to the curb and we silently got out of the car. The storm that had threatened most of the night had finally moved in, causing cold rain to needle at my cheeks. The wind kicked up, sweeping and howling within the man-made canyons. I tugged the collar of my jacket up to block the worst of it as I walked briskly toward the motel.

A neon sign flickered intermittently above the entrance,

casting an eerie glow over the wet, cracked pavement. When I imagined Serena staying in a place like this, my disdain for the seedy motel only deepened.

The air carried a peculiar mix of stale cigarette smoke, marijuana, and an indistinct mustiness. The check-in counter had a sign noting that the attendant was at lunch. I scoffed. It was nearing midnight. Clearly, the desk staff had chosen not to return.

"This place is a dump," Zeke remarked. I glanced his way to see his eyes sweep over the dubious surroundings, carefully taking in every inch of the place with his hawk-like gaze. His distaste mirrored mine. The motel's infamous seedy reputation had preceded it, a fact that now seemed irrefutable as we ventured further down the corridor.

We reached the bank of elevators, and I pulled out the keycard that I'd taken from Serena's purse. The envelope had room number 310 written on it. Pressing the button for the third floor, we ascended in silence. When the doors opened, we were greeted with a dimly lit hallway. The poor lighting couldn't mask the faded gold wallpaper peeling at the edges. The red carpet was stained and worn, and the banged up wooden trim work was caked with layers of chipped paint.

The only solace I got from being here was the knowledge that Serena would never have to return—at least not if I had anything to do with it. The more I looked around, the more disgusted I became. If it were up to me, I'd have the place leveled.

When we reached her assigned room, I unlocked the door and pushed it open, but stopped on the threshold. I hadn't expected the room to be in better condition than the hallway, but I didn't anticipate finding complete and utter chaos. Clothes had been tossed from suitcases and left strewn across the floor. Dresser drawers were pulled out and emptied with reckless abandon. This wasn't a mess created by laziness or sloppy living. It was bold destruction driven by something sinister.

The hairs on the back of my neck stood on end as I scanned the room. The bed bore the brunt of it. The sheets were a tangled mess atop a mattress that had been sliced open and shredded six ways to Sunday. Bedside lamps lay toppled, and pillow stuffing littered every square surface. The cracked mirror on the dresser reflected the aftermath of the upheaval, its broken pieces littered on the floor.

"What a mess…" I said as I stepped further into the trashed space.

I glanced behind me at Zeke. His right hand was inside his suit coat, fingers wrapped around the grip of his 9mm. His jacket was tailored so precisely, that only a trained eye would notice the holster and firearm. But I knew it was there. It was a job requirement.

"This is bad," Zeke muttered as he took in the damage. His sharp eyes darted around the room for any signs of immediate danger. Appearing satisfied that there wasn't any, he turned back toward the door and inspected the handle. Running his pointer finger along the jamb, he shook his head. "No damage here. Whoever did this had to have had key access to the room. But check this out."

"What is it?"

Zeke closed the door so I could see the backside. Someone had spray painted a misshapen spiral with a childlike drawing of an eye. Its jagged and irregular lines seemed as though they'd been put there by a trembling hand. A rough oval encircled the design, giving it an unfinished, chaotic appearance, almost as if its creator had been hurried.

Zeke ran a finger over the paint.

"Paint is dry. Hard to tell if this is recent. What do you think it's supposed to be?" he asked.

I shook my head. "No idea."

"Kind of looks like a snake with an eye that's too big."

There was a disconcerting stillness to the air, and unease settled in the pit of my stomach. This went beyond intrusion of someone's personal space. What happened here was violent.

"What do you think, Zeke? Random theft or something else?"

"Nah. A regular thief would have wanted to get in, take anything of value, and get out undetected. Destroying the place and spray-painting graffiti would be a waste of time."

"This motel is such a dive. That spray painted thing behind the door may be old and completely unrelated to this."

"True. But, I'm certain this wasn't random. The way every drawer is pulled out, the mattress—this place was deliberately tossed. The question is, what were they looking for?" he said with a slight edge to his voice.

I thought about the ruby necklace Serena had been wearing. That alone made her an easy target, but something told me that the necklace wasn't what the intruders were looking for.

I made my way around to the other side of the bed and began to collect Serena's personal belongings. Instinct warned me to use caution, and I was careful not to touch anything other than the items we'd be taking with us.

As I gathered her clothing, I noticed a leather-bound journal with a worn cover and frayed edges lying on a discarded T-shirt. Picking it up, I flipped through some of its pages. They were filled with cursive writing, hand drawn maps, and symbols I didn't recognize.

"What is it?" Zeke asked from behind me. I turned to see him looking at me expectantly.

"I'm not sure. Looks like a journal of some sort."

"We should call the police," he advised.

"I don't know if..." My words died on my tongue when I noticed thin lines of white powder dusting the dresser. I was no stranger to drugs, and would recognize the remnants of those precise lines anywhere.

Cocaine.

My stomach tightened. Seeing it felt surreal, like an unimportant detail in an old crime movie. I hesitated as painful memories threatened to resurface. The room suddenly felt colder.

I took a step closer, the outside edges of what was left of the mirror catching my reflection. In it, I saw a younger version of myself. My jaw hardened and I looked away, refusing to let the ghosts from my past in. I needed to focus on the current situation.

Did the coke belong to Serena?

The question circled in my mind, but she just didn't seem the type. Or perhaps a random junkie had gotten in. It might explain the trashed room, but I couldn't be sure. A hundred possibilities raced through my head, but none of the answers made sense. My eyes shifted back to the slashed mattress, and then to the spray-painted door. A chill raced down my spine. I wasn't easily rattled, but instinct warned me that something bigger was in play.

"Let's hold off on calling the police," I told Zeke.

"Why?"

I considered how little I knew about the woman fast asleep at my penthouse. If she was in danger, she'd be safe at my place—but only if nobody knew she was there. My building had security, but it was minimal at best. Zeke recently contracted a firm to bring the systems up to date, but they hadn't begun the work yet.

"Something isn't sitting right with me. I need to find out more about Serena, and you and I both know that cops will only complicate matters. I don't want them sniffing around anything related to me, even if I don't have a direct connection to what happened here. Call it gut instinct, but let's try to figure this out on our own first. For now, we'll just collect her personal things and get out of here. Be careful not to touch anything else."

"Are you sure that's the right move, boss?" Zeke asked. His voice was heavy with doubt, but he was already pulling a linen handkerchief from his breast pocket.

I watched as he began wiping down the door area to remove any fingerprints we might have left, fighting off momentary indecision about the risks. The last thing I needed was to be connected to a scene like this. While I doubted the motel had much in terms of security, Zeke would need to check for CCTV cameras to eliminate any evidence of our being here. Street cams were another matter entirely, but Zeke had connections. I needed to trust my instincts.

"No, I'm not sure this is the right move. But something is telling me to play it this way for now. When we get back, I want you to get in touch with your contacts and find out everything there is to know about Serena Martinelli."

AN HOUR LATER, I stepped off the elevator and entered the main foyer of my quiet penthouse. Zeke was two floors down in his apartment, already collecting as much information as he could find on the woman sleeping in my bed. He had a wide network of contacts and resources at his disposal, and I knew he would bring back any relevant information he found.

I rolled her suitcases into the living room, and then reached into my jacket pocket to pull out the leather-bound journal. I had planned on retreating to my office to study it but decided to check on her first.

My bedroom was still and hushed when I entered, with only Serena's gentle breaths breaking the silence. The storm clouds had cleared, making room for the moon to shine through the large windows. Moving to her, I reached down and placed my palm over her forehead. She still felt warm, but not as fiery hot as she'd been earlier.

I watched the rise and fall of her chest while she slept. Taking the cloth from the basin on the nightstand, I gently wiped her brow. She didn't even stir. I continued to stare down at her, unable to tear my gaze away from the way the moonlight accentuated the soft lines of her face. Dark lashes lined her closed lids, concealing the blue eyes that reminded me of a raging ocean.

She shifted to her side, tucking her hands between her face and the pillow. A lazy curl fell across her cheek, obstructing my view. I pushed it back behind her ear so I could continue admiring her flawless skin.

Even in sickness, she was beautiful. In fact, she may have been the most beautiful woman I'd ever laid eyes on. I didn't know how this bewitching Italian princess could possibly connect to the violent destruction that Zeke and I had found at the Midtown.

"Who are you, Serena Martinelli?" I whispered.

CHAPTER SEVEN

Serena

Sheets of rain slice through the night sky, the heavy droplets furiously battering against the windows. The raw power of Mother Nature is on full display tonight, her fierce winds strong enough to wrench a shutter from its latch. It thumps loudly against the stucco walls of my parents' home as the storm rages on.

Bang! Bang!

The shutter's relentless pounding echoes through the house as it slams into the side of the house again and again. I consider rising to secure it, but I don't want to release my father's hand. I rake my gaze over his still form, unable to fathom how he deteriorated so quickly. His once vital, sturdy, and strong body had become so weak in just a few short months.

"Serena," he says in a hoarse whisper. "Fix the shutter."

"Yes, Papa." Reluctantly, I release his hand, hurry across the terracotta floor to the window, and open the glass pane.

Reaching past the ornamental security bars and out into the rainy night, I pull the shutter closed once again and secure the latch.

My father offers me a small smile once I return to my chair next to his bed. "Such a good girl, Serena. You always were. Did the shutter damage the stucco?"

"I didn't see anything. I'm sure it's fine, Papa. Please stop worrying. You need to rest."

"I have to worry while I still can, princess. I'll be resting forever soon enough, and I don't want your mother to have to deal with damage to the house after I'm gone."

I blink back tears and shake my head. "You're talking nonsense. You'll be back to your old self in no time. You'll see."

He doesn't respond to what we both know is a lie. He simply gives me another weak smile and closes his eyes. I take his hand in mine once more, noting how cold it had gotten in the short time it took me to secure the shutter. His circulation is getting worse by the day, but at least the stomach pain and vomiting has stopped—thanks to the morphine and antinausea medication prescribed by the doctor.

I glance up when I hear my mother come into the room.

"How is he?" she asks.

"He seems more comfortable than yesterday. I just wish we could get him well enough to get on a plane. The doctors in the U.S. have access to so much more."

"No more talk about America. Italy is my home, Serena," my father says fervently. I turn back to him as he attempts to sit up.

"Carlo, lie down," my mother scolds.

"No. There are things I have to say, Sylvia," he insists.

Not wanting him to struggle, my mother hurries to his bedside where the two of us work to get him upright against the headboard. I frown when I hear his labored breathing, signaling how much the simple act of sitting up taxes his frail body.

I fold my arms across my chest and give him a pointed look.

"You're so stubborn, Papa. I don't know why you couldn't say whatever it is you have to say while you were lying down."

Ignoring me, he turns to my mother. "Sylvia, go fetch my leather book. The bigger one."

"The map book? You can't possibly want to start drawing in that old thing now!"

"Sylvia Martinelli, if you even so much as try to argue with me…" He can't finish the veiled threat before he begins violently coughing. Speaking with any sort of conviction takes all the strength he has.

"Mulo!" my mother mutters in Italian. "Serena is right. You're as stubborn as a mule." Stalking over to the corner desk where my father keeps his many research journals, she rifles through the contents of the top drawer. Pulling out the largest of the brown leather-bound journals, she brushes invisible dust from the top of it and brings it to him.

Without a word, he places the book on his lap and gingerly flips through the pages until he finds the one he wants. With one red, swollen finger, he points to a map of the Roman Forum and begins tracing the lines as if trying to commit them to memory. It's a peculiar thing for him to do—after all, he's the one who had drawn it.

My throat tightens as I watch him move his hand along the worn paper until he comes to an X on the bottom right page.

"X marks the spot," he says in barely a whisper.

My mother shoves a loose lock of salt and pepper hair back into her bun and huffs out an impatient breath. My frustration matches hers. If these truly are my father's final hours, I don't want to spend them talking about ghosts.

With the book still balancing on his lap, he reaches for my mother's hand and brings her finger to the X on the page. All her frustration melts away, and a look of understanding passes between them—as if they're sharing decades of emotions in a single moment.

"You worked so hard to find them," she murmurs, eyes full of sadness and heartbreak.

It's killing me to watch her suffer—to watch them both suffer. I blink back tears and return to the window. I peer out through the shutter's slats and watch the rain batter the streets. As the wind whistles and whips, I can't help but think the storm's fury is a sign from the heavens. It's as if the angels are expressing all the rage I feel in my heart.

"Serena, let me tell you about Cleopatra and Mark Antony," my father says.

I turn away from the window and back to him. "I know their story, Papa."

"Historians say their ending was so epic, even Shakespeare himself couldn't have written it better," he continues as if I hadn't spoken.

"Yes, you've told me the story a thousand times," I remind him, wishing he would save his strength rather than go off on what is sure to be a long-winded tale. "Cleopatra attempted a fake suicide that resulted in Antony's death. When she learned what happened, a heartbroken Cleopatra killed herself with poison. I used the story in my dissertation, Papa. You don't need to tell me again."

"Let me tell it to you anyway. Come sit."

Suppressing a sigh, I return to my chair beside his bed. My mother sits on the opposite side with a wary expression.

"Carlo, maybe just tell the short version. You don't want to overdo it."

He pays her no mind and turns his attention to me.

"Cleopatra was a cunning and masterful leader," he begins. "From the moment Mark Antony met her, he was smitten to the point of obsession. Cleopatra knew this and used it to her advantage. She needed Antony's protection to expand her power, and he needed her riches to fund his armies in the East. She threw extravagant parties for the Romans and flaunted her wealth. She drank and flirted with Antony, who was determined to surpass her extravagance by throwing parties of his own."

"But his parties were never as good as Cleopatra's," I continue with a small smile, having heard the story so often that I know it by heart. "Eventually, they fell in love, and Antony impregnated Cleopatra, only to leave her and return to Rome to marry another woman. While he was there, Cleopatra gave birth to twins."

"That's correct! Alexander Helios and Cleopatra Selene," my father adds with eyes brighter than I've seen them in weeks. "They are the key to all of this, Serena."

My brows push together in confusion. In all the times I've heard my father speak of Cleopatra and Mark Antony, he's never once focused on their children.

"They are the key to all of what, Papa?"

My father gives me a knowing smile, then looks down at his book and pulls out a folded piece of paper. He unfolds it to reveal a sizable rubbing of old Roman cursive that I've never seen before.

"Six months ago, I came across a stone tablet and took this rubbing of it," my father explains. "It's the proof that Mark Antony and Cleopatra's ashes are in Rome, Serena—not in Egypt. But some have gone to great lengths to keep this information hidden. They will kill to protect the secret and—"

My father's words cut off as he's overcome with another coughing fit. My mother hurries to grab a tissue from the dresser and hands it to him. He holds it to his mouth as his body convulses and spasms. To my horror, when he pulls the tissue away, it's stained red with blood.

"Papa, let me get you a drink. You've been talking too much. You need to—" He grips my hand with such force, I'm taken by surprise. I didn't think he had that much strength left in him.

"Trust your intuition, Serena. X marks the spot—I'm sure of it. But it's dangerous and you'll have to be careful. Be smarter *than me. Promise to see my work through to the end. You must find Cleopatra and Mark Antony."*

For the briefest moment, I consider my glassblowing workshop and my passion to create. The art calls to me, even now, as I stare into my father's glassy, yellowing eyes. They're so full of desperation. I have little choice but to give this dying man —my hero for as long as I can remember—my solemn vow.

My dreams no longer matter.

I will do anything for my father, even if it means giving up the thing I love the most.

"I promise, Papa. I will find them."

I SLOWLY EMERGED from the darkness of sleep, my face scrunched as if I'd been crying. The weight of grief pressed upon me like a lead blanket, while my mind swirled with remnants of the haunting dream. The flashback of my father's final days was as clear as when it originally happened.

I inhaled a shaky breath and opened my eyes, feeling emotionally wrung out. My head throbbed mercilessly, a relentless ache pulsing behind my temples. I blinked, struggling to focus on my surroundings.

Disoriented from the dream that felt too close to reality, it took me a minute to remember where I was. The scent on the soft pillows—his scent—was all I needed to bring me back to the present day.

As if materializing from the shadows themselves, Anton's silhouette became visible in the dark room. He leaned down, turning on the bedside lamp. I allowed my eyes to adjust to the light, and met his observant and assessing onyx gaze. He stared with an intensity that sent shivers cascading down my spine.

"How are you feeling?" His voice was low and gravelly, cutting through the silence like warm whiskey, its timbre sending a burning awareness through my veins.

Ignoring the uptick in my heart rate, I frowned and considered how I felt. Flashes from my dream came forth, and grief washed over me once again. I could almost smell the antiseptic from my mother's meticulous cleaning in the air. The sound of my father's voice still echoed in my mind. The rain whipping against the house, the chill of fear I'd felt in my bones... Reliving it was all too much to bear.

I struggled to find my voice, unsure how to articulate the storm of emotions raging within me. I didn't want to talk about my dream or how it made me feel—at least not at that moment. Not when my head felt like it might explode.

"I...I don't know," I managed to whisper, my words barely audible in the quiet of the room. I adjusted the blankets around me, noticing how he tracked my every move as I folded back the sheet and shifted to a sitting position. The small action made the piercing pain in my skull that much worse. I winced and brought a hand to the back of my head.

"Are you alright?"

"My head is pounding."

"There's ibuprofen on the nightstand. Let me get you some fresh water and—"

"No, it's okay," I said. "It's not that kind of headache. It's the bobby pins in my hair. They've been there since Monday afternoon."

When he sat down on the edge of the bed, I could feel the heat radiating from his body. Strangely, all I could think about was curling into him, needing a comforting embrace amidst the turmoil left behind by the dream. It was an effort to stop myself from doing exactly that, acutely aware of the vulnerable position I was in.

Anton lifted a hand toward my face. Instinctively, I pulled back. Despite my headache, I had the wherewithal to remember that my skin was sticky from fever sweats, and I hadn't showered in a few days. I was, for lack of a better word, completely gross, and didn't want to be touched by another human while in this state. Anton, by contrast, was handsome and perfect, smelling like soap and pine and sin.

"Why did you shy away?" he asked.

"I'm just…" I paused, embarrassed as I struggled to find words.

His hand reached out again, tentative but determined, as he brushed aside a limp lock of hair that had fallen across my forehead. The contact sent a jolt of awareness coursing through me, igniting a blazing fire in the depths of my soul.

And then, to my surprise, he began to remove the pins from my hair.

CHAPTER EIGHT

Anton

I sat on the edge of the bed, carefully removing the bobby pins that held together Serena's complex hairstyle. It was hard to see in the dim light, so I had to feel my way around.

She wasn't burning up, and I was pleased that her fever had broken. She wore nothing but my oversized T-shirt, the soft fabric draping over her curves in a way that made my dick twitch. Despite her illness, she projected the same sex appeal and quiet strength that I'd found intriguing the moment I met her outside the Met Gala.

"What time is it?" she asked.

"Just after one in the morning."

"I feel wide awake. My body must still be on Italy time. But that doesn't explain why you're awake at this hour."

"Couldn't sleep," I told her with a noncommittal shrug. I could have explained further, revealing that being the owner of Club O usually kept me up well past midnight. However, I wasn't sure how she would respond to learning that I owned a sex club, nor did I know her well enough to divulge one of my biggest secrets.

As one pin after another came loose in my fingers, Serena's locks fell around her shoulders like a dark chocolate curtain. Her hair, once meticulously styled for the gala, now tumbled in silky waves against her skin. Her eyes fluttered closed and a soft sigh escaped her lips. It was as if the tension were melting away with the removal of each pin.

I watched her reaction with curiosity, wondering about her ability to place such blind trust in me. There was something intimate and raw about the moment, stirring unfamiliar thoughts and desires deep within me.

"How do you know how to do that?" she asked.

"Do what?"

"Hair. Most men don't even know what a bobby pin is."

"I've seen my mother remove pins from her hair enough times. It isn't all that difficult."

"Does she wear her hair up regularly?"

"Before she died, yes."

"Oh, I'm sorry," Serena murmured.

Not wanting to invite a conversation about my mother's death, I didn't reply. I continued to work on Serena's hair instead. There had to be at least a hundred pins wedged in every which way. It was no wonder she had a headache.

When I tugged the final one free, the last tendril fell to complete the messy masterpiece.

"All done," I told her, letting my fingers linger on the dark strands, savoring the satiny feel of them. I envisioned it braided, trialing down the middle of her back, ready to be wrapped around my hand the moment I wanted her.

Serena tilted her head slightly, meeting my gaze with interest. There was a question there, unspoken yet palpable.

"That feels so much better," she finally said. "Thank you."

"You're welcome."

Silence fell and she glanced down awkwardly.

"I, ah... I should probably get dressed. I need to return to my motel and check out."

"I've taken care of it."

Her head snapped back up to look at me, her expression heavy with concern. "You took care of it? But what about my belongings?"

"I retrieved your things while you were sleeping, just like I told you I would."

She frowned as if searching her memory before saying, "That's right. I remember you mentioning that. Were there any problems with check out?"

"No issues," I replied quickly, deliberately not mentioning that her hotel room had been ransacked. A part of me wanted to confront her about what I'd found at the Midtown, but I needed more answers about who she was first. It would be best to wait for the background check so that I'd know who I was dealing with. Hopefully, Zeke would have information for me by the time the sun came up.

"I should have gone with you. I'm sorry. I just felt so out of it. Getting sick had not been on my agenda for this trip, but I have more of a clear head now." She paused, her eyes darting around the room, suddenly looking panicked. "I need to call home. My mother will be out of her mind with worry when she finds out I'm not back as planned. Where's my phone?"

Before I could answer, she slid out of the bed and moved quickly toward the chaise lounge to where her belongings were. Pulling her cellphone from her purse, she muttered something before tossing the phone back onto the chaise. It took me a second to figure out that she was speaking to herself in Italian.

Amused by her unintelligible ramblings, I felt the corners of my mouth pull up. "What's wrong?"

"I need to find my charger. The battery is dead."

"There's a charging cord in the nightstand." Reaching for the drawer, I pulled out the charger and handed it to her. "Do you always check in with your mother?"

"Not always, but ever since my father…" Serena seemed to get lost in thought for a moment before shaking her head. "It's barely seven in the morning in Italy. I don't want to wake her if she's sleeping. I'll just let my phone charge for a bit, then call her in an hour. She should be up by then."

She raked both hands through her hair. The simple action of raising her arms caused the T-shirt to rise above the tops of her thighs, exposing the red thong she wore underneath. Catching herself, she quickly pulled down on the hem as a visible flush of heat spread to her cheeks.

I raised a brow at her show of modesty.

"No need to be shy, princess. I've already seen most of what there is to see."

Her blush deepened and I suppressed a smile.

"Look, Anton," she began, choosing not to acknowledge my comment. "I'm feeling better, but it seems like I might be here for a bit yet—at least until I can get my affairs in order and figure out what I need to do next. I don't want to impose, but is it okay if I took a quick shower? It'll be good to wash off the sweat before I attempt civilized society again."

I nodded. "Of course."

I motioned for her to follow me into the ensuite bathroom. The smooth marble floors were cool beneath my bare feet as I pointed out where she could find clean towels and toiletries. Then I went over to the large, walk-in shower, and turned the valves to adjust the temperature of the waterfall shower head. The sound of running water filled the room, and I turned back to face Serena.

My breath caught as I took in the sight of her underneath the muted lighting. I was normally a satin and lace kind of guy, and if the mood struck, I could get into leather, too. But the way she stood there, barefoot in my white cotton T-shirt, I didn't think I'd ever seen anything sexier.

A vision of her naked body in my shower, water flowing hot and wet over every curve, flooded my mind. The muscles in my arms and chest tensed, betraying the sudden wave of pure, carnal desire that washed over me.

I craved her. Desperately.

I barely knew her, yet all I wanted to do was take her to my bed and worship her tight body, licking and biting every sensual curve before savagely claiming her as mine.

Fuck. What is this woman doing to me?

I shook my head and stepped away from the shower. After making my way back toward the bathroom door, I turned to face her again. Suppressing my thoughts, I cleared my suddenly dry throat and said, "Take all the time you need."

Leaving her alone with the steam of the shower so she could feel human again, I withdrew to the bedroom, my mind and body buzzing.

Restless, I moved into the living room and headed toward the wet bar. After pouring two fingers of Bowmore 27 single malt over a ball of ice, I went into my office and looked out the large windows overlooking 5th Avenue. I lifted the glass to my mouth, feeling the cool liquid over my tongue just before the burn hit the back of my throat.

I ran a hand through my hair as I took in the nighttime view of the city. I had barely lived here long enough to appreciate its luxuries, but they weren't why I'd bought it. My interest in the property was rooted in its historical significance.

Having developed a fascination with the rich and powerful throughout history, I couldn't pass up the opportunity to buy the home that had once belonged to the late Jacqueline Kennedy Onassis. I had to have it. The purchase may have seemed ostentatious to anyone who knew where I'd come from, but it didn't matter what they thought. The street rat they once knew was dead. My home symbolized who I was now—and I would never go back.

Sitting on the northeast corner of 85th Street, the penthouse was only one block north of the Metropolitan Museum of Art, the very place I'd met mystery woman in my shower.

My thoughts drifted back to Serena once again, the image of her delicate silhouette veiled by steam haunting my mind. She was a complex puzzle, each piece more alluring and captivating than the last. But for every one I put into place, there were others I couldn't match. They only added to her mystery, and for some reason, that made me desire her even more. I didn't want ordinary and only coveted the extraordinary—and Serena checked all the boxes I craved.

I tried to push aside the feelings she incited, burying them beneath layers of control and detachment that had served me well over the years. Still, there was no denying how much she affected me. It didn't matter if she was a mystery. I wanted her naked and kneeling. I imagined her under me, her legs wrapped around my hips as I drove into her. I hadn't lied when I told her I didn't ogle her body when I undressed her.

But I wasn't blind either—and Serena was perfection.

I needed relief. Something—or someone—to ease this unwelcome sexual frustration. But it was the dead of night, and I couldn't think of anyone who would be available for a late-night rendezvous. For once, I regretted my own strict rule about not hooking up with the patrons of Club O. At least there, willing bodies were around at all hours of the day. However, even if that were an obstacle of my own design, I didn't want just any woman.

I wanted Serena.

Lost in thought, I swirled the whiskey in my glass, the ball clinking against the sides. The faint sound of the shower shutting off caught my attention. Serena would emerge soon, wrapped in a towel, her skin glistening with droplets of water.

I tried not to think about all the things I wanted to do to her and tilted the glass until the last of the whiskey flowed past my lips. The liquor burned my throat, and I savored the layers of sweet toffee, subtle spices, and hints of oak. Setting the glass on the desk, I went back to the living room.

A door creaked quietly, and I glanced down the short hallway that led to the bedrooms. Serena stepped out, her skin glowing pink from the heat of the shower. Droplets of water traced paths down her delicate collarbone, disappearing into the towel that wrapped around her body.

I eyed her carefully, wondering what it would take for me to get this Italian goddess to submit to me. She didn't strike me as someone who took a lover without consideration. She would need to be wined and dined and given the respect she deserved. But that didn't stop me from imaging her reaction if I decided to rip that towel from her body, bend her over the back of the sofa, and begin to make every one of my fantasies a reality.

She stared at me with a mix of uncertainty and something more challenging, as if she expected me to either look away or make a move toward her. She was wary—as she should be.

If she had any idea about what I was thinking... About what I want to do...

"Thanks for the shower," she finally said, albeit hesitantly as she bit her lower lip. "Where are my things so that I can get dressed?"

With a lift of my chin, I nodded toward the sofa—and the two pieces of luggage tucked against it.

Serena went to the suitcases. She tried to maneuver both of them with her free hand, while the other struggled to keep the towel clutched to her body. I smirked. As much as I would have loved to see the plush terrycloth fall to her feet, I thought better of it. She would be too much of a temptation. My self-control was good, but I wasn't sure if I wanted to test it right then.

Instead, I moved to help her. She flashed me a grateful smile when I took over, then followed behind me as I pulled the baggage through the bedroom and into the bathroom.

With a half nod, I turned, and went back to the bedroom to allow her privacy. However, before crossing the threshold into the hallway, I noticed the bathroom door slowly shift open. The latch was faulty. I had meant to get it fixed, but it hadn't been a priority. After all, I lived alone and never brought women into my space. It didn't matter to me if the door to the ensuite bath latched properly.

As the door opened further, the more I could see. Serena's back was to me, bent over, as she rifled through the contents of her suitcase. The towel was still wrapped around her, but barely covered her backside. It draped low on her back, kissing the skin where her ass began to curve.

Mesmerized, I couldn't tear my eyes away from her as she shifted to stand. She gracefully unwrapped the towel, letting it fall to the floor. It was wrong to stare, but I couldn't help myself. Every line and curve of her body was like a work of art, beckoning me to explore it further. The gentle bend of her spine led to the delicate lines of her waist and the curve of her hips. Her olive skin was smooth and flawless, her movements a testament to effortless grace.

She glanced at the mirror and our eyes met. I froze, holding her gaze. Instead of rushing to close the door like I thought she would, she stood perfectly still. I couldn't move as her stare drilled into me through the reflection. The tension between us crackled like electricity and something flashed in her eyes.

Curiosity. Confusion. Fear.

I thought it might be a combination of all three.

I allowed my eyes to travel over the front of her body reflected in the mirror. I took in the smooth slope of her shoulders, her tight breasts and erect nipples, down to the soft lines of her stomach and the thin patch of hair at the apex of her thighs.

A mischievous smile tugged at the corner of my lips when I watched her conflicted expression shift to challenging. She straightened her spine, turned, and took a calculated step toward me. Her movements were fluid and determined. But just as I thought she would emerge from the bathroom completely naked, she instead reached for the door and closed it with deliberate force. The click of the lock signified that the door was truly latched this time.

I let out the breath I hadn't realized I was holding.

"Fuck," I muttered under my breath. I barely knew this woman, yet somehow, I was certain she would be my undoing.

CHAPTER NINE

Serena

The steam from the shower swirled in the air. Pressing my back to the door, I closed my eyes and counted to ten. I inhaled deeply on each count, but still I couldn't suppress the arousal that rocked me to the core. I opened my eyes once more. The air seemed to shimmer, as if there were sparks of electricity crackling and dancing all around.

Anton's gaze had burned into me, scorching hot, and left me aching. His onyx eyes had been filled with a mix of desire and something deeper. The way he'd looked at me made my pulse quicken, causing a rush of heat to spread through my body, creating a throbbing ache between my legs. Despite having a solid wood door between us, I could feel the intensity of his stare even now.

I wasn't sure how long I'd allowed him to look at me. A few seconds. A minute. In those moments, all sense of time had ceased to exist. I didn't know what had come over me.

Why did I let him stare for so long?
I bit my lower lip.

The question should have been, why did I *want* him to stare?

My cheeks flushed with embarrassment when I thought about how easily I could have melted into him—a perfect stranger—while he was pulling the bobby pins from my hair. I didn't know anyone in New York, I was almost broke, and I was in the home of a man who had seen me naked—twice—without my permission. And oddly, I was okay with all of it.

Am I so desperate for affection that I can just ignore the precarious spot I'm in?

Anton's proximity was more potent than any drug could ever hope to be. He was dangerous, and he stirred something in me that I hadn't felt in too long.

Desire.

Moving to the mirror, I ran a brush through my wet hair and considered the reasons that could explain my surprising ease with the situation.

Why Anton and why now?

I'd avoided men for the better part of the past year. I learned the hard way that no good could come from having one in my life. They couldn't be trusted, and I'd happily committed to being the hero in my own story.

But then I met Anton Romano—the man who dared me to trustfall.

I'd never encountered anyone quite like him. The feelings he stirred were hot and addicting, and not at all welcomed. Not when so much was at stake.

Once I was dressed, I felt more like a human being with a clear head. Ideally, I'd love to be on a plane home today. But I also knew that booking a same-day international flight to Italy would likely pose a challenge to my already thin wallet. I'd probably need to find a hotel to crash in until I could get an affordable flight. I just wasn't sure if the cost savings would be worth it. However, before I did anything, I had to call home.

Moving to the bedroom, I retrieved my cell phone from Anton's nightstand. I began to dial my mother but paused when I caught a glimmer of something inside the bedroom closet. The door had been left open a crack, allowing a glimpse of what was inside. Curious, I pushed it just enough so I could see better.

The closet screamed luxury, with perfectly organized rows of suits, each tailored to perfection. Stepping further into the space, I couldn't help but run my fingers over the luxurious material. Like the bathroom, not a thing was out of place. Each suit hung perfectly—almost too perfectly—presenting like a museum showcasing masculine colors and styles. I marveled at the meticulous organization.

But what had caught my eye from the bedroom were the sparkling glints reflecting off a large display of cufflinks. They shimmered in the soft light, each pair more dazzling than the next. From classic gold to sparkling gemstones, they highlighted Anton's impeccable taste. It was clear that no expense had been spared, yet I found the sophisticated accessories to be at odds with the dangerous vibe he gave off.

Who are you, Anton Romano?

I suspected he had a story. What it was, I didn't know. He both intrigued and scared me, yet I still wanted to know more about the man behind the polished exterior. Perhaps, in another life, I might have been afforded the opportunity. But not in this one. I had responsibilities that dictated my every move, and men who looked like Anton Romano were not on the agenda.

With a sigh, I left the closet and headed out of the bedroom with my suitcases in tow. When I stepped into the hallway, I was confronted with a sizzling sound and the smell of bacon. My stomach growled. Following the scent, I navigated through the penthouse in search of the kitchen.

Despite my unease about the unfamiliar setting, it was hard

not to appreciate the lavish surroundings. The penthouse was a sweeping display of luxury, from the modern crystal chandeliers hanging from the high ceilings to the plush, deep burgundy couches. The walls were painted with rich colors and adorned with expensive artwork, and the tall windows offered breathtaking views of New York City.

I entered the kitchen at the same time Anton placed a steaming plate of scrambled eggs, bacon, fresh fruit, and toast on the black marble topped island. Like the rest of the penthouse, the kitchen was sleek and modern, with polished stainless-steel appliances and granite countertops. The walls were painted a warm gray with glossy cream-colored cabinetry lining them.

Despite its splendor, the décor seemed to blur into the background. All I was able to see was Anton.

When I'd first met him outside the Met Gala, he looked debonair and irresistible in a tuxedo, exuding wealth and privilege. But here, in the penthouse, he looked different—more casual and at ease in his dark denim and T-shirt.

I felt a tightening in my core. The casual version of Anton was so much more potent. Seeing him like this was deadly, making him seem more relatable even though we lived worlds apart.

His jeans were comfortably loose, yet still managed to mold around his hips and thighs. His fitted T-shirt accentuated his broad chest and thick muscular arms. Music was playing. I recognized "In The End" by Linkin Park coming from speakers hidden somewhere in the room. The dark lyrics about personal struggle only seemed to amplify Anton's sex appeal.

The muscles in his shoulder rippled as he leaned forward, bracing both palms on the countertop. My stomach twisted, and my heart raced.

Focus. Put one foot in front of the other. You aren't sixteen.

As I approached the large island in the center of the room, I practiced nonchalance. I wanted to appear confident, even though I felt anything but.

Anton glanced down at my suitcases and frowned. He seemed annoyed to see them but didn't comment.

"Sit," he told me, pointing to one of the six cushioned barstools that lined the long countertop.

"What is this?"

"Food. You haven't eaten in two days." I shifted my eyes to meet his ever-observant stare. Heat rose into my cheeks as I recalled his gaze on my body. He spoke so casually—as if he hadn't just seen me stark naked in his bathroom.

It was awkward.

Once again, I asked myself why I'd allowed him to stare for so long.

I was about to insist that I wasn't hungry and should head out, but my traitorous stomach growled again. Reluctantly, I decided to at least have a fast meal before attempting to find a hotel room.

"Thank you. You didn't have to do this, but I appreciate it all the same. I'll eat quick, call my mother, and then—" I paused, noticing that he wasn't making a plate for himself. "Aren't you going to eat?"

"I don't like to eat before bed."

"Oh, I…" I frowned, once again aware of the time. My body clock was so screwed up. "I'm sorry to keep you up so late."

"Don't apologize. Although this is a little later than usual, it's not far from the norm. Rarely do I fall asleep before one in the morning."

"Oh?"

"I keep late hours and don't typically get up until eight or nine. It all depends on the day," he explained. "Weekdays, I just try to be up before the market opens."

Market?

I frowned and thought back to what Madeleine had told me

about Anton the night of the gala. He must be referring to the stock market. Madeleine had said he'd made his money on cryptocurrency and was a millionaire many times over.

"I don't know much about stocks or crypto," I admitted. "I just assumed people involved in that line of work started their days early."

Anton raised an eyebrow. "So, you know who I am then?"

I shrugged, wondering if I should be embarrassed that I hadn't known until Madeleine told me.

"My dress designer, Madeleine, filled me in after you left the gala."

"I see." He pressed his lips together in a tight line, clearly displeased about something. "What else did she say?"

"Not much. She just said that you'd made your way with cryptocurrency. Is that what's keeping you up late tonight? Worried about the current value of Bitcoin?" I teased, attempting to ease the sudden tension.

He didn't answer me. Instead, has glanced down at my plate and said, "You should eat before it gets cold."

He took a seat on one of the stools further down the island. His careful gaze was intimidating, so I quickly looked away and began to eat the eggs.

"I haven't had bacon and eggs in years," I told him.

He raised a curious brow. "Do you not like them?"

"Oh, no. I do, very much. It's just very American. Bacon and eggs aren't really a thing in Italy. Back home, a typical breakfast is hard roll with Nutella or sweet biscuits. Sometimes we'll add toast with thin slices of meat, like prosciutto, salami, or mortadella."

He didn't say anything but continued to watch me curiously. Every once in a while, he'd take a small sip from the glass that sat in front of him. It contained an amber liquid that I assumed was some kind of whiskey or scotch. He swirled it, causing the large ball of ice to clink against the sides of the glass before raising it to his lips. The action caused his T-shirt sleeve to shift just enough for me to catch a glimpse of dark ink curling over his bicep. The sharp lines disappeared under his shirt, teasing at a story I suddenly wanted to know more about.

My pulse quickened as I imagined tracing the design with my fingertips and wondered what other secrets might be under his shirt.

"Do you like to cook?" I asked between bites, needing a distraction from the inappropriate thoughts in my head.

"Not particularly."

His response was cool, and he didn't seem to be in a talkative mood. Still, I was intrigued by the stranger whose bed I'd slept in, so I pressed on.

"Have you thought about hiring a chef or a housekeeper?"

"I haven't considered bringing on anyone after my last household employee didn't work out."

"Oh?"

"I hired a majordomo about a year ago, but it didn't go well."

"Wow. Fancy—and not cheap from what I've heard. Was the person not any good?"

"On the contrary, he was stellar. His training was impeccable. I was the problem. I didn't like his hovering."

"But isn't part of his job to do exactly that in order to better serve you?"

"Perhaps. But I like my privacy. I don't easily trust strangers, especially in my personal space."

I pressed my lips together and contemplated his words, thinking back to the night we met. Although he divulged very little about himself, he'd been charming and convincing when he told me to trustfall. The suggestion had come easy to him, yet here he was talking as if he trusted nothing and no one.

"That sounds strange coming from the person who expected me to trustfall so effortlessly. Why so many trust issues, Mr. Romano?"

"Why so many questions, Dr. Martinelli?" he countered. I met his onyx gaze and found him studying me with a mixture of amusement and something else I couldn't quite place. He broke eye contact first, shifting to look down at my plate. "You aren't eating."

"You're changing the subject," I pointed out as I added more eggs to my fork.

He eyed me again, seeming hesitant. It was if he were assessing how much he wanted to say.

"I'm a private person. I don't live a conventional lifestyle. The fewer people I let into my circle, the better."

I frowned, mentally dissecting his response as I nibbled on a strip of bacon. I stole a glance in his direction, wishing I could get a read on him. At times, he seemed so much the gentleman. And at others, he gave off an edgy vibe that made him seem more calculating and ruthless.

I could sense his intense appraisal of me, and I did my best to ignore it. However, after several moments, his persistent observation won, and I met his stare. As nice as he was to look at, the most captivating thing about him were his eyes. It was nearly impossible to resist the piercing onyx that seemed to see through to the most secretive parts of my soul. Their intensity caused a flush to creep up my neck to my face.

He slid off his stool and made his way toward me, his swagger ever so prominent. When he leaned against the counter next to me, I swallowed hard.

He was close.

Too close.

My breath caught.

"You're blushing," he stated matter-of-factly. The corned of his mouth twitched with amusement.

My eyes widened. Mortification crept in.

"Am I?" I looked away, feeling the burn in my cheeks deepen.

"Yes, you are."

"Maybe the fever is coming back," I muttered awkwardly. Looking at the plate, I scraped the last of the eggs into a neat pile before bringing them to my mouth. Swallowing them down, I shifted off the stool. "Thank you for the breakfast and the shower. I have a few calls I need to make, so if you'll excuse me..."

I made to step around him, but he moved in front of me, blocking my path.

"No, you don't. Not yet," he said, catching my arm.

He studied me with such an intense scrutiny, I felt like I was being hunted by a lion. My insides twisted into knots. He was preparing to pounce on his prey. If I let my guard down, he could easily strip my soul bare. No man had ever affected me this way, and I didn't know how to respond to it.

"The longer I wait, the longer I'm stuck in New York. I love the city, but I can't financially afford to waste time dawdling. The sooner I..." I sucked in a breath when his hand lifted to tuck a strand of hair behind my ear.

"You worry too much about money."

"Says the guy who has tons of it," I replied. The words came out breathy despite my attempt at sarcasm. I just couldn't think while he was standing so close.

His piercing gaze remained fixed on mine. I was exposed in my khaki capris and off-the-shoulder sweater. My cheeks flushed deeper under the intense examination. I couldn't decipher the thoughts behind his stoic expression, but a hint of uncertainty flickered in his eyes. His unrelenting stare made me suddenly aware of every movement I made.

"Who are you, Serena Martinelli?" he asked, breaking the tense silence.

"I'm sorry?"

His eyes shone with a predatory gleam as his hand traced the curve of my shoulder. I bit down on my lower lip, my heart seeming to stop at his touch.

"You're nervous," he said in a deep, throaty voice.

"No, I'm not." The lie was obvious.

"Why are you afraid?"

"I'm not afraid. Cautious would be a better word. I don't know the first thing about you. My surroundings are unfamiliar and you're…"

You're making me feel things I shouldn't feel.

But I didn't complete the sentence. I couldn't.

"I'm what?" he pressed.

"Nothing." Unable to withstand his blistering gaze, I turned my head and focused on the undefined gold veins in the black marble countertop.

"Look at me, princess," he demanded, using one hand to turn my chin towards him. There was something dark and dangerous lurking behind those piercing onyx eyes, and I wondered if he was going to kiss me.

My insides trembled. I couldn't speak. I was a complete mess. The air was thick and suffocating, making it hard for me to breathe. His nearness clouded my senses, shattering any intelligent or rational thought. I tried to take a step back, but he grabbed hold of my hand and held it firmly.

He leaned in closer, and his breath warmed the side of my neck. The scent of pine mingled with something fresh and clean enveloped me. It was intoxicating and left me feeling helpless.

"I want to suggest something," he murmured. "But I can't help but feel like it will be a bad idea."

"What do you mean?" I asked, my voice barely a whisper.

He pulled away and took a moment before responding, as if selecting his words carefully.

"I've been around women my whole life. I usually have no problem understanding them, but you're a puzzle." A sardonic grin tugged at the corners of his mouth. "It's a puzzle I want to solve, and that includes learning why you were at the Met Gala. You mentioned seeking investors."

"Oh, um. Ye—yes," I stuttered, caught off guard by the shift in conversation. It felt like ages since that night, yet it was the sole reason I'd come to America in the first place.

"I want to hear more about it. But not right now. It's been a long couple of days, and I need to get some sleep. We'll have dinner together—tonight. Be ready to go at seven."

I blinked at the finality in his tone.

Did he just order me to have dinner with him?

It was as if there would be no discussion about it whatsoever. I bristled. Instinct wanted me to resist. I wasn't one to take orders without question.

But that was a different version of myself. Things had changed, and I was in no position to challenge anyone—especially someone like Anton. He wanted to know why I was at the gala, and that question opened the door to a discussion I desperately needed to have. Anton had money—and lots of it. He might be the solution to all my financial problems.

I most likely wouldn't get a flight out until tomorrow or the day after at the earliest. What harm could come from having a simple dinner with the man? I had to eat, after all, and I'd be foolish to squander the golden opportunity.

He took a few steps back and I exhaled, suddenly able to breathe again.

"I suppose I can do that," I agreed, my mind already spinning with ideas of how to pitch my proposal to him.

Anton nodded, looking pleased as if the matter were settled.

"Good. Now, since I've allowed you to take over my bedroom, I'm going to lie down in one of the guestrooms. Feel free to use the penthouse to do what you need to do. However, my office is off limits. The wi-fi is my last name, R-O-M-A-N-O. The password is Rebecca67, capital R."

And with that, he turned and headed toward the bedroom. I

was left gaping, unsure what to think about this strange turn of events.

I didn't know what he expected me to do all day—or I should say, all night—in this lavish space, but if it bought me time until I had to shell out more cash for a hotel room, I was more than happy to make do. I began a mental list of all the calls I had to make and emails I needed to send.

I also found myself questioning who Rebecca—capital R—was to Anton.

FOUR HOURS LATER, I stared out the massive windows of the living room. The city lights twinkled like a thousand tiny stars. Dawn was fast approaching, and my thoughts were a chaotic whirlpool as I struggled to digest the bizarre situation I was in.

I'd tried to call my mother, but she hadn't answered. More than likely, she was busy at the shop on Via Fillungo where she sold hand-sewn dresses to locals and tourists. In a way, I was relieved that she hadn't picked up the phone. It allowed me to leave her a brief, nondescript voicemail explaining my travel delay, saving me from an incredibly awkward explanation. I could practically hear her shock and disapproval if I'd have told her exactly where I was and how I'd come to be here—never mind that a strange man had undressed me and tucked me into his bed.

An image of my mother making the holy sign of the cross filled my mind and I smiled. No doubt, this would make her feel compelled to attend church twice a day for the next month.

I had a good relationship with my mother, but she wasn't who I needed at that moment. I needed Caterina, my best friend. Her familiar voice was the anchor I desperately wanted, but she hadn't answered my call either. All I could do was send her a quick text asking her to call me back. That had been three hours ago.

I reached up and rubbed my temples before moving my hands around to squeeze the base of my neck. From the whirlwind events of the Met Gala to my unexpected sickness, everything was a blur. Add in how I'd willfully allowed a stranger who looked like a Greek god to see me naked, and it was all too much.

This wasn't who I was, but somehow things just seemed to be happening to me. I wasn't known for spontaneity. Structure and order defined my days. Strangely, a part of me was drawn to the chaos. It both fascinated and terrified me.

What am I doing here?

I pinched the bridge of my nose as I further contemplated the situation.

I should leave before Anton wakes.

I could easily touch base with him about dinner once I was settled in a hotel. However, I wasn't sold on the idea of having dinner either. After all, there was no reason we couldn't conduct business over the phone—long distance, where I wouldn't be distracted by those onyx eyes. Heaven knows, it would be much easier to present a proposal if I didn't have to physically look at him. He was so attractive, it hurt.

Perhaps I should skip it.

An evening with Anton would only heighten this unexplainable desire I had for him. It was better if I kept a safe distance.

I glanced around the penthouse as if somehow the walls would provide the answer to what I should do. The expensive artwork and sconces stared back, silent witnesses to my struggle. They offered no guidance, only more uncertainty.

Pressing my lips together in a tight line, I shook my head. I'd indulged in nonsense long enough. Decision made, I went to the master suite to collect my things. It was time to go.

CHAPTER TEN

Anton

My feet thudded against the revolving belt of the treadmill, propelling me through the final mile in my home gym. Beads of sweat dripped down my face, mingling with the salty traces already staining my skin. I welcomed the burning sensation in my muscles and the steady rhythm of my breath. A good cardio workout was exactly what I needed to clear my head—especially after the shock I'd experienced after I woke up.

She was gone. Really gone.

I wasn't sure why it had bothered me so much. Perhaps because she'd left without so much as a goodbye. Her suitcases had vanished, and if it weren't for the lingering traces of her perfume, it was as if she hadn't been there at all.

But even as I pushed myself to run faster and harder, my mind couldn't escape the memories of Serena Martinelli. They had plagued my sleep and every waking thought since our first meeting. The fitful dreams during the night had left me feeling like I'd barely slept at all, igniting a wildfire within me and exposing just how mundane my life had become.

Before meeting her, I'd been content. I had money and could do whatever I wanted, yet now everything seemed dull. Finding the Brutus Denarius was important to me, but the idea of obtaining the coin was suddenly far less important than uncovering the truth about Serena. She was extraordinary, and I wanted to know more about her.

As I reached the end of my run, exhaustion burned in my muscles. I hit the kill switch on the treadmill and slowed my pace until the belt came to a stop. I pulled the sound buds from my ears and set them on the bench press, silencing the Imagine Dragons album that I'd been listening to. My chest heaved as I caught my breath, sweat dripping down my face and neck. Grabbing a nearby hand towel, I closed my eyes and wiped it away. Behind my lids, Serena's piercing blue gaze invaded my mind, an alluring vision searing into me.

I couldn't help but imagine what she would look like with her lashes lowered in submission. I liked to indulge my Dominant side when the mood struck, and Serena had hit every pressure point. She'd be an unlikely sub. She had too much fire and strength in her to follow a command without question. But that didn't mean I wasn't up for the challenge. I wanted her naked body kneeling before me. The image was both tantalizing and maddening, sending an electric jolt of desire straight to my groin.

Get a grip.

Shaking off these thoughts, I chided myself for being so consumed by a woman I barely knew. But try as I might, I couldn't deny the intense pull she had over me.

Tossing the towel onto the ground, I left the gym and made my way to the master suite.

As I entered my bedroom, I tried not to look at my bed—the place she'd slept for two days. Even that was now a reminder of her. Striding past it, I grabbed a change of clothes from the closet and headed toward the bathroom. Pushing the heavy door closed, I heard the satisfying click of the latch—the very same one that had failed Serena, leaving her exposed and naked in front of me. I kicked off my sneakers and stripped out of my damp workout clothes. After adjusting the shower valves to my preferred temperature, I stepped under the steaming water and braced myself against the wall tiles. I let out a sigh as the heat soothed my muscles.

But even in this peaceful moment, thoughts of Serena didn't fade. I couldn't recall a time in my life when a women had gotten under my skin as much as she had, and I wasn't sure what to do about it. I wanted to know her story. The unknown was both exhilarating and dangerous for someone like me.

If she was in some sort of trouble, she could bring unwanted attention. The press was already circling me like hungry wolves scenting fresh prey. I was a shiny new penny to them. They'd have a field day if they ever found out that their newly minted crypto billionaire was also the owner of a sex club. It would open Pandora's Box and risked exposing secrets that were long dead and buried.

What would Serena think if she knew where I came from?

I shook my head. I had to think about this rationally. I'd just met the woman mere days ago, and she'd been asleep for the better part of that time. So many things could go wrong if I divulged too much. It was better to keep my focus, and ensure finding the Brutus Denarius was my only goal. If she had it, I was confident I could get it for the right price. After all, Serena needed money, and I had plenty of it. If I happened to seduce her into my bed during the process, it would be a satisfying bonus. I'd wanted her under me, hot and submissive, since day the moment I'd laid eyes on her.

The problem was, I had no idea where to find her.

AN HOUR LATER, I approached the main entrance to Cornerstone Tower. A sleek ornamental spire soared high above the building, piercing the sky. It was a bold symbol of the ruthless and powerful entrepreneurs who occupied the coveted office space in the renowned skyscraper.

I pushed through the revolving doors and made my way across the vestibule to the bank of elevators. I gave a brief nod to the uniformed guard behind the polished mahogany security desk before entering my floor number into the keypad.

On the forty-second floor, the doors opened to reveal a long corridor that divided the floor into two sections. One half was occupied by the Davenport Accounting Firm, and the other half belonged to me.

My office staff was minimal, only Zeke and Myla McKinnon, my personal secretary. I didn't need a lot of space, and I certainly didn't need a floor the size of half a city block—but needs and wants were two different things.

My personal office at Romano LLC was spacious, and I'd made sure it had a view. The conference room was impressive, if rarely used, while Zeke and Myla had sizable offices of their own. Each was secured by a fingerprint access panel, making the waiting area the only space accessible to the public.

If truth be told, I much preferred my office at Club O, but it wasn't a place for respectable people to conduct business. The office at Cornerstone Tower had a purpose, but it was for show more than anything else.

Myla exited her office to greet me in the reception area. Dressed in a short black skirt that hugged her hips and a tiny siren red top that left little to the imagination, Myla wasn't what some would call a traditional assistant. She came from my world —a dark world that we'd once shared a long time ago. The former prostitute had only been sixteen when I'd saved her from wasting away in the underbelly of society. Because of that, I had her loyalty. And her discretion.

Myla was also a genius with numbers and extremely organized. Her efficiency made her a valuable asset to the empire I'd just begun to amass. While I analyzed the crypto markets and dabbled in venture capitalism by day, she and Zeke kept track of business matters at the club that required my attention by night.

"Good evening, Mr. Romano," Myla said. Her voice was naturally sultry, which had worked to her advantage in her former life.

"Myla," I replied with a nod. "Have the monthly expenses been added to the books?"

"Yes, sir. Included is the updated invoice from J&D Liquor Distribution. However, it still isn't correct, despite my numerous attempts to get their accounting department to adjust it. You're being taxed double by the state because of it."

"As if we aren't already taxed enough by New York State," I muttered. "Don't worry about it. I know Josh, one of the owners of J&D. I'll call him personally to get it straightened out. What else do you have for me?"

"New additions to the payroll need your John Hancock," she said, handing me a manilla folder. "And Zeke left an envelope on your desk. He said it was a personal matter that you wanted him to look into."

My ears perked up. It had to be the background report on Serena.

"Thank you, Myla."

Without another word, I went straight to my office.

Taking a seat in the black leather chair behind my desk, I set the messenger bag that I'd brought with me that morning on the floor. I pulled a letter opener from the top drawer and sliced open the envelope Zeke had left. Inside was a printout and a sticky note with Zeke's handwriting.

Boss, she's squeaky clean. Not even a parking ticket. Hale wasn't able to find more than this, but admitted her foreign residence made things harder to dig up. The only red flag is her debt load. She's about 250k deep, but most of it is in student loans. Let me know if I should ask Hale to keep digging. - Z

This wasn't a good sign. Hale Fulton was the best in his field. If he hadn't found anything, there was nothing to find. Frowning, I peeled off the sticky note and began reading through the background report.

FULL NAME: Serena Amara Martinelli
DOB: August 1, 1992
PLACE OF BIRTH: Mesa, Arizona (St. John Medical Center)
PHYSICAL DESCRIPTION:
Height: 5 feet 7 inches
Approximate Weight : 135 lbs.
Hair: dark brown
Eyes: blue
ADDRESS:
Current address: unlisted/unknown (*possible apt. rental in Rome, Italy)
Previous address: Via Guglielmo Marconi, 11, 55022 Bagni di Lucca LU, Italy
PHONE: +39 0583-953857 (*disconnected 2 months ago, updated number not found)
CITIZENSHIP: Dual: United States and Italy
PARENTS:
Carlo Martinelli (father, October 2, 1962 – November 15, 2022)
Sylvia Martinelli (mother, March 30, 1964 –)
SIBLINGS: None
RELATIONSHIP STATUS: None found
EDUCATION:
School (gr. K) - Mesa, Arizona: Desert Bloom Academy

School (gr. 1-4) - Pompeii, Italy: Vesuvio Primary School
School (gr. 5-6) - Athens, Greece: Acropolis Intermediate Academy
School (gr. 7-8) - Phoenix, Arizona: Copper Canyon Middle School
School (gr. 9-10) - Phoenix, Arizona: Saguaro Vista Preparatory Academy
School (gr. 11-12) - Lucca, Italy: Lucchese Classical Lyceum
College: Arizona State University
College: Sapienza University of Rome
College: Università degli Studi di Firenze, Doctor of Philosophy (PhD) in Archaeology
OCCUPATION:
Professor of Archaeology, RPA, American University of Rome
Roman Discovery, Fieldwork, Dig Director
SOCIAL MEDIA PLATFORMS: Facebook Only
CLUBS & ORGANIZATIONS: Archaeological Institute of America
CRIMINAL BACKGROUND: None
BANK & CREDIT INFORMATION:
Banca Intesa Sanpaolo: checking account balance: €1731.42
No savings found
No U.S. bank accounts found
Credit Debt: €39,393
Loan Debt: €226,569
VEHICLE MAKE AND MODEL: Fiat Panda

I read through the document once more, although I already knew there wasn't anything hiding in the text. Dr. Serena Amara Martinelli lived a very normal—very boring—life. She had little money and high debt. Based on the way she'd jumped schools, it looked like she'd moved around a lot too. But since she was a minor, it was most likely due to her parents.

I didn't know what kind of skeletons I'd been expecting, but I'd thought there might be a clue that would explain why her hotel room had been tossed. Perhaps it really was just a random break in.

I leaned over the side of the chair, reaching into my messenger bag to retrieve the leather-bound journal that I'd swiped from Serena's motel room. Placing it in front of me, I ran my hand over the soft cover, worn from years of use. I opened it, the pages crackling softly under my fingers.

The first few pages were filled with neat handwriting with tight loops and sharp angles. I wasn't sure if it was Serena's or someone else's. The more I flipped, the stranger it got. Folded maps lay between the pages, old and frayed, sketched with symbols I couldn't make sense of. Some were detailed, with tiny notations in the margins, while others looked like half-finished rough outlines of places I didn't recognize.

My eyes caught on a particular symbol sketched within the journal. It seemed to carry significant meaning, as the pattern was repeated on several pages. It reminded me of a coiled snake with loops spiraling unevenly. The snake's eye was out of proportion, its oversized pupil irregular.

While not quite exact, it was eerily similar to the spray-painted design on the back of the Midtown motel room door. The more I looked at it, the more I was convinced there was a connection—another riddle without a key.

There were references to Cleopatra and Mark Antony throughout the book as well. I was vaguely familiar with the stories, or at least the version everyone else knew about their tumultuous love affair. But my knowledge was limited. Whoever had written in this journal wrote about them as if they'd known them personally. They seemed to be chasing something deeper, in search of more than just history.

I flipped back to a map page that had one corner folded down. There were small marks drawn across the map connecting cities and ruins. It was like a treasure hunt—except it provided no clues to what I was looking for.

Seeing so many ancient references was like viewing a time warp to another place. It reminded me of my coin collection. My eyes settled on the framed watercolor painting across the room. Behind the canvas, a hidden safe was nestled in the wall. It held my collection of ancient coins. I didn't have to leave my chair to picture the glass case and empty velvet slot where the Brutus Denarius should have been. But the coin was out of my reach, much like the answers I sought to find about Serena.

I sat back in the chair and breathed deeply, allowing her face to face fill my mind. The lack of information in the background check and the journal was nothing short of irritating. Neither told me where to find her. Even her current address was unknown. If she was living in Rome as suspected, trying to locate her in the densely populated city would be like trying to find a needle in a haystack.

Frustrated to have learned almost nothing of substance, I returned the leather journal to my bag, slipping Serena's background check in alongside it. Needing a distraction, I opened the manilla envelope Myla had given me with the new hire information.

I began to sign in the required spots, trusting that Zeke had fully vetted each and every person. Once that was done, I shot off an email to Josh at J&D requesting a call time, and then began reading and sorting the invoices that needed my attention.

The rest of the day was spent analyzing market trends and making portfolio adjustments where necessary. Before I knew it, over ten hours had passed. The only break I'd taken was to meet Alexander Stone for a working lunch. The real estate tycoon had presented several investment opportunities to me, ones I was eager to look more into. Crypto had made my fortune, but I had concerns about its environmental impact. The sooner I got out of the digital currency market, the better.

The idea made me think about a meeting I'd had last week with a potential club member. He had also made his fortune through digital assets on the blockchain, making him a very recognizable member of society. He'd wanted my personal assurances that his membership at Club O would remain a secret. Of course, that was never a guarantee, but we had plenty of safeguards in place. I gave him the rundown of the ways we protect our members and explained the vested interest every member had in maintaining privacy. Satisfied, he readily wrote me a hefty check for an annual membership.

Club O's fees weren't cheap, and his membership alone paid the salary of every service employee in the place. I may have made my fortune on crypto, but club revenue was a sizable source of my income. I could sell my crypto portfolio tomorrow and have more than enough money to last a lifetime.

So why don't I?

I pressed my lips in a tight line, knowing the answer. I needed security before I sold—a guarantee that I would never again be without money. That's where Alexander Stone came in. He understood my situation better than most and knew ways I could diversify my income.

Leaning back, I rubbed my hand over the back of my neck, massaging the tight muscles. I was exhausted, but my workday was far from over. Club O needed my attention. With all the recent hiring, I wanted to see for myself how the staff changes were working out.

Pulling out my phone, I sent Zeke a text.

TODAY 3:31 PM: ME

7:31 PM, Me: I'm headed to the club. Are you there?

His reply came almost instantly.

> **7:31 PM: ZEKE**
> Yep. I'll come get you.

> **7:32 PM: ME**
> Don't waste your time. I took the Aston Martin this morning. I'll be at the club in less than 15 minutes.

> **7:32 PM: ZEKE**
> We need to get you a Volvo.

> **7:33 PM: ME**
> I'll leave the bulletproof beast to you. I like my car. See you soon.

Pocketing the phone, I secured my office and turned off the lights. As I made my way to the parking garage, thoughts of Serena were not far from my mind.

I WALKED through the main vestibule of Club O, passing the mosaic wall and rock garden, appreciating the calming sound the built-in waterfall provided. I'd already introduced myself to the new staff and spent time watching them in action. I approved of Zeke's hiring choices and thought they were going to work out well. They understood that it was a privilege to be inside these walls, and they were paid handsomely to keep its secrets.

Normally I enjoyed a hands-on approach to the club. I loved the control, and was involved in every facet of the business. But my heart wasn't in it today. Tonight, all I could think about was Serena. I had to find her. My obsession went beyond physical attraction. It ran deeper in ways I couldn't explain. Perhaps it was because I knew she'd be a challenge—the biggest one I'd ever face—and I never shied away from a challenge.

As I moved through the halls of sin, I decided to grab a quick nightcap at the bar before heading back to the penthouse. I passed through the throngs of people in the common area on my way to the lounge. The door leading down to The Dungeon opened, and music by Dua Lipa filtered up, amplifying the monthly Blinded By Lust party in the sub club. The blindfold play night was always popular, and the place was packed. When the door closed, the atmosphere of quiet seduction returned.

"Pappy Van Winkle, neat," I said to Brock, one of the more seasoned bartenders.

"Busting out the expensive bourbon tonight, boss? What's the occasion?"

"No occasion. It's just been a long a day."

Three long days, but who's counting?

Glancing down the polished mahogany bar, I noticed Amber Hawthorne on the prowl. She was dressed in a tight black dress with her long, dark locks secured in a braid. Just as beautiful and as sultry as always, she stood out in any crowd. She wore a green wristband again today, and I found myself seriously thinking about breaking my cardinal rule.

When she looked my way, her eyes immediately lowered like an obedient submissive, her chin angling down. Amber was a well-trained sub. If I gave her the signal, she'd drop to her knees without question. I'd be able to wrap my hand around the braid that trailed down her back with confidence, knowing she'd do everything she could to please me.

Taking a step toward her, I put a finger under her chin and tilted her head up to look at me. Hazel eyes met mine—not the deep ocean blues that I hadn't been able to stop thinking about.

It was then that I realized how much I'd been obsessing over Serena. Since the moment I'd seen her, I wanted her legs wrapped around my waist and craved her cries for more. No woman had commanded my desired the way she did. And when I looked at Amber, I felt nothing.

There was only one woman I wanted underneath me, but I had no idea where she was.

Lowering my hand, I gave Amber a small smile to soften the rejection I was about to deliver.

"Boss." I glanced to my left to see Zeke approaching. "Sorry to interrupt, but I thought you'd want to know right away."

"What is it?"

He glanced at Amber, then back at me before seeming to carefully choose his words. "News about the good doctor."

Any thought of letting Amber down easy disappeared.

Turning back to her, I gave her a pointed stare. "You know the rules, darling. I don't get involved with club members. Now, move along."

Undeterred, she slid her hand up my forearm and over my bicep.

"We'd be good together, you know," she said. Another time, perhaps we would have. But now was not it.

"I said no. Walk away, Amber," I barked, ignoring her pouty response to my command. I turned my attention back to Zeke. "What have you got?"

"A few things. Luckily, the security system at the Midtown motel was weak, and they don't have any CCTV cameras. And it was by pure happenstance that the street cams in that area were down for maintenance. As far as anyone knows, we were never at the motel."

"Good. Any news on Serena's whereabouts?"

A corner of Zeke's mouth turned up in a smirk. "Yep. I found her."

I raised an eyebrow. "And you didn't feel the need to tell me that first?"

"Come on. You know me. I like to save the best for last. She's right outside the gates to the club. I spotted her on one of the perimeter cameras while I was training a new hire on the security system."

"She's here?" I asked incredulously.

"Not *here* per se, but nearby. As soon as I saw her, I came to tell you. If you want to catch her, she should still be on the block."

My mind began to race. A person didn't accidentally loiter beyond the gates. To the outside world, the people within these walls were freaks. Although experience taught me that the most judgmental voices were the ones who often harbored the filthiest desires.

Be that as it may, sex clubs were not part of civilized conversations, so I couldn't think of a single way she could have found out about Club O.

"How in the hell did she find this place?"

"Not sure if she did, boss. Looked like she was just out for a walk."

"Well, I'm about to find out."

CHAPTER ELEVEN

Serena

I wandered aimlessly on the sidewalks of New York, determined to find some semblance of peace before I got on a plane to return home. The past few days had felt like a whirlwind, even if I had been sleeping for half the time.

After I'd left Anton's penthouse, I tried to get a room at the motel I'd been staying at before, but when I arrived at the Midtown, I'd found it swarming with police. Everything had been roped off with crime tape. I overheard some of the conversations had by those loitering around and was able to piece together fragments of their chatter. A member of the hotel staff had been found dead. The presence of crime tape suggested foul play. I recalled Anton's warnings about the seedy motel, and I was glad I hadn't been there for whatever had gone down.

Not left with much choice, I ended up at a hotel a few blocks south. It was nice, clean, and three times the price. But I was past the point of caring. Cash would be low for the foreseeable future, so I'd pulled out the emergency credit card. Within thirty minutes, my only zero balance card carried the financial burden of a hotel room, a one-way ticket to Rome, and an overpriced bottle of Sauvignon Blanc.

Living in Italy had trained my tastebuds to appreciate a fine wine, and this bottle had failed to hit the mark. But beggars couldn't afford to be choosey. It was an unnecessary splurge, but I'd earned it, and had happily consumed two glasses of the mediocre wine before heading out for a walk.

I meandered slowly, appreciating that I had nowhere to be for the evening—even if that hadn't been the original plan. When I left the penthouse, it was merely to create some space. Once I was settled, I had every intention of calling Anton about dinner, but then I realized I didn't have his phone number. After hours of indecision, I decided I would have looked stupid if I went back after leaving so abruptly. So, now here I was, committed to looking him up once I was back in Italy where I could safely do business over the phone.

I browsed the store fronts and landmarks as I walked. It was getting late. Other than a smattering of restaurants and bars, most places had closed up hours ago.

My thoughts wandered back to my short time with Anton. I pictured piercing onyx eyes, razor sharp cheekbones, and the knowing smile that made my pulse quicken and my stomach twist. I was familiar with desire, even if it had been a long time since I'd last felt it.

I'd wanted to give myself over to it—to flirt, to fall into a game of seduction, and see where it led to. In hindsight, I wasn't sure why I hadn't. I was a grown woman after all, not a blushing virgin, despite what my mother might think. Catholic guilt was real, and she was quick to lay it on thick whenever the opportunity presented itself.

I'd never been promiscuous and had always been in a steady relationship with the men I took to my bed. Perhaps that was why I'd hesitated with Anton. I didn't know *how* to have a one-night stand. Emotional connection held too much value for me to allow one to happen.

I wasn't sure how far I'd walked or where I was, but it didn't matter to me at that moment. The noise from Midtown Manhattan had long since quieted, and I found myself on less eventful streets with few cars and even fewer pedestrians. My mother would say that a woman walking alone a night in such a big city was reckless. Perhaps it was. That was the thing about parents. No matter how old we were, some lessons stayed with us forever. The GPS on my cell might get me back to where I needed to be, but echoes of her warnings ensured I stayed ultra-aware of my surroundings.

A flash of light to my left caught my attention. At first glance, it looked like I was staring down a dark alley. However, upon closer inspection, I realized it was a driveway. The light had come from a car's headlights as it turned and disappeared into blackness. I squinted into the night, trying to make out where the car had gone but the moonless sky left me blind.

As if they had a mind of their own, my feet began to walk in that direction. After a few moments, I was able to make out the outline of a large, wrought iron gate. I continued up the drive, slowing my steps when I realized the gate was closed.

I was about to turn back, but a shimmer glass to the left of the nondescript entry caught my eye. Illuminated only by a nearby streetlight, the tall glass casement was built into one of the two stone pillars flanking the entrance. The statue inside is what gave me reason to pause.

I placed my hand on the brick pillar, needing a closer look at the artistry of the carved stone statue. It was a full body rendition of a woman with her head tipped back slightly. One hand covered a naked breast while the other was buried between her thighs. Her gaze stared out into the unknown, defiant almost, as she captured her pleasure.

At her feet, glass flames rose up to meet her, a symbol of the burning hot orgasm that she'd gifted to herself. The blown glass was a balance of color and form, blue and orange flames that evoked a sense of movement and energy. The vibrant colors gave life to the gray marble statue centered within. The translucency and depth of the glass made it feel alive with the flickering essence of fire, allowing light to pass through and enhance the vivid colors.

"Beautiful," I whispered.

I found myself wondering what I looked like in the throes of an orgasm—what I would look like to Anton if I'd allowed his hand to press between my legs.

Would I look like this woman? Could I allow the world to completely fall away, fully embracing the sensuality of the moment?

Emotion washed over me without warning, and I blinked back the unexpected tears.

What the hell is wrong with me?

I wasn't the overly emotional type. I was most like caused by the two glasses of wine I'd consumed. Fantasizing about a what-if moment with a man I barely knew was pointless. I'd probably never see him again. That's what I'd wanted, after all—to conduct potential business over the phone so I didn't have to look into those gorgeous eyes.

I needed to go back to my hotel. Wandering aimlessly in the dark, having no idea where I was, was foolish and dangerous. I pivoted to retrace my steps but stopped short when I crashed into something—or someone.

"Oh!"

My hands came up between me and the person in front of me only to find a wall of hard muscle. I looked up and found myself staring into the pair of onyx eyes I'd been trying to avoid.

Anton.

He felt all too familiar, his expression exactly same as the night we met—scorching hot—burning into my memory. I couldn't get a read on them then, and I couldn't get a read on them now. All I saw was an assortment of complex layers that were undecipherable.

There wasn't even an inch of space between our bodies. I could feel the heat coming off him as my thighs brushed intimately against his. One strong hand cupped my elbow while the other rested at the small of my back, his fingers splaying possessively.

"Princess. We really need to stop meeting like this." His words were innately sexy, and I wondered if that was deliberate or if the huskiness in his voice was part of his natural sex appeal.

"Hi," I said, my voice breathier than I'd intended.

"I thought we were having dinner together tonight, but you disappeared on me."

"Yeah… I, ah…" I was embarrassed by my abrupt departure—especially after the way he'd taken care of me while I was sick. The least I could have done was left a note. "I'm sorry. I was going to call. I just wasn't comfortable imposing anymore. I thought it was best for me to find a hotel."

He pressed his lips together in a tight line, seeming annoyed by my answer. "What are you doing out here all alone?"

My stomach flipped and I blinked, my heart beginning to race as I recalled what I'd been thinking about right before he showed up. I flushed as if he could possibly know, trying to ignore how every second of contact with him only made more nerve endings come to life. I craved his touch on every part of me.

My eyes darted to the sculpture of the naked woman, and too many erotic possibilities filled my head. My nipples tightened, tingling and hardening to embarrassing peaks. I stepped away quickly, hoping he wouldn't notice. The hand at my elbow fell to his side, but the other shifted to rest on my hip. I tried to ignore it and flashed him an uncomfortable smile.

"I could ask the same of you. Do billionaires regularly take nighttime strolls by themselves?"

"Some would say that's the only safe time for us to take a casual walk. Less chance of being seen."

"Is that what you were doing?"

His eyes narrowed and I could feel the twitch of his hand at my hip, carefully accessing me as he weighed his response.

"I had business in the area that ended earlier than expected. A walk seemed like a good idea, so here I am."

There seemed to be a challenge in his deep, rough-edged voice, as if daring me to question him. I gave him a casual once over. My modest skinny jeans, cream-colored gauzy shirt, and navy flats made me look like a peasant next to his pristine white shirt, dark tailored pants, and tie. He was clearly dressed for business, yet I couldn't help but wonder what kind of business dealings a crypto trader would have at this time of night.

"This feels like déjà vu. Except this time, we know each other better," I said casually, my tone holding more confidence than I felt.

"Yes, we do. Much, *much* better," he acknowledged, emphasizing his words in a suggestive way. "But not nearly as well as I would like."

Heat rushed into my cheeks as he held my gaze captive. His dark eyes twinkled in the dim streetlights, and a devilish smile turned up one corner of his mouth. It was blatantly sensual, and I knew he was thinking about the times he saw me naked.

I stared at him, unable to deny the desire building inside me. It was an ache I couldn't describe. His hand on my hip was possessive—as if he didn't need permission—intensifying my desperate want for him. All I had to do was lean in. It was so tempting.

Liquid courage flowed through my veins, the two glasses of wine I'd consumed giving me a jolt of confidence to explore the possibilities. God knew, without the aid of alcohol, I was anything but confident in front of this man.

I groaned inwardly and cursed the wine. It was making me reckless, enticing me to toss away my inhibitions without a second thought. Pushing aside all thoughts of stripping him bare right there on the street, I returned his smile and took another step back to create a respectable distance between us.

"I was just admiring the statue," I said, angling my head in the direction of the display case.

Anton glanced up at the life-sized marble. "She's beautiful."

"My thoughts exactly. She completes the flames. Or perhaps the flames complete her."

He turned back to me, his gaze curious. "You have a sharp eye. One wouldn't look right without the other."

I studied the glass and marble artwork inside the case. "I always thought the flames were missing something."

"Are you familiar with them?" he asked, his question revealing his surprise.

I glanced his way and smiled. "Of course, I recognize them. I'm the creator. I don't know how the flames came to be here, but I'd recognize my art anywhere."

"I'm sorry. But did you just say you're the creator?" His normally reserved expression took on a look of disbelief.

"Yes. I created this piece a few years back."

"I didn't know you were an artist."

"I wouldn't go so far as to say I'm an artist. Blowing glass is a part-time hobby that I mastered when I was in college. But I only create when I need to." I shrugged. "Not enough to make a living on, but it helped pay for a bit of my college expenses."

"A hobby? No. This is more than a hobby. It's real talent. Clearly the purchaser of the piece thought so too, or it wouldn't be displayed here so prominently."

I silently considered the flames. I recalled shaping the molten glass with the blowpipe and manipulating the form. The end result was a vibrant exchange of colors, where the calming blue contrasted with bright orange.

Still, despite its beauty, my glass creation paled in comparison to the sculpture of the woman placed strategically behind it. She defined art. Even though I loved what I had created, I'd always felt that the flames were missing something, and now I knew why. They needed the passionate woman to give reason for their existence.

"Perhaps," I said with a small sigh. "I'll admit, I'd hated to part with this particular piece. I'd always felt that this was one of my better works. But life happens. I had bills to pay, and a gallery in Florence offered me a price I couldn't turn down. I often wondered who the gallery had sold it to, now here it is in front of me, against all odds. I mean, the chances of me stumbling upon it an ocean away must be slim to none."

"Ironic indeed," Anton mused.

My eyes darted to look beyond the iron gates but all I could see was a driveway disappearing into the darkness. "What is this place, anyway?"

"Private property," he replied evenly.

I looked at him, thinking he would explain more, but he didn't. Instead, Anton's gaze bore into mine, his expression inexplicably intimate. I returned his dark, magnetic stare, attempting to measure what he might be thinking. Those piercing onyx eyes held steady. And once again, my thoughts drifted to what he would be like in bed.

Unable to stand his scrutiny any longer, I tore my gaze from his and turned my head to look at the glass case once more.

"My parents' neighbor, Enzo, had a little glassblowing shop. I was fascinated by the art and used to watch him work for hours. During my third year of upper secondary school—or eleventh grade as it's called in the States—he began to teach me," I explained.

My thoughts strayed to the past, remembering my first solo piece created under Enzo's supervision.

"Go on," Anton prodded.

"He passed away suddenly, leaving his glassblowing workshop to me. He had no family, so I suppose it made sense since I was the only person who spent time with him. I'd lose myself in the shop for hours, allowing time to just slip away." I paused again as I recalled what it had felt like to be in the heated embrace of a roaring furnace. I breathed deep, imagining that I was filling my lungs right before pushing air into the blowpipe, giving life to an unknown creation. "It's like weaving magic from fire and sand."

"You love it," he stated.

Blinking, I pulled myself from my reverie and angled my head to look at him. He scanned my face, studying me as if I were the work of art, and not the statue beside us.

"I do. Very much."

"Yet you dig up bones for a living. Another mystery," he added. "Why archaeology over doing what you truly love?"

He posed the question as if it had a simple answer. The truth stalled in my throat, and I stayed silent for the span of a few heartbeats. Perhaps it was because a small part of me was disappointed in myself for not following my dreams. I had always considered myself strong and independent, yet I'd chosen to walk a path that had been predetermined for me rather than forge my own.

"Like I said, there was no money in it. So, I chose archaeology for my father."

He moved closer to me once again, reaching for my hand and encasing it in his. As much as I knew I should pull away, I couldn't bring myself to. Instead, I found my fingers involuntarily lacing through his.

His free hand moved up, his thumb tracing the line of my jaw. I shivered from the contact.

"You intrigue me." The low, erotic rumble of those three little words made my stomach flip. Powerful, unbridled heat sizzled though my veins as his penetrating gaze seemed to bore deeper. "I keep asking myself the same question over and over again. Who are you, Serena Martinelli?"

"I'm nobody."

"We both know that's a lie, princess. You're unique and extraordinary. It's why I'm attracted to you. I'm bored by the mundane and, somehow, I know I'd never get bored with you."

"I'm really not that interesting," I insisted. My words sounded hoarse and breathy, even to my own ears. My reaction to him was unlike anything I'd ever experienced before, and I didn't understand it.

"I disagree. You're fascinating, and it's why I want you."

I sucked in a breath as my world seemed to tip on its axis.

"Excuse me?"

"You heard me."

"Don't you have a girlfriend?"

"No. What makes you think that?" he asked, sounding genuinely surprised.

"Your wi-fi password. It's Rebecca. Who is that?"

The corner of his mouth turned up in a sardonic smile. "Jealous, princess?"

"No," I lied, despite knowing I had no business being jealous. It shouldn't matter if he had a girlfriend. I had no claim to him.

"Rebecca was my mother's name," Anton explained, and I suddenly felt extremely foolish.

"Oh."

"You don't have to worry about other women, Serena. Relationships are more effort than they're worth." I tended to agree but didn't let on as he continued. "I'm not a hearts and roses kind of guy."

My brows pushed together. "What's that supposed to mean?"

"It means that despite my desire for you, I don't know if we'd be a good match. You seem like you would need...more. And romance isn't my thing."

I never had any illusions that he was the romantic type. On the contrary, I thought he was the exact opposite. My eyes skimmed over his corded neck and strong, square jaw. Five o'clock stubble darkened his features, making me wonder what it would feel like brushing against the insides of my thighs right before his mouth closed over my sex.

"Who said I wanted romance?" I challenged.

"You seem the type."

"You don't know me well enough to know what type I am."

"I'm a pretty good judge."

"I might surprise you."

"Alright, princess. I'll indulge in this game of cat and mouse. But let me warn you. I'm the predator, and I always catch my prey." He stepped closer to me, filling the space as if he owned it.

"And when you do?" My voice was steady even if my heart was racing. I held my breath, preparing for an answer that I somehow knew would shatter the fragile foundation I was standing on.

"I don't play in the conventional way. I fuck. And I fuck hard. If or when that time comes for us, I won't be gentle. I'll possess you in a way that will make you forget any other man ever existed. Do you think you can handle that?"

A ripple moved down my spine, raising the hairs on the back of my neck. My nipples hardened almost painfully, and my body hummed to life. I wasn't sure how or when the conversation took such a dramatic turn, but I was here for it. Angling my chin in defiance, I embraced his suggestion.

"I think you underestimate my wants and desires, Mr. Romano. I'm a thirty-one-year-old woman in tune with my sexuality. You seem to suggest that I don't appreciate a good, hard fuck. As for possession, no man owns me."

"Make no mistake. When the time comes, you will *want* me to own you." His eyes darkened and he leaned forward. I thought he might kiss me right there on the street. I breathed in, preparing for the thing I so desperately wanted. But instead, he bypassed my parted lips and brought his mouth close to my ear. Then he whispered, "When you look at that statue in the flames, what do you see?"

My body purred as Anton invaded my senses. Without thinking, I gave him my unvarnished opinion.

"She's a woman who understands and accepts who she is. Unafraid to bend to her own needs, she defies societal norms and takes what she wants, owning her pleasure without seeking permission." The words tumbled out of me, making me feel exposed and vulnerable.

And then, unexpectedly, tears pricked at the corners of my eyes when I realized how much the marble statue revealed about myself. I wasn't her, but I wanted to be.

"What else?" he asked, the heat of his words like a caress over the shell of my ear. The air turned heavy, and it felt like Anton and I were the only two people in the world.

"I-I don't know," I stammered.

"I think you do. You're just holding back because of the stigmas surrounding pleasure and fantasy. There are far too many of them. Why live life pretending pleasure—in all its forms—doesn't exist? I want you to let go of everything you know and tell me what you desire."

My heart raced as I considered his demand. What I was thinking—what I was feeling—seemed sacrilegious. But I told him anyway.

"I want to be her. I want to know what that kind of unashamed pleasure feels like." The words were barely a whisper. I should be horrified by the revelation, yet I wasn't. I didn't know what it was about this man that made me divulge so much raw emotion. For a moment, I wondered if it was because I knew he would understand.

"I want you to do something for me."

"What?" My breath hitched as his mouth moved to hover over mine. His lips couldn't have been more than an inch away.

"Trustfall. Can you do that?"

That single request was as smooth as velvet. The cautious side of me warned that I was approaching dangerous territory, but I didn't care to listen to it. It was all too easy to let every ounce of my self-preservation to slip away. Unable to stop the word from slipping from my tongue, I gave him the answer he was searching for.

"Yes."

CHAPTER TWELVE

Anton

A surge of victory came over me, even though I'd only just begun the battle. The odds of her being here—directly outside my club—had to be slim to none. Yet here she was confessing her desires, her gaze as potent as the flames she'd created. Perhaps I was wrong to assume she wouldn't be accepting of Club O and all the forms of salacious behavior that accompanied it. It was time I stopped asking myself who Serena was, and dig deeper to find out.

I released her hand to wrap an arm around her slim waist, pulling her tight to me. My free hand came up to cup the side of her neck. Her pulse was racing.

"You shouldn't be so quick to trust me, princess. I'm not a nice guy." She inhaled sharply, but she didn't pull away. Her stormy blue gaze never wavered. "When I see something I want, I make it mine. And I want you. In my bed and screaming my name. Does that scare you?"

Her breath caught again, as if she were surprised by my brutal honesty, but there was no mistaking the desire swirling in her eyes.

"No. Not afraid. I'm just..." She paused, seeming to search for the right words.

I took us a step forward, forcing her to move backward until she was pressed against one of the stone columns flanking the driveway to Club O. My cock ached painfully. All I wanted to do was carry her into one of the private rooms of my club and fuck her until I sated this irrational need that I had for her.

But I didn't do that. Instead, I pressed my body close to hers and placed my hands against the stone on the sides of her head. When she closed her eyes in silent surrender, I nearly groaned. With her caged between my arms, I leaned down and pressed a soft kiss to her lips.

I was gentle, making the kiss a complete contradiction to my crude words and hard cock. But that was the point. I knew Serena couldn't be rushed. I just want to give her something to think about.

I didn't use my tongue, but focused on her pouty lower lip, pulling it into my mouth briefly before releasing her. I stared into her eyes to see a raging ocean reflecting back at me. Serena would be fire in bed. I was sure of it, and in that moment, I'd never wanted to bury myself in a woman more. I took a deep breath, restraining myself from shoving those tight pants down her hips and doing exactly that.

I cupped the side of her cheek.

"I will have you eventually, princess. I want you in a proper bed when I take you, someplace where I can take my time worshipping your body."

She angled her head to the side, cradling it in the palm of my hand.

"My flight back to Italy leaves on Friday morning," she whispered.

I studied her. I didn't know if that was statement of fact or if she was trying to send a message that we only had one more day. Whether we ended up in bed or not, this wouldn't be the end—at least not if I had anything to do with it. I had to see her again.

"What are you saying?" I asked.

"I might not need romance, but I also don't do casual sex, Anton."

"That doesn't surprise me. I never thought you were a woman who took a man to bed with little regard." I paused and stepped back, angling my head with curiosity. "Serena, tell me why you came to New York looking for investors. What do you need the money for?"

Her expression shifted, like she'd been expecting the question but wasn't quite ready to answer. She let out a small sigh, tucking a loose strand of hair behind her ear.

"I need funding for the dig I've been working in Rome. It's a project that started with my father. I made a promise to him before he died and now... Well, it's complicated. We're excavating a site that might have connections to Cleopatra's final days. The problem is, my team and I are running out of resources, and I've sunk a sizable chunk of my personal savings into the dig just to keep it going."

I considered the contents of the leather-bound journal I'd been looking at earlier, and the grid maps it contained suddenly made more sense. Rather than let on that I had it in my possession, I only nodded, encouraging her to continue.

"I have enough money to cover my apartment rent in Rome until the end of the month. After that, my lease is up, and I'll most likely have to move. I'll need to try selling more of my handblown glass pieces to a gallery in Florence. If all goes well, I'll keep a roof over my head, but it would never be enough to fund a full dig. The permits alone cost a small fortune."

She looked at me, as if gauging my reaction. I was quiet for a moment, absorbing everything she'd just laid out.

"Where is your apartment in Rome?" I asked, deliberately prodding for the information so she couldn't disappear on me again.

"Trastevere," she replied, a faint smile tugging at her lips. "The flat is small but comfortable, tucked away on a narrow street. You can hear church bells in the morning, and there is a market just around the corner. It's become my home away from home—at least through the end of the month."

Her smile faded, as if her new reality was just sinking in. She was holding onto more than just an apartment. It seemed more like a dream—a dream that was slowly slipping away.

"This is important to you."

"Yes, it is."

I narrowed my gaze, coming to a decision.

"Give me one month," I said, taking an impulsive risk.

She looked at me with confusion. "What's in one month?"

"It's when I'll give you whatever funding you need for your project."

She blinked, her face awash with disbelief.

"Anton, I appreciate the offer. Really, I do. This morning, I was fully ready to pitch my case to you, but I've come to realize that it wouldn't make sense. Subconsciously, I think that may be why I left your place without notice. Funding for archeological digs typically comes from research grants offered by universities, governments, or private institutions—all of whom have a vested interest. You don't check any of those boxes and asking you for the money would make me feel like a fraud."

"You don't have to ask. I'm going to give it to you."

"Buy why? What's in it for you?"

"I told you I wasn't a nice guy, Serena. I don't do anything without there being a benefit to me—especially when it comes to my money. There are strings attached to it."

"What kind of strings?"

She bit down on her lower lip, something I'd come to

recognize as her tell. She did it when she was nervous. I studied her face, memorizing every detail so that I could get a true measure of her reaction to what I was about to offer.

"I said I wanted a month—I meant one month with you. I'm willing to come to Italy if that's what you'd prefer. For the most part, I can manage my business from anywhere in the world. During that time, I want to get to know you better. I want your mind and your body, and after thirty days, I'll provide you with whatever money you need."

"You c-can't—" she sputtered, her words halting as her eyes widened. She shook her head in disbelief. "You can't treat my body like a Wall Street transaction or a commodity to be traded."

"Are you saying you don't want the money?"

"I'm saying that I'm not going to trade sexual favors in order to get the funding I need."

I shrugged, having already known she would refuse my offer —for now. The corners of my mouth turned up in a half smile. I was amused by her ever-changing facial expressions. They were a mix of shock, horror, and disbelief. But there were also flickers of curiosity and desire that betrayed her indignation. It made my cock twitch.

"That would be your loss, princess. But I may have an alternative option."

Her brows pushed together with a frown as she waited for me to pull the other ace from my sleeve.

"What's that?" she asked cautiously.

"We can discuss it over dinner. Krystina's Place tomorrow night. I know the restaurant owner and feel confident that we can have a conversation there with minimal interruptions."

"And if I say no?"

"We'll go back to option one. I'll come to Italy, and we'll spend a month having fantastic sex."

Serena pressed her lips together in annoyance, making me want to kiss that smirk right off her face.

"Don't be so arrogant."

I moved closer, forcing her back so she was pressed against the pillar once more. Reaching up, I wrapped a hand around her neck, allowing my thumb to rest on the pulse at her throat.

"It's not arrogance if I'm right." I leaned in. To my satisfaction, she didn't pull away. I felt the heat flush her neck as her eyes darkened to a deep blue. They brimmed with possibilities as I moved close enough to feel her exhale on my lips. "Your pulse is racing. It betrays you. I dare say that the idea of spending a month together intrigues you."

"I never said anything to the contrary. I just said I wouldn't allow my body to be treated like a transaction." Her voice was breathy, betraying her confidence and exposing her desires. When her lips parted, I nearly groaned.

"Let me touch you, princess."

"You are touching me."

"I mean really touch you. I want to show you how good we could be, to give you the freedom to be the female sculpture in the flames."

She let out a quiet whimper as arousal seeped into her eyes. She hid her sexual need better than most women, but I could still sense it—hot and wanting. The pulse in her neck quickened under my palm as I lowered my head. Our breaths mingled and she angled her head, surrendering her mouth to mine.

Her lips were soft and full, parting to allow my tongue access. Electric shockwaves coursed between us, and she released a small moan. I responded by pushing my mouth harder against hers. Her need tasted too damn good, showing me that she wanted this as much as I did.

I kissed her desperately and passionately, teasing her with the promise of more. Adrenaline coursed through me and my cock throbbed. I pulled her tighter against my chest, and she melted into me, giving me all the encouragement I needed to lower my hand and squeeze her firm ass. I couldn't wait for the day when I'd see it flushed red from the sting of my palm.

I pushed my hips against her, allowing her to feel how rock hard my cock was. She gasped, swiveling her pelvis, our bodies meeting for a slow, gentle grind. It just made me burn for her all the more. I devoured her, our tongues twisting and tasting as she angled her head so I could take more.

And I wanted more.

I needed more.

I thought about the club, just mere steps away.

I could take her to one of the private rooms and... No. Now is not the time.

Tearing my lips from hers, I took a second to read her hooded ocean blue eyes. All I saw was desire and longing behind those thick lashes.

"Tell me what you want." When she didn't respond, I slipped a hand under her shirt until I felt the warm, olive skin at her waist. I pressed my lips to the side of her neck, trailing soft kisses along her collar bone as I moved my hand up to cup one of her breasts. I began to massage over the lacy fabric. "This—is this what you want?"

"Anton," she murmured against my lips. "What if someone walks by?"

"Let them watch," I growled.

She moaned softly at the suggestion of being caught, my words bolstering her enough to let go. Her fingers curled through my hair, then moved down to my shoulders and back, touching as if she couldn't get enough.

"Anton, we shouldn't. I shouldn't." Her protest was weak.

"Tell me to stop," I challenged.

"No. I don't want that either," she breathed. Her words were barely audible in the night air. "I want you to touch me."

Using two hands, I continued my exploration under her gauzy shirt, greedily pulling down the cups of her bra. Her breasts spilled free, allowing me to pinch her hard nipples. She arched, encouraging me to take more. I twisted one peak while slowly caressing the other, mixing both pain and pleasure. When she released a sigh of pleasure, I nearly came on the spot.

There was no doubt—Serena and I would by explosive in bed.

Sliding one hand down to the apex of her thighs, I applied pressure between her legs. Even through her jeans, I could feel her heat. She lifted her hips against my hand to get better friction. Her hands snaked around the base of my neck, pulling me in and searching for more.

The woman was driving me fucking wild and I'd barely even done anything with her yet.

Needing more skin-to-skin contact, I swiftly unbuttoned her pants. When she showed no sign of protest, I pushed the boundaries and dipped my hand under the waistband of her panties. My fingers connected with her slit, finding her hot, wet, and ready. I imagined her spread out before me, open to the mercy of my tongue. My fingers. My cock.

I released a groan.

"Fuck. I love that you're already wet," I murmured against her lips. I circled her hard clit for a moment, then drove a finger inside her heated well. Her breath hitched and her hips pushed upward, taking what I offered with fevered urgency. I increased my tempo, stroking and building momentum until she was whimpering with need.

"Come for me, princess. I want you to come on my hand."

She kissed me frantically, and my fingers thrusted deeper to massage her walls, only pulling out to trace wet circles around her throbbing nub. Her body tensed, and her shallow breaths began to come faster. I knew she was close, so I quickened the pace. If she refused to see me again tomorrow, I wanted to give her this memory at least—to make her see that if she gave us a chance, we'd be fire together.

When I thought she was almost there, I tore my mouth from hers so I could see her face. I wanted to watch her as she fell apart. Spinning her around to reverse our positions, I pushed my back against the pillar and took her chin with my free hand.

"Look up behind me. See the woman in the flames. Be her, Serena."

She did exactly as I'd told her. I continued to rotate my finger on that tight bundle of nerves, flexing my fingers with more urgency until I could feel the slight tremors of her building orgasm. Within minutes, her eyes grew wide, rolling before they snapped closed. Seconds later, I was rewarded with her muted cry of pleasure as she shattered under my palm.

As her ecstasy slowly faded to pulsing aftershocks, she lifted her head, her eyes fluttering open to look at me. I smiled at her glazed expression. Lowering my head, I gave her a slow, languid kiss. The minutes slipped by as she stayed wrapped in my arms—five, ten. I wasn't sure. All time seemed to have stopped. When I pulled away, she didn't mask the heat in her gaze.

"I can't believe I allowed that to happen in public," she said, stepping back so she could shift her clothing back into place.

I chuckled.

"It's a moonless night and nobody is around." I didn't mention the security cameras that were just over head. More than likely, Zeke was witness to the whole thing. It's why I made sure to keep her clothes relatively intact and body covered. Just the idea of another man seeing her made me irrationally jealous.

"It might be dark, but still..." She trailed off, glancing around.

Gripping her chin between my thumb and forefinger, I angled her head until her gaze met mine.

"That was just a taste. Dinner with me tomorrow night. We can discuss things further. And perhaps we can even finish what we started here tonight."

"Wait, what?" she asked, her glazed eyes suddenly snappping back to reality.

Releasing her, I chuckled and took another step back.

"Give me your phone," I told her. She frowned, but didn't hesitate handing over the cellphone that she pulled from her shoulder bag. Going into her contact list, I programmed my phone number and email address, then sent myself a text text message so that I would have her number as well. "Where are you staying?"

"Summit Suites."

I nodded in approval, happy to hear she had chosen a more reputable hotel. "I'll walk you back."

"It's not far. I can find my own way. But thanks."

My instinct was to argue with her. It was getting late, and I didn't like the idea of her walking the streets alone. It was a relatively safe area, but New York was unpredictable. I was about to press the issue but noted the stubborn set to her jaw. If she were mine, there would be no debate.

But she wasn't mine—yet.

I pressed my lips together, annoyed by the situation.

"I'm glad you didn't go back to the Midtown," I finally replied.

"Honestly, I tried to. The place is cheap. But when I got there, I found that something must have happened. The place was swarming with police and there was crime scene tape everywhere."

My brow furrowed as my mind flashed back to her ransacked room. If she had gone back there, she most likely would have been informed of the vandalized hotel room. But vandalization was hardly reason for cops and crime tape.

"Crime scene tape, huh? I wonder what happened." I kept my words casual, hoping to get more information.

"I don't know. I heard loiterers talking. I guess a hotel staff member was found dead."

Quiet alarm bells began sounding in my head. I recalled the hotel employee who'd gone to lunch but never returned. A trashed room was one thing. I'd been there, and the possibility of being linked to a murder scene brought my presence at the hotel to a whole new level. I would need to get Zeke on the situation immediately to find out what was going on. It didn't matter if we hadn't been spotted on camera. There was always the risk of being connected in some other way.

Not wanting to let on that anything was amiss, I brought the conversation back to tomorrow night's dinner.

"I'll text you tomorrow afternoon to confirm pick up, but plan to be ready by six."

"You're serious about dinner?"

"Very. And I'm even more serious about my offer to fund your project. Thirty days, princess. Think about it. Until then," I paused just long enough to place a chaste kiss to her lips. "Remember the woman in the flames. You deserve to be her."

"Anton, I—"

I turned on my heel and ignored her when she called after me. I hated to walk away, wanting nothing more than to take her to my bed tonight. But that would've led to regrets that I didn't want her to have. She needed space to process what happened here tonight.

Using a hidden path that led to the natural stone wall surrounding Club O, I ducked out of sight. I had no intention of going back into the club. Instead, I headed for my car to go home, opting to call Zeke about what happened at the Midtown rather than discuss it in person. I was still sporting a raging hard on, and walking through a sea of twisting bodies in the club was the last thing I needed to do—not when the object of my desire was still out of reach.

But I'd have Serena soon enough.

For tonight, a shower was calling my name—a very cold one.

CHAPTER THIRTEEN

Anton

The room is wrong—stretching and shifting like it's alive. The wallpaper melts, streaks of dark green bleeding into brown, and the air reeks of metal and sweat. She's there, her back pressed to the bed, her head lolling to one side, hair sticking to her damp face. Her arm hangs limp as another man climbs on top of her.

"Mom!" My voice doesn't sound like mine. It echoes too loudly, like shouting underwater. No matter how hard I try, my legs won't move. The threadbare carpet feels like quicksand, pulling me deeper, keeping me rooted in place. I struggle harder, chest burning, heart pounding so loudly it drowns out everything else.

I want to go to her, but I can't. Not with the way Jerry holds me tight. The rough hands on my shoulders are strong as iron. I twist, kick, and scream, but he won't let go. His face is shadowed and blurred next to mine.

But I can hear him laughing.

His low, raspy chuckle makes my stomach churn.

"Watch," he hisses, his breath hot and foul against my ear. "This is the life she chose. And this is going to be her fate night after night until you do what I want. Do you understand me, street rat?"

My mother's chest rises and falls, but too slowly.

Too shallowly.

There's a needle still buried in her skin.

Her lips are blue.

Her eyes flutter open for a split second, glassy and unfocused, as the man above her pumps his hips ruthlessly. I try not to look, but I can't block him from my periphery.

I squeeze my eyes shut tight, trying to block everything out. But I can still hear.

Jerry's laugh.

The squeak of the bed.

The stranger's grunts as he fucks my mother.

A strangled gurgle.

I open my eyes.

My mother.

I swear she looks at me, her mouth moving like she's trying to say something—but nothing comes out. Then her eyes close.

I scream again, louder this time, begging her to wake up. To fight. To stay. But Jerry only laughs harder, the sound sharp and cruel, slicing through me like a knife.

The room tilts, the colors bleeding faster, the shadows swallowing everything. Her face is fading, her body sinking into the couch like it's eating her whole.

My muscles burn as I fight harder to get to her, but it's useless. I'm strong, but Jerry is always stronger. His grip tightens, pinning me in place.

"Stop!" I beg, choking on the word, tears streaming down my face. "Please—don't do this!"

The needle falls from my mother's arm, hitting the floor with a deafening clink. Her eyes stare vacant at the ceiling.

The room starts to spin.

Jerry's laughter is back again—a horrible, gut-wrenching sound that rings in my ears as the room dissolves into darkness.

I JOLTED UPRIGHT, gasping for air. Sweat clung to my skin, cold and sticky, and my T-shirt was plastered to my back. My heart pounded so hard it hurt, each beat echoing in my ears. I pressed my palms to my face, trying to steady my breathing, but the images wouldn't leave.

Her lifeless body.

His laughter.

The sound of that goddamn needle hitting the floor.

It all clung to me like a second skin.

My chest heaved as if I'd been running for miles. The room was dark, the only light coming from moonlit sky, but it was enough to remind me that I was in my bedroom at the penthouse.

I wasn't there.

It wasn't then.

That was another time and place—a nightmare best left buried.

Nonetheless, I still felt sick. My stomach churned, twisting itself into knots. My hands shook as I reached for the glass of water on the nightstand, but I couldn't hold it steady. The water sloshed over the rim, dripping onto my fingers, but I didn't care. I drank it anyway, desperate for something—anything—to ground me.

It didn't help. The dream lingered, the memory as clear as it had been when it happened. I hadn't thought about that moment in years. I thought I'd buried it, locked it away where it couldn't hurt me anymore. But tonight, she came back.

And he came back.

The weight of it hit me all over again. I leaned forward, elbows on my knees, and let my head hang. My fingers gripped my hair, tugging hard, as if pulling it would somehow erase the pain.

"Fuck!"

It didn't matter that there was nobody around to hear me. My chest was tight. I couldn't get enough air, and my throat burned. I hated this. Hated how that night still owned me. No matter how far I'd come or how much time had passed, in my dreams, I was always dragged back to that filthy room, forced to watch the woman I loved most destroy herself while I was held down, powerless.

I swung my legs over the side of the bed and sat on the edge, staring out at the glittering skyline. New York, the city that never slept, was alive outside. But inside, it felt as empty as I did. No matter how high I climbed or how much I built, the past still found a way to drag me back down.

I wiped my face, the sweat cooling on my skin. I stared through the glass windows, not looking at anything in particular as I waited for my heart to slow. I needed to push the ghosts back where they belonged, but they never left quietly.

I glanced toward the empty side of the bed and, for a brief, foolish moment, wished Serena was here. I wanted her soothing presence in a way I couldn't explain. The thought hit me like a sucker punch, leaving me unsettled.

Serena could never see me like this—shaken, drenched in sweat, and fighting nightmares I should've conquered years ago. She deserved better than the mess I kept hidden behind the mask.

Standing, I snatched my phone off the charger on my nightstand and pulled up Serena's contact info. Her name glowed on the screen, a lifeline in the darkness, but my thumb hovered, unsure. My jaw clenched, the internal battle raging. It was after three in the morning. Waking her now would be selfish—

desperate, even—and yet, just the thought of hearing her voice was like oxygen I desperately needed to live.

Fighting the instinct to call her, I opened another app instead and pulled up her location. The little blue dot blinked back at me from the map, steady and unmoving. She was at her hotel. Safe.

I knew I was bordering on stalking. It was Possessive. Controlling. Wrong. My behavior caused a sour taste in the back of my throat. When I'd programmed my number into her phone, I'd turned on location sharing. I'd told myself it was practical, a precaution after she'd disappeared on me once, but now that little blue dot felt like something else entirely.

I sank onto the edge of the bed, phone still in hand, staring at the map as my thoughts spiraled. I hated myself in that moment —hated how broken I still was after all these years. Hated that even in this sleek penthouse, a symbol of the empire I'd built, I couldn't escape the shadows of my past.

The dream, like it always did, had ripped me open and left me raw. My chest ached, the need to reach out to Serena still gnawing at me, but she couldn't know about this—about where I came from. That part of me was dead and buried.

Leaning back against the pillows, I closed my eyes and tried to steady my breathing. The blue dot burned into my mind, giving me just enough comfort to surrender to the darkness of sleep once again.

CHAPTER FOURTEEN

Serena

I'd spent the night wrestling with my own desires, my body restless and my mind captive to the memory of Anton's touch. Falling asleep had been a losing battle. The phantom sensation of his hands on my skin had haunted me and kept the Sandman at bay. It wasn't just the heat of his kiss or the forbidden thrill of the moment. It was the way he commanded me, body and soul, as if surrendering to him was an inevitability. With Anton, it wasn't just lust. It was hunger—a fire that burned through every layer of restraint I'd carefully built.

By dawn, I gave up the pretense of sleep and slid out of bed. The glow of my laptop illuminated the small hotel room as I sorted emails, dove into grant applications, and scoured the Archaeological Institute of America's website looking for philanthropy and government organizations that might be interested in supporting my dig. I wasn't surprised to see there was little interest in funding a site that had already been thoroughly mapped and excavated. Most considered my father's project—now my project—a fool's mission. Private funding would be my only option.

I continued to search for opportunities, but every line of text felt like static as my thoughts continued to drift back to Anton's proposition.

One month.

Thirty days with him, on his terms, in exchange for the funding I so desperately needed for my dig.

The terms were maddeningly simple, yet they weighed heavily on me. I couldn't deny that the idea of being with him didn't exactly feel like a punishment. A month in the orbit of a man as magnetic and dangerously alluring as Anton Romano might destroy me, but it would be a sweet demise.

Still, the idea of being bought—of selling pieces of myself, even for my father's dream—left a bitter taste in my mouth. I just wished I could shake off the notion that I'd be some sort of commodity to him.

Frustrated, I picked up my phone and dialed Caterina. My best friend had always been my compass, grounding me when the storm of my emotions threatened to sweep me away. I'd called her yesterday after checking into my new hotel, but she hadn't picked up. Things between us had felt off as of late—distant almost. I made a mental note to make time to catch up with her more regularly.

As the phone rang, I drummed my fingers anxiously against the desk, praying she'd answer this time.

"Hello, lovely." Caterina's voice spilled through the line like warm honey, thick with sunshine and familiarity.

"Hey!" A breath I hadn't realized I was holding escaped me. "God, it's so good to hear your voice. It's been weeks!"

"You, too! How was New York?"

I hesitated, staring at the city outside my window. "Kind of crazy, actually. I'm still here."

"Still there? Why?" she asked, the concern sharp in her voice. "I saw that you called a few times, but I figured I'd just catch up with you this weekend. I thought you were supposed to be home on Tuesday."

"Yeah, I was," I murmured, moving to the bed and flopping down. I propped myself on one elbow and sighed. "It's a long story."

And so, I told her. Over the next fifteen minutes, I spilled everything—the electric first encounter with Anton at the Met Gala, the fever that had left me sick in his penthouse, and what it felt like to be in the presence of a man who was both too much and not enough. I ended the tale with what had happened last night—the moment that had consumed me since he'd silently walked away. It had been so surreal, and a part of me wondered if I'd imagined the whole thing.

Caterina's reactions came in sharp bursts of laughter, gasps, and drawn-out silences that spoke volumes. I told her everything —except for one thing. His name. I wanted her raw, unfiltered responses, free from the reality of who he was.

When I finally fell quiet, my heart was hammering from the memories. Caterina let out a long, low whistle.

"Rena, you Jezebel," she said in awe, but her tone was laced with amusement. "Making out with a gorgeous stranger right there on the street? Who are you and what have you done with my friend?"

A flush crept up my neck.

"I don't know," I admitted, pressing my fingers to my temples. "That's the problem. It's not me. I don't do things like that. I don't know what came over me."

"Oh, sweetheart." She let out a rich, knowing laugh. "I know exactly what came over you—an insanely sexy man made you feel something again. And it's about damn time, too."

A small, helpless sound escaped me as my head fell back against the pillows. "I don't know why I let it happen."

"That's a lie," my mind whispered.

I did know. It was the way he looked at me, like I was a challenge he was eager to accept. The way his touch lingered like an unrealized promise. The way his lips had branded mine, stealing my breath, my control, my logic. The way he'd dared me to be the woman in the flames.

Caterina scoffed. "Oh, please. How or why it happened doesn't matter. If he's as hot as you say he is, then why the hell not? It's not like you're some blushing virgin."

"It's not about that," I said, my voice softer now. My gaze drifted to the city skyline, to the place where I knew he was, waiting. "I just need to be careful. He's interested in funding the dig, but…" My pulse skittered. "It's more than that. He's not just any other guy, Cat."

"What do you mean?"

I swallowed, heart thudding. "Have you ever heard of Anton Romano?"

A long pause followed my question. The silence stretched on, and I began to wonder if she'd lost the connection before she finally spoke.

"As in the Anton Romano?" Her voice turned hushed, almost reverent. "Billionaire, crypto king, international enigma? *That* Anton Romano?"

I closed my eyes. "Yeah," I murmured. "That's him."

Another pause. Then, almost breathlessly, "Are you telling me that you had one of the hottest, most earth-shattering hookups known to man with Anton Fucking Romano?"

"Yes, Cat!" I said, exasperated. But then I lowered my voice so it was barely above a whisper. "That's exactly what I'm saying. And it's why I'm calling. He wants to see me tonight to talk over dinner. I just don't know if I should go."

"Rena, don't be ridiculous."

"I'm not being ridiculous," I argued, sitting up a little

straighter. "He's interested in funding the dig. I have to play this right, but his offer doesn't come without...stipulations."

"What kind of stipulations?"

I hesitated, not sure if I wanted to divulge the rest. In the end, my need to unload won out. "He'll give me everything I need in exchange for thirty days."

"Thirty days to do what?"

A smirk tugged at the corners of my mouth. "Me."

She laughed, a sound that was equal parts delight and disbelief. "Let me get this straight. Richer-than-sin Anton Romano made you see stars, and now he's offering to bankroll your dig if he can spend a month *doing* you?"

"Something like that," I muttered, still unable to believe I was considering any of this.

"This is like something out of a romance novel."

"I would hardly call this romance. More like a cautionary tale."

"Nope. This is a real-life *Indecent Proposal*," she insisted.

I considered the 90s movie starring Demi Moore. Like the heroine in the movie, I'd taken a gamble. I had followed my father's path despite my reservations, betting against the odds that I'd unlock Cleopatra and Mark Antony's mysteries. The gamble had cost me everything. Now my only choices were to give up my father's dream or give up a piece of myself to keep the dream alive. I was in a no-win situation, and Anton held a double-sided lucky coin.

"In a way, it very much is an indecent proposal. I basically said as much, too. I don't want to be treated like a business transaction, Cat."

"I was only teasing. Don't over complicate it. Money aside, that man is fine as hell. And you hooked up with him before he made you that offer. The interest is clearly there. You should go for it. See what happens. When was the last time you had sex?"

"Cat!"

"What?" The feigned innocence in her tone was palpable.

I smirked. "Subtlety has never been your thing."

"Answer the question, Rena."

Sighing, I pinched the bridge of my nose, hating what I was about to admit. "I haven't been with anyone since Cade."

"It's been a year since you two split."

"Ten months," I corrected.

"Close enough. You need to get out there and start dating again and now seems as good of a time as any. I mean, Anton seems like a decent guy. He didn't have to nurse you back to health. He could have easily sent you home with a driver and a 'get well soon' card. The fact that he didn't speaks volumes. Do you like him?"

I chewed on my lip for a moment before responding. "Yeah, I like him. He's charming, smart, and there's definitely an attraction there."

"So what's the problem?"

"I'm just too busy to date. I've been doing just fine with my rechargeable friend."

"That's not the same and you know it. If I were offered this thirty-day deal, I would want to find out if we were compatible in bed first—a hot alleyway make-out session isn't enough. What if he's into some weird shit? At the very least, have yourself a one-night stand and find out. They are completely underrated in my opinion."

I laughed. "I will admit, the idea of no emotional attachment is appealing."

"Exactly."

"I'm just not sure if I want to jump back into this arena anytime soon."

"Why not?"

"You know why." I paused, frowning before asking, "Have you seen them around by any chance?"

I didn't have to elaborate on who *them* was. Caterina knew.

The moment the words left my lips, a sharp silence filled the line, heavy with our shared history.

Cade. Briana.

The two people who had shattered my trust in a way I hadn't even thought possible.

"Fuck Cade Rosenberg," Caterina spat, her voice laced with venom. "He and Briana can take a flying leap for all I care."

I let out a dry laugh, though there was no humor in it. "I take it you've seen them."

"This past weekend," she admitted. "At La Terrazza."

My stomach twisted, a sharp, unpleasant pang striking through my ribs. Of course it had to be there. Our place. The rooftop bar that had once been my safe haven, where I had spent countless nights sipping cocktails under the Florence skyline with my three friends, laughing and making memories. The first weekend of every month had been ours—mine, Caterina's, and Briana's.

Until Briana had blown my world apart by having an affair with Cade.

Now it appeared as if she wanted to take La Terrazza, too.

Was there anything she wouldn't steal from me?

"What the hell," I muttered, rubbing a hand over my forehead.

Finding out she had been sleeping with Cade behind my back had been a devastating kind of heartbreak, but what had come after had been worse. The way they had twisted everything, rewriting the narrative until I was the unreasonable one, had hurt even more.

Cade had insisted it had just happened, that he never meant to hurt me, that I was the one who had driven him away with my "emotional distance" while I helped my mother care for my father.

His words echoed in my mind.

"You never let me in, Serena. You know how hard that was for me. I tried, but you kept shutting me out."

As if his betrayal had somehow been my fault. As if I had been the one to push him into her arms. It was nothing but manufactured regret.

And Briana—her gaslighting had been even worse. She had looked me straight in the eye, with that pitying expression she always wore so well, and had the audacity to say I was overreacting. She claimed that Cade never loved me, and if he had, he wouldn't have run into her waiting arms.

Even now, their words burned like fresh wounds that refused to heal. It wasn't the affair that bothered me the most—it was the way they had made me doubt myself.

And now, they were at La Terrazza, parading their relationship around a place that had once been ours.

I exhaled sharply, forcing the bile down.

"To hell with them," I bit out. "I dare them to show up again while we're there. We'll make it so awkward, they won't want to return."

Caterina huffed. "I might have told Alessio to spit in their drinks."

That startled a laugh out of me. I could just picture it—Alessio, the longtime barista at La Terrazza, giving them his signature unimpressed stare as he leaned in to accidentally contaminate their cocktails.

The brief moment of amusement faded, replaced by an old familiar pain. A heavy weight pressed down on my chest, the betrayal sitting there, cold and resolute. I was done crying over them. Done being angry. But the sting of what they had done, the way they had tried to make me believe I was the problem—that was harder to shake.

Maybe I had no control over the past, but I sure as hell wasn't going to let them take anything else from me.

Certainly not La Terrazza.

And definitely not my peace.

"Back to my dilemma with Anton," I said quickly, needing to change the subject. I refused to succumb to the bitter, hollow ache that thoughts of Cade and Briana always provoked.

"I don't see how this is a dilemma."

"Humor me. I want your honest opinion about what I should do."

Caterina sighed. "I already told you. Let yourself live a little and see if the two of you jive. Go to dinner with the guy. Hell, have sex with him until dawn, too. It will be good for you. But it doesn't have to be more than that if you don't want it to be."

"And what about this proposal? A month with me in exchange for money."

"Would it be so bad?"

I frowned. "I think we're choosing the wrong movie. This is more like Julia Roberts in *Pretty Woman*. While this is a far cry from the story of a rich man and a prostitute, it still gives me the same vibes."

I shifted to sit on the edge of the hotel bed, my phone pressed to my ear as I absentmindedly picked at the hem of my shirt.

"So, I'll say it again. Would it be so bad?" Caterina pressed. "I mean, just think about the clothes Richard Gere bought her!"

I rolled my eyes. "I can buy my own clothes, thank you very much."

"Oh, shit. That reminds me. What are you going to wear tonight?"

"I don't know. I hadn't even thought about that." I flopped down on the bed again, suddenly stressed about my lack of wardrobe choices. I reached up and rubbed my temple. "The only clothes I brought with me are my gala dress and some casual pieces—nothing even close to suitable for going out."

"Well, you're in New York," Caterina pointed out. "There's no shortage of places to shop. Surely you can find something."

I bit my lip, thinking back to the store I'd passed the night before, just down the street from the hotel. The window display had caught my eye, especially the red skirt and matching heels on the mannequin. It was a consignment shop, which would be perfect for my small budget.

"Actually, there's a store near the hotel. I walked by it last night. They had this gorgeous red skirt and heels in the window. It might be exactly what I need."

"Red, huh?" Caterina replied thoughtfully. "That could work. And you could add that ruby necklace from Madeleine, too."

I thought about the necklace with the deep red stone, and how it caught the light like fire. It was on loan, and I could only imagine it's worth. I couldn't chance wearing it for a casual night out.

"I can't. It was only supposed to be for the gala, not a night out on the town. Madeleine has already arranged the insured shipping. I have to return it as soon as I get home."

"Rena, come on," Caterina pressed. "You're going out for dinner in New York, not running errands around Lucca. That necklace would be stunning on you. And who knows? Maybe it'll give you the confidence boost you need for sexy time."

I laughed, imagining my friend waggling her eyebrows. I was about to brush off the idea again, but then I paused, recalling how Anton had seemed to admire the necklace—the way his dark eyes had lingered on me. When he undressed me while I was unconscious, he'd removed everything but my panties and the necklace.

Was that deliberate?

Getting up from the bed, I began to pace the room. Having dinner with him tonight wasn't just a casual thing. He was influential, powerful, and dangerous. And I wanted him—desperately. An ache formed between my legs just thinking about how we might be. But being around him also made me feel off-balance.

I closed my eyes and imagined myself on Anton's arm,

strolling into a restaurant with him—a red skirt hugging my hips and the ruby necklace resting just above my breasts, gleaming like a secret only I knew. Perhaps Caterina was right.

"Maybe I should wear it," I murmured.

"You'll look amazing, trust me," she said, triumph in her voice. "Anton Romano won't know what hit him."

Her confidence was infectious, and after I hung up the phone, I found myself eyeing the ruby necklace I'd worn to the gala. Maybe it would give me the confidence I needed to be bold—to be the woman in the flames as Anton had suggested.

Perhaps tonight wasn't just about a business proposal and dinner, and more about embracing the fire he ignited in me—and if I was going to play with fire, I had damn well better dress for an inferno.

CHAPTER FIFTEEN

Serena

A sleek, black Volvo SUV pulled up to the curb, its dark windows reflecting the setting sun and city lights. I smoothed down the red skirt and black satin tank top I'd purchased that afternoon from the consignment shop. Nerves and anticipation tingled in my stomach as I stepped out of the hotel lobby, the cool evening air brushing my bare shoulders.

I had expected Anton to emerge from the vehicle, his usual confidence on full display, but when the door opened, it wasn't his face I saw. A driver I didn't recognize came around the car.

He stood a few feet away, arms crossed over his chest, the sharp lines of his suit doing nothing to hide the solid frame beneath. His hair was dark but just beginning to gray at the temples, a subtle sign of experience rather than age. Broad shoulders, a strong jaw, and eyes that missed nothing made him look like a man who had spent years standing between danger and the people who paid him.

He offered me a stiff nod.

"Serena Martinelli?" he asked, his expression carefully neutral.

"Yes, that's me."

"My name is Zeke Kristof. I'm here to take you to Mr. Romano. Right this way, please."

Disappointment flickered through me, sharper than I wanted to admit. I hadn't realized how much I wanted Anton's onyx gaze on me. I loved the way his eyes lingered just long enough, even if it made me feel ambiguous in a maddening sort of way.

Zeke opened the back door, and I climbed into the car. Settling back against the buttery leather seats, I absently stared out at the buildings as Zeke merged into the traffic. The quiet purr of the engine and the smooth glide of the SUV should have been calming, but my pulse only quickened as I began thinking about the whole purpose of this dinner tonight.

Anton said he wanted a month with me, but he'd also hinted at an alternative option. I didn't know what it might be, and I couldn't help but wonder if this was all a game to him—keeping me waiting, letting the anticipation build until I didn't know whether I was more frustrated or turned on by his machinations.

So lost in thought, I hadn't realized we'd arrived at our destination until Zeke climbed out of the Volvo. He rounded the vehicle to open my door, his movements crisp and professional.

"Ma'am," he said politely, offering a hand to help me out. I accepted it, letting him guide me to the curb.

I looked up as Zeke escorted me to the main entrance of the restaurant. *Krystina's Place* arched in an elegant font over the door. I took a deep breath, my nerves tightening with every step. I didn't know what to expect once inside.

Would Anton be there to great me?

Or would I sit alone at a table waiting for him to appear?

A little voice in my head whispered that this was stupid, and I shouldn't be here. I wasn't even sure why I'd agreed to this night in the first place. When I thought back, I was pretty sure I hadn't. Yet, somehow, here I was. This was more than just dinner with an insanely handsome and wealthy man—it was the dance, the chase, the electric tension that had me craving more, even when I knew I should be guarding everything that I was.

Once I was inside, Zeke retreated to the vehicle and I was left alone. Looking around, I took stock of my surroundings. The restaurant was all polished mahogany wood with low, amber lighting. The only sounds were the murmur of voices blending with subtle piano music and the soft clink of glassware. The air was thick with the rich scent of truffle oil, garlic, and fresh bread. The vibe was luxury layered with just a hint of intimacy.

"May I help you?"

I refocused my attention on the attractive man standing before me. He had olive skin and thick dark hair. His smile was easy, but there was mischief in his eyes that added to his devilishly handsome appearance.

"Um, yes. My name is Serena Martinelli. I'm here to meet—"

"Yes, yes," he interrupted. "I am Matteo Donati, the restaurant owner. Pleased to meet you. Your dining partner is expecting you. Please follow me."

I frowned.

Dining partner?

Matteo didn't elaborate and I wasn't given the chance to ask for clarification since he'd already turned away. I had little choice but to follow him.

His broad frame cut a path through the warmly lit room as he offered a charming smile to everyone he passed. When he came to a stop at a doorway, he extended his arm to me.

"*Mia signora,*" he said, his voice smooth. I took his arm, and he led me deeper into the restaurant, my heels clicking softly against the marble floor as we moved away from the bustle of the main dining area and toward the back of the building. My heart pounded a little faster with each step, anticipation winding tight inside me.

At the end of the corridor, a heavy velvet curtain separated the dining room from beyond. Matteo paused, his hand on the thick fabric, glancing down at me with a knowing smile before he pulled it aside. Behind the curtain was a private dining area meant only for the privileged few, deliberately created to avoid prying eyes.

And there he was—Anton.

He stood when he saw me, backlit by the soft flicker of candlelight. My breath caught. He was dressed in a dark suit that was tailored to perfection, the crisp lines a stark contrast to the raw power he always carried around with him. His onyx eyes found mine immediately, sharp and intense, sending a rush of heat to the apex of my thighs.

A slow, familiar smile tugged at the corner of his lips, the kind of smile that said he knew exactly what he was doing to me —how he could make my pulse jump with a single look.

"Serena," he said, his voice low. It was like warm whiskey sliding through me until my knees felt weak. He stepped forward, reaching for me. When his fingers found mine, the touch sparked an electric jolt. Savage, carnal thoughts filled my mind.

"Anton," I managed, my voice a little unsteady. My heart hammered in my chest. It didn't matter what game he was playing—I'd lost the moment I'd laid eyes him. I would agree to any bargain he dared to strike, and he knew it.

"Thank you, Matteo," Anton said after Matteo released my arm. "I appreciate you arranging the private room on short notice for me. As you can imagine, discretion is hard to come by."

"It was no trouble at all. While I trust my staff, I'll be your server tonight. I just received a shipment of your favorite Cabernet Sauvignon from Ornellaia. Shall I bring a bottle?"

Anton looked to me. "Is red wine okay with you?"

"Yes, it's fine. Thank you."

Giving us both a short nod, Matteo rushed out, leaving me alone with Anton.

Anton came around the table set for two and pulled a chair out for me. I smiled and moved to sit down, taking in the private space around us.

The room was small and intimate, all dark wood and soft leather. Wine bottles were lined up in a glass case on the far wall, and a fire crackled in the corner. It was a world apart from the bustling city outside. Seductive and intimate, it was the kind of setting that left no room for secrets.

After Anton pushed my chair in, his hand brushed over my arm, lingering momentarily before he took his seat across from me. I wanted to seem unaffected by his touch—to match his calm and collected gaze. But I couldn't stop the way my breath quickened or the flush that warmed my skin. That small touch was a collision of everything I'd been craving and everything I'd tried to ignore since last night.

"I apologize for not picking you up myself," Anton said. "I figured you'd prefer it that way."

I raised a curious eyebrow. "Why do you say that?"

"The press has begun to take an interest in me, and I'm still learning how to navigate it. While Matteo does a good job of protecting his patrons' privacy, there's always someone quick with a camera phone. I didn't think you'd appreciate being featured in tabloid headlines."

"Is that why he referred to you as my dining partner when I walked in?"

"Exactly. If the wrong person heard my name, it could bring problems later."

As I unfolded my napkin, I caught the glint of his cufflinks—polished gold, each one set with a deep green emerald. I remembered the collection I had seen in his bedroom, neatly arranged in the velvet-lined cases.

"You collect cufflinks," I said, angling my chin toward his wrist and watching for his reaction. "I don't mean to pry. I just happened to notice the collection in your bedroom."

For the briefest moment, he hesitated. Then, as if deciding not to not point out my snooping, he simply nodded. "Yes. But it's more than just an ordinary collection. Each pair has history."

I shifted my gaze back to the jewelry on his cuffs. "Those are beautiful."

His lips curved slightly.

"These belonged to a Hungarian count in the 1800s—legend says he lost them in a card game. The ones I wore to the Met Gala were platinum set with black diamonds." He glanced up, meeting my gaze with quiet amusement. "They used to belong to Al Capone."

Anton leaned back in his chair, as if waiting for my reaction to his mention of the notorious gangster. When I said nothing, his sharp and unwavering gaze landed on the ruby necklace resting below my collarbone. I reached up instinctively and glanced down to look at it. The low light of the room glinted off the deep red stone, making it sparkle even more than usual.

"That's quite a remarkable piece. Where did you get it?" Anton asked, his voice a velvet caress that sent a shiver down my spine. It occurred to me then that I could easily listen to him talk for the rest of the night and never feel more content. It was hypnotic, unapologetic, and alluring.

My fingers brushed over the smooth, cool surface of the ruby.

"It's on loan," I said, trying to sound nonchalant. "From Madeleine, the fashion designer I introduced you to at the Gala."

His brows lifted slightly, a hint of intrigue flashing in his eyes. "How do you know Madeleine?"

"She's an old friend of my mother's," I explained, resting my elbows on the table and trying to read his expression. "She's been very supportive of my family over the years."

"Supportive," he repeated. His gaze flicked back to the necklace. "It must be quite the friendship if she's loaning out rubies and couture."

There it was again, that quiet, unrelenting scrutiny that made me feel both exposed and alive all at once. He wasn't just looking at me; he was dissecting me, peeling back layers with every word.

I took a sip of water, suddenly nervous, although I wasn't sure why. Perhaps it was pride. I hated that I was in a position to beg. Or perhaps it was his eyes—his gaze so potent that I sometimes found it hard to form an intelligent thought.

"She supported my father's work. When my mother mentioned I needed help funding a dig in Rome, Madeleine stepped in. She's always been loyal to my family."

He tilted his head, his lips curving into a faint smile that didn't quite reach his eyes. "Loyalty like that doesn't come cheap."

"What do you mean?"

"It's just a curious observation. Attending the Met Gala isn't an affordable evening out, especially for someone short on cash as you claim to be."

Heat rose to my cheeks, but I refused to look away from him.

"Madeleine took care of it," I said, my voice steady. "She provided the dress, the necklace, and the ticket. She didn't explain how, and I didn't ask. I was just grateful for the opportunity."

Anton's gaze didn't waver, his expression unreadable as he leaned forward. "Serena, do you know how much it costs to attend that event?"

I frowned, unsure if he was testing me or genuinely curious. "How much?"

"This year, tickets started at fifty thousand, capping at around seventy-five thousand."

"Dollars?"

"Yes."

My eyes widened as my stomach dropped. That was obscene—a number so far removed from my reality that it might as well have been spoken in another language.

"I had no idea," I managed, my voice barely above a whisper.

He nodded, his eyes never leaving mine. "That's before you factor in the clothing, jewelry, and other expenses. Being that she's a designer, she may have purchased a table, which would have lowered the ticket cost, but the difference is marginal."

I leaned back in my chair, my mind racing.

Madeleine had spent all that—just to showcase her work?

And I hadn't even walked the red carpet. I ran out before the cameras could get a single picture. Although I hadn't looked, there were undoubtably pictures from the Met Gala all over social media—and most likely, I wasn't in a single one. If I was, it was by pure accident.

I felt so foolish—and guilty. If only I could go back in time, I'd show Madeliene the depth of my gratitude.

"I can't believe she spent so much," I murmured, more to myself than to him. "I was too caught up in my own insecurities. It wasn't my world. I felt out of place. And then I got sick."

His brows furrowed and, for a moment, his carefully controlled expression slipped to reveal a flicker of something I couldn't quite place. Amusement? Concern? Or was it curiosity?

"I don't know why you felt insecure. You looked the part," he said, his voice low and steady.

He said it like it was an undeniable truth, sending a thrill through me that I quickly tamped down.

"Looks can be deceiving," I said, forcing a smile.

He studied me for a moment, his gaze intense and probing. "Yes, they can."

The air between us was heavy, charged with words left unspoken. He was a puzzle, each piece more abstract than the last, and I couldn't tell if I was any closer to solving him or just getting more confused by the strategy.

"You intrigue me, Serena. You have this aura about you that I can't explain. It makes me want to know more about you. Tell me about your upbringing. Your family, your childhood."

The request caught me off guard. But something in the way he asked made me want to share.

"I can't say my life was very interesting, but it wasn't boring. My family moved around quite a bit when I was young," I told him, tracing the rim of my water glass with my fingertip. "My father's work took us to different countries. I don't think we ever stayed anywhere for more than a couple of years."

Before I could delve deeper into my childhood tales, Matteo returned with a bottle of the wine. His timing felt both fortuitous and frustrating.

"Here we are. The *Ornellaia* Cabernet Sauvignon," he announced with a theatrical flourish, showcasing the bottle like a prized possession. He proceeded to expertly uncork the wine, filling our glasses with a practiced hand. The rich aroma of blackberries and oak hit my senses.

"Thank you," I said after he placed a glass in front of me.

"*Prego.*" Setting the bottle down, he began to describe the evening's specials. "We have a delightful risotto *ai funghi* that's been prepared with freshly foraged porcini mushrooms."

Anton leaned back in his chair, a small smile playing on his lips as he listened to Matteo's description of the specials. Occasionally his gaze would shift to me, a silent question dancing in the depths of his dark eyes.

"Why don't you surprise us, Matteo?" Anton said finally, his voice smooth and confident. "I've never gone wrong with your recommendations. What do you say, Serena? Do you trust Matteo to choose for us?"

Trust.

I seemed to be doing a lot of that when it came to Anton.

I smiled and shrugged before I could overthink it. It was only food, after all.

"Sure."

Matteo's eyes sparkled with a mix of mischief and pride at being entrusted with our meal selection. He gave us a quick nod before leaving us alone once more.

I glanced at Anton. He'd said he wanted to know more about me, but I wondered how much he already knew. He was a man who thrived on control, on knowing more than anyone else in the room. And yet, as he raised his glass to mine, there was something in his eyes that told me he was just as curious about me as I was about him. I could see it in the way he watched me, his gaze holding steady as if he were trying to read every thought in my mind.

The air between us crackled with inexplicable anticipation as he studied me with an intensity that made my heart flutter. Light from the flickering fire painted his features with sort of a mesmerizing allure, accentuating the depth of his onyx eyes and the sharp angles of his jawline. The silence between us was pregnant with silent words, each moment stretching taut like a finely tuned string.

"You were telling me about your upbringing. You'd said that you moved around a lot," Anton finally said, settling back in his chair as he returned to our previous conversation.

A small sigh escaped me as I thought back to my childhood of constant change and disruption.

"Oh, yes. There was always a dig or another great discovery to make," I replied, my tone both weary and derisive. I didn't want to talk about the frustration and loneliness that came with always having to start over.

"You didn't enjoy it?" Anton asked, his dark eyes probing.

I shrugged, trying to brush off the topic.

"Not many kids like being uprooted from their friends time and time again," I said dryly. I took a sip of the red wine, savoring the velvety richness. "But it was a long time ago. When I look back, I had a good life—even if it wasn't ideal. What about you? Where did you grow up?"

"Now that's the million-dollar question, isn't it?"

I raised an eyebrow. "Is it?"

A guarded look crossed his features.

"My childhood is not something I choose to discuss," he said firmly.

"But mine is?" I couldn't help feeling a twinge of annoyance at the double standard.

"I'm just trying to get to know you better, princess. I think it's only fair to want to know who I'll be giving money to."

His words cut through me, reminding me that this wasn't a game. I realized then that it was time to address the real reason for this dinner.

"About that," I said, jumping on the chance to cut through the small talk. "Can we just discuss why I'm really here?"

"You don't waste time," he replied with amusement. "Are you ready to agree to the thirty days? I promise, one month under me, wearing nothing but that ruby necklace, will be worth your while."

I pressed my lips tightly together, annoyed that his crude words caused a flutter in my belly.

"The necklace will be returned as soon as I get back to Rome. And no, I'm not agreeing to anything yet. You said you had an alternative."

Anton's lips curled into a sly smile, his eyes glinting with satisfaction at my directness. Setting his glass of wine down with deliberate precision, he leaned forward slightly, the firelight casting a warm glow over his features.

"I can't tell you how much I admire your directness," he murmured, the timbre of his voice low and velvety.

The air hummed between us, reminding me of the moment right before a storm breaks. His gaze held mine in an unyielding grip as he reached across the table, his fingers lightly tracing the hand wrapped around the delicate stem of my wine glass. The subtle touch sent a shiver down my spine, reminding me of what his hands had felt like on my body. It awakened a cascade of sensations that I shouldn't be feeling. At least not now—not at a moment when so much was on the line.

"The alternative, Anton." The words were barely a whisper. I couldn't think past his heated gaze. "Tell me what my alternative is."

"So be it. Yes, I want you, but you have something else that I want, too. Either way, you'll have to give up something—whether it be your body or a possession."

My breathing quickened at his words, every breath feeling like a dare. A flush crept up my neck despite my efforts to remain composed.

"I don't have any possessions that you could possible want."

"On the contrary, I think you do."

"It's unlikely. But prey, tell."

His answer was as simple as it was surprising.

"The Brutus Denarius."

CHAPTER SIXTEEN

Serena

T*he Brutus Denarius.*
 I pulled my eyes from Anton's, my gaze fixating on the flickering votive candle at the center of the table. The setting around me blurred as my mind raced, thinking about the gift from my father—a secret that belonged in a museum. The coins weight, both physical and emotional, seemed to press upon me even from a distance.

"Why so quiet, princess?" Anton's smooth voice cut through my reverie.

I lifted my gaze to meet his piercing onyx eyes, forcing a polite smile. "I'm just wondering what would make you think I have a coin of such value."

"So, you've heard of it then?"

"Of course. It's the Ides of March coin, struck by Marcus Junius Brutus to celebrate the assassination of Julius Caesar."

"Correct. It features a bust of Brutus, one of the assassins.

It's one of the rarest ancient Roman coins, minted in both silver and gold. Fewer than one hundred silver coins are known to exist, but only two gold are known to have survived. They are currently located in a museum in France. But rumor has it that you may have a third."

My eyes widened in surprise before I quickly recovered. While things like ancient coins were commonly discussed within my circle of peers, normal people typically didn't have such detailed knowledge about ancient artifacts. But then again, Anton was anything but normal.

How could he know I have that coin in particular?

He was correct about the rumor. But he was wrong in thinking there was only one more. There were actually three more coins that nobody knew about—and I had all three of them hidden inside a small safe in my flat in Rome.

I knew their importance, yet I'd never told a soul about them. Mark Antony had melted down almost all the coins for reuse, but my father had discovered three of them on a dig in Athens. He'd gifted them to me the day I received my acceptance letter from the Sapienza University of Rome, setting me on the path to where I am today.

I recalled my father's words on that day. With him, everything had been a lesson, including his gift.

"For your graduation, I'm giving you three coins. The number three has always been important in ancient cultures, symbolizing ideas like balance, completeness, and the divine— like the Holy Trinity in Christianity or the three sides of the Egyptian sun god. In Pythagorean philosophy, three was seen as the perfect number, standing for wisdom and understanding— both of which you'll need to uncover the truth. These coins are also tied to the story of Brutus spreading lies about Mark Antony after Caesar's death. Like Antony and Cleopatra, you'll have to navigate through the lies to find the truth."

My father often spoke in riddles, and that day had been no

different. The coins were the last thing he'd ever given me. Shortly after that, he became sick. There was no way I would give them up—to a museum or to Anton. They held too much sentimental value.

I shifted my attention back to Anton and contemplated my answer. His gaze narrowed and my pulse quickened as I took in his imposing figure. He was studying me through fierce eyes, almost as if I were an unsuspecting lamb—the prey hunted by the wolf.

"The idea that I might have the Brutus Denarius is ridiculous," I said, hoping I sounded convincing.

I thought I saw a flicker of disappointment cross his face, but his expression was so impassive, I couldn't be sure. Leaning back in his chair, he folded his arms and considered me carefully.

"I don't believe you."

I raised a brow. "And why is that?"

"The lighting might be dim, but I can spot a terrible poker face. I'm good at reading people, particularly their tells."

"I don't have a tell."

"Oh, but you do, princess. You bite down on your lower lip when you're nervous, and you're doing that right now."

I sucked in a breath, releasing the lip that had been trapped between my teeth. I hadn't even realized I was doing it. Angling my chin, I stared defiantly at him.

"So what if I was biting my lip? That doesn't mean I have the coin. Besides, whether I have it or not is irrelevant. It would never be for sale. A coin of that value belongs in a museum."

"Why a museum? So random people can look upon it, never fully understanding its importance?"

He wasn't wrong.

I pressed my lips together in a tight line. "Why is the coin of interest to you anyways?"

"Like my cufflinks, I collect things of historical significance—particularly ancient coins. Not ordinary coins, but ones that hold importance. Mundane, boring, and common things are of no interest to me. I covet the rarest in the world, and I already have six of the top ten in my private collection. Unfortunately, a few are out of reach, having been placed in museums or possibly lost forever. I had believed the Brutus Denarius to be amongst the unobtainable until I read an article about a different Dr. Martinelli."

"My late father," I stated, giving clarity to the identify confusion that often occurred in my professional circles. "Dr. Carlo Martinelli."

"As I eventually figured out, but not before I went looking for him at The Met Gala. You can imagine my surprise when I found you instead. I can't say I was disappointed," he added suggestively, his eyes darkening. I tried to ignore the little flip in my stomach. "It's said that your father found a collection of Roman coins while in Greece. A gold Brutus Denarius was supposedly among them."

My brow furrowed, trying to remember the details of the article he was referring to so I didn't mix it up with the truth.

"If I recall, that article was full of inaccuracies. It was mostly rumors made up by jealous peers who were intent on sabotaging my father's theories. There weren't any Brutus Denarius coins in the jug." Even to my own ears, the venom in my voice was obvious as I continued the lie—anger sparked by loyalty to my father. I made a conscious effort to even my tone. "The article was pure speculation. If such a coin had been found, it would have been extraordinary."

"You seem very... passionate about your position."

The way he seemed to draw out the word "passionate" caused an involuntary shiver to course through me. I took a sip of wine to steady myself.

"For years, my father was dismissed by his peers. Your

mention of the article reminded me how upsetting it was for my mother and me."

"And here I thought your vehemence was a way to punctuate your denial about the coin. But I am curious to hear more about your father's theories that stirred such controversy." He paused, seeming to search for the right words. "Whether I give you the money you need in exchange for a coin or in exchange for, shall we say—"

"A pound of flesh?" I offered.

A wicked smile played on his lips. "A dramatic take, but it fits."

My stomach did another little flip, and I tore my gaze from his. Needing something to do, I reached for my wineglass again. Rather than take a sip, I toyed with the stem for a moment before speaking. "My father had a lot of theories. What is it that you want to know?"

"For starters, why was he not taken seriously by his peers?"

I pressed my lips together into a tight line as more memories rushed to the surface.

"My father didn't agree with many scholars. Most archeologists believe that Cleopatra and Mark Antony are buried in a lost city in Egypt, but my father's maps told a different story. Decades of research led him to Rome. He had had everything mapped out—from the Arch of Constantine to the three tall columns of the Temple of Castor and Pollux, everything led him to an unexcavated location not far from where Julius Caesar's ashes are believed to be."

I recalled my father's words when I was barely sixteen years old. He had chartered a helicopter to get a bird's-eye view of the landscape of the Forum and had taken me along with him.

"Do you see the area where the vegetation is thinner, Serena? The plants grow thick above buried wooden structures and more thinly above the stone ones. There's something there—I can feel it in my bones. I don't care what they say. My maps are

correct. If someone as famous as Julius Caesar could be cremated and buried here, is it so outlandish to think the infamous Cleopatra and her lover would not be nearby as well?"

It had been fourteen years since we'd taken that flight, but I could still hear the words as if he'd said them only yesterday.

"I spent many years alongside my father studying that location," I continued. "He believed Cleopatra and Mark Antony were there with every fiber of his being."

"And do you think they are?"

I frowned and then sighed. "I don't know. We've narrowed down the terrain and have made a lot of progress. There's not much left to search. My team and I just need more time. But time is money."

"Money you don't have." Anton's eyes never left mine as he continued, his voice dropping to a low, seductive timbre. "Alright. We'll forget the Brutus Denarius. If you say you don't have the coin, so be it. We'll just go back to the original plan."

Just as I was about to open my mouth to respond, the conversation was interrupted once again by Matteo's arrival. He was carrying a tray thick with the rich aroma of garlic and parmesan. The combined scents wafted through the air. I inhaled deeply, allowing their familiarity to calm my racing heart.

"*Signore, signora!* I present to you tonight's specialties," he announced with a flourish, setting down plates of steaming risotto and perfectly grilled sea bass. "*Risotto alla Milanese* and *branzino alla griglia. Buon appetito!*"

After Matteo retreated, Anton raised his wine glass.

"To new partnerships," he toasted.

"But I haven't agreed to anything."

"You will," he said confidently, his dark eyes searing into me.

My core tightened until an ache began to form low in my belly. The conversation had changed. It had gone from academic to sexual in the blink of an eye. There was a challenge in his expression, as if he dared me to deny his proposition.

"Your arrogance never ceases to amaze me. But I'll admit, your proposal is intriguing," I acknowledged, choosing my words carefully. "I'm just not sure I'm comfortable with what it may entail."

Anton's lips curved into a knowing smile. "Comfort zones are meant to be pushed, princess. Perhaps my toast should have been made to testing boundaries."

I hesitated before raising my own glass, suddenly uneasy about the boundaries he wanted to test.

"To... mutual understanding," I finally said.

We began to eat, the silence disrupted only by the soft clink of cutlery against the plates. I savored the rich flavors, trying to focus on the meal rather than the conversation Anton was sure to continue. However, the effort was in vain. I couldn't stop my mind from racing.

If I agreed to Anton's proposal, it could save the excavation, allowing me to continue the pursuit of my father's dream.

But at what cost? My integrity? My very sense of self?

Or maybe I should just give up one of the Brutus Denarius coins.

As soon as the thought popped into my mind, I dismissed it. I was a sucker for things with sentimental value, and the ancient coin held too much to give up.

"I can practically see the wheels in your head turning," Anton said after a few bites, his tone deceptively casual.

I stabbed at the risotto, buying time.

"I think I understand your offer," I said finally, meeting his gaze. "But I need more details so that I can consider all the ramifications."

Anton's eyes gleamed with a predatory intensity as he leaned closer.

"Let me be explicit, Serena. I will fully fund your excavation in Rome for the next year. In exchange, I want thirty days of unrestricted access to your body. When I want you to kneel, you'll kneel. When I want you spread out before me, you'll obey without question. And when I'm not inside you, I want access to your mind—days full of intelligent conversation. I want to learn how you think. You won't deny me any part of yourself. Is that detailed enough for you?"

My breath caught as my fork clattered against the plate. I blinked—once, twice—my mind reeling from a tumultuous mix of shock, outrage, and unabashed desire.

"I...that's..." I stammered, struggling to form a coherent thought.

Internal conflict raged within me, taking the form of past memories and dreams for the future. I saw the potential to uncover the secrets that had eluded my father—to bring an end to the hunt so that I could finally focus on finding out who I really was. I'd made a promise to him—one that I fully intended to see through. But chasing ghosts wasn't what I wanted to do with my life forever.

I thought about my small glass blowing shop in Lucca. It reminded me of the flames I'd created, and of the marble woman who stood with them.

Anton's words echoed in my mind.

"Remember the woman in the flames, princess. You deserve to be her."

I met his gaze again and considered his proposal. His desire for unrestricted access to all parts of me—both physically and intellectually—oddly thrilled me. He'd only hinted at the possibilities that lay ahead, and I wanted to know more.

But there were rules.

I may have defied my Catholic upbringing by having sex before marriage, but I had standards—and a hot, toe-curling love affair with a sexy billionaire I barely knew didn't fit into my neatly defined box. Add in that I'd be doing it in exchange for money, and well...

Just thinking about it required a visit to the confessional.

Who am I kidding? At this rate, I'll burst into flames just entering the church.

Tearing my eyes from his, I looked down at my half-eaten plate of food.

"This was a bad idea. I should go," I said, my voice barely above a whisper.

Anton reached across the table, his fingers brushing against mine. The slight touch sent shock waves through my system, and I stood abruptly. My eyes darted toward the exit.

"Serena," Anton's deep voice resonated through the room as he rose from his seat. His movements were fluid, almost predatory, as he came around the table to me. Before I could retreat further, his hand encircled my wrist. His touch was gentle yet unyielding, halting any escape I may have contemplated.

"Thank you for dinner, Anton. Everything was lovely, but I—"

"You think you want to run, but deep down, I know you don't."

"Anton, two people as different as us are not compatible."

He grinned, a gleam in his eye suddenly turning wicked. "Have you already forgotten last night?"

Heat flooded my cheeks, and I looked away. "Of course not."

Taking hold of my chin with his thumb and forefinger, he tilted my head back. The silence sizzled with tension. Anton's eyes flickered to my lips, and before I could process what was happening, he leaned in, capturing my mouth in a searing kiss.

The world tilted on its axis. The kiss was passionate and intense, reviving the sensations he'd made me feel last night. In the dark. Pushed up against the stone wall. My analytical mind short-circuited, forgetting all the what-ifs as Anton's lips moved against mine.

His hand slid to my lower back, pulling me closer. Involuntarily, my fingers curled into the lapels of his expertly tailored suit. The scent of his cologne, a heady mix of sandalwood and citrus, enveloped my senses as our tongues danced.

When we finally broke apart, I was breathless. It was a real struggle to regain my composure.

"Anton, I—"

"Come back to the penthouse," he murmured, his thumb tracing my jawline. "Let me show you how good it can be—how good we can be."

My heart raced, his words sliding over me like warm whiskey as I lost myself in his endless onyx eyes. Whenever he regarded me like that, I found myself speechless. I wasn't sure how much more I could take. It was ridiculous, really. Every time I looked at him, my heart would begin pitter-pattering like a schoolgirl with a crush on the star football player. That steady beat had now quickly evolved into a strong thumping in my chest. His mere presence was unsettling. He made me feel unbalanced, and I found it difficult to stay composed when he looked at me that way.

A slow leisurely smile began to form on his face. I was mesmerized, and he knew it.

"I don't know if I can do this," I protested weakly, even as my body yearned to lean into his touch.

"You can, princess."

I took a deep breath, feeling as though I stood on the precipice of a life-altering decision. Somehow, I knew if I agreed to go back to his place, my life would never be the same.

"You're serious about all of this? Not just tonight, but about the funding and spending a month with me."

"I assure you. I've never been more serious about anything in my life."

I studied his gaze, trying to see past the desire swirling in those onyx eyes, looking for answers before I took a giant leap of faith.

It wasn't just about the money or all the strings attached to it. I wanted him. Desperately. I didn't know what the future held, nor did I want to worry about it. I only cared about this moment. If nothing happened beyond tonight, so be it. This was about me and allowing myself to feel—to being selfish and taking without regret for once in my life.

Bless me Father, for I am about to sin...

"Okay, Anton. I'll be with you tonight."

CHAPTER SEVENTEEN

Anton

The alley behind Krystina's Place was dark, lit only by the dim glow of a flickering streetlamp near the end of the building. The faint hum of the city surrounded us, muffled by the high brick walls of the restaurant. I held the back door open for Serena, and she stepped through, her heels clicking softly against the pavement.

"Is there a reason we couldn't go out the front door?" she asked, glancing over her shoulder at me.

"We could have. We also could have been met with flashing cameras and tomorrow's headline. Prying eyes, remember?"

"Ah, that's right. I guess I'm not used to being in the company of someone so popular," she teased. Her lips curved in a cautious yet playful smile, while her eyes maintained the spark of desire.

I was pleased that she didn't appear ruffled by the absurd lengths we had to go to just to avoid the ever-growing presence of the press. More than likely, nobody lurked in the bushes ready to take my picture, but Zeke's constant talk about security was starting to make me paranoid.

"I've barely gotten used to it myself," I admitted, adjusting the lapels of my suit coat. "But you should heed the warning, princess. You're about to spend thirty days with me. I'll try to protect you, but my sudden popularity could come with a price."

"Such arrogance. I haven't agreed to anything yet," she said with a *tsk*.

"Predicting the inevitable isn't arrogance. I'm just confident."

I led her to the Aston Martin parked discreetly at the edge of the alley. The sleek silver body gleamed under the streetlamp, its presence understated yet impossible to ignore. It was a car that matched me in every way—powerful, precise, and designed to reveal only what I wanted others to see. I opened the passenger door for Serena, and she slid inside with fluid grace.

As I settled into the driver's seat, the light scent of her jasmine perfume filled the interior. It was intoxicating and entirely too distracting. I started the car, the engine roaring to life with a deep growl, and pulled out onto the street.

The city lights blurred as we drove toward the penthouse, the rhythmic hum of the tires on asphalt the only sound. I flipped on the radio, keeping the volume low yet loud enough for Halsey's husky voice to cut through the silence.

Serena shifted in her seat, crossing her legs and resting her elbow on the door. Her gaze lingered on me, and I could almost feel the press of her thoughts, sharp and probing.

"If I'm going to do this, I need to know you better, too," she announced, her voice soft but firm. It wasn't a request. It was a demand.

I smiled, appreciating the no nonsense approach. A part of me was attracted to her assertiveness—but another part wanted to take her over me knee for pursuing a topic I had no interest in discussing.

"Details complicate relationships," I said.

"Well, I need them all the same."

"Why?"

"Call me old-fashioned. Or maybe it's my mother's religious influence. I just can't jump into bed with a stranger."

I grinned. "We're hardly strangers anymore, princess."

"You know what I mean!" she said, not bothering to mask her exasperation.

"You said it was your mother's religious influence. Was it not your father's, as well?" I asked, hoping to divert the conversation to her.

"My father didn't believe in organized religion, but he respected my mother's beliefs. As a result, I got a little of both. My mother raised me in her religion, but I'm practical like my father, and I ask questions."

"Such as?"

"The Bible is a man-made book, and like man, there are flaws. The stories in it seem to have been chosen to fit a narrative."

I raised a brow and peered over at her, suddenly more curious about her than ever before. Religion was a complex mix of personal, cultural, and family influences. I'd never practiced any religion, but I was intrigued by what her beliefs might be.

"And what do you think that narrative is?" I asked.

"One of the most obvious flaws is the number of gospels. The Bible tells us that Jesus had twelve disciples. Have you ever wondered why there are only four gospels—Matthew, Mark, Luke, and John? Some believe that the other eight gospels weren't included because they portray the faults of Jesus Christ."

"I can't say that I've ever thought about it. I didn't have a religious upbringing."

She sighed. "Some might say you're fortunate in that regard.

The Catholic faith has a long, bloody history. Regardless of what I believe or don't believe, Catholic guilt is a very real thing."

I smiled, amused by the concept. I'd long fallen short of any divine expectation. My immorality ran deep, and I wouldn't have it any other way.

"Tell me more about this guilt," I prodded.

Angling her body, she turned toward me. "I think you're changing the subject. I'm supposed to be getting to know you better, remember?"

I glanced over and met her pointed gaze.

"Fine. What do you want to know?"

"Everything," she replied without hesitation. "Like, where did you go to college?"

"I didn't."

"Oh, it was wrong of me to assume. I just…" Her cheeks flushed with embarrassment.

"I'm not ashamed about not receiving higher education, nor should you feel awkward about asking. I had an interest in going, but simply didn't need it. I'm good at spotting trends and used that to my advantage. I taught myself everything I needed to know to get to where I am today without the need of a classroom."

"And clearly, you excelled at it. How about your family? You haven't talked about them."

I exhaled through my nose, keeping my eyes fixed on the road ahead. "That's because there's not much to talk about."

She tilted her head, studying me like I was a puzzle she was determined to solve.

"Tell me about your parents."

"I don't know who my father is, and I already told you my mother died. She passed when I was young. That's all there is to it." I kept my tone measured, even as a knot formed in my chest. It was the kind of ache that came from buried memories clawing their way to the surface. Images of my mother's lifeless body, a needle protruding from her arm, filled my mind.

My hands tightened on the wheel.

Don't think about it.

"That's not all there is to it,' Serena persisted. "Everyone comes from somewhere, Anton. You have a past—a story. You didn't just appear out of thin air as a billionaire with a penthouse and a penchant for secrecy."

I clenched my jaw. She didn't understand—couldn't understand. My past wasn't something I shared. Not with anyone. Zeke was the only person alive who knew everything, and that was how it would stay. It was better to not answer her questions—especially now that I knew about this so-called Catholic guilt.

What the hell is that all about anyway?

And here I'd worried about what she'd think if she ever learned I owned a sex club. How could I tell her that I was raised by a prostitute? Hearing the truth about my upbringing would lead to too many questions that I couldn't answer. Serena was as worldly as she was innocent, and I'd be damned before I corrupted her with my sordid past.

She was quiet, so I glanced her way again. Her brows knitted together, her lips pressing into a tight line.

"My mother died of a drug overdose," I said finally, the words bitter on my tongue. It was the only truth I could offer, the piece that was already public record. Anything more would be stepping into dangerous territory.

She blinked, clearly surprised by my admission.

"I'm sorry," she said softly. "That must've been...difficult."

I shrugged, feigning indifference. "It was a long time ago."

"How long?"

"I was fourteen."

Silence stretched between us, heavy and charged.

That's right, princess. Too old to be called a child, yet not a man. And I've been fending for myself ever since.

I could feel her wanting to ask more, to dig deeper. And for a moment, I wondered what it would be like to tell her everything—to lay it all bare. But the thought was fleeting, chased away by the familiar sting of shame.

"Did you have anyone else?" she tentatively asked. "After she passed?"

"No," I said, my tone sharp enough to end the conversation. The less she knew, the better—for both of us.

I glanced at her out of the corner of my eye, seeing the hurt flicker across her face before she masked it. She seemed to be contemplating what I'd said. I hated the way her expression twisted something in my chest, but I pushed the feeling aside. I didn't need or want her sympathy.

The rest of the drive passed without conversation, the air between us filled with unspoken words. I turned up the volume on the radio, allowing a song by Sakoya to fill the awkward silence. I smirked at the irony that this particular song just happened to be streaming. It was a combination of moody beats, exploring themes of surrender and desire, and the tension between control and letting go. It was exactly how I envisioned tonight playing out.

However, the closer we got to the penthouse, the more I felt Serena retreating into herself. Things were not going as planned. Her natural warmth had been replaced by a chilling uneasiness. It was a stark contrast to her usual self, and it unnerved me more than I cared to admit.

When we arrived at the penthouse, I pulled into the secure underground garage and parked in my reserved spot. I stepped out of the car and rounded to her side, opening the door for her. She slid out without meeting my eyes, her movements brisk and deliberate.

The doorman greeted us with a polite nod as we entered, his

practiced smile as fake is it always was. His name was Patrick something or another, and he'd come with the building. Zeke had run a check on him, and his background came back clean. But there was something about him that I didn't like. I just wasn't sure what it was.

I barely acknowledged him as we passed, and typed in the code for the private elevator that would take us to the top floor. The doors slid open with a soft chime, and we stepped inside.

The silence was almost unbearable now, the hum of the elevator doing little to drown out the weight of everything left unsaid. I glanced at Serena, standing with her arms crossed, and her gaze fixed on the polished metal doors. She was stunning, even in her quiet contemplation, but the distance between us was insurmountable. I found myself wishing I could bridge the gap, to offer her something more than the cold detachment I'd given her. But I knew better. Trust was a luxury I couldn't afford—not when it came to my past.

The doors slid open, revealing the foyer of my penthouse. I gestured for her to step out first, but she hesitated for a fraction of a second, her eyes meeting mine with a mix of frustration and something softer.

That softness stirred something foreign inside me. I didn't just want this woman. I needed her like the air I breathed, and all the talk in the car had taken up precious oxygen.

"Fuck the conversation from earlier, Serena. None of it matters. Only this does."

Without another word, I slipped my arm around her waist and yanked her to me. I didn't hesitate or ask permission before I crushed my mouth to hers. Fueled by absolute lust, I devoured her with the intent of kissing her senseless. I didn't know what possessed me to do it.

Maybe it was her cheeks that had flushed scarlet when she'd spoken about not going to bed with a stranger.

Perhaps it was her tell—that slight bite of her lower lip.

Or perhaps it was her mystery and the answers that evaded me.

Or maybe I just needed to crush that goddamn Catholic guilt.

I only knew that I had to have this woman.

I shoved my tongue through her parted lips, my need to taste her completely unleashed. I refused her any sort of finesse and took her mouth fully—like a storm. Unbreakable. Powerful. Unrelenting.

I nipped at her lower lip before moving down her jawline to baptize her neck with hot, open-mouthed kisses. I breathed her intoxicating scent, an irresistible mix of ripe plums and jasmine. It was utterly captivating.

I gently tugged on her earlobe, drawing a soft gasp from her lips. I groaned from her sudden inhale, her response like a lightning bolt to my cock. Gathering her hair in my hand, I gave it a slight tug, urging her back until she was pressed against the elevator door frame. I pinned her there, attacking her mouth again.

She returned my kiss fervently as I held her in place. I pressed the full force of my weight against her, her body boneless in my arms. She knew what I wanted the moment I placed my cards on the table. And from the way she pushed her hips against me, I could tell she was ready to play the hand that had been delt.

She released a soft moan, and it was all I could do not to hike up her little skirt and bury my cock into her velvet heat. To be lost in her—in everything that made up this fiery Italian princess.

"Fuck, how I want you. Here. Now," I growled. But I knew I needed to slow things down, even if only for a short time. I didn't want to take her like this—like a feral animal against a wall. Serena deserved so much more if I wanted her to give this a chance—to give us a chance.

Summoning all the willpower that I could manage, I tore my mouth away from hers. Swallowing hard, I studied her face. She was flushed, her hair in disarray from my hands, and she was panting. As delicious as she looked in this state, I tamped down my desire so I could focus on finesse.

"After you," I said, my voice steady.

Her long lashes dropped before lifting to boldly meet my stare. Then she nodded and stepped out. I followed, the sound of the elevator doors closing behind us, the final punctuation mark on a kiss unlike any other I'd ever had before. When I laced my fingers through hers, she glanced up at me. I watched as her demeanor shifted, her eyes glimmering with a barrage of conflicting emotions—desire, longing, apprehension.

When I tugged her hand, bringing her further into the penthouse, she didn't resist. She wanted this, but there was so much I needed her to give.

I wanted her to beg.

I wanted her hands tied behind her back as I plunged my cock into her mouth. I pictured her ass high in the air, and I imagined what she'd feel like when took her from behind. I wanted to feel her nails raking across my back, and I wanted her screams.

But most importantly, I wanted her surrender.

I just wasn't sure if that was something Serena was capable of.

CHAPTER EIGHTEEN

Serena

"Fuck, how I want you. Here. Now."

Anton's words hung in the air like a loaded gun pointed directly at my heart before ricocheting through my body. I repeated them in my head as he led me to his bedroom, the ache between my legs nearly unbearable.

When we reached the primary suite, he reached for the switch on the wall. After he adjusted the dimmer, a romantic glow flooded the space, casting long shadows over the sleek lines of his bedroom furniture. He unbuttoned his cuffs, rolling them back just enough to reveal his muscular forearms.

"I'll be right back," he said. Then, he left the room.

I stood there, unsure what I should do, as I listened to the faint clink of glass from down the hall. A moment later, I heard the pop of a cork. When he returned, he was holding a tumbler of whiskey in one hand and a glass of red wine in the other. He handed me the wine, his fingers grazing mine just long enough to send a curl of heat through me.

He took a slow, deliberate sip before setting his glass on the nightstand. I watched as he crossed the room to the console table and pressed a button. Soft music filled the air, haunting and cinematic. It unfolded like a slow-burning storm with a ghostly piano melody.

Each note lingered in the air like a whispered secret as Anton returned to me. I caught the scent of sweet, oaky whiskey on his breath. He stepped closer, his gaze dark with intent, making him look dangerously sexy. I exhaled slowly, feeling the sexual tension stretch tighter than ever.

This was it—the point of no return.

My mind spun with possibilities, trying to decide if I wanted out of this impossible situation. I was torn between giving in to this burning desire to finally be with him and holding onto my principles. Whichever path I chose, I would have to sacrifice something. The thought made my heart race and my cheeks flush with anxiety. But as I looked into Anton's intense gaze, I couldn't deny that I wanted tonight to happen.

I craved him. Desperately. And I couldn't recall a time in my life when I needed anything more.

Anton shifted to sit on the bed, pulling me down beside him and looping my legs over his lap. Then he kissed me—lightly at first, but it was a graze that drove me completely wild. I whimpered against his lips, and he seemed to take that as encouragement. Within mere seconds, the kiss went from seductive to feverish. He was passionately demanding, taking what he needed.

I was acutely aware of the music as it progressed. The percussion grew heavier, a heartbeat-like rhythm that pulsed beneath the melody, creating a sense of urgency that matched our heated kiss. I gave willingly, allowing our tongues to dance as his hands moved possessively up and down my back. They progressed over my ribs and to my waist, skimming the sides of my breasts on the way down. I shivered at the contact, the fervent ache between my legs building to impossible heights.

Shifting my position, I raised my skirt so I could straddle his hips. He gripped my hair at the roots, the pull a sweet ache as he tugged my head back. He nipped his way across the line of my jaw, his hot breath a whisper on my neck before moving down to my cleavage.

He pulled down a strap of my black satin tank with one hand, while his other ran up my leg and under my skirt. He massaged my thigh, shoving my skirt further up as he went, brushing past the strap of the lace thong at my hip and around to cup my nearly bare behind. He held me firmly, pulling my tank down to expose a red lace-covered nipple.

"I like you in lace," he murmured. "But I think I'll like you without it even better."

Using one finger, he pushed down the cup of my bra until my breast was bare. Sliding my other strap down, he repeated the process until my chest was completely exposed. My nipples pebbled from the appreciative way he gazed at them. A moan escaped me as he leaned in to kiss the area around one tightened peak.

He kneaded my breasts, pinching the erect nipples between his thumb and forefinger before capturing one with his teeth. I hissed at the same time he slid a finger under my panties. The throbbing between my spread thighs intensified, and I ached to be satisfied.

"Anton, I need you to touch me."

"I will, princess. I've been fantasizing about seeing you spread out before me for too long. I want to look at you—all of you. Then I'll touch you. Taste you. Claim you," he said, punctuating each statement with a kiss.

"Yes." The word came out as an exhale as my head lolled

back. He could do whatever he wanted to me. I was already completely lost to this man.

Grabbing hold of my hips, he lifted us both from the bed with little effort. Setting me on my feet, he looped one finger through the side of my thong and said, "Time to take these off."

He tugged my panties to my feet so I could step out. He kissed his way back up my legs, starting near my ankles, then moving his lips over my knees until he reached the apex of my thighs. A fire burned in my belly, and I couldn't think straight. But instead of putting his tongue where I wanted him to, he continued his tease by slowly pulling my skirt down my legs and kissing every inch as he went.

Once I was completely exposed from the waist down, he removed my tank and bra, leaving me stark naked in front of him.

Stepping back, he cast a look of admiration over my body. "You're so fucking gorgeous."

I blushed, but it wasn't because I felt self-conscious. The flush was born from desire. There was something about him that made me feel confident in a way I never had before. It was incredibly liberating.

Taking me by the waist, he surprised me by pushing me back toward the bed and tossing me until I felt the cool satin under my backside. I hadn't expected to be treated like a ragdoll, but I couldn't say that I minded it.

Anton crawled over my body, using one hand to raise my arms above my head. His onyx eyes held steady on my gaze as he pinned my wrists together. Then he leaned down, crushing his mouth so hard to mine, I was sure my lips would be swollen tomorrow. I kissed him back with the same urgency, our tongues dancing as I became acutely aware of the strain of his erection through his pants.

I shifted a leg up to loop it around his hips, needing to feel the friction against my bare sex. I tried to pull my hands free so that I could grip his hips, but he kept them firmly pressed against the bed.

"Keep them above your head. You're mine, and for tonight, I'm in charge. You'll only touch me when I tell you to, or I'll bind these wrists together."

His words elicited a gasp from me. Whenever he stated the unexpected, all thoughts seemed to escape me. This time was no different. Bondage wasn't anything I'd ever gotten into, but the idea was unexpectedly arousing. I wanted him to tie me up.

So, I let my inhibitions melt away, losing myself to the moment—to him.

Keeping my arms above my head, I arched my back as he nipped his way around my collarbone. His free hand brushed along the curve of my breast, pausing only to flick at a tight peak before sliding down over my stomach to the juncture of my thighs. When he ran a finger through my wet slit, my breath caught, a gasp of unadulterated pleasure.

His fingers began a slow circle around my clit as he moved down my body. He didn't stop until he was kneeling on the floor, positioned between my legs that dangled over the edge of the bed.

"Open wide for me, princess. I want to look at your pussy."

Holy hell.

Doing as he asked, I spread my legs. Never before had I felt so free. It was as if I'd waited a whole lifetime for this moment.

Pushing my knees up with both hands, he spread my thighs further. Then he returned to the slow exploration of my most intimate parts, lazily circling my clit with his thumb. He spread the moisture around before sliding two fingers inside, stretching me for the invasion that was yet to come.

I moaned as my back arched and stomach tightened. I was coming apart at the seams.

"You like this?"

"Yes, don't stop!" I begged shamelessly.

Lowering his head, he pressed his mouth against my folds as his fingers dug into my thighs. Instantly, an electric shock surged through my body, extracting a cry from my lips. His tongue pushed in and out of me, flicking and filling me with the most intense pleasure I'd ever felt.

"Come for me, Serena," he murmured between licks. "Then I'm going to fuck you. Hard."

Fire coursed through me at his words, the ache turning into something vicious. I needed to know what he'd feel like inside me. The idea of him filling me and finally satisfying this desperate need I had for him was enough to send me reeling over the edge.

"I'm there!" I gasped. The words had barely passed my lips when wave after wave of the sweetest, most intense ecstasy careened through me. It started low and deep, bursting in a display of a thousand colors. My body shuddered and convulsed, but Anton didn't stop the merciless flicks of his tongue. I squirmed, but he held me to the spot. With his firm grip on my hips, his tongue moved, slowing to a tortuous ache.

"Come again," he ordered.

It was as if my mind, heart, and body were not my own, but something only he commanded. It wasn't long before the tightening sensation began to build deep in my belly once again. As he sucked on my clit, his fingers circled my walls. The second orgasm was just over the horizon, but he kept me on edge, never quite allowing me to get there. I bucked involuntarily, craving the relief he was teasing. I was beyond the point of wanting.

I reached down and gripped his hair. Much to my dismay, he pulled back.

"Hands above your head," he ordered.

"Dammit, Anton," I cursed, throwing my arms back on his order. He was driving me insane. I was beyond desperate, completely lost in an ocean of sensations.

I felt the curve of his smile against my folds as he returned to finish what he'd started. He plunged his fingers deeper into my core and increased the intensity of his tongue. When he pulled his fingers out, slipping them down to apply gentle pressure against my back entrance, there was no holding my cry of pleasure. What he was doing to my body was more than just sinful. I was sure to go straight to hell after tonight.

Within seconds, my insides constricted, and my mind went hazy. In one blinding moment, white-hot pleasure shot through my veins. I cried out, unable to suppress my screams.

Time stood still. Or perhaps it was slowly passing without me. Seconds. Minutes. Hours. All had lost any semblance of meaning. I was only aware of the tingling sensation all over my body as I slowly opened my eyes to see Anton standing at the side of the bed. His gaze feasted hungrily on my body as he unfastened the last button of his dress shirt.

My breath caught as he shrugged it off, the fabric sliding from his shoulders to reveal the hard, defined body I had only imagined until now. Broad and toned, every muscle seemed carved with the kind of strength that came from years of discipline. The soft glow of the bedside lamp traced the lines of his chest, the sharp cut of his abdomen, the defined curve of his biceps.

But it was the tattoo that held me captive.

Black ink stretched over his shoulder, a bold design of fascinating angles and sharp curves. It moved with him, accentuating the powerful lines of his body. At first glance, it seemed abstract, but the longer I looked, the more I could see fragments of symbols woven into the design, their meaning just out of reach. There was something primal about it, as if the ink carried a story only he knew. The details were precise, every line purposeful. The tattoo had been etched onto him with intent rather than impulse. It wasn't just random—it belonged to him in a way that made it feel almost alive.

After he removed his pants, my gaze returned to the beautiful lines of his body. The man would make any sculptor weep. He was magnificent in every sense of the word. From his muscular thighs to the rippled power of his rock-hard abs, he was the perfect specimen of the alpha male.

He stood still for a moment, allowing me a moment to take in the rest of him. My gaze traveled down past his tapered *V* to settle on his long, thick erection that looked impossibly hard. When my eyes met his once more, I found a dangerous glint in his stare, those deep pools of onyx a violent inferno of desire.

His lips parted slightly as he moved to the bed, sliding up my torso and taking the lobe of my ear between his teeth. I heard a rustle, and realized he was sheathing a condom over his length. A shiver ran through me at what was about to come.

His erection pressed hard against my heat as his lips moved around to capture mine. Fisting his hand in my hair, he roughly yanked my head back to ravage my mouth. His teeth bit into my lower lip, the sharp sensation cutting through me and intensifying the ache in my belly.

I needed him inside me—right now.

He reached between us to position his tip to my entrance, and then he pushed into me with painstaking restraint. I inhaled sharply as he pierced me, stretching me inch by divine inch until he was rooted deep in my essence.

"You're so wet. And hot. Fuck, Serena." His guttural tone sounded almost unhinged—as if he was barely hanging on to control.

I tightened my legs around him. Taking my hands, he braced them on his shoulders and began to move inside me. As if made for each other, we easily found our rhythm. His motions were determined, matching me thrust after thrust. His rippled muscles bunched beneath my palms as he pounded into me. I didn't think it was possible, but I was already ready to come again.

"Oh, God!" I gasped.

"Give it to me," he growled with satisfaction. "I want to feel your nails on my back as you come. Let that sweet pussy tighten around me."

Reaching between us, he began to circle my clit with his finger as he pushed deeper inside me. My muscles clenched involuntarily as he brought me closer and closer to that glorious peak. He knew exactly what to do to please me—hitting every pleasure point designed to torment me just long enough to ensure my climax would be cataclysmic. It was delicious, mind-blowing bliss that I'd never before experienced.

With every inch of his length buried inside me, I dug my nails into his shoulders. I was right on the cusp and could barely think, bracing myself for that spellbinding moment when I would be sent over the edge. Trembling, I lost more of myself with every passing moment. I became desperate, the promise of release all-consuming.

He pulled out and then used his strong hands to grip my hips and flip me over. It wasn't slow or graceful—it was animalistic and desperate. His roughness didn't bother me. It was the exact opposite. I loved this aggressiveness—the feeling of being owned.

With me on my knees, he pushed into me again with a hard thrust. Over and over again, he plunged impossibly deeper, reaching under me to grip my breasts, pinching my nipples into painful peaks.

Then his hand came down, smacking my ass once. Twice. A third time. I cried out as he drove us both toward ecstasy. I was mindless, wildly grinding against him as he powered forward until I split apart at the seams, overcome with a sensation of blinding heat.

"Anton!" I cried out.

Colors flashed before my eyes as the rush surged through me. My sensitive tissues rippled, spasming uncontrollably in a long, shattering, heart-pounding orgasm. My fingernails clawed at the sheets when I felt him tense. I matched his thrusts, waiting for the moment he would follow me into the abyss of mindless release.

With one last plunge, his body quivered before momentarily falling still. When his breath hitched, and I felt the delicious pulsating of his cock, we spiraled together as his climax burst forth.

CHAPTER NINETEEN

Anton

Serena lay curled against me, her warm skin impossibly soft. Her breathing eventually steadied as her hand absently traced patterns over my chest. The aftershocks of several mind-blowing orgasms hung in the air like a satisfied sigh. The smell of sex and something uniquely hers lingered, arousing and intoxicating.

Her dark hair spilled across the pillow like ink, a stark contrast to the cream-colored sheets. In the faint glow from the moon and the city lights through the windows, she looked almost angelic. The soft curve of her lips, the delicate slope of her nose, the way her lashes fanned against her cheeks when she blinked—it was all impossibly perfect, almost too much for a man like me to take in without losing his grip on reality.

"What are you thinking about?" she asked after we lay there in quiet for a long while. Her voice was low and husky, making me want to sink into her once more.

"I'm thinking about how beautiful you are, and about how long it will be before I'm buried inside you again."

Her lips curved into a faint smile, and she tilted her head to look up at me, her eyes catching the moonlight.

"That's a dangerous answer," she teased.

"Dangerous is relative," I replied, brushing a strand of hair from her face.

The simple fact was that my answer was as raw as it was true. I liked sex. Plain and simple. Emotional strings were never part of the equation, yet Serena took up more headspace than I cared to admit. She was all I thought about—even if I hadn't yet solved the mysteries surrounding her.

I trusted my instincts, and my gut told me she was exactly who she claimed to be. Yet the woman I was coming to know was at complete odds with the violence I'd seen in her ravaged hotel room. That alone made me pause. As annoyed as I was to have these thoughts invade my mind at a moment like this, I couldn't ignore them. They gnawed at me like a piece of a puzzle that didn't fit.

Someone had been searching for something, but what? And why her?

I should just ask her, but instinct made me hesitated. If I wanted answers, she might be able to provide them. But if she couldn't, finding out what happened would only upset her. I didn't want that.

I slid my fingers along the curve of her shoulder, my thoughts scattered. Between the perfection of the moment and the inability to find the truth, I wasn't sure where to settle. I wondered if she had any idea what she did to me—how her presence was a constant test of my carefully constructed control.

She propped herself up on one elbow, the sheet sliding slightly to reveal more of her olive skin. My gaze flicked down to her bare breasts.

God help me, the woman is breathtaking, and she isn't even trying.

I forced myself to bring my gaze back to her face.

"Tell me something," I said, my voice low but steady. "Something about you I don't already know."

"Like what?"

I thought about the leatherbound journal full of notes and drawings. It was old and well worn, the writing style far too masculine to belong to Serena. I suspected it had once belonged to her father. Perhaps if I could understand more about her dynamic with him, I'd find the answers I was looking for.

"Your father," I said, stating the words before I could rethink them. "How did he die?"

Her expression shifted, the lightness in her features fading into something more guarded. For a moment, I thought she wouldn't answer, but then she sighed softly.

"Not my idea of pillow talk," she began, her voice tinged with a distant sadness. "His death wasn't sudden. He was sick for months. It started with him feeling weak all the time, then came nausea and weight loss. His skin became red and swollen, and he complained about his fingers and toes feeling like pins and needles. There was chest pain, too. He just kept getting worse from a whole slew of symptoms that didn't make any sense."

"What did the doctors say it was?" I asked, sitting up slightly.

"They couldn't figure it out," she said with a small shake of her head. Her fingers absently plucked the edge of the sheet. "They tried tests, various treatments, but nothing worked. Nobody knew why he was sick. Hospitals in Lucca are limited. I wanted to bring him back to the States, but he was too weak to travel. By the time he passed, they still didn't have answers. Heart disease was listed on the death certificate, but I know that wasn't it."

She paused, her brow furrowing as though she was reliving it.

"What do you think it was?"

"I don't know."

"Was he in pain?" I asked.

"He said he wasn't, but I know he only said that so my mother didn't worry. She never left his side. It was awful to watch. She and I did everything we could to make him comfortable, but..." She looked down, her expression tightening. "It wasn't enough."

Her voice was calm, but I could feel the undercurrent of frustration and sadness in her words. I reached out again, brushing another strand of hair from her face.

"You were close to him," I said.

She nodded, and her eyes took on a faraway look. "He was everything to me. Losing him was like losing a piece of myself."

For the first time, I began to see why she was so desperate to push aside her own wants and desires to fulfill her father's dream. It was a selfless act that I couldn't fully understand. It went against everything I knew about humanity.

"Cade couldn't handle my reaction to my father's death," she continued. Her expression shifted, a spark of anger flaring in her eyes.

I frowned. "Cade?"

"My ex-fiancé."

Jealousy hit instantly, and much harder than it should have.

Since when do I get jealous?

I felt my body tense, and I slid out of bed before she could notice. I needed a moment to process the foreign emotion, realizing that it wasn't the first time I'd felt it when it came to Serena. Crossing to the minibar near the window, I poured myself a whiskey.

"Drink?" I asked, glancing over my shoulder.

She shook her head. "No, thanks."

"You were saying?" I said, keeping my tone casual. As much as I didn't want to hear about her ex-lover, she was talking and I needed answers.

"He hated how much time I spent helping my mother with my father. He said I was neglecting him, that I cared more about my parents than I did about him. He always made me feel like I was in the wrong. And for a time, I believed I was. He was the master at manipulation, somehow painting a different reality that made me question everything."

Gaslighting.

The word echoed in my mind, though I didn't say it aloud.

"Did you love him?"

"I thought I did. But then I learned that love wasn't supposed to be toxic."

"Sounds like a real gem," I said, unable to keep the sarcasm out of my voice. "Is that why you split up? Because he was toxic?"

She gave a humorless laugh, the sound almost startling in the quiet room. "He slept with my best friend. That was the end for me."

Her tone was matter-of-fact, but her eyes betrayed her. There was anger there, a deep-seated betrayal that would leave scars no matter how long it had been.

"He didn't deserve you," I said.

She tilted her head, a faint smile playing at her lips. "I know that now."

I paced the room, pausing only to take another sip of whiskey. I used the burn to ground me as I mulled over her story. What she revealed to night was nothing out of the ordinary, yet I couldn't shake the feeling that I was missing something.

I drained the rest of my drink, setting the glass on the nightstand before sliding back into bed.

"What time is your flight tomorrow?" I asked, changing the subject.

"One fifteen," she said. "I'll need to be at the airport a couple of hours before that though."

"Zeke will drive you," I said, earning a skeptical look.

"I can catch a cab."

"I know you can, but I'd prefer it if Zeke drove you."

She rolled her eyes but didn't argue.

"I'll be in Italy within the week," I continued. "It will be easier for us to be more ourselves there, in a country where I'm less recognizable. That's when our thirty days start."

She raised a brow, her lips curving into a playful smile. "Once again, your arrogance astounds me. We still haven't agreed to any terms."

I slid a hand along her waist, running my fingertips over the smooth skin at her stomach before moving up to cup one of her breasts.

"Tell me your terms, Serena."

Her breath hitched as I skimmed my index finger over a nipple, circling the hard peak.

"Oh, I um…I was thinking—" She hissed through her teeth when I pinched the ridged point. "I was thinking we should take it day by day. Or maybe week to week. A month is long."

"Is it?" Leaning over, I captured her nipple with my mouth. I rolled my tongue, pausing only to ask, "How much money do you need every month?"

"Holy Mother of God. Anton, I don't know how you expect me to talk while you're doing that."

"You seem to be doing just fine," I teased.

She shoved a lock of hair from her eyes, flustered.

"It varies depending on what we need in any given month," she said.

"I need more details," I prodded as I slid a hand down between her legs. My fingers found her soaked pussy, and she moaned.

"Anton, do you want me to talk, or do you want sex?"

"I love how you react when I touch you. Can't we do both?"

"I can't..." Her breath hitched when I applied pressure to her clit.

"I can't focus on words while you play."

I chuckled and pulled my hand away. "Alright. Talk now. I'll own that pussy after."

She all but purred before letting out a reluctant sigh. Shifting to prop herself up on a pillow, she took a moment to collect herself before continuing. "My project manager will know the exact breakdown. There's the cost of securing permits, machinery rentals, supplies for excavating, mapping, and recording. If we use aerial reconnaissance to search for patterns, the spend jumps significantly. There's also the lab where we process findings. Fortunately, the fieldwork team is made up of volunteers and students."

"How much money, Serena?" I repeated, even if I didn't particularly care about the cost. She could say she needed ten million dollars, and I'd hand it over without question.

"On average, the dig costs around thirty thousand per month, give or take. Our spend since the start of the project has exceeded five hundred thousand."

"That's a lot of money," I mused, toying with her. "I don't think I can take things day by day, or week to week. I want a full month commitment."

"But—"

"A full month and I'll give you five hundred thousand up front. That should be enough to keep your dig funded for a good long while—and well past the year I originally proposed." She began to shake her head, but I silenced her with a finger before she could speak. "You know what I'm going to say, don't you?"

"No."

"Yes, you do."

She held my gaze steady, her blue eyes a raging storm of emotion.

After a moment, she nodded.

"Trustfall."

"That's right, princess. Take the money and don't ask questions. Now, where was I?"

Lowering my head, I recaptured her nipple between my teeth. When I slid my hand down to her wet slit, her back arched in surrender, and I smiled to myself.

Tonight, she was mine, and that was enough.

CHAPTER TWENTY

Anton

The bright afternoon sun streamed through the tall windows of my penthouse, casting beams of light across the sleek furniture. The space felt cavernous and silent without Serena's presence. She'd left hours ago, Zeke driving her to the airport late in the morning, but I could still feel her here. The sound of her voice lingered, and her scent clung to the bed sheets.

I stared at my computer screen, trying to shake the restlessness that gnawed at me. It was why I opted to work from home rather than go into the office. Work at Cornerstone Tower could wait, as well as the meeting I was supposed to have with Kent Leahy, a portfolio manager at Fourth Bank Market Equities. I didn't have the patience for stock tickers, trends, and spreadsheets today. Thankfully, my assistant had been quick to respond when I'd emailed her earlier.

To: Myla McKinnon

Subject: Out of Office

Myla,

I won't be in the office today. I need you to push my meeting with Kent Leahy to tomorrow. If that doesn't work for him, it will have to wait until next month since I'm leaving for Italy later this week. I'll also need you to look at my schedule for the next 30 days. I'll be out of the country for much, if not all, of that time. My scheduled meetings will have to shift to video conference. Please arrange accordingly. If something urgent comes up, handle it as you see fit.

Anton

Her reply had been immediate, a curt acknowledgment that she'd take care of things. I trusted her implicitly, but the heaviness in my chest had nothing to do with work.

It was Serena.

I could have gone for to the airport with her and Zeke, but I told her I had work to do. It wasn't a lie, per se. I truly did have to go to Club O to check on a few things before beginning work at my day job, but it felt dishonest all the same.

I wished I could Serena her about the club, but I couldn't take the risk—and it wasn't just because I was afraid of being outed publicly. Even if I could trust her with the secret, the more she talked about her Catholic mother, the more I was convinced that she wouldn't understand. It didn't matter if, last night, she'd said some of the dirtiest things I'd ever heard—words that made my dick hard just thinking about them. When she told me that some lessons were ingrained in people, I knew keeping the club's existence from her was the right thing to do. At least for now.

My instincts about people were rarely wrong, and something

about her had rung true from the moment we met. She wasn't hiding who she was or pretending to be someone else. If she was, she deserved an Oscar. No, Serena was genuine—raw, complicated, and utterly unguarded in ways that disarmed me.

Still, the mysteries surrounding her consumed me. The motel break in might have been random, but there was something about it that didn't sit right with me. Especially now that I knew a staff member had been murdered. I wanted to shake it off as happenstance, but I couldn't.

I opened my laptop and began sifting through news articles until I found the one that mentioned the death at the Midtown Hotel. Clicking on it, I began to read.

> *"A man was found dead behind The Midtown Motel late this afternoon. He was the victim of a stabbing. The man, whose identity has not yet been released, was reported missing after the day shift employee discovered he was absent from his usual post at the front desk. Police later located his body near a dumpster behind the building. Authorities are investigating the circumstances surrounding the death and are asking anyone with information to come forward."*

I skimmed the rest of the article, and it appeared as though the police didn't have any leads. When I thought about the motel break-in, the murder only raised more questions than it answered.

I leaned back in my chair, rubbing my hand over my chin. Things had to be related, but I struggled to connect the dots. I considered what Serena had said about her father's death and wondered how that might fit in. It might not be related to the situation at the Midtown at all, but there seemed to be too many mysteries surrounding Serena to ignore it. The symptoms she'd described had been too specific.

I changed my internet search to try to identify a possible cause for his passing. This proved to be more difficult. Italian death certificates weren't easy to access, especially for someone with no familial ties. Still, money and connections could open most doors, even in Europe. A few emails and some discreet inquiries later, and I was confident I'd have a copy of Carlo Martinelli's records within a day or two.

While waiting for responses, I shifted my focus to something more immediate. Serena had been vague about the doctors' inability to diagnose her father's illness, so I typed the symptoms into the search bar, refining the terms until a pattern emerged.

"Poison?" I murmured.

Every search result described chronic arsenic poisoning as fatigue, nausea, weight loss, red and swollen skin, organ failure, and several other horrific symptoms.

The dark and unsettling possibility that he might have been murdered flashed in my mind.

If it had been arsenic poisoning, I wasn't sure how any competent doctor could have missed something so obvious. My pulse quickened as I scanned the many articles on the topic, searching for more details. It was unnerving how closely the description mirrored what Serena had told me. I wondered if the doctors had ordered a heavy metal test.

If her father had been poisoned, it could have been accidental. But I wasn't ready to dismiss the symptoms as random. And when I considered the break-in at her hotel—the calculated way someone had appeared to be searching for something—the pieces just didn't fit. Once I had a copy of the death certificate, I would assign Zeke the task of tracking down medical records.

I was halfway through a detailed article about heavy metals in the bloodstream when my phone rang, breaking my concentration. I glanced at the screen. Alexander Stone was calling.

"Alexander," I said, leaning back in my chair.

"Anton," he replied, his tone as smooth and self-assured as always. "How are things?"

"Busy," I said, though it wasn't entirely true. My schedule was only as busy as I allowed. It was one of the perks of being a self-made billionaire that I thoroughly enjoyed. "And you?"

"Never a dull moment," he said with a chuckle. "I wanted to discuss the waterfront property we talked about last month. We've got an opening to move on it, but the timing is tight."

We talked briefly about the logistics, including acquiring the land and navigating the red tape, but my mind wasn't fully in the conversation. As Alexander outlined potential profit margins, I quickly realized it was a no-lose opportunity.

"All of it sounds great. And you're right. We'd be foolish not to move now," I said.

"Great. I'll get Stephen to draft a good faith contract. He should have it ready for us to sign within a day or two."

Alexander and I shared the same law firm, and Stephen Kinsley was one of the best. He was also a member of Club O. I trusted that he would ensure the best deal possible.

"Sounds good, Alex. I'll be on the lookout for it."

As Alexander spoke about potential contract concerns, I typed a quick email to Myla, making her aware of the incoming documents.

"How's the family, Alex?" I asked once it was clear we were past the business portion of the call.

"Good," he said, his tone softening. "Really good."

"I haven't seen you at the club recently."

"Krystina's got her hands full with Eva and Turning Stone Advertising. She thrives on chaos," he said with a laugh. "But you're right. It's been a while. We should stop by soon."

"Yes, you should. I'm glad to hear things are going well for you," I said, meaning it. Alexander and Krystina had a relationship I admired. The couple had been through a lot yet had come out stronger for it. I had no intention of settling down, but if I did, I imagined my future would look something like theirs.

We wrapped up the call after a few more minutes of small talk, and I returned to my research.

The more I read, the more I realized my arsenic theory wasn't just plausible—it was probable. The symptoms Serena described matched too perfectly to ignore.

I picked up my phone again and dialed Zeke.

"Boss," he answered on the second ring.

"Where are you?"

"Just about to leave for the club."

"I need to run something by you. Are you able to come to the penthouse?"

"On my way."

Zeke arrived a short while later. He stepped into the office and frowned what he saw my concerned expression. Closing the door behind him, he waited for me to speak.

"Sit," I said, gesturing to the chair across from me.

He did as instructed, his sharp eyes scanning my face. "What's going on?"

I leaned forward, resting my elbows on the desk. "I need your take on something."

I outlined what Serena had told me about her father's death, then walked Zeke through what I'd found on arsenic poisoning and the latest news about the murder at The Midtown. He listened without interrupting, his expression unreadable.

When I finished, he leaned back in his chair, crossing his arms over his chest. "You think someone poisoned her old man?"

"It's possible," I said. "But if that's the case, why? And is it connected to the motel?"

"Connecting them is a stretch. I mean, we're talking about a crime stretching across two continents." Zeke paused and frowned. I could see the wheels turning in his head. "Unless whoever broke into her room was looking for something related to her father."

"It's a theory," I said.

He shook his head slowly, his gaze narrowing. "If someone wanted him dead, they had to have a reason. Money? Revenge? He didn't exactly have the kind of job that makes enemies."

"Unless he found something he wasn't supposed to," I countered.

Zeke raised his eyebrows, appearing skeptical. "You aren't the type to entertain conspiracies."

"No, I'm not. There's just something about this that isn't sitting right. I feel like it's all connected somehow. Call it a hunch."

Zeke frowned again, considering the possibility. "You think Serena knows more than she's letting on?"

"No," I said firmly. "If she did, she wouldn't have described his symptoms so openly or casually mention the murder at The Midtown. I don't think she's hiding anything."

Zeke studied me for a long moment before nodding. "Alright. What's the next step?"

"I want you to get with Hale. Expand the background check you did on Serena to include anyone she's had significant contact with over the past decade," I said. "And see what you can dig up on her father's work—specifically, anything he was working on right before he died. His medical records would be helpful, too. Also, some guy named Cade. He's Serena's ex. I don't have a last name."

Zeke stood, his expression resolute. "You got it. Anything else?"

"If I think of something, I'll call."

"Boss, are you that serious about this girl?"

I hesitated, not sure how to answer him. I was serious about everything when it came to Serena, but there wasn't a commitment like Zeke was implying.

"Serious in a way, but not like you think. We have a financial arrangement, and I will be spending a month with her in Italy—which brings me to the other reason I called you here. Since I have no other security that I trust as much as you, I'll need you to come come with me. We'll have to work out who is going to run Club O while I'm gone."

Zeke reached up and rubbed his hand over his jaw. If he had any thoughts about this impromptu trip to Italy, he didn't let on. Instead, he asked, "Does she have the Brutus Denarius?"

I shook my head. "That's not the reason for this trip. But to answer your question, no. She said she doesn't have it."

"Okay, then. You're the boss," he added with a shrug. "I'll start packing for Italy. The recent hires at Club O are solid, and Myla knows the business as well as we do. I think she can handle things while we're away."

"Perfect," I said. Pausing, I recalled the worry I had about the press while leaving the restaurant the previous night. Add in the concern about Serena being mixed up in some sort of criminal plot, and the need to amp up security suddenly felt more real. "One more thing, Zeke. You're right about the need for more security."

He didn't bother to hide his sigh of relief. "I've already been working on a team. Just waiting for you to give me the green light."

I considered the time I would be spending with Serena in Italy. I wanted just a few more weeks of peace—without the presence of watchful eyes. Call it intuition, but somehow, I knew that when I returned to New York, a twenty-four-hour security detail would no longer be an option. It would be a necessity.

"Have them in place after when we get back."

CHAPTER TWENTY-ONE

One Week Later
Rome, Italy

Serena

I blinked back the tears glossing over my eyes as I sifted through a soil sample, trying not to dwell on the fact that today was the final day excavating the Roman Forum—or at least it would be for the foreseeable future.

I'd been blindsided that morning, the rug viciously ripped out from under my feet when I found out that what little funding we had left for the excavation had been pulled earlier than expected for unexplained reasons. I was supposed to have cash flow until the end of the month, and losing it left me in a panic. Our permits expired today, and I didn't have the funds to extend them. It meant I would financially need Anton sooner than expected.

I thought about him—he was never far from my mind. Despite his promises, I hadn't heard from him since I'd left New York. He said he'd be here within a week, but seven days had passed without a word. I couldn't count how many times I'd picked up the phone to text him. I'd type out a message, then backspace the entire thing in frustration.

A part of me thought that my days with him had only been imagined. But then I remembered my last night in the city. In his bed. His hands on my body—making me feel things I'd never before imagined. Even now, the memory of his touch caused a growing ache between my legs.

I scowled, and my face flushed, but it wasn't from desire. I was embarrassed, wondering if he'd only used me for a cheep thrill. It wouldn't be hard to believe I was exactly that. After all, he had no vested interest in a project like mine. Perhaps the carrot he'd dangled was just a tease meant to lure me into his bed.

The more I thought about it the more I was convinced I'd probably never see him again, but the idea of not looking into those gorgeous onyx eyes caused an unwelcomed pain in my chest. I missed him, even though I shouldn't. Or perhaps it wasn't him I was missing but rather the feelings he evoked. Anton made me want again, opening a part of myself that I'd shuttered long ago.

And I hated him for it.

Shaking off the unwanted emotions, I refocused my attention on the fragments appearing in the dirt as I sifted. When the sifter was nearly empty, I noticed a small, triangular-shaped stone resting on the screen. Pulling a small whisk broom from my work belt, I began to brush away the loose dirt. After careful examination, it didn't take long to figure out I was staring at a rock. Not a long-lost relic. Not an ancient coin. Not a piece of broken pottery—simply a rock. At this point, I would even have settled for porphyry, but the columns of igneous rock that surrounded me didn't want to give up any secrets today.

I looked up and scanned the Forum. The clear skies and warmer than average temperatures had made for perfect digging conditions. The frosty winter temperatures had fallen away weeks ago, clearing a path for an early spring and what was sure to be a hot summer. Tall Italian stone pines dotted the landscape, creating an umbrella canopy across the seven hills.

Despite the splendor, I felt numb, and I couldn't bring myself to appreciate it—at least not today.

My unshed tears began to well until one slid down my cheek. Everything I'd been working for—everything my father had worked for—was likely coming to an end. I'd failed him.

"Find anything good?" said a male voice from behind me. I glanced back to see Jared Griffin walking toward me. He was a recruit from Texas who'd volunteered to be on the archeological fieldwork team.

Standing, I dusted my hands off on my jeans. I quickly brushed my tears away, not wanting to be seen having a moment of weakness in front of a team member.

"It was nothing. Just a meaningless stone—nothing that will generate new funding," I replied, struggling to keep the melancholy from my voice.

"Don't sweat it. You know how these things work. We'll get a new donor, you'll see." Jared tried to reassure me. He didn't know about my deal with Anton—yet. And that was assuming there still was a deal. While Jared was forever the optimist, I never celebrated until I had proof of funds.

"Time will tell," I murmured.

"Our work would have stalled anyway due to the summer holiday travelers. They make it too hard to focus. Tourist traffic has already picked up, and you know this place will be swarming before long."

I nodded in agreement. That was the problem with digging in a popular area. The tourists often had little care for the clearly marked excavation site, and the *Polizia di Stato* had to make regular patrols to make sure people didn't cross the line into dangerous zones.

"Maybe you're right, Jared. For now, it's getting late, and I still have to get with the city about our permits. I'm hoping they'll grant us an exception and allow us to leave things as they are. I don't want to have to backfill all the trenches if I can help it."

Jared's eyes widened and he groaned. "We'll lose so much if we have to start from scratch."

I pursed my lips and tried to tamp down the apprehension I felt. If Anton didn't follow through on his promise, there was a very high probability that we'd never get to finish our work here.

"I'm going to tell the crew to call it and start packing up the site. Have you seen Craig anywhere?" I asked, wondering why I hadn't seen my lead researcher all day.

"He's actually headed this way now," Jared said, pointing to the right. I followed his finger to see Craig Davies jogging toward us.

"Your ears must have been ringing. I was just looking for you," I remarked when Craig reached us.

"Hiya, Serena. I was stuck in the lab all bloody day and just heard about our funding getting pulled early. That's rubbish!" he said with disgust. Craig's British slang was always most prominent when he was upset by something. He shook his head, the action causing his wire-rimmed glasses to slide down his nose. Pushing them back into place, he continued. "So much work has gone into this. Absolutely gutting news, it is. Anyway, I came to find you because there's a strange bloke here looking for you. He said his name is Anton something or other."

My heart skipped a beat.

Anton.

The name echoed through me, stirring a jolt of something I dared not acknowledge. And once again, images of our last night together flashed in my mind. The best sex of my life. His eyes had been dark and intense, like he was peeling back the layers to find my soul. I could almost feel the way his hands had slid over my skin, making me forget where I was until my only focus was on the desperate heat of the moment.

"What did he say?" I asked as casually as I could.

"Not much. He showed up in a black Maserati right after I arrived. Asked to see Dr. Martinelli. I figured you might be busy, so I asked him why he was looking for you. I thought maybe I could help. He said you were expecting him. Shall I tell him to bugger off?"

"No," I said, albeit a little too quickly. "I can handle it. Where is he now?"

"Last I saw, he was near the trailer. He's with some other guy in a suit. The pair will be hard to miss," Craig said.

Most likely, Zeke was the second suit.

"Why do you say that?" I asked.

"Because they are the only fellows gallivanting around in the dust wearing posh suits and shiny shoes."

Jared snorted, but I ignored him. Turning away from Jared and Craig, I began walking down Via Sacra, the main pedestrian road in the Forum.

When I reached the crew trailer, I looked around. In the distance, I saw the sleek Maserati parked illegally near the bottom of Capitoline Hill but there was no sign of Anton or Zeke. Scanning the area, I stopped short when I spotted the tops of two heads, their bodies hidden behind a large soil heap. The absence of hardhats set me on alert. If they were field workers, they'd know better than to go into a trench without the proper gear. It was an unsafe location, even for an experienced excavator. Whoever it was didn't belong there.

Probably a tourist. Dammit!

I hurried off to shoo the people away from the freshly dug hole.

"Hey, you two!" I called to them. "*È pericoloso!* It's dangerous! You need to clear that area."

They began to make their way up the bank and around the large pile of dirt and rock sediment until they came into full view.

And lo and behold.

The two careless fools were none other than Anton and Zeke.

Despite my irritation, I couldn't help but notice the way the men moved. They didn't walk side-by-side. Instead, Zeke followed slightly behind, looking around conspicuously, a certain amount of intimidation in his stride. If I didn't already know he was a bodyguard, it would be apparent now.

I turned my attention to Anton. He looked especially sexy today in dark sunglasses, his broad frame filling out his perfectly tailored black suit. He strode toward me with an air of grace and confidence, as if he owned the world and everything in it.

But this wasn't his world—it was mine.

And he was breaking all the rules.

"Are you crazy? You can't just go walking around a dig like you're out for a stroll," I scolded.

"Hello to you, too, princess."

"I'm serious. We haven't secured the balk."

His brows rose over the top of his sunglasses before he slowly removed them. "I'm sorry? The balk?"

I sighed, forgetting that I wasn't speaking to someone versed in my world.

"The balk. It's a wall of earth meant to maintain structural integrity. It could crumble if someone simply stepped or pushed against the wrong area."

"You look different," he said, rather than acknowledge his wrongdoing.

I looked down at my dusty pants, suddenly self-conscious

about the grime on my hands. The last time he saw me, my nails had been perfectly manicured. Now, I was a mess. I automatically reached up to smooth my dark hair behind my ears.

"It's impossible to stay clean in this line of work."

The corner of his mouth turned up in a lopsided grin. "I like you dirty."

My eyes widened, and my pulse quickened as heat crept up my neck. He was a respectable distance away, but it didn't feel that way. He was just so *there*, radiating with authority. Heat surged in his eyes, the palpable wave making me dizzy.

An unhurried smile curved his lips—lips that looked like they belonged on a fallen angel amidst a storm. He was so sure of himself. Arrogant. Gorgeous as sin, and he knew it. That confidence is what drew me to him in the first place.

"I haven't heard from you. Where have you been?" My voice came out sharper than I intended, but it didn't matter. I crossed my arms, a weak shield against the force of him. Anything less would invite him to trample over me. It was becoming our routine. He intimidated, and I pushed back. Somewhere in between, I lost more of myself to him than I ever intended.

A maddening smirk played on his lips, daring me to rise to whatever challenge he was preparing to throw my way. Zeke loomed silently behind him, as stoic and immovable as ever, his presence adding a measure of importance to Anton's arrival.

"I told you I'd be here within a week, princess," he said, his voice smooth as silk and just as dangerous. "And here I am."

I glared at him, my irritation clawing its way to the surface.

"Within a week," I repeated. "But no calls, no texts, no clue when to expect you. A little communication would have been appreciated."

His smirk deepened, his dark eyes glinting with amusement—or was it satisfaction? His gaze swept over me slowly, deliberately, as though cataloging every inch of me. From my dusty boots to the braid over my shoulder, he took it all in. But it wasn't just an innocent appraisal—it was a touchless caress, reminding me of the power he wielded.

"Careful, or I might think you missed me." His smirk tilted into a grin, the kind that made my pulse falter.

I stiffened under his scrutiny, heat rising to my face.

"No." I snapped, though we both knew it was a lie. "I just don't appreciate being left in the dark, Anton. Not when people are counting on me."

"You're right. And I'm sorry. I'm not used to…" He paused, then held my gaze. "I'm not used to answering to people."

I rolled my eyes and turned away, refusing to let him see how his words—or his presence—unnerved me.

"I'm not someone you have to answer to. It would have been a courtesy, that's all. Especially given…well, given everything," I said, my tone clipped as I tried to busy myself with one of the tools hooked to my belt. I didn't want him to know how utterly discarded I'd felt only moments before he'd shown up. "My team has begun packing up the dig site. Today's the last day for us for a while. The permits expire at midnight."

"Packing up?" He crossed his arms, shifting his weight to one foot like he belonged there—as if this dusty, sun-scorched place could ever match the glossy perfection of him. "Can't you extend the permits?"

I signed. "Not without money. And I'm all out of that. I'm headed back to Lucca shortly."

He frowned, his displeasure evident in every line of his face. "Why aren't you staying in Rome? I've booked the penthouse suite at the St. Regis."

"Well, I hope you didn't pre-pay for that fancy hotel," I said, still irritated over his seven days of radio silence to care much about his inconvenience. If he'd called or texted, he would have been aware of the situation. "I can't stay. My apartment lease is up, too. That's why I'm going back to Lucca."

For a moment, surprise flickered in his eyes, quickly replaced by something more measured. "You're moving that quickly?"

I shrugged, aiming for nonchalance even though his attention was suffocating.

"I'm used to not keeping roots anywhere for very long. The apartment was a fully furnished rental. All I had to pack were my personal belongings, and I did that this morning. My car is already loaded. My mother is expecting me tonight."

Anton straightened, his posture shifting from casual to full-blown alpha male in a way that made my heart stumble.

"Your mother? No. I'll book a new hotel in Lucca. You'll stay with me."

He wasn't asking. I was quickly learning that Anton never asked.

He commanded.

I nearly laughed out loud. "I can't stay with you. Not only would my mother never forgive me for living in sin, but I have a lot to figure out. Until I have a concrete plan for what comes next, I'm just going to stay at my mother's house. No sense in starting a new lease when I'm not sure where I'll be in a few weeks."

"But our agreement—"

"Did not include sleepovers."

"You're a grown woman who doesn't need to ask permission from a parent."

"It's not about asking permission. It's about showing respect for my mother and her beliefs. I don't agree with her, but I don't need to flaunt it." I paused, sighing. "Don't worry. I'll still keep my end of the deal—assuming we still have a deal."

"Of course we have a deal. I promised you five hundred thousand, and I'm a man of my word." He held my gaze, unyielding, as he seemed to come to a decision. "Give me your mother's address."

My pulse quickened, but I didn't know why. Perhaps it was his commanding tone. Or maybe it was his furious expression—as if he wanted nothing more than to take me over his knee. Surprisingly, I would have welcomed it. I'd rather enjoyed the sting of his palm on the one and only night we'd shared.

I rattled off the address like it didn't matter—like he didn't matter—despite my racing heart.

"I'll be in touch later once I have a hotel," he said, his voice low and edgy. "I expect you to hold your end of the bargain. Plan on seeing me tonight, princess."

And with that, he turned, walking away with that infuriating confidence. Zeke trailed after him like the silent shadow he was. I watched them go with my arms crossed, my body locked in place as my mind churned with a mix of frustration and the desire I didn't want to acknowledge.

He walked like he owned the world. Maybe he did.

Or maybe he just owned me.

CHAPTER TWENTY-TWO

Serena

The sun-bleached facade of my mother's house came into view as I turned onto the cobblestone street. It was modest, with weathered terracotta tiles on the roof and pale-yellow stucco walls adorned with climbing vines that bloomed with pink and white flowers in the summer. A wrought-iron gate framed the tiny front garden, where herbs and potted plants lined the walkway.

I killed the engine of my Fiat Panda. Stepping out of the car, I slung my purse over my shoulder and retrieved one of the large duffle bags with my belongings from the back seat. I inhaled deeply, letting the familiar scent of basil and lemongrass soothe the nerves that had been tightening since that morning. This house was home—at least as close to one as I'd had since before my father passed.

The door swung open before I reached it. My mother stood there, her smile bright and her arms outstretched.

"Serena! *Amore mio, sei a casa finalmente!*"

Her voice was like music, lilting and warm, full of the kind of love only a mother could express. She looked as she always did—effortlessly put-together despite her simple attire. Her dark hair, streaked with silver, was swept into a loose chignon. She wore a fitted cardigan over a floral dress that swayed at her knees. The apron tied around her waist was dusted with flour.

"*Ciao*, Mamma," I said, stepping into her embrace.

She kissed both my cheeks before pulling back to look at me, her hands framing my face. Her deep blue eyes—so much like my own—scanned me as if trying to assess any changes in me.

"You look thin," she said, her brows creasing. "Did you not eat while you were in New York? Americans and their terrible food."

"I ate plenty, Mamma." I hated to lie. But if I told her the truth, that would require more explanation than I wasn't ready to give. I'd had plenty to eat while I was in New York, although I'd skipped a few meals when I was sick. When I got back to Italy, money stress had robbed me of my appetite, and I'd eaten very little over the past week. I wasn't sure how much weight I'd lost, but my clothes were fitting a tiny bit looser.

She waved me inside, chattering as she led me through the familiar hallway.

"Tell me about New York. Did you make time for yourself while you were there? Did you go to any of the museums? Did you meet anyone interesting?"

I hesitated, placing my bag by the door. I understood what she was asking in not so many words. She knew why my trip to the United States was important, and she wanted to know if I got the funding for the dig.

"It was...busy," I said, keeping my tone vague. I wasn't ready to talk about Anton, or how I'd gotten the money I needed. "I'm still trying to sort through things. There are a lot of decisions to make and things to do now that I'm home. It will be a bit before I head back to Rome. The permits expired, although I managed to get a temporary fourteen-day extension before I left Rome today."

"So you plan on continuing?"

I looked away, not sure if I was ready to admit the truth to her. My mother had supported my father, and she understood why I wanted to continue his search. She'd been there and had heard the promise I made. However, if I didn't succeed, I was certain she wouldn't be disappointed. As encouraging as she was, my mother would have liked to see me follow a different path—one that didn't include chasing ghosts.

"I'm not sure, Mamma," I finally said quietly.

"I see. How long do you think you'll be home?"

I smiled, knowing she'd be happy to learn I was back for more than my usual weekend.

"Funding to continue work is on the way, but I still have to get that sorted out. I'll be home for couple of weeks at least."

"Wonderful! You'll have time to relax. Maybe create some new glass pieces? And there is so much happening in town this week! Did you know the festival starts tomorrow? Oh, and the *Mercato Antiquario* is back. You must go—it's the best one yet!"

I smiled again as she rattled on about her findings at the antique market. As she continued, I walked to the small desk in the corner of the living room where she usually piled the mail that came for me while I was away. I started sorting through it, separating bills from junk, while she recounted the latest town gossip.

Halfway through the stack, I came across an envelope with the insignia of a gallery in Florence. My pulse quickened as I opened it. Inside was a check—the payment for my last set of blown glass pieces—and a letter.

I scanned the words quickly. They were requesting more work, praising my craftsmanship and asking if I could create additional pieces for their upcoming exhibit. Relief washed over me.

"Good news?" my mother asked, pausing her monologue to peer over at me.

"Great news," I said, smiling. "The gallery in Florence wants more glasswork. It's been a rough few months. This will really help me get caught up."

"*Che meraviglia!*" she exclaimed, clapping her hands together. "You are so talented, Serena. Your father would be proud."

Her words made my chest tighten. We both knew proud wasn't the right word. While he appreciated my talent, he saw it as a hobby. If I ever spent too much time in my workshop, he'd tell me I was wasting opportunities, saying my time would be better spent digging in the field.

"I'm going to head upstairs to unpack a few things, Mamma."

"Go, go. I've just finished prepping the *fiocchetti*. I'll wait to do the rest until you come down."

"I shouldn't be long," I said, leaning in to hug her. "I'm so happy to be home. I missed you."

Stepping away, I grabbed my duffle bag and headed upstairs.

The floor creaked beneath my feet as I pushed open the door to my old bedroom. The scent of lavender and vanilla sachets hit me first. It was faint but familiar, as if the ghost of my teenage self still lingered in the air. Nothing had really changed much since then. The walls were still painted that pale yellow I'd insisted on when I was fourteen, a color I'd declared sunshine chic, but now just seemed tired and faded.

My bed sat against the far wall, its iron frame slightly bent from so many international moves. The floral quilt my mother had sewn was still draped over it, a patchwork of soft pinks, yellows, and greens. I ran my hand over it as I passed, fingers catching on a tear near the corner. A mismatched assortment of pillows sat haphazardly at the headboard, looking more decorative than inviting.

The shelves above the desk were cluttered with relics of a past life. Dusty trophies from school debates, a lopsided clay pot I'd made in art class, and a row of paperback novels with cracked spines still occupied the wooden ledges. My collection of Cleopatra biographies stood out, their worn covers a reminder of my fascination with the queen ever since I was a little kid. Back then, she'd seemed untouchable—powerful and untamed. Now, I wasn't so sure.

This room belonged to a girl who used to scribble hieroglyphs in her notebooks and dream about becoming an archaeologist. I barely recognized that person anymore. Somewhere along the way, I'd gotten lost. While I hadn't lost sight of the goal, I also didn't know where I belonged anymore.

I set the duffle on the bed and unzipped it, the sound harsh in the quiet room, and started unpacking. As I folded my shirts, I noticed they smelled faintly of Rome—clean, yet a mix of dust and stone clung to them. I stacked them in the narrow dresser that bore scratches from years of slamming its drawers shut.

I caught sight of the corkboard above the desk, its corners still dotted with faded pushpins. Pictures of old friends—some smiling, some mid-laugh—stared back at me, their edges yellowing and curled from age. A photo of me with my parents stood out in the center. It was taken on my final day of secondary school, right after we'd moved into this house. We were standing by the front gate, my father's arm draped protectively around my shoulders. I looked so young, so sure of myself.

That girl was naïve, and didn't know how much she'd change over the years. The pictures pre-dated Cade and Briana, and all the heartache they would eventually cause. It was before my father got sick, leaving an empty space in my heart that could never be filled.

I shook my head and turned back to place the empty duffle in the closet. Heading to the shared bathroom down the hallway, I took a moment to wash my face and hands, removing the grime from the day. After towel drying, I planned to go to my car and retrieve my other bags but paused when I heard a sharp knock at the front door.

Walking out into the hallway, I yelled, "I'm on my way down, Mamma. I'll get it."

Opening the front door, I froze. Anton stood there, looking impossibly handsome. His piercing onyx eyes locked onto mine with an intensity that sent my pulse racing. At first, I wasn't sure how he'd known to find me here, but then I remembered that I'd given him the address so he could find a nearby hotel.

"Anton," I said, my voice faltering.

"Princess," The corners of his mouth lifted in a faint smile.

"I wasn't expecting you to come here. I thought you were going to a hotel, and we'd meet up later."

My mother appeared behind me, forcing me to maintain my composure. Her eyes widened as she took him in, her lips parting in surprise.

"And who is this?" she asked.

"Mamma, this is Anton Romano," I said, stepping aside and motioning him in. "Anton, this is my mother, Sylvia Martinelli."

Anton extended a hand, his charm effortless. "It's a pleasure to meet you, Mrs. Martinelli."

My mother took his hand, her cheeks tinged with pink. "Please, call me Sylvia. Serena, you did not tell me we were expecting such a handsome guest this evening."

"Oh, I um… " I stammered, shooting Anton a questioning look. "Anton is interested in investing in the Rome dig. We met in New York. I wasn't expecting him. I—"

"It's no bother at all! I've made plenty," my mother declared, never once taking her observant gaze off Anton. "You'll join us for dinner, yes?"

My eyes widened.

Oh, no...

It was nearing eight o'clock. It had been a long day in the field, and I was tired from the four-hour drive from Rome to Lucca. I was not mentally prepared for this.

Anton chuckled, the sound low and warm. "Thank you, Sylvia. I wasn't planning to impose. I've booked a room at the Hotel Villa Bianca, just a few blocks away. I was only stopping by to see if Serena wanted to join me for a bite to eat. We have... business matters to discuss."

My mother waved this off as if it were absurd. "Nonsense! You'll eat here. I insist."

I opened my mouth to protest, but Anton spoke first. "Thank you. I'd be honored."

Of course, he would accept.

He thrived in situations like this—completely unflappable and utterly in control. I, on the other hand, was suddenly very aware of how awkward this was sure to be.

"Well," my mother said, clapping her hands together. "Come, Anton. Sit, relax. I've made *fiocchetti* with pears and parmesan cream. Serena, go pick out a nice wine for us."

I shot Anton a look of exasperation, but he just smiled, clearly amused. It wasn't long before my mother began fussing over him, peppering him with questions about his business in New York.

I resigned myself to my fate. It was going to be a long evening.

CHAPTER TWENTY-THREE

Anton

Dinner was an experience, and not just because it had been a while since I'd enjoyed a home-cooked meal. The delicate folds of pasta in cream sauce with sweet pear was incredible, and the women seated across from me were truly fascinating to watch.

Sylvia was a force of nature, commanding the tiny dining room with an energy that filled every corner. She laughed easily, her hands gesturing animatedly as she recounted stories about the locals and the antics of her neighbor's mischievous dog. It was all so...domestic, and it was a far cry from anything I'd ever experienced.

But I was more taken with Serena. She was different, relaxed in a way I hadn't seen before. Her careful guard had seemed to soften—her laughter more genuine and her smile unreserved. She leaned forward, listening to her mother with rapt attention, occasionally throwing in her own quips.

I enjoyed observing people. It helped me to understand them better so I could anticipate their actions. The stock market and crypto exchange were reactionary, and I wouldn't have amassed my fortune if I couldn't predict human behavior. But studying Serena was different somehow. Watching her was a lesson in grace.

I leaned back in my chair, rolling the last sip of wine over my tongue as I watched them. Sylvia's dark hair, streaked with silver, gleamed under the dim light, the curve of her face an echo of Serena's. She and her mother shared a closeness that was foreign to me. Their conversations seemed to move like a dance of words and silent looks of understanding. It was a kind of affection I'd never witnessed before up close—a bond that should have felt natural but instead twisted something deep in my gut.

It made me feel like an intruder.

I wasn't the jealous type. Not in the petty, insecure way most men were. This felt like jealousy, yet different somehow. Perhaps it was my curiosity about their relationship that caused the strange, hollow ache inside me. Or maybe it was something darker. My own mother was buried in a past I rarely allowed myself to think about. Sitting at a table like this—exchanging laughter, sharing a meal—was so alien that it may as well have been fiction. I couldn't help wonder that, if given the right opportunity and set of circumstances, my own mother and I might have had this.

I dragged my gaze from Sylvia to Serena, tracking every subtle movement and nuance of expression, needing to understand. Serena must have felt my scrutiny, and she turned. When our eyes met, everything else seemed to fade. The look she gave me was inquisitive, as if she were wondering what I was thinking. After a moment, her shoulders stiffened and something in her eyes shifted. I noticed the increasing rise and fall of her chest, and quickly realized Serena was no longer thinking about the words her mother was saying.

I glanced down, watching her fingers curl ever so slightly around her napkin. Her lips parted, just barely, and my pulse kicked up. I wanted to know what was going on behind those ocean blue eyes. The space between us grew charged with tension. It called to something central in me—to something possessive.

"Dessert?" Sylvia's voice broke the moment. She was blissfully unaware of the silent fire igniting between her daughter and me as she reached for a small tray of pastries on the counter.

Serena blinked, bringing herself back to the present as she straightened in her chair. "None for me, thank you," she said quickly, her voice light but firm, her eyes still tethered to mine. "Anton has had a long day of travel. I'm sure he must be exhausted."

It took every ounce of self-control not to smirk.

"Not particularly," I countered, keeping my tone deliberately casual.

My gaze remained steady on hers. Serena shot me a sharp look, her irritation barely masked. She feigned a yawn, but I wasn't fooled. Not for a second.

"It's getting late," she persisted.

I arched a brow, amusement flickering through me.

Is this forced tiredness for my benefit, or her mother's?

It didn't matter. If she thought she was getting rid of me that easily, she was sorely mistaken. The dinner I'd just shared with mother and daughter was nothing more than an interlude. The real game—the one Serena and I were playing—was just beginning.

Sylvia glanced at the clock on the wall. "Oh! I didn't even realize it was nearing ten. Time gets away from me when I'm enjoying good company. You should take Anton next door before he leaves, Serena. Show him the workshop."

The sudden shift in topic seemed to catch Serena off guard.

"The workshop?"

"Yes, of course!" Sylvia's voice was bright with enthusiasm before she turned her attention on me. "You can't come all this way and not see it. Serena is so talented, Anton. You wouldn't believe the things she can do with glass."

"I'd love to see it," I said.

Sylvia began clearing plates. "I'll take care of cleaning up. I'm actually starting to get a little tired myself. I'll probably turn in soon. Serena, don't forget to lock up when you get back."

Serena hesitated, her lips parting as if to protest, but her mother gave her a look that brooked no argument.

"Okay, Mamma."

Sylvia turned back to me, smiling warmly. "Thank you for joining us tonight, Anton. It was a pleasure having you here."

"The pleasure was mine," I said, standing and offering my hand.

She took it, her grip firm and confident. "You're always welcome in our home."

Home.

The foreign word seemed to linger in the air as Serena grabbed a set of keys from the counter. Without another word, she led me outside.

The night was cool, a breeze carrying the faint scent of citrus through the narrow path between the house and the workshop.

"Sorry about that," Serena said, seeming uncomfortable as we walked.

"For what?"

"For her... enthusiasm. It really is late. I can't imagine seeing my workshop was high on your priority list."

I chuckled. "I thought your mother was charming. As for my priorities, I won't deny that I had other ideas for you tonight."

Serena glanced at me, her expression unreadable. "I haven't been to the workshop in months. Dust will have settled. You aren't really dressed for this."

"It's of no concern. Clothes can be washed and replaced."

She didn't respond but slowed her pace as we reached the workshop. The building was small, a mix of wood and aged brick walls that bore the marks of decades of use. Serena unlocked the door and stepped inside, flicking on a light that illuminated the space with a warm, golden glow.

The workshop was simple. Wooden benches lined the walls, each one cluttered with tools, shards of glass, and half-finished projects. Shelves were filled with jars of colored glass fragments, their hues catching the light like jewels.

"It's nothing fancy but it works," Serena said, walking ahead of me. She moved to one of the workbenches, her fingers trailing over the tools with a kind of reverence.

My eyes landed on a finished piece resting on a shelf—a glass sculpture of a bird in flight, the wings delicate and translucent. The attention to detail was exquisite.

"Did you make that?" I asked, nodding toward it.

She looked over and nodded. "That was one of my first solo pieces. I was just a teenager when I made it."

"It's stunning," I said, meaning it.

A faint blush crept up her cheeks, and she busied herself with straightening tools on the workbench. "Glass is...unpredictable. It can shatter if you're not careful, but if you handle it right, it transforms into something beautiful. I like that about it."

I mulled over her words for a moment and found myself watching her more closely. There was something about the way she moved in this space—comfortable, confident, and completely in her element.

"Show me how you do it."

"Blow glass?"

"Yes."

She laughed. "It takes hours for the furnace to reach temp. Another day, maybe."

I stepped toward her. "Tomorrow then."

"I suppose that could work. I have a commission I need to start on, and tomorrow is as good of a time as any."

She paused, and her brow furrowed. Her lips pursed contemplatively, seemingly lost in thought as she looked around the workspace. Just the idea of seeing her work—seeing her create something as sensual as the flames on display in front of my club—was enough to make me want to take her right here and now. Knowing she was the creator of such a provocative work of art reminded me that she was the only one who had ever triggered such deep, carnal desires in me.

I thought about when I'd first seen the glass flames at a silent auction in New York. They had been the talk of the event, stunning in their beauty and mystery. The auctioneer had mentioned that they'd been recently acquired from a gallery in Florence. The moment I saw them, I knew I had to have them. Now knowing that Serena had created them felt like too much of a coincidence. I didn't believe in one almighty God or any of the Catholic teachings Serena had mentioned. But I did believe in fate.

"It will be an early morning," she continued. "I'll have to get up before six to light the furnace and—"

I silenced her words by roughly pulling her to me. I'd been patient enough all through dinner. I needed to taste her—to feel her.

"Come back to my hotel, princess. Spend the night with me," I murmured, my voice low and coaxing. I caught the soft scent of her perfume, a stark contrast to the fire in her gaze.

Serena tensed and let out a breathy laugh, shaking her head as she glanced away. "I can't."

"Yes, you can." I reached for her hand, placing it between us and running my thumb over her knuckles. She didn't pull away, but she didn't relax either.

"Not tonight. It would be too...obvious. It's my mother," she said finally, her voice tinged with something between exasperation and amusement. But I also detected a hint of longing.

I arched a brow. "Need I remind you again? You're a grown woman, Serena. You don't need your mother's permission."

She sighed, biting her lip, that internal battle playing out across her face.

"You don't understand. I'm happy you're here, and I want to be with you again—more than you know. This isn't about permission," she said, and paused to let out a sardonic laugh. Then she exhaled slowly, meeting my gaze. "If it were about getting permission, I'd still be a virgin. My mother just has this way of seeing things. She's spent her whole life in the church—praying, confessing, believing every word of it. She takes her faith very seriously."

I watched her, reading the hesitation in her eyes, seeing the struggle between desire and guilt. She wasn't making excuses—this was real for her. It didn't matter if Serena didn't share her mother's beliefs. This was about a lifetime of faith, of timeless prayers and careful obedience, all pressing down on her shoulders.

She sighed again, then turned away from me, crossing the room to the window. Separating the wood blinds with two fingers, she peered out into the night. The house where I'd just enjoyed dinner was dark. No lights were on in the windows. No shadows moved behind the curtains.

I waited, watching the tension in Serena's shoulders melt away. Then, slowly, she let the blinds fall back into place. Turning, she reached behind her, and I heard the snap of the door lock.

"But my mother has gone to bed. While that doesn't mean I'll go back to your hotel, it does mean we're alone."

She moved toward me with deliberate slowness, each step measured, her body drawn to mine as if by some invisible force. Her eyes, dark and smoldering with something dangerous, never left me. The air between us thickened, pulsing with anticipation. With need.

When she reached me, she hesitated for just a fraction of a second, her breath warm against my lips. Then, with a tilt of her head, she closed the distance. Her lips pressed against mine, soft yet insistent, testing at first before deepening with quiet desperation.

She tasted like wine and something intrinsically her—a sweet and intoxicating flavor that I knew would ruin me for anyone else. I slid a hand around the curve of her waist, pulling her closer, feeling the heat of her body against mine. She responded instantly, her fingers tangling in my hair as her nails grazed lightly against my scalp.

A soft sigh escaped her, and that sound sent a surge of possession through me. I tilted my head, taking control, parting her lips as I deepened the kiss. She met me stroke for stroke, her body arching into mine, her surrender making something dark and fundamental flare inside me.

I wanted more.

Needed more.

But I also wanted to savor this—every shaky breath, every subtle tremor, every inch of her pressed against me. I let my fingers trail up her spine, slow and deliberate, reveling in the way she shivered beneath my touch. She was fire and silk. Resistance and surrender.

Then, to my surprise, she dropped to her knees and began unbuckling my pants. Deft fingers made quick work, and it wasn't long before I was free from the constraint of clothing.

When she took the full weight of me in her hand, I hissed. "Fuck, Serena. You look exquisite on your knees."

She wrapped her perfect lips around my cock. Any thoughts I had about taking her back to my hotel disappeared. She was now in control, and surprisingly, I was happy to let her take over.

Gabbing the back of her head, I fisted her hair and pushed deeper into her throat. I glanced down and found myself completely taken by the vision of her working over my length. She had one hand resting on the outside of my thigh, while the other hand wrapped around the base of my cock.

And her mouth...

Those perfect lips performed miracles of epic proportion.

She met my gaze, her eyes smoldering with a secret only she understood. Then she pulled back, running her tongue slowly and deliberately down the entire length of my erection. She did it again, flicking her tongue over the sensitive tip, her eyes never breaking contact with mine.

I moaned and I could feel her smile around my cock before she tightened her suction once more. This was a measured tease, and it made me want her that much more. I was coming apart, and I wouldn't be able to hold back much longer. It was pure torture, and she knew it—and I wanted nothing more than to punish her for it.

Stepping back, I pulled her to her feet. After stripping her shirt over her head, I pushed her until she was against the worktable in the center of the room. I gripped her shoulders, pressing her back until her spine was horizontal, and covered her body with mine. Burying my face in her neck, I breathed deeply, inhaling her scent. I peppered kisses along her jaw, moving to nip at her ear. She threw her head back, welcoming me to take more.

I was suddenly desperate. It had been too long since I'd been inside her. I needed to feel that hot, wet heat again.

Reaching under her to unhook her bra, I shoved it up roughly over her breasts. Then I bit down, capturing a nipple. Her back arched as the taut peaks hardened in response.

I moved a hand down her belly unfastening the button and zipper, I pushed the restrictive material down enough to make room for my fingers. When I made contact with her wet slit, she moaned—and it just might have been the sexiest sound I'd ever heard.

"Jesus Christ, Serena," I grunted. "You're so wet. I want to fuck you. Right here. Right now."

I circled her nub with my forefinger, wanting her to come before I plunged my cock into her. I was desperate to have her and knew I wouldn't be gentle when the time came.

"Yes. Just like that!" she cried out.

Her eyes locked on mine, and all I saw was a blazing inferno of desire as I continued to push her higher and higher. I wished we were somewhere else—my hotel, my club, anywhere. Fucking her like a savage on a slab of wood in a dusty garage didn't seem fitting for a woman who deserved to be worshipped, but I was at the point of no return. The promise of her sweet pussy was too much.

"I want your orgasm, princess. I need to feel you tighten around my finger."

"Please, Anton. Make me come," she begged.

My eyes closed at the sound of my name falling from her lips. If I could live in this moment for the rest of my life, with the feel of her body trembling for me, I would die a happy man.

"I will, princess. And then I'm going to take you right here on this table."

She moaned again, and within moments, her body stiffened and shuddered, surrendering to her climax.

I didn't give her a moment to come down before pulling my fingers free and sliding her pants all the way down her legs. I made quick work of the condom, then cupped her ass and pulled her closer to me. I paused only for a moment so that I could lean down and press my lips to her soft, warm mouth. The ragged edge of her kiss was a sharp contrast to how sweet she tasted, making me moan into her mouth.

She ground her hips against me, seeking my cock. Grabbing her waist, I held her, controlling the motion. Then, positioning myself at her entrance, I shifted my feet to get the leverage I needed and pushed in deep, driving all the way home.

She let out a gasp as her body worked to accommodate my girth. I waited, letting her intense heat soak me.

"That's it. Take all of me like a good girl. Feel it."

Her rippling heat drove me wild as I began to pump into her. When she wrapped those glorious legs of hers around my hips and rose up to meet me, I hissed through clenched teeth and pushed harder. Over and over again, I impaled her.

It was as if I couldn't get close enough.

I needed more than her body.

I needed to possess her.

To own her.

"Anton," she moaned, her eyes a violent inferno of blue flames. The moaning of my name eventually turned into a plea. She was beautiful—absolutely stunning, and her sounds only made me harder.

"Yeah, that's it. Say my name again, princess. I want to hear you scream it."

Invigorated by the feel of her slick, tight walls, I increased the speed of my thrusts. By the time I felt her orgasm start to clench around my cock, I was ready to explode. When she came, her cry of release was all I needed to lose myself in her. I came with such a violent force, I was left shuddering and trembling in her arms.

Time seemed to stand still, and I wasn't sure how long we lay there before Serena finally said, "I should get dressed."

"I like you naked," I murmured, shifting my weight so she could sit up.

She turned her head slightly, meeting my gaze with a look that was both exasperated and amused. "I'm sure you do."

She stretched, the action making it impossible not to run my hand over her smooth, olive skin. I traced my fingers along the curve of her hip, feeling the warmth of her body and watching the way her breath hitched.

When she moved to stand, I stood with her, pulling my pants back on as I watched her collect articles of clothing that were strewn about. Reaching down, I hooked a finger through a belt loop of her jeans and held them open for her to step into.

"Thank you," she murmured. "But I've got it."

I didn't let go of the pants. Instead, I pulled them up her legs. Once they were in place, I slowly raised the zipper and fastened the button. Leaning in, I brought my lips to the shell of her ear. "I like taking care of you, princess. You'll need to get used to it if we're going to spend the next month together."

She let out a small laugh, shaking her head. "About that. Does this count as day one?"

"I suppose it can."

She looked at me for a moment, seeming to consider the situation. "I can't spend all day, everyday, with you. I have a glasswork commission, and I should take advantage of this time away from the dig site to complete it."

I shrugged. "I have work of my own to do. And when I don't, I'll watch your craft. I believe you mentioned starting early tomorrow."

A flicker of something passed through her expression—hesitation, maybe. Then intrigue. "You really want to sit and watch me make glass?"

"I like watching you."

Her face flushed, and her lips parted slightly as if she wanted to protest.

"It will take the morning for the furnace to reach temp," she said finally. "Be here at noon."

I met her gaze, letting a slow, deliberate smile play on my lips as I thought about fucking her again right here on this table. "Noon it is, princess."

CHAPTER TWENTY-FOUR

Serena

Gravel crunched beneath my feet as I walked toward my workshop. The sun had barely peeked over the horizon, casting a warm glow that promised a beautiful day. The morning air was crisp, and I shivered as I zipped up my old work sweatshirt. The cold wouldn't last. Within the hour, the heat from the furnace would chase away the remnants of the dawn's chill, leaving only the dry, suffocating warmth that came with molten glass.

I stepped into the workshop, inhaling the familiar scent of ash, metal, and charred wood. It was comforting and grounding. My space. The furnace sat silent for now, its massive structure looming in the room like a sleeping beast. I moved to it automatically, checking the temperature gauge before flipping the switches that would bring it back to life.

A low hum filled the workshop as flames ignited behind the heavy steel doors. Soon, the heat would build to nearly two thousand degrees, and I could begin work. While I waited, I tied my hair back, looping the long tresses into a loose ponytail, and began clearing a workspace.

The glass dust and stray shards from my last session needed sweeping, and my tools needed organizing. I wiped down the marver table so the smooth surface was ready to shape and cool hot glass. I checked my blowpipes, making sure the punty rods were still in good shape. It was a meditative process, and the rhythm of preparation helped quiet my mind, letting me drift as I moved around the workshop.

I paused by the display shelf near the back where some of my older pieces sat. I studied a delicate glass rose, a twisting ribbon of bright pink. Its petals were so thin, they looked like they might shatter with the slightest touch. That particular freeform piece had taken me weeks to perfect.

Then, there was the one I always lingered on—a simple glass heart, smooth and clear except for a thin crack running through its center. I ran my fingers over it, the flaw catching against my skin. Imperfect and beautifully broken. I'd created it the day I had found out Cade was cheating on me with Briana. While I liked to think I'd moved on from that painful part of my life, the glass heart reminded me to never forget—and to never again love so freely.

With a breath, I straightened and turned back to my workbench, my mind shifting to what came next. I thought about the gallery in Florence, and the sort of pieces they preferred. They had specifically requested something unique, and unlike anything else I'd given them. An idea had been simmering in my mind since the moment I'd read their letter, but now, I finally settled on it.

I would create a swan, its wings stretched wide, frozen in that moment just before flight.

I already could envision the delicate curve of the neck and the feathered detail of its wings. It would be a challenge, but that was the beauty of glass. The push and pull between control and chaos, between what I saw in my mind and what the heat and fire would allow, was unlike anything words could describe. If I did it right, the piece might catch a pretty penny.

I began sketching the first lines of the design, losing myself in the drawing and not paying attention to the time. The gentle purr of a car engine coming from outside pulled me from my concentration. I glanced up at the clock. It was nearing noon. My heart skipped a few moments later when I heard footfalls outside the workshop.

Anton.

I wiped my hands on my jeans and headed for the door to greet him. I watched his approach through the side window, and my pulse kicked up another notch despite myself. My stomach tightened, my lust for him always shimmering just below the surface.

He hadn't called or texted to say he was on his way. He simply arrived, unannounced and right on time, carrying that effortless confidence that said he expected to be welcomed.

And may the devil take me, but I was more than ready to invite him inside.

"Hey," I said after opening the door.

"Good morning, beautiful." He gave me a slight nod, the corner of his mouth turning up in the most delicious, lopsided smile I'd ever seen.

I glanced behind him to see Zeke standing by the car. "Zeke is welcome to come in as well," I offered.

Anton waved me off as he stepped inside. "He has business to attend to. I told him I'd text him when we're ready to leave."

"Business?"

"Yes. I've asked him to research a few things."

"Oh? A lead on more ancient coins," I suggested, my tone teasing.

"Something like that." His reply was vague, as if no further explanation were needed. I frowned and was about to prod further, but he brushed past me and walked toward the table. After removing his jacket, he pulled an envelope from the inside pocket and placed the contents on the table. "The contract. I figured we could get this out of the way first."

I glanced down at the single sheet of paper before me, then frowned when I saw what was written on it.

"What are the terms? This only asks for bank details."

"There are no terms. I can't force you to spend thirty days with me. I'm just going to trust you to keep your word. All I need is your bank information for the wire transfer." Pausing, he pointed to a section on the paper. "Once you fill this out, I'll have Zeke handle the rest. The transfer will be instant."

I blinked, confused about the situation. I struggled to find words, unable to do anything but stare at him.

"You're serious?" I finally asked.

Anton's expression didn't waver. "I don't say things I don't mean, Serena."

His voice was firm, leaving no room for doubt or space for me to question his decision. Looking down, I picked up the piece of paper.

This is too easy—too simple.

After all the back and forth, the teasing, the power plays, I didn't understand why he would just hand over five hundred thousand dollars.

I hesitated, my gaze flicking from the form to Anton.

"So that's it? You're just giving me the money. No stipulations. No games."

He leaned in, his presence commanding. His gaze locked onto mine, dark and unrelenting. "The stipulation is that you don't go back on your word. I don't play games with the things I want, Serena. And I want this—I want you."

A war waged inside me. I wasn't used to things being given

so freely, especially from men like Anton Romano. But there was no deception in his face. Just absolute certainty.

He gestured to the paper. "Write down your bank details, Serena. Let's get this done."

I exhaled slowly, glancing down at the form once more, still unable to believe what he was offering. The only thing he required was my bank information. There wasn't even a signature line binding me to my verbal promise.

Reaching for my phone, I pulled up my banking app. After I verified the numbers, I copied the information onto the form.

Anton didn't look away. He just watched me, his presence a tangible force pressing in around me. As I finished writing, a strange mix of relief and apprehension settled in my chest. I wasn't sure if I had just won this game of chess or if I had set myself up for a checkmate.

I handed the paperback back to Anton.

"Good. I'm glad we got that business out of the way," he said with a nod. After folding the paper and placing it back inside the envelope, his eyes landed on my drawing of the swan. "I see you're hard at work already."

"Just sketching out what I want to create. It helps if I have a visual before I begin molding the glass. The gallery wanted something distinctive. The swan will take several days to complete, but if I capture it right, I hope it'll catch a good price."

His gaze swept over me, moving slowly up and down my body. He wasn't even trying to be subtle. "You didn't want to create more flames like the ones in New York?"

Warmth spread through me, and I flushed. I hated that he could slip past my defenses so easily. All it took was a look and a few well-placed words, and I was putty in his hands. It was frustrating and intoxicating all at the same time.

"I've already told you. The flames felt incomplete until I saw them with that statue."

"So why don't you create a different glass version of the woman instead? Perhaps in your own likeness."

My face flushed an even deeper shade of pink, and I looked away. Moving over to my tools, I said, "Even if I wanted to, my oven isn't large enough to create something that big."

"I could buy you a bigger oven."

I suppressed an eyeroll and retrieved a fresh blowpipe. Ignoring his comment, I asked, "Are you ready to watch me work?"

His lips curved. "I was hoping for something a little more interactive."

I raised a brow. "Oh?"

"I don't want you to just watch you. I want to try." He leaned against the worktable, arms crossing over his chest as he studied me. His expression was full of mischief with a hint of desire smoldering in those ruthless onyx eyes.

I laughed. "Get whatever you're thinking right out of your head. This won't be like the movies. There won't be any sexy Demi Moore and Patrick Swayze pottery moments while the oven is on. The heat will melt your skin from your bones if you're not careful. It's best if I show you first."

I gestured for him to follow me. The heat had built to full strength now, making the air around the furnace thick and heavy. Beads of sweat gathered at the back of my neck almost instantly, and Anton tugged at the collar of his shirt before rolling up his sleeves.

"First lesson," I said, dipping the end of my pipe into the furnace to gather the red-hot glass. "You need to keep the liquid glass moving. If it stays still too long, gravity takes over, and you lose control."

He watched intently as I turned the pipe, the glowing blob of molten glass clinging to the end like honey. When I pulled it out, it pulsed with heat, the color shifting between bright orange and deep gold. I moved to the marver, rolling it against the smooth surface to shape it before glancing at him.

"Stand behind me and give me your hands—but no funny business. I don't want either of us to get burned."

Anton stepped behind me, his body close enough that I felt his warmth even against the oppressive heat coming off the furnace.

"Is the pipe hot?" he asked.

"It's warm, but not too hot to touch. I have gloves, but they're generally not recommended for glassblowing. They can hinder the dexterity needed to handle the pipe and shape the glass, potentially increasing the risk of burns."

Wrapping his arms around me, I guided his hands around the end of the pipe, constantly shifting the orb. After a few moments, I let go, allowing him to repeat the movements I'd just shown him. His hold was steady, but the weight seemed to surprise him, making him adjust his grip.

"Keep it turning," I reminded him, reaching out to guide him over the marver. His muscles tensed beneath my touch, and for a brief second, the air between us shifted, thickening with something far hotter than the furnace.

His gaze flicked to mine, and I knew that if I leaned in just a fraction—if I so much as breathed the wrong way—he'd close the distance between our lips that were already too close.

Not wanting to risk an accident, I ducked out from between his arms and stepped back.

"Not bad." My voice was steady—barely. I turned toward the end of the blowpipe and leaned against the counter, needing something solid to hang on to.

I watched as Anton rolled the glass a few more times before setting the pipe down. "I'm not sure how you'll make that blob into a swan. I can't even begin to envision it."

Smiling, I picked up the pipe and returned it to the furnace.

The heat wrapped around me like a second skin as I gathered more glass, the glowing mass dripping like honey before I moved to shape it against the marver once again.

"This is where the magic happens," I murmured, more to myself than to Anton.

I felt his gaze on me, watching as I worked, but I didn't look at him. Instead, I turned my focus inward, letting my hands move with practiced precision, allowing instinct to take over. I had done this hundreds of times before—gather, shape, blow, refine—but each piece was different. Each one had its own life and temperament. Glass was unpredictable, and if you didn't respect it, it would betray you.

I shaped the glowing mass with a block of soaked wood, steam hissing as the heat met moisture. The smell of burning wood mixed with melted glass filled the air. It was a scent I had grown to love over the years. My arms ached from the constant movement and the weight of the pipe, but I welcomed the strain. It meant the piece was coming to life.

Anton moved closer. Smooth words and that sexy smile had been replaced by an intense stare as he continued to watch me work.

I dipped the pipe back into the furnace for a second gather, layering more molten glass over the base shape. I worked quickly, shaping the body of the swan, coaxing the form into existence with careful turns and calculated motions. The body elongated, smoothing under my hands as I rolled it on the marver, creating the graceful curve of the neck.

The wings were next—the tricky part that could ruin everything.

I switched to my jacks, the steel blades sliding against the glass with practiced ease, carving feathered details into the soft heat before it could cool too much. My brow furrowed in concentration, making every movement precise. Each adjustment was crucial. The glass fought me, resisting the shape I demanded of it, but I didn't back down. I knew how far to push, how much heat to use, and how to make it yield without breaking.

Minutes stretched into what felt like forever, the world outside my workshop fading into nothing. It was just me, the glass, and the fire.

When I finally pulled the pipe away, the swan stood proud on the punty, wings stretched wide, frozen in the moment before flight. The translucent glass still glowed with residual heat, the delicate details catching the light, throwing shimmering reflections across the walls.

I let out a slow breath, my muscles aching from effort, my skin damp with sweat. What I'd created wasn't the final product for the gallery, but rather a miniature replica. In the coming days, I'd study the creation to find areas for improvement for the final, larger swan that I'd eventually craft.

"Incredible," Anton murmured, breaking me from my reverie.

I turned to him and found his eyes locked on me. There was something in his expression, something unreadable and potent.

I swallowed, setting my tools down as a different kind of heat surged through me.

"It's not the final product. This was just the practice run," I said, my voice lower than I intended. "It still needs to cool in the annealer overnight, then I'll study the imperfections."

He stepped toward me, never taking his eyes off mine. The usual sexual tension between us began to shift into something heavier and far more real.

I looked away and wiped my hands on a rag. The adrenaline that always came from creating still coursed through my veins, making me feel restless. Angling my head to look at Anton, I found him watching me, his onyx eyes sharp and thoughtful.

When he spoke, his words were slow and deliberate.

"Watching you do this is easily one of my new favorite things. You should give up the rest."

I frowned. "The rest of what?"

"Archaeology. You should give it up and do this instead." He gestured to the glass swan, still glowing faintly with heat.

I let out a breathy laugh, shaking my head. "Anton—"

"I'm serious." He took another step closer until our bodies were almost touching. Taking my chin between his thumb and forefinger, he spoke again in a low but firm voice. "I've seen you in the field covered in dirt, Serena. It was only briefly, but I witnessed enough to know it didn't suit you. But this? I can see the passion in your eyes. Blowing glass is what you were meant to do."

I opened my mouth to argue, but the words didn't come.

He wasn't wrong.

I stepped away, moving to adjust the settings on the furnace, giving myself a moment to think. The days and weeks leading up to meeting Anton had been beyond stressful. From worrying about funds running out to the late nights spent poring over old maps and endless theories about Cleopatra and Mark Antony—it had all been too much. It was everything my father had dedicated his life to, and everything I had spent my adult life chasing. But the money to keep going and the answers to the riddles were always just out of reach.

And I was exhausted from it all.

But in my workshop, covered in sweat and glass dust with my muscles aching, I felt alive.

I tightened my grip on the edge of the workbench, my breath coming slower now, deeper.

"This is my last excavation," I admitted softly. Anton stayed quiet, letting me speak. I swallowed the lump in my throat, my chest tightening. "If we don't find anything this time, I'm done. I haven't told my mother yet, but I can't keep chasing ghosts. This has always been about my father. It was his dream. He spent his whole life searching, always believing he was just one step away from finding Cleopatra and Mark Antony. After he died, I just couldn't let it go. I thought if I found them and finished what he'd started, it would mean something."

"You need to do what makes you happy, princess."

I turned back to Anton then, meeting his gaze head-on. "It's your fault I started questioning this—questioning everything. It started the moment you told me to trustfall."

His brows lifted slightly, but he didn't speak.

I let out a slow breath.

"You dared me to fall without questioning whether everything would be alright—to blindly jump into an uncomfortable situation and trust that someone or something would catch me—even if the very thing I had to trust was myself. Your words made me realize that I don't have to keep doing this. I can trust my instincts and follow my own path, no matter how foreign it may be." I paused and looked around the workshop. "And today...today reminded me what it feels like to create. To make something beautiful with my own hands, instead of digging up the remnants of someone else's past."

A long silence stretched between us. Then Anton exhaled, a slow, knowing smile tugging at his lips.

"And here I worried that I'd be a bad influence on you."

I laughed, shaking my head. "Who said you weren't?"

His smile widened, but there was something softer in his eyes now.

"For what it's worth," he said, stepping closer, "I think you made your decision long before meeting me. You just needed to convince yourself."

I looked back at the swan, my first real piece in months, and something settled inside me. Maybe he was right. I just hadn't wanted to face it.

Anton stretched, rolling his shoulders.

"Come on, princess. Let's get out of here, go into town, and do something that doesn't involve talking about glass and old bones." He pulled out his phone, already dialing before I could respond. He turned away slightly as the call connected. Looking back at me, he held my eyes steady. "Zeke, I need you to come back and pick us up. I have a princess who deserves to be spoiled."

CHAPTER TWENTY-FIVE

Serena

Lucca came alive in the late afternoon, its narrow cobblestone streets humming with activity. The medieval walls that once protected the city now enclosed a world of old charm, where history lingered in the worn bricks and flower-draped balconies.

The scent of espresso and freshly baked bread drifted from cafés, mingling with the distant notes of a street musician playing an old Italian love song on a violin. It was the kind of place that made you want to slow down, breathe deeply, and get lost in the romance of it all.

Anton walked beside me, his stride easy and confident. He seemed to belong in a place like this, even with his quiet luxury and sophistication. He fit against this backdrop just as easily as he did in a penthouse suite or the halls of a museum. It was as if the world and everything in it had been built to accommodate him.

And yet, despite his polished appearance, there was something undeniably predatory about him. He was like a wolf playing civilized for the afternoon, never forgetting what he truly was beneath the suit and charm. He might travel with a bodyguard, but Anton was an intimidating force all by himself.

I glanced at Zeke following closely behind us. Tall and broad-shouldered, he had the presence of a man who knew he was the most dangerous thing in the room. He was dressed casually enough—a dark shirt and tailored slacks—but there was no mistaking what he was. His sharp eyes never stopped scanning, tracking every person who passed, and assessing every potential threat no matter how harmless they might have seemed.

I wasn't sure what to think about his looming presence, so I did my best to ignore it.

We turned onto a quieter street lined with boutique shops and art galleries. We wandered with no agenda in mind. I pointed out famous landmarks, telling him the history of Lucca and its well-preserved city walls. I was so familiar with the town that I barely noticed the everyday things like the olive oil displays in the store windows or the hand-stitched Italian leather stands on the streets. But Anton noted everything, and I was enjoying seeing things through the eyes of a newcomer.

When he stopped abruptly, I turned and asked, "What is it?"

He pulled me toward a small jewelry shop, its window filled with delicate, handcrafted Italian necklaces and earrings.

"That necklace," he said and pointed to a simple ruby heart on a thin gold chain. The deep red stone seemed to flicker in the late afternoon sun. It wasn't large or flashy, yet it still demanded attention. "It reminds me of the ruby you wore at the Met Gala. Do you still have it?"

I shook my head. "No, I sent it back to Madeleine as soon as I returned to Italy."

He turned, his gaze lingering on me, his expression unreadable.

"That's a shame. It suited you."

I looked back at the ruby heart again and shrugged. "I've never been much into jewelry."

Reaching up, he traced a line along my collarbone. My core tightened, and I sucked in a sharp breath, once again surprised by my instant reaction to him.

"This necklace makes me think of the first time I saw you—and the first time I fucked you. You were wearing a ruby around your neck, and nothing else." The quiet way he gave voice the memory made my pulse stutter. "This neck was made for jewels, princess. And I'm going to give them to you."

"Anton, I don't really need—" I paused when a flicker of movement caught my eye in the reflection of the jewelry store window. Zeke stood a few feet away, watchful as always. I shifted my attention back to Anton, ready to continue my protest, but he had already slipped inside the store. "Oh, for crying out loud."

I shook my head, then entered the store. He'd already done enough for me. The last thing he needed to do was buy me jewelry. I had no use for such frivolity.

I caught up to him just as he was speaking to the shop owner, an older man with sharp, perceptive eyes. The exchange between them was brief, but Anton's decisive tone left no room for negotiation.

"Ah, *signore*," the shopkeeper said, nodding appreciatively as he retrieved the necklace from its velvet display. "An excellent choice. A piece like this—it speaks. Understated, but full of fire. Like your *bella donna, sì?*"

Anton's lips curved slightly. "Exactly."

"Anton," I hissed, reaching for his arm. "You don't have to buy me that."

His head turned slowly, his eyes pinning me in place. "I know."

"Then don't." I kept my voice low, aware of the shopkeeper's keen gaze and the few other customers browsing nearby. "I don't need jewelry. I don't even *wear* jewelry."

The older man let out a low chuckle as he set the necklace onto a velvet tray. "Ah, but that is because no one has given you the right jewelry before."

Anton smirked. "She's just being stubborn."

"She is a woman," the shopkeeper said with a shrug. "But a man who knows what he wants? He does not hesitate."

I scowled at his presumptiveness and glanced down at the necklace on the tray. The price tag was plainly visible, and I nearly choked at the cost. I was pretty sure that amount was enough to feed a small village for a day. I quickly looked back up at Anton, not bothering to hide my shock.

Something dark flickered in his expression. "It's my money to spend, and I want you to have this."

I shook my head. "I can't accept."

His jaw tightened, his mouth hardening into a firm line. "Yes, you will."

"You don't get to order me around. Just because you have money doesn't mean you should be so frivolous with it."

"Serena." His commanding voice made me stop short. Taking my arm, he steered me away from the counter and whispered, "You don't know a damn thing about me or my past to make any sort of judgement about what I should or shouldn't do with my money."

I blinked, surprised by his words. "That's only because you haven't wanted to share it with me."

"I came from the streets," he continued, his gaze dark and unrelenting. The shift in his tone froze me in place. "No money. No power. All I ever had were the clothes on my back. Now I have more money than I know what do with, and nobody to spend it on. So, if I want to buy something for you, I expect you to accept the gift without arguing."

My eyes widened. The gravity in his voice had caught me off

guard. I had never heard him talk about his life before finding wealth. He'd only allowed glimpses into that part of himself— and it was limited at best. Now, all I wanted was to know more.

"I'm sorry, Anton. I don't mean to sound ungrateful."

The shopkeeper, seemingly unaffected by the charged moment between us, spoke up. "Would the lady like to try it on?"

Anton met my gaze, the intensity there making my breath hitch. "Yes, she would."

"Ah, you see? A man with means does not ask permission to cherish a woman. He simply does it." The shopkeeper slid the necklace toward him. "Go on, *signore*. See how it looks on her."

Anton didn't hesitate. He lifted the delicate gold chain, stepping behind me and brushing my hair to the side. The deliberate way his fingers grazed my skin sent heat curling low in my stomach.

I exhaled as the clasp clicked into place, feeling the weight of both the necklace and Anton's unwavering stare. I looked at our reflection in the mirror behind the glass display case. The ruby heart rested just below the hollow of my throat, its deep crimson catching the warm lighting in the store.

It wasn't an extravagant piece, and it was significantly smaller than the heavy ruby I'd worn to the Met Gala. But none of that mattered when I caught the way Anton was looking at me —and not the necklace. The desire in his gaze made me feel like the rarest jewel in existence. I'd never had a man look at me the way he was at that moment. It was unnerving.

"Perfect," the shopkeeper murmured with approval.

Anton's fingertips traced the pendant.

"Yes," he agreed, his voice a husky whisper. "It is."

"I—" My voice caught. I had no idea what to say.

"Do you like it?" he asked, and I detected a challenge beneath the question.

I could have told him again that it was unnecessary—that I

had no need for gifts. Or that the last thing I wanted was to be kept. But the truth was, I did like it. Maybe too much.

So instead, I nodded. "It's beautiful."

A satisfied hum rumbled in his chest. "Good."

I swallowed, my throat suddenly dry as Anton moved behind me, his fingers grazing the sensitive skin at the nape of my neck as he unfastened the delicate chain. A slow shiver worked its way down my spine.

After placing the necklace back on the tray, he stepped away and reached for his wallet.

"Anton," I tried again, still uncomfortable with such an extravagant gift. But the words died in my throat as he handed his black card to the shop owner. He took it with a deferential nod, moving swiftly to process the payment.

"It's done, Serena," Anton said smoothly, slipping his wallet back into his jacket. "No point in arguing about it now."

The transaction wrapped up quickly, and before I knew it, I had a gift bag in hand as Anton led me back onto the sunlit streets of Lucca. Zeke was waiting outside. He was trying—and failing—to be subtle.

I sighed, wondering if he would always be with us. "Does Zeke follow you everywhere?"

Anton's lips twitched. "That's kind of his job, princess."

"I know, but…" I let out a frustrated breath. "I guess I'm just not used to having someone watch me all the time."

"I trust Zeke with my life. You'll get used to it."

I wasn't sure I wanted to, but I didn't admit that part out loud. As Anton reached down to thread his fingers through mine, it seemed like the most natural thing in the world. Maybe —just maybe—there were some things I wouldn't mind getting used to.

That thought scared me. This thing between us was dangerous. Immediate. Real.

And if I wasn't careful, I could fall for him far too easily.

Don't be foolish. This is a business arrangement. Nothing more.

"We're getting gelato," Anton announced after we passed a group of teenagers licking the frozen treat from tiny spoons.

I arched a brow. "Are we?"

His lips twitched. "Yes. You look like you need something sweet after all that unnecessary protesting."

"Fine," I relented. "I happen to know just the place. But I'm paying."

CHAPTER TWENTY-SIX

Anton

I sat at the sleek glass desk in my hotel suite staring at my computer screen. The sheer curtains billowed around the open window, and the quiet hum of the street below filtered through. I barely noticed. My focus was locked on the fluctuating numbers spread across multiple windows—U.S. stock trends, shifting cryptocurrency valuations, and market volatility indicators.

Years of experience had sharpened my instincts, allowing me to read these movements like a second language, letting me know exactly when to pivot and when to hold. A slight downturn in tech stocks caught my eye, but it was the erratic behavior of Bitcoin that held my attention. There was an opportunity buried beneath the panic of minor investors, and I could already see how to exploit it. However, I was looking to offload my crypto portfolio, not expand it.

Leaning back in my chair, I reached for the mug of coffee that had long since turned cold. I took a sip as I picked up my phone, scanning through the messages. One from Myla stood out. I tapped the screen and dialed her number. She answered on the first ring.

"Tell me you have good news," I said.

"Depends on how you define good," Myla replied, her tone even. "The nondisclosures for the contractors renovating the private lounges have been signed and filed. They should begin work sometime next week."

"And the completion date?" I hated any disruptions for the members at Club O, but the lounge renovations were needed.

"Pending no unforeseen problems, the rooms should only be down for five days."

"Good. Keep me apprised on the progress. What about the update for the new security system?"

"Almost finished. But I would feel better if Zeke could give it his stamp of approval before I sign off on anything."

"I agree. I'll see about sending him back to New York early to help with that. Anything else?"

"That should be it. How are things in Italy?" she asked.

I pressed my lips together, not sure how to describe how things were going. I'd been here for two solid weeks. During that time Serena and I had settled into an easy routine. We spent most afternoons and all of our evenings together, and I had enjoyed several more dinners in the company of Sylvia Martinelli. After that first dinner, she discovered who I was. While most people's behavior would have changed once they learned of my status, Sylvia remained as kind as she had on the day I met her.

She was a lovely woman, and it was easy to see why Serena didn't want to disappoint her. Hell, even *I* was beginning to care about her approval. I'd never followed a curfew once in my life, yet I completely understood the need for one now—but understanding didn't mean that I liked it.

I wanted more from Serena—freedom from rules and time restrictions. I hadn't planned on things being like this when I came to Italy. My eyes drifted back to the charts on my screen. Markets were predictable. My predicament with Serena was not. And in my world, control was everything. The days were slipping away. I had two weeks left with her, and I needed to take command of what remained of our time together.

"It's different. Quieter and more…domestic," I told Myla, lacking a better word to describe the situation.

She laughed. "Domestic is not how I would describe you."

I was about to agree, but the line beeped to signal another incoming call. I glanced at the screen. It was Serena. I quickly ended the call with Myla and clicked over.

"Afternoon, princess. I was just thinking about you."

"Were you now?" she mused, her voice carrying a teasing lilt. "That sounds dangerous."

I leaned back in my chair, allowing the sound of her voice to wash over me. "You have no idea."

She hummed in response, and I could almost picture her—leaning against the wood table in her workshop, her eyes sparkling the way they always did when she was toying with me. "What exactly were you thinking about?"

I let the question hang between us for a moment, my mind shifting gears.

"A few things," I said smoothly. "Like how long it's been since I've had you pinned beneath me with my cock inside you. Or how much I love the sound of you moaning my name."

There was a sharp intake of breath on the other end. "You're insatiable."

I bit back a chuckle. "I think you like that about me."

"It's too early for me to handle your shenanigans."

"It's well past noon."

She exhaled, and when she spoke again, she sounded frustrated. "I know. It's been a long morning. I'm calling to let you know that the dig permits have been delayed. We won't be able to resume work in Rome for another two weeks."

That caught my attention. Two more weeks in Lucca meant another two weeks with a curfew. That would never do. I was too old for this shit, and I'd been patient long enough.

"Why so long?" I asked, already thinking about putting Zeke on the problem. Perhaps he could find a way to speed things along. Money talks, and I wasn't opposed to greasing a few palms if it meant getting Serena all to myself.

"Italian bureaucracy." She sighed. "But at least my team will be heading back to the lab on Monday to process some of the more recent findings."

I tapped my fingers against the desk, considering this new information. "And what about you?"

"I'll still be here in Lucca for a little longer. I want to finish this piece for the gallery before going back to Rome," she said. "But I wanted to ask you something. My best friend, Caterina, will be in Florence for the weekend. She recently took a job in London, so we don't get to see each other very often. When she comes back to Italy to visit her parents, we try to meet up at a place called La Terrazza, our favorite rooftop bar. I was thinking…maybe the two of us can drive to Florence this evening and meet her for dinner? What do you think?"

I smiled to myself, already seeing this as an opportunity to seize control.

"I'd love to," I said, mentally formulating a plan. "Florence is what? About an hour and a half drive? Let's spend the night."

She hesitated for only a moment before seeming to catch on.

"Ahhh, yes. We should absolutely spend the night. I mean, we'll probably have a few drinks afterall. We wouldn't want to drink and drive. And I just thought of something else," she added. "I think you also need to see the Uffizi Gallery, the Duomo, Piazza della Signoria. There's also the Galleria dell'Accademia. Oh, dear. We might have to spend the whole *weekend* in Florence."

I smiled at her playful tone. This was Serena's way to respectfully escape her watchful, church-going mother.

And I was here for it.

"Dinner tonight with Caterina it is. But after that, I want you all to myself. And Serena," I added, pausing for effect. "I really hope you don't plan on visiting any of the places you just named. I have other plans in mind—no dress code required."

"Noted. I'll pack light, Mr. Romano."

Fuck me.

I nearly groaned at the way my name sounded on her lips. I had wanted uninterrupted time, and now I had it. Tonight couldn't come soon enough.

After the call ended, I shifted my attention back to the computer to book the hotel stay. I wanted somewhere discreet and intimate, luxury without the flash. A large bed was non-negotiable, but that was hard to come by in Italy. I could never understand Europe's aversion to king-sized beds.

A sharp knock on my hotel room door pulled me from my search. I pushed back from my desk, rolling my shoulders before making my way over. Most likely, it was Zeke. He'd been hard at work doing the research that I'd asked him to do, and I was hoping he finally had some answers for me.

When I opened the door, Zeke stood on the other side with a black folder in his hand. He almost always looked serious, but right then, his somber expression was enough to set my nerves on edge.

"What is it?" I asked, stepping aside so he could come in.

"I got in touch with Hale Fulton like you asked. He found a little more on Serena's father's death. The information was limited, so he put me in touch with a contact he has here in Italy. The local guy got me pictures, archived records, and some other info. There's a lot to go over. Let's sit down."

He let out a short breath and set the folder on the small table near the window. Opening it, he pulled out a photograph.

I glanced down at it. A man I didn't recognize stared back at me—mid-thirties, dark hair, sharp jawline, attractive. I didn't know why, but the image of him pissed me off immediately.

I frowned. "Who the hell is this?"

"This is Cade Rosenberg, Serena's ex-boyfriend."

My jaw tightened as I stared at the photo. Something in my gut twisted. Just the image of him sparked a jealousy so foreign, my hands curled into fists. I hated knowing there was a time when he had touched her—kissed her—or that she might have looked at him the way she sometimes looked at me.

Taking a calming breath, I kept my voice level and asked, "What did you find out about him?"

"Look at the back of his neck," Zeke said as he flipped through more pictures to reveal a close-up image beneath the original.

It was a tattoo—a symbol that I recognized. The first time I'd seen the twisting shape, it had been spraypainted on the back of Serena's motel room door in New York. However, I hadn't realized what it was at the time. I had also seen the symbol scrawled in the margins of Serena's father's leather journal. While I hadn't made the connection to the haphazard paint job at the motel, seeing it now in tattoo form made the link more obvious.

I looked at Zeke, my jaw tight. "What is this symbol?"

Zeke leaned against the table and crossed his arms. "That's what I'm trying to figure out. Now that I've seen it, I find myself seeing it everywhere. Graffiti in back alleys. Carved into old stone near the Roman Forum."

"It was also in her father's research notes—in the journal I took from the motel room."

"Do you still have it?" he asked.

"I do, but it's back in New York. I'd meant to bring it with me so that I could return it to Serena, but I forgot it."

"The symbol is in too many places for me to think this isn't all connected somehow. Also, your instinct about arsenic is most likely correct. I had a medical examiner in the States look over Carlo Martinelli's records. While they couldn't say for sure without an autopsy, every sign points to arsenic poisoning."

I exhaled slowly.

"So he was murdered?"

"It's a theory. Could be that Serena's father, in all his digging into the past, stumbled onto something he shouldn't have."

I met Zeke's gaze. "And what about Cade? Do you think he had something to do with it?"

Zeke shrugged. "I'm still waiting on the background report for him. But I think it's suspicious as hell that Serena's father was most likely poisoned and her ex-boyfriend is literally branded with the symbol that was found in her motel and her father's research notes. Too much doesn't make sense. At least not yet. I still have more digging to do."

"I need to tell Serena about the break in. I should ask her about the symbol, too." I sighed and turned away, dragging a hand through my hair. I didn't know how to tell her about my suspicions, or why I'd kept all of this from her in the first place. The theories seemed so outlandish. Even worse was adding Cade to the mix. I didn't know how he fit in either.

I scowled just thinking about him.

What else does she know about him that she hasn't told me?

Zeke studied me. "You're pissed."

I shot him a look and began to pace the room.

"Pissed is not the right word for it. I'm frustrated. I wanted answers, but this only created more questions. I don't know how to approach Serena about it. I don't want to stress her if this turns out to be all one big coincidence. But if it's not, I don't want to get her involved in something potentially dangerous."

I stopped pacing and looked at Zeke. His expression was grim.

"Boss, I hate to break it to you, but I think she's already in the thick of it."

CHAPTER TWENTY-SEVEN

Anton

A few hours later, Serena and I sat in the backseat of the Maserati as it passed through a break in the stone wall surrounding Lucca. The hum of the engine could barely be heard, a Rolling Stones song playing on the radio and drowning the outside noises as Zeke guided us onto the open road.

I settled deeper into the seat, stretching my legs out in front of me while Serena curled hers beneath her. Her body was angled slightly toward the window as she absently scrolled through her phone. I watched her, studying the little things—the way her lips pressed together when she was concentrating, and the subtle crease that formed between her brows when she was trying to understand. It had been four weeks since our chance meeting in front of the Met, and since then, it had felt as if my sole purpose in life was to memorize these little details about her.

She was completely absorbed in whatever she was reading,

unaware of my scrutiny. My gaze drifted lower, tracing the curve of her bare thigh and the way the fabric of her sundress slid up just enough to tease me. A slow heat coiled in my gut, but I tamped it down. We had a long drive ahead of us.

Zeke remained silent behind the wheel, his eyes locked on the road as the countryside blurred past. I turned my attention out the window, and before long, my thoughts drifted to a place I didn't want them to go—the end date for my thirty-day arrangement with Serena.

I hadn't expected to feel this way about her—to want more. More time. More of her.

I knew how this was supposed to go. I had set the terms and drawn the boundaries. But Serena had blurred them from the beginning, slipping through the cracks of my control like sand through my fingers.

And I had let her.

The problem was, she knew very little about me. I'd made sure of that. I exhaled slowly, forcing myself to think logically. It would have been so much easier if I'd kept it all about the Brutus Denarius. Chasing the coin was a challenge I understood. But then I'd laid eyes on Serena, an Italian princess, and all thoughts of hunting down a coin had disappeared.

From that point on, my orderly life had flipped on its axis. I didn't understand, nor could I predict, what would happen with the woman who sat beside me. I wanted her more than I ever wanted another woman. Yet there were still so many questions that I had no answers to—her father's death, the motel, the symbol Zeke had uncovered, and how Serena tied into it all.

Serena shifted beside me, drawing my attention back to her. She must have sensed me watching because she glanced up, her head angling inquisitively.

"What?"

I gave her a deliberate once over. "Just enjoying the view."

She rolled her eyes. "Smooth. Real smooth."

I chuckled. "It's true."

A blush crept up her neck, and she turned back to her phone, but not before I caught the small smile she tried to hide.

I let the silence settle between us again, but my mind remained restless. I needed to talk to her about her father—about the possibility that he hadn't just died, but that he may have been murdered. My jaw tightened as I considered how upsetting it would be for her to hear. I didn't want to bring it up now. Not yet. I didn't want anything to ruin the weekend.

Once we get back to Lucca, I'll ask her about it and tell her my suspicions.

The soft vibration of Serena's phone cut through the quiet hum of the SUV. Seated beside me, she frowned at the screen. Her fingers moved swiftly over the glass, then hesitated. I watched the shift in her expression. Disappointment settled into her features before she looked up at me.

"Caterina just canceled," she said, her voice even. I frowned, catching the underlying frustration. She turned the phone toward me, the text message glowing against the dim interior.

> TODAY 3:45 PM: CATERINA
> Something came up at work. I never made it out of London. Sorry, Rena. Next time?

I glanced back at her. "Rena?"

"It's her nickname for me. It carried over from high school."

I frowned, not liking the shortened version of Serena's name. It wasn't elegant enough.

"I wonder what happened to delay her," I said, rather than voice my thoughts.

Serena shook her head, her focus still on the screen.

"I don't know. I just keep thinking…" She seemed lost in thought.

"What is it?"

"Caterina and I have been friends for a long time. We met

when we were only fourteen. Cat and Rena, the dynamic duo. We were inseparable until my parent made me move to Italy just after my sophomore year. We lost touch for a bit, but reconnected when I moved back to attend Arizona State. We picked back up right where we left off, and things were great for the longest time. It wasn't until…" She sighed and set the phone aside, staring out the window. "There was a time Cat would have called to explain. It wouldn't have been a text. But she's changed. I don't know. Maybe I'm making more out of it than there really is."

I studied her, trying to understand what she might be feeling. I didn't have many close friends, and the people I was closest to were tied to business. Casual friendships were something I never allowed myself. But despite my inexperience, I knew distance between friends didn't happen overnight.

"Has this happened before?" I asked.

"Yeah, but it started with small things—like missed calls. This isn't the first time she's canceled plans. After graduating from Arizona State, we both moved to Italy for our master's degrees. She studied in Florence, and I went to the University of Rome. That's where I met Briana, another friend—or I should say, ex-friend." She shook her head, disgusted. "Cat, Briana, and I meshed really well. La Terrazza, the restaurant we are supposed to go to tonight, was our favorite hangout spot. But then one day, all went to hell. Remember when I told you that Cade cheated on me?"

My fists clenched involuntarily. "Yes."

"Briana was the friend he slept with. The weirdness between Cat and me started after Briana left our little trio," she continued, almost to herself. "Things just never felt the same."

She trailed off, shaking her head again as if she weren't sure how to finish the thought.

I took her hand in mine, circling my finger on the underside of her palm. I had no intention of letting her spiral over this and potentially ruin the weekend.

"I know it bothers you, but I can't say that I'm upset about not meeting her. Her loss is my gain. Now I get you all to myself."

Her gaze snapped back to mine, a flicker of amusement chasing away the disappointment. "That's your takeaway from this?"

I grinned. "I warned you that I wasn't a nice guy, princess. Selfishness is one of my most redeeming qualities."

I pulled out my phone and scrolled through restaurant options near our hotel in Florence. La Terrazza was out. I didn't want Serena sitting through dinner with a forced smile, pretending she wasn't thinking about her so-called friends. Instead, I chose a spot just down the street from the hotel, an intimate restaurant with a menu that didn't require overthinking.

The weekend was now completely ours, and I intended to make full use of it. A slow smile tugged at my lips as an idea began to take shape. I recalled the night outside of Club O when Serena admitted to wanting to be the woman in the flames. So far, our sex had been vanilla—conventional, yet still hot as hell. I hadn't attempted to pull her into my world or test her limits.

It was time to change that.

Opening a different browser page, I typed in a new search. It didn't take long to find what I was looking for.

Florence, you don't disappoint.

I shifted slightly, turning to face her. "Change of plans. I found a restaurant down the street from the hotel we can eat at. What we do after that all depends on you."

She arched a brow. "What do you mean?"

"I want to take you out to a club," I said, deliberately vague.

Her expression turned wary. "A club?"

"It's upscale. Exclusive. Do you have anything suitable to wear?"

She thought for a moment, then shrugged. "Possibly. Why?"

"Because if you didn't, I'd want to make time for you to shop."

"I have a black dress that should work," she mused. "But I'll be honest. I'm not sure what girls wear to night clubs these days. I haven't been clubbing since undergrad. Aren't we too old for this sort of thing?"

The corners of my mouth turned up, thinking about the patrons at Club O. They came in all shapes and ages, and the dress attire was never the same. In some rooms, clothing was optional. But I wasn't about to suggest that to Serena—yet. Tonight was a test. I needed to know if my time with her could extend beyond these thirty days. A part of me already knew Serena was going to fuck up my life plan, but Club O was part of my very identity. I would never give it up. I just wasn't sure how receptive she would be to this sort of lifestyle.

Leaning in, I whispered, "Trustfall, princess. I'm taking the lead. Tonight, I want you to truly let go and be the woman in the flames."

Her eyes widened, and she angled her head curiously. Surprisingly, she didn't press for more details.

"Alright. You're the boss," she said, shifting to rest her head on my shoulder.

I wrapped my arm around her, pleased she was being so agreeable. Although she didn't know about my club in New York, I had standards, and the club I found in Florence seemed to check all the boxes. However, information online could be deceiving. While Serena and I ate dinner, I would send Zeke ahead to make sure it was up to snuff.

THE NIGHT AIR in Florence carried an odd mix of car exhaust, garlic, and fresh bread as Serena and I walked down the narrow street toward Rosso Fiore, the restaurant I had chosen. The city was alive, buzzing with conversation. Laughter spilled from cafes and wine bars, but my focus was solely on the woman beside me.

When she'd stepped out of the bathroom at the hotel, I'd nearly told her dinner was canceled. I'd always thought Serena had an effortless kind of sex appeal, but tonight, she looked every bit the seductive princess who had haunted my dreams for weeks.

Her dress was a sleek black number that clung to her curves like it had been sewn onto her body—and it was fucking lethal. The plunging neckline teased just enough to make me want more, and the slit at her thigh made me hard on the spot. Her dark, espresso-brown hair cascaded in glossy waves down her back, catching the light with hints of warm chestnut. Silken and thick, it framed her face with effortless sophistication.

She'd opted to wear the ruby necklace I'd bought for her, too. She'd paired it with strappy red heels that accentuated the graceful lines of her legs. Later, I planned to bury my cock in her while she wore nothing but the necklace and those matching fuck-me shoes.

While the outfit was undeniably sexy, it was still on the conservative side for where I planned to take her after dinner. But all things considered, it might be for the best. The club was a world apart from anything she was used to.

I slid a hand to the small of her back, turning her down the street that would take us to the restaurant. This area was quieter than the main drag and there was little to illuminate our path. The only light came from a single streetlamp, casting long shadows against the buildings.

We passed a dark alleyway a few blocks from the restaurant. Out of the corner of my eye, I saw movement. A woman was on her knees before a man. Her hands gripped his belt, her shoulders tight.

And beside them, a boy.

Instantly, I tensed. He looked to be around six, maybe seven. Small. Thin. His arms wrapped tightly around himself as he stood a few feet away, his body angled just enough so that he didn't have to watch. His face was partially hidden in the shadows, but his gaze lifted, and he looked straight at me.

Our eyes locked and my breath seemed to freeze in my lungs.

I knew that look—the kind of quiet acceptance that came from knowing the world wouldn't save you from cruelty. He was surviving, and survival meant looking away. Pretending not to hear. Not to see.

Looking at the boy was like looking into a mirror at a child version of myself. A coldness settled in my bones, the air around me suddenly too thick. I turned before Serena could notice— before she could see what I had seen. Before she could ask questions that I wasn't willing to answer.

"The restaurant is across the street. Let's cross here," I murmured quietly, ensuring my voice didn't betray the storm of emotion churning inside me.

We moved away from the alley, away from the ghosts of a past that refused disappear, and didn't look back.

CHAPTER TWENTY-EIGHT

Serena

I'd gone out to dinner with men countless times. They were often predictable dates filled with polite conversation and laughter—sometimes genuine and other times forced just to get through the evening. But dinners with Anton always felt like something else entirely. There was nothing performative about him, nor did his behavior seem to be about impressing me. It was more about owning the moment—and owning me.

Our dinner tonight had been lovely—romantic even. But under it all, something else simmered. I felt like I was being claimed. The sexual tension radiating from him was palpable. Every glance he cast in my direction felt like a promise of something dark, possessive, and positively irresistible. It wrapped around me like a silk rope, seductive and inescapable, making it impossible to focus on polite dinner conversation.

By the time we left the restaurant and began making our way to the night club, my body was thrumming with anticipation. A part of me wanted to skip the club altogether, go back to the hotel room, and strip him out of that perfect shirt and tie. However, Anton had requested to take the lead tonight, and I was too curious about what he had in mind to suggest altering our plans.

Despite spending so much time in Florence, I had never ventured far from the city center. Where we were headed now was off the beaten path, and nowhere near any of the tourist areas. When Zeke had pulled up to the nondescript building to drop us off, there was no signage visible, yet there was still a vibe that screamed exclusivity. Judging by the expensive cars parked nearby and the velvet rope guarded by a bouncer dressed in all black, that was intentional. It didn't seem like the kind of club that advertised. It was the kind of place you had to know about—the kind of place someone like Anton would know about.

As we approached the entrance, I began to second guess my willingness to let him take charge. Bass pulsed through the pavement, the thrum of house music vibrating in my chest. We hadn't even gone inside yet, and I was already starting to feel out of my element.

To my surprise, we didn't pause at the line to get inside. Instead, Anton placed a hand on the small of my back and guided me straight to the entrance. He held up his phone so the broad-shouldered man guarding the door could see the screen. He gave Anton a quiet nod of acknowledgment before unclipping the rope and stepping aside so we could pass.

"What did you show him?" I asked, glancing back at the line to get in.

"VIP pass. I had Zeke check out the place earlier. He arranged it for us."

Of course, he had that kind of pull. What is this life?

This sort of treatment was foreign to me, and I wasn't sure how I felt about it. I considered the hotel Anton had booked for us for the weekend, and way the staff had fawned all over us after we arrived. Luxury didn't even begin to describe it.

A part of me thoroughly enjoyed the white-glove service, but another part of me was uncomfortable with it. I didn't know how to handle the special treatment any more than I knew how to ignore the jealous looks we received from the people in line outside the club. I wasn't used to this kind of privilege.

I glanced up to read the scripted gold letters on the large sign just inside the door, above an entrance to a long corridor.

Eclipse Night Club: Meet. Dance. Play

I was surprised to see the words in English and not Italian. It made me wonder if the club catered to a more international crowd.

The further we moved down the hallway, the louder everything became. Anton showed our pass once more to a woman behind a counter, and I couldn't help but notice the shroud of secrecy that cloaked everything here. She nodded her head toward a second doorman, and he motioned us through another set of doors to the club.

Once inside, Eclipse was an assault on the senses. The lights pulsed in sync with the music, neon blues and purples casting waves of color over the crowd. The dance floor was packed with bodies, and the air was thick with perfume, sweat, and something expensive that I couldn't quiet place. Whatever it was reminded me of tuberose, rich and intoxicating.

Floor-to-ceiling mirrors reflected the scene back at us, making the space feel even larger. A DJ stood elevated at the far end of the room, controlling the flow of sound with precision, his hands gliding over the mixer as if conducting an orchestra. I recognized the popular Katy Perry tune almost instantly. As *Dark Horse* pumped through the speakers, I couldn't help but compare the lyrics to my relationship with Anton. He was the perfect storm, something I didn't quite understand yet couldn't resist—like playing with magic.

I continued to scan the crowd, barely having a chance to take it all in before I noticed the way the women were dressed—or rather, the way they weren't dressed like me. I was surrounded by sheer fabrics and sky-high heels, dresses that were mere suggestions of clothing and left very little to the imagination. Some dared to wear nothing but lingerie, their exposed skin glittering under the lights.

I glanced down at my black dress, then leaned in toward Anton. Pressing up on my tiptoes, I spoke into his ear so that I could be heard above the music.

"I can't say I would wear any of the outfits I'm seeing here, but I'm severely overdressed. I should've worn something different."

He turned his head slightly, his dark gaze sweeping over me in a way that sent a shiver down my spine.

"You're perfect."

"I look like I'm going to a cocktail party, not—" I gestured at the crowd of barely-clothed women dancing like they were performing some kind of ritual. "I don't even know what's happening here."

Anton chuckled. "Come on, princess. Let's get a drink."

As if sensing my hesitation, Anton's fingers curled around my wrist, guiding me through the mass of bodies toward the bar. His grip was firm and possessive, his presence commanding as people instinctively stepped aside to let him pass. The polished bar stretched the length of the wall, illuminated by soft blue under-lighting. Shelves of liquor bottles glowed against a mirrored backdrop, their reflections casting fractured patterns of light.

Anton leaned against the bar, catching the attention of the bartender. She was striking—long legs, high cheekbones, and a perfect figure poured into a barely-there black bodysuit. Like everything else in this place, she shimmered under the lights. Her sleek ponytail emphasized her high cheekbones, and when she turned to Anton, her lips curved into a practiced, sultry smile.

"What can I get you?" she asked, her voice smooth and directed entirely at Anton.

"We have a VIP table and bottle service arranged," he told her.

She tilted her head, already reaching beneath the bar to retrieve a menu. "Right this way."

She stepped out from behind the counter, her outfit clinging to her every movement as she guided us toward a raised VIP section. It was hard not to notice the glances club patrons gave us as we passed. The eyes of both men and women noticeably lingered on me more than Anton, and I wasn't sure if it was because I looked like an imposter in my conservative dress or if it was something else. All I knew was that I couldn't shake the sense of being stalked.

Anton's hand remained on my back, a silent reassurance. Or perhaps it was a warning to those who stared for a little too long. I couldn't be sure. The entire environment was surreal.

The bartender led us to a private booth along the edge of the dance floor, elevated from the main floor but with a perfect view of the crowd.

"Your server will be right with you," she purred before turning back toward the bar.

I exhaled, settling into the plush seating as Anton took the spot beside me, his arm stretching casually over the back of the booth. Then he turned to me, his gaze sharp and assessing.

"What are you thinking?" he asked, his voice barely audible over the pounding bass.

I hesitated, scanning the dance floor. Everywhere I looked, women draped themselves over the men, their bodies pressed too closely to be mistaken for casual dancing. The more I watched, the more my heart raced, intuition kicking into overdrive.

"Just trying to take it all in, I guess," I said cautiously. "Is this how women dress in clubs nowadays?"

"This isn't a typical club, princess." He paused, allowing his fingers to casually brush my bare thigh. "This place caters to a more diverse clientele, and they're selective about who they let in."

A shiver ran through me. I had already come to that conclusion.

"What kind of club is it?" I asked, bracing myself for the answer.

Before he could reply, our server appeared. She was a stunning woman with an impossibly toned figure, her outfit just as revealing as the bartender's. She focused her attention on Anton, her smile practiced and poised.

"What can I get you?" she asked. Her accent was French, solidifying my suspicions about the international crowd.

Anton didn't spare the menu a glance. "We'll take a bottle of Louis XIII."

Her brows lifted slightly, seeming impressed. "Excellent choice. Is the standard selection of mixers okay?"

"That's fine."

"Yes, *monsieur*. I'll be right back," she said with a nod before walking away with hips swaying as if she knew all eyes were on her.

I turned to Anton. "What's Louis XIII?"

"Cognac. I'll drink it straight, but I wasn't sure about your preference and figured a variety of mixers would be best."

"You don't want me to drink liquor straight. I'd be drunk in a hot second if I did that," I said with a laugh. However, after having only been here for fifteen minutes, I was beginning to think liquid courage might not be a bad idea. I should have had more wine at dinner.

Anton shifted closer, his fingers trailing up my arm. A shiver of goosebumps raced down my spine despite the heat of the room. Leaning in until I could feel his warm breath on my ear, he said, "Watch the crowd. Tell me what you see."

I did as he said, letting my gaze wander. The scene before me was charged, electric. If it weren't for the way most of the women dressed, one might assume it was a normal night club. But this place was anything but normal. The people moved in a rhythm that was more carnal than casual. I wasn't sure how to define it yet, and I didn't want to give voice to my suspicions.

My eyes zeroed in on a woman in a skin-tight red dress with a deep plunging neckline. She leaned against a glass partition, her head thrown back as a man pressed against her, his hands gripping her waist in a way that made it very clear they were doing more than dancing. A few minutes later, they made their way to an open doorway in the back corner of the room. A guard stepped aside to let them pass, and they disappeared from my line of sight.

My eyes shifted back to the dance floor. Another couple was in the corner, her arms wrapped around his neck, their bodies moving in a slow, intimate rhythm. Watching them seemed wrong—as if I were intruding on something deeply personal. A few moments later, they too disappeared through the mysterious doorway. But this time, when the man keeping guard moved back into position, his eyes met mine. I looked away quickly, heat flooding my cheeks over being caught staring.

Everywhere I looked, there were overabundant displays of shameless touching in an environment that seemed to welcome indulgence. I'd been to France and Germany. I'd heard the stories about their provocative, illicit club scene. But surely Anton wouldn't have brought me to one of *those* clubs. It was probably just my imagination running over time.

I swallowed, shifting in my seat, needing to know the answer.

"Give it to me straight, Anton. What is this place exactly?"

His fingers traced slow, lazy circles on my thigh as he

studied me. His dark eyes held mine, full of heat and something far more dangerous. It was as if he were memorizing every line of my face so he could best assess my reaction to what he was about to say.

When he finally spoke, his tone was direct and to the point. "It's a sex club."

CHAPTER TWENTY-NINE

Serena

I blinked, biting my lower lip, fingers clenching and unclenching.

A sex club.

My instincts were right but hearing him say it out loud made it so much more real. While I knew places like this existed, I never expected to find myself in one. My gaze drifted back to the dance floor. Bodies moved together in ways that blurred the lines between dancing and foreplay, charging the air with heat and unspoken invitations.

Strangely, I wasn't scandalized. One would think all that Catholic guilt would come rushing back, but it didn't. I held no judgment for the people who indulged in this kind of thing. If anything, I was fascinated by the freedom of it, the sheer abandon with which they gave in to pleasure. But that didn't mean it was for me.

I turned to Anton, who was watching me carefully, reading my every reaction.

"This isn't my scene," I admitted. "I don't mind that it exists, but it's just…not my thing."

"Don't be so quick to dismiss it. There's a stigma surrounding this lifestyle, but it's not always the way some might imagine it."

My heart rate kicked up another notch. I wasn't sure what he was hinting at.

Before he could elaborate further, our server returned, setting down a crystal bottle of Louis XIII cognac alongside a silver tray of mixers. Anton didn't acknowledge her beyond a nod, already reaching for the bottle. He poured himself a measure of the dark amber liquid. Then he poured mine, but instead of leaving it untouched, he added a generous amount of ginger ale before sliding the glass toward me.

"Thank you," I said, picking it up and talking a long gulp. The warmth of the cognac mixed with the crispness of the ginger ale slid down my throat. It was smooth, expensive, and did nothing to ease the tension building in my body. I downed the rest of the drink quickly.

When I lowered the glass and set it back on the table, Anton's brows raised in surprise.

I shrugged. "I was thirsty."

His expression didn't change, but there was a new warning in his eyes.

"Slow down," he said. "Inebriation in a place like this isn't good for anyone. I want you to have a clear head."

"I know my limits," I insisted.

He pressed his lips together in a tight line, appearing to mentally deliberate the situation before standing and extending a hand to me. "Come dance with me."

I hesitated, glancing behind him at the crowd, then back into his onyx eyes. Thing were happening on that dance floor—things

I wasn't sure if I was ready for—yet I still found myself reaching for his hand.

Anton led me toward the mass of people, his grip just as firm and possessive as it had been when we'd entered the club. The thrumming bass matched the beat of my heart as we stepped into the crowd, pushing through the press of twisting bodies. The air was thick with the scent of perfume, alcohol, and sex. Hands roamed freely, and lips brushed against necks as fingers tangled in hair. The atmosphere was spellbinding—dark, primitive, and erotic. I was suddenly hyperaware of everything around me. The heat of it all was suffocating yet intoxicating.

And then there was Anton.

He turned to face me, his hands settling at my waist, pulling me flush against him. My breath caught as his body pressed into mine, strong and unwavering. He didn't move right away but stood there. Waiting. Watching me. Testing me.

"You're tense," he murmured. "Relax your hips. Let me control the pace."

I let out a shaky exhale and forced myself to loosen, looping my arms around his neck. Then he started to move, his grip guiding me into the rhythm of the music. His pace wasn't fast. It was slow, deliberate and commanding as the DJ mixed into a new song. The melody was equal parts obsession and confusion, matching the storm of emotion raging through me.

I followed Anton's lead, my body molding to his in a way that felt incredibly natural. The heat between us quickly grew, spiraling into something dangerous until every move—every press of his hips and slide of his hands on my body—was charged with a sizzling energy that compared to nothing else. A part of me hated how effortlessly he made me forget my reservations. But I also relished it. I *liked* who I became when I was with Anton.

Every move he made felt like both a tease and a challenge. Each rotation of his pelvis against mine made me forget who I was, and I found myself thinking about the couple who'd disappeared through the door in the corner.

Where did they go to?

What happened in the spaces beyond this room?

Anton dipped his head slightly, his nose grazing along my temple before his lips hovered just over the shell of my ear.

"Can you feel the energy of this place?" he murmured.

"Yes." The word was barely above a whisper. I swallowed, my fingers tightening on his shoulders.

"There's misconception about these clubs, particularly by close-minded people. Not everyone comes here for sex. Some explicitly plan for it, but it's so much more than that. Half of the people on this dance floor have come solely for the sexually charged environment. Then they'll go home and make their own fun after."

I couldn't deny what he was saying. Sexually charged was an understatement. Being here—pressed against Anton—watching the sensual dancing and touches of those around us was a turn-on like I'd never before experienced. I could feel the tightening in my core and the wet heat forming between my legs. There was no doubt. I knew the sex between us would be explosive tonight.

Over his shoulder, I watched as another couple disappeared through the door in the corner of the room.

"Anton, what's through that door?"

"Most likely, the playrooms."

My eyes widened, not needing him to explain what sort of play went on.

"The doorway to sin," I murmured, more to myself than to him. "I think I'll stay out here tonight."

I felt Anton's chest vibrate as he laughed. "We aren't going through that door, princess. I have other things in mind for us."

"Such as?"

He pulled back to look at me, his dark eyes smoldering.

"Come with me. There's a loft area upstairs. I want to show you something."

Intrigued yet apprehensive at the same time, I allowed Anton to lead me toward a narrow staircase tucked away in the opposite corner from the doorway to sin. The music pulsed around us, each beat matching the erratic pace of my heart as we ascended. The stairwell opened into a loft area with low lighting and leather couches. There were a few couples lounging about, talking and enjoying their drinks, and looking very normal all things considered.

At the far end of the loft, Anton stopped in front of a glass wall. Beyond it, a dark room came into view. The sight hit me like a jolt.

Naked bodies were everywhere, and not a single one seemed to care or notice the people in the loft staring down at them. They were too busy with each other. Some couples separated themselves from others, keeping their sexual escapades monogamous. But there were other areas of the room that entertained larger groups of people, everyone moving so in sync, it was hard to tell where one person ended and the other began. They surrendered to rhythm and desire just as the space demanded they should.

I placed my hands on the cool railing lining the glass wall, my heart hammering.

This is insane. What am I doing here?

I'd never before felt so out of place, yet I also didn't want to leave. It was wrong to stare, but the dampness forming between my legs was proof of my arousal. I couldn't look away. Watching the people below was provocative and voyeuristic in a way that sent an unexpected heat coursing through my veins.

Anton stepped behind me, his body close enough to feel but not quite touching. I leaned back into him, my gaze settling on a woman who was being taken from behind by her lover. She glanced at a nearby couple, and there seemed to be some kind of silent communication before the pairs moved together and...

Are they swapping?

"Sometimes, it's not about participating," he murmured, his voice low. "It's more about seeing what turns you on."

My throat constricted, and I angled my head to look at him.

"Is this...is this what turns you on?" I asked, praying to everything holy that Anton didn't expect to share me with others. That was never going to happen.

He smiled, but didn't answer. Instead, he skimmed his hand down my hip, reaching around to the front. Moving lower, his hand slid up under my dress. He paused when he reached the lace band of my thigh-high. His eyes burned even darker, churning with a new hunger.

"I'm a sucker for thigh-highs, princess. Leave them on later."

"Okay," I whispered as his hand traveled up further. My breath caught in my throat when I realized what he wanted to do. "Anton, wait. People could see."

He grinned. "That's the point, princess. But if it bothers you, don't worry. We can see them through the glass, but they can't see us."

I turned my head away from him, focusing again on the people below. For some reason, knowing the glass was only one way gave me the nerve to study the people a little more carefully.

It wasn't long before the intense ache between my legs bordered on painful, and I began to wonder if I was overthinking the entire situation.

Sex doesn't need to be so serious. It can be fun, too. These are all consenting adults after all.

Still, I wasn't sure if I had it in me to let go of all inhibitions the way these other people did. They seemed so free, and if there was one thing I wasn't used to feeling, it was the freedom to be myself without constraint.

"Part your legs, Serena. I want to feel you." Anton's command was firm, cutting through my moment of indecision.

I glanced back up at him, meeting his heated onyx stare. And for the first time all night, I stopped thinking and did exactly what he told me to do. I let go, allowing myself to be truly free, and let him take control. Slowly, I shifted to part my legs, allowing him better access.

He placed a knuckle under my chin and traced my bottom lip with his thumb. My lips parted when he cupped my cheek and pressed his lips to mine in a punishing kiss. The hand between my legs shifted higher, his fingers curling around the edge of my panties until he could push them aside. When he made contact with my most sensitive spot, I gasped.

I was soaked.

"Oh, princess. You have no idea how happy it makes me to know that you're turned on by this place."

Shame washed over me, but it was short-lived. I was too consumed by the moment. I would contemplate my guilt and sinful debauchery another time.

My nipples tightened as he slid his fingertip over my folds until he found a slick bundle of nerves. He swiped over it. Once. Twice. Three times.

"Mother Mary," I moaned into his mouth. I wanted this—wanted him to touch me in the worst possible way. It didn't matter if people were mere feet away. Everyone in this place was lost in themselves, uninterested in what was going on between Anton and me. And if by some chance they were watching, strangely, I didn't mind.

I turned my attention back to the people below as Anton's finger found my center. I felt his cock grow hard in his pants as he rimmed my soaked opening in a torturous circular pattern. I moaned again, meeting his gaze reflected in the glass. His stare was intense as he moved in and out, paying special attention to my clit.

I closed my eyes and gave into the delicious tightening in my belly, pushing up against his hand and chasing a bliss that could only be found from his merciless touch.

"Do you want to come?" he asked.

"Yes." The word came out harsh and fast, my brazen need for release all consuming.

"You don't disappoint, princess," he said in my ear. "Your response is everything I was hoping for and more. But we're done here." And then all at once, the release I craved was viciously snatched away when he removed his hands from my body. I opened my eyes in shock, breathless from one of the most erotic experiences I'd ever had.

"What are you doing?" I asked, unable to keep the accusation from my voice.

A wicked smile formed on his lips. "We're going back to the hotel. There are too many things I want to do to you—in private."

I didn't argue.

I followed him out of the club, my mind and body reeling. A part of me couldn't believe that I'd allowed things to happen the way that they did—but I loved every minute of it at the same time.

I thought about the night in New York City when I ran into Anton while on a walk. I hadn't cared about public spaces then either. That was another thing I'd have to think about later—exhibitionism. I'd never considered it before, but I was starting to wonder if exhibitionism was a kink I wasn't aware of having before now.

CHAPTER THIRTY

Serena

On the ride back to Hotel Aureo Firenze, the sexual tension could be cut with a knife. Just a few hours earlier, I had said that places like Eclipse weren't really my thing. However, my reaction to being in that environment said otherwise. I couldn't remember a time in my life when I'd been so turned on. The only thing keeping me from crawling on top of Anton and stripping him bare right there in the car was the fact that Zeke sat in the driver's seat.

The moment we arrived at the hotel, the staff moved like clockwork. The doorman greeted us despite the late hour, tipping his hat as he opened the car door for us. A concierge stood ready, discreetly acknowledging Anton with a respectful nod. Even among the wealthy elite that frequented this place, Anton exuded a presence that demanded deference.

Just as we reached the marble steps leading inside, a flash of light cut through the darkness.

"Mr. Romano!" a voice called out, sharp and eager.

We both looked to see who was speaking. A man clad in a wrinkled blazer gripped a camera with a telephoto lens.

"Shit," Anton muttered. "Fucking paparazzi."

"Who's your date tonight?" the man continued. "Care to comment on—"

Zeke was on him before he could finish the statement, creating a solid wall between us and the man who had somehow tracked Anton to this place.

He stumbled back as Zeke loomed over him.

"Get lost," Zeke growled, his voice low and dangerous. The man tried to peer around him to take another photo, but in one violent motion, Zeke knocked the camera out of his hand. Pieces scattered all over the concrete.

I gasped.

"Hurry up. We need to get inside," Anton advised. He didn't seem rattled by the intrusion, but his grip tightened around my wrist as he pulled me forward, his pace quickening. I stole a glance at him as we entered the grand lobby, catching the tense set of his jaw and the flicker of irritation in his eyes.

"What was that all about?"

"It's what Zeke has been warning me about. I just hope that guy wasn't tracking us from the club." He exhaled sharply, rubbing a hand over his jaw. "Things might have to change in the days and weeks ahead."

I didn't ask what he meant by *things*. I already knew the answer. If I was going to continue being with him, even if we agreed it would only be for a short time, that meant accepting everything else that came with his world—and his world didn't allow for anonymity.

We reached the private elevator that would take us to the penthouse, I stepped inside and exhaled the breath I hadn't realized I'd been holding. Anton reached for me, placing his hand possessively on my hip. The air inside the elevator suddenly grew tense, but it wasn't caused by the intrusive reporter. This was something else—something darker that had been left unfinished from the club.

I could feel the heat radiating from Anton. His hand flexed on my hip. It was a reminder that he could touch and take if he wanted to, and that I'd willingly give without question. I wasn't sure when or how it had happened, but I already knew I'd lost pieces of myself to him.

When the doors opened to the hotel's penthouse suite, I was awed once again by its breathtaking vaulted ceilings and floor-to-ceiling windows that overlooked the city. The décor was sleek, modern yet indulgent, with deep leather furnishings and gold accents that screamed exclusivity.

I crossed the entryway, barely giving myself a moment to consider my next move before Anton's presence consumed everything. He seemed everywhere all at once. The energy from the club hadn't waned. If anything, it had intensified. The unadulterated lust, the restraint, the denied orgasm, and boundaries that neither one of us had a chance to voice all invaded my senses at once.

I turned to him, my pulse seeming to falter at the look in his eyes—carnal, shrewd, hungry.

Anton took a slow step forward, backing me up against the nearest wall, his hands bracing on either side of me. His lips curled in a way that made him look dangerous.

"Tell me what you want, Serena."

I swallowed, remembering how I'd felt in the club. When I was there, I'd surrendered in the same way the woman in the flames had. I'd given into my desires without restraint, and I wanted to go back to that moment. Lifting my chin with a confidence I didn't really feel, I looked him square in the eye.

"I want all of it. Do what you said you were going to do tonight. Take the lead."

"Do you know that that means?"

My breath hitched, anticipation snapping through me like a live wire.

"Not exactly. But I want to find out."

"Then follow me."

My pulse quickened with every step I took toward the bedroom. Anticipation curled low in my stomach, a delicious ache that tightened with each passing second. My breathing became shallow and uneven, half from nerves and half from an acute awareness of what was to come. I wasn't afraid, but I was on the edge of something I couldn't define, and every part of me burned to experience it.

When we reached the side of the four-poster bed, Anton turned me to face him.

"Take your clothes off. But leave those fuck-me shoes and thigh-highs on. And this." He paused, reaching up to touch the ruby heart at my neck.

"The necklace?"

"Yes. I like seeing you in jewels. It will also serve as a reminder that you're not like me, and I need to take things slow."

My eyes widened and my already rapid heartrate intensified, unsure what he meant. I closed my eyes.

Trustfall.

This was what I wanted. Reaching up, I tugged at the zipper near my neck. The little black dress pooled at my feet, leaving only my thigh-highs, bra, and panties. Anton eyed me appreciatively. Then he stepped back and pulled his phone from his pocket. He fiddled with it for a moment until music filtered from the wireless speaker on the dresser.

The low, sultry bass of *Pleasure* by Two Feet pulsed through the room. Each strum of the guitar slid temptingly over my skin, creating a mood not all that dissimilar to that of the club. In just a few short seconds, the air in the room started to sizzle like the wick of a bomb waiting to go off. It was more than just sensual background music—it was a promise and a silent invitation, charging the space until I felt ready to combust.

Anton returned to me, a wicked gleam in his eyes. His gaze skimmed up and down my body, fanning the fire building in the pit of my stomach. I loved the way he looked at me.

"Close your eyes, princess. Listen to the music. Focus on my hands when I touch you. Tonight, I'll give you more pleasure than you've ever imagined."

Goosebumps prickled from head to toe as he placed his hands on my shoulders. Slipping his fingers under the straps of my lacy black bra, he slid them down my arms with a torturous slowness, before unhooking the clasp in the back. He tossed the lingerie to the floor and began to roll my nipples between his fingers. A jolt of pleasure surged through me, and I moaned under his touch.

"How does this feel?" he asked, pinching each peak harder.

"So good," I breathed as he continued to squeeze my tight points firmly between his fingers and thumb. He plucked for a moment longer before shifting to capture one nipple in his mouth. I relished the feel of his tongue as he sucked and nipped.

Anton stepped back and loosened his silver tie with slow, practiced fingers. I watched him unbuttoned his dress shirt one clasp at a time, transfixed. My mouth went dry as he shrugged out of it, revealing the black ink that swept across his shoulder in bold, complex lines. With his shirt removed, he stood before me with only his slacks and a tie hung loosely around his neck. His skin was smooth and tanned, stretching over hard chest muscles and an abdomen cut like stone. He wasn't just beautiful—the man before me was magnificently carved raw power.

His hands slid down my belly, making quick work of removing my panties. He coaxed them down my legs, and I stepped out of them. Now I was completely bare save for the thigh-highs, and I was left feeling vulnerable and exposed.

"Get up on the bed. Kneel so you're sitting on your heels. Then I want you to spread your knees, keeping your thighs open. I want your pussy completely accessible to me."

Climbing onto the mattress, I did as he instructed. Wild sexual anticipation coursed through my veins as I shifted into position. Sitting this way made me painfully aware of how exposed I was to him. Once I was situated, Anton moved around the bed, removing his necktie as he came up behind me.

"I'm going to bind your wrists now," he told me. "Bring your hands behind your back."

Once again, I did as he asked, and he began loop the silver silk tie around my wrists. He bound me slowly and purposefully. I wasn't sure if this was his attempt at easing me into things, or if it was a deliberate display of seduction. Whatever it was relaxed me. I wasn't nervous or afraid, but more curious and anxious for what would come next.

"Are you okay?" he asked after ensuring the knot would hold steadfast.

"Yes. I'm good," I said truthfully.

Anton came back around the bed to stand in front of me, the lacing of his abs flexing with his every move.

Leaning in so his breath was hot on my ear, he said, "I like you kneeling."

I considered his words. I'd read enough romance novels in college to know this was the submissive position—or at least a variation of one. I wondered if that was Anton's kink.

"Are you into the whole Dom/sub thing?" I asked, genuinely curious and also unsure if I could get into that sort of thing.

"Only when it suits my mood. I don't live the formal lifestyle, nor have I had any desire to. But I do like my women to submit to me in the bedroom."

"But you like the control," I asserted.

"Now you're learning, princess." He slid a hand down

between my legs, through the patch of curls to meet my slit. He growled his appreciation when he found me still wet and began circling his index finger around my pulsing little bundle of nerves.

I moaned when he dipped his finger inside, then brought it up to his mouth to taste me. His onyx eyes burned into mine as he rolled his finger around his tongue.

"I love the taste of you."

Returning his hand to the sensitive spot between my thighs, his fingers pushed deeper and harder while his other hand reached up to pinch and pull at the rigid peak of one of my breasts. He knew all the right ways to touch me, and it didn't take long before I was on edge. I began pumping my hips against his hand, welcoming every unholy thing he made me feel, unable to control my burning need for release.

But just like at the club, he didn't let me come. Instead, he removed his fingers and began a torturously slow circuit over my pleasure button. I throbbed under his touch, swollen and sensitive, the perpetual rhythm driving me wild.

"Anton, please. Get me there," I begged.

He pressed himself to the edge of the bed, pushing against my knee until I could feel his manhood straining through his pants. The motion of his fingers picked up speed, and I couldn't take it anymore. My breath hitched, and my insides began to convulse, hitting that coveted shattering point as a kaleidoscope of colors flashed before my eyes.

It took me a few minutes for my vision to return to normal. Tremors coursed through my body, the aftereffects of one of the most intense orgasms I'd ever had.

"Shift up on the bed so you're sitting with your back against the headboard," Anton ordered. "You have the sexiest mouth, and I want to fuck it."

He didn't wait for my consent, but I had no desire to protest either. Within moments, I was sitting up with Anton positioned in front of me. He gripped the base of his cock with one hand, and the other moved to take hold of the back of my neck. He stroked his thick member, bringing it to my waiting lips.

I ran my tongue around the smooth crown, and he groaned. I took more of him into my mouth, wrapping my lips around his head, and flattening my tongue against the tip. He was thick and soft as his ridges slid back and forth over my lips.

"Oh, yeah. Suck on it, princess," he said hoarsely. He entwined both of his hands in my hair, wrapping the strands in his fists as he thrust himself deeper into my mouth. I opened my throat, accepting his assault, sucking and twisting my tongue around his thick shaft while he pumped.

He hissed, pulling back suddenly, his breathing ragged. "Fuck, what are you trying to do to me?"

I licked the excess saliva from my lips, giving him a sly smile. "Did I do something wrong? You said you wanted to fuck my mouth."

"I don't like that kind of language from you."

I raised a brow in surprise. "Am I not allowed to swear?"

He pressed his lips together in a tight line, clearly displeased. "Apparently, not."

"And what happens if I don't listen?" I was deliberately toying with him now, partly amused by the situation while also wanting to see how far I could push him.

"I might have to punish you."

"Is that an offer, sir?"

His gaze darkened. "You continue to surprise me, Serena. You're a complete contradiction. You talk about Catholic guilt like it's a living thing, yet you let your desires rule you. Which is it?"

"I told you I wasn't practicing. And after being in that club tonight, I'm pretty sure I'm going straight to hell. No passing go, and I certainly won't be allowed to collect two hundred dollars.

So, if that's where I'm headed, I want to make sure I live life doing things that make me feel good. And this—the freedom I felt tonight—was like shedding this extra layer of skin I hadn't even realized I was wearing. If I'm already damned, then let me go down burning."

He studied me for a moment, as if he couldn't quite believe what I was saying. And if I was being completely honest with myself, I wasn't sure if I believed it either. I only knew what I felt at this moment—what I felt for him.

"You are incredible." Leaning down, he crushed his mouth to mine in a hard, burning kiss. Tearing his lips away, he looked at me through desperate eyes. "I need to feel you. Now. Flip onto your stomach, face down."

As I shifted onto my belly, Anton got off the bed. I heard the sound of his belt buckle hitting the floor as he removed his pants. There was the familiar telltale tear of packaging, and I knew he was sheeting his length with a condom.

When Anton finally climbed back onto the bed, his naked weight pressed against my backside, and his erection rested heavily between my thighs. Pushing my legs further apart with his knees, he positioned himself just outside of my entrance. With renewed awareness, I yearned to be filled by him.

"Are you ready for me?" he asked, his voice a hoarse whisper in my ear.

"More than ready," I breathed.

One of his hands moved back between my legs, sliding down my crack. His finger pressed against the puckered hole, testing it for weakness, and I gasped.

"Have you ever been taken here?" he asked, his voice raspy.

"No."

"It will be up to me how I get to enjoy you, and one day, this too will be mine."

In that moment, all I could think of was one word.

Possession.

Everything that had happened tonight—from the moment we walked into the club to the way I'd allowed him take control of my body in this room—was a statement of his claim on me. My body was an erotic buffet that was his for the feasting.

And he was making damn sure I knew it.

CHAPTER THIRTY-ONE

Anton

I pressed into the liquid heat that had gathered between her legs, stretching her with my girth. Inch by inch, I fed her my length, claiming her.

"I will do whatever I want to your body, however I want to do it. This pussy is mine, princess. Do you understand me?"

"Yes. I'm yours," she said between pants.

The sound of her ragged breathing was nearly enough to make me come, and I couldn't wait any longer. I gripped her hips, preparing for an explosive ride.

"I'm not going to hold back. You're going to take me—all of me."

Then I began to move. I started slow, but I wasn't gentle. I pushed in hard, her breath catching as she absorbed each stab of pleasure. I rocked into her over and over again, working her into a desperate fever.

"I want you to come like this," I told her, leaning in to kiss the shell of her ear as my hips pumped. I kissed down her neck and shoulders, pushing into her hot well until she began to tremble. Then, yanking her hips up, I pushed forward until the tip of my cock was pressing against her very core. Instantly, she cried out from the pressure of me being so deep.

"Oh, God!" she gasped in shock.

And that's when I felt it. Pleasure shot through my veins as the walls of her pussy began to constrict around me. She sheathed my cock in heat, pulsing with desire. I pulled back slowly, then drove all the way home.

Again and again, I impaled her with a savage rhythm, needing to feel her orgasm more than I needed my own. Her body writhed with pleasure, taking all that I could give. I gave her bottom a sharp slap, testing her response. She had liked it the last time I did it, but I had restrained myself, not wanting to push her too far.

She moaned, so I hit her again. But this time, I struck hard enough to make her skin turn pink.

"Yes!" she cried out. "Please. Again!"

Fuck, this woman.

I groaned and brought my hand down on her ass a third time. I continued to spank her until she began to vibrate around my cock, ever closer to that teetering edge. Her pussy tightened with each smack as she met me thrust for thrust, pushing back with surprising strength. Without being able to brace herself with her hands, matching my thrusts couldn't have been easy.

Still, I continued to possess her. And when she finally came, the visual she created as the climax rocketed through her body compared to nothing else. Her back arched as her hands strained against the tie binding her wrists. Her sex tightened like a vise, and I knew I wouldn't last much longer.

With my cock still buried inside her, I moved to untie her

wrists. Once she was free, I pulled out of her wet heat and flipped onto my back. Then I dragged her over the top of me, positioning her to straddle my hips.

"Ride me, princess."

Her eyes widened in surprise, but the shock didn't last. Her expression quickly turned dark, blue eyes burning with a provocative and sultry glow, conveying a need I couldn't describe. She slid her hands down my stomach, wrapping her slender fingers around the base of my cock. Rising up on her knees, she positioned her body so she could slowly lower down, taking me fully into her.

The groan that passed my lips came from the gut, deep and rasping. She constricted around me, her heat like silk, wrapping me in her warmth. When she began to move, I raked my eyes over her as she rode me with her head thrown back in shameless bliss. Her breasts bounced with every move, her pace destined to push me over the edge. Serena was a goddess in bed, driving me to the point of madness. I was so close, but I couldn't come yet. Not without her. I wanted her orgasm first.

"Think about the club, Serena. What it felt like being there. One day, I'm going to fuck you in a place like that—where everyone can hear your screams."

She moaned at my words, and her eyes turned glassy, as if she were living in an alternate world. My cock throbbed and pulsed, the pleasure like liquid gold running through my veins.

"I'm going to come. Meet me there," she pleaded.

Her desperation nearly broke my sanity. I was completely lost in her. In this. In the moment. I thrust up hard, matching her movements while she drove me to an unbelievable height. The pace grew erratic, more jerking and demanding. Our gazes locked, and she tightened around me. I pushed up, piercing her, and she cried out my name.

"Anton!"

"Give it to me now, Serena," I demanded, my voice rough.

At my words, she exploded like a bomb, but I didn't stop moving. I continued to piston up into her, my hands digging into her hips, demanding her to take it. Her back arched and she cried out. This time, I didn't hold back. I allowed myself to fall with her. My body went taut, straining so tight I thought I would burst apart at the seams, my orgasm hitting from every direction. Rushes of white and color flashed before my eyes, dizzying and all-consuming.

Serena collapsed down on top of me. I could feel her heart racing in her chest, the beat matching my own hammering pulse. With heavy breaths, I began tracing small circles up and down her spine. A warm feeling settled over me, as if I could stay in this moment for the rest of my life. I didn't know it could be like this.

Such contentment was foreign, and I wasn't sure how I felt about it. It was far too easy to lose myself in this woman, and that was dangerous. There were too many things she didn't know about my past—things she could *never* know. Even with all the mystery surrounding her, I knew Serena defined everything that was good in this world. I was the opposite. I'd done things I wasn't proud of. I'd crossed lines that I shouldn't have yet bore no regret for the things I'd done. For me, it was about survival.

Despite knowing I didn't deserve my Italian princess, I couldn't help but give in to this flashpoint in time—even it was only for another couple of weeks. It didn't matter if I wanted her beyond our agreement. I was a realist. A relationship with Serena would never last. I was too tainted. Too corrupt.

When she shifted off me and settled into the crook of my arm, I closed my eyes. I tried not to think about all the lines I'd blurred in my lifetime, choosing to focus on the soft, warm body of the woman beside me. Within minutes, I fell into my own peaceful sleep.

FLASHES of light cut through my slumber like pieces of shattered glass.

I open my eyes and realize the light had been turned on.

My stomach growls. I'm hungry. I'm always hungry.

The air in the room is thick with the scent of stale cigarettes and cheap perfume, but beneath it is something worse—something rotten.

I turn when I hear the creak of the door.

I look up but I already know who it is before I see him. I would recognize that smell of stale whiskey, weed, and bad cologne anywhere.

Jerry steps inside, his boots too heavy. There's someone with him—a shadow in the doorway, broad and faceless. My stomach knots, the way it always does when Jerry lingers too long.

I look around, but I'm alone. I wish my mother was here. She always takes care of Jerry when he comes in. She'd convince him to go somewhere else.

Somewhere away from me.

But she isn't here now.

She's gone, off with a john, probably so high she doesn't remember I exist.

"Look at you," Jerry murmurs, his voice smooth, coaxing. Like he's trying to tame something wild. "Getting older, aren't you?"

Something in his tone prickles down my spine, a warning before the strike.

I don't trust it—I don't trust him.

I bolt from the mattress, but I'm too slow.

Pain blooms, sharp and sudden, as Jerry's hands find me, yanking me back and twisting my arms.

The shadow moves in, and the world tilts as I'm slammed onto the mattress, face down.

Panic.

A scream locks in my throat, claws at my ribs, but no sound comes out.

The bed sinks beneath their weight.

The room is too small.

The air is too thick.

The walls press in, and my mind splinters, retreating somewhere far, far away.

A part of me fractures.

A blur of heat, of breath, of hands that don't belong to me.

The pain is overwhelming.

Then—nothing as darkness swallows everything whole.

MY BODY JOLTED AWAKE, heart slamming against my ribs like a wild animal trying to escape its cage. My breath came in sharp, ragged gasps, my skin damp with cold sweat. Darkness coiled around me, thick and suffocating.

Another body pressed against my backside, holding me down. My pulse pounded like a war drum, a deafening rhythm of terror. I lunged away, twisting violently, my instincts taking over before reason could catch up. A growl tore from my throat as I wrenched free, flipping the attacker beneath me. My forearm crushed against their throat while my freehand captured their wrists above their head.

The shadow writhed, gasping, but I held firm. I had him now. I had *him*.

"Not this time," I snarled.

My grip tightened. The bastard wouldn't take this from me. Not again—never again.

But something was wrong.

The face beneath me blurred, flickering between past and present like a broken film reel. Jerry's smirk. The stranger's grin.

And then, ocean blue eyes were staring back at me, wide with shock and fear.

No, no, no.

Reality came crashing back, blindsiding me with the horror of what I'd just done. My grip loosened instantly, my breath still ragged as I stared down at my beautiful Italian princess.

"Serena," I rasped.

CHAPTER THIRTY-TWO

Anton

A sob-like gasp choked from Serena's lips. Her wide, terrified eyes locked onto mine, pulling me out of the abyss. My breath stilled, the room around me slamming into focus.

The moonlight filtering in through heavy drapes. The hotel. The suite.

The now.

Not then.

Jerry was gone. I'd made sure of that.

My arm was still pressed against her throat, her body pinned beneath mine. I trembled as I pulled away so fast, it was like I'd touched fire. A ragged curse tore from my lips, and I scrambled off her toward the edge of the bed.

I ran a shaky hand down my face, trying to force fresh air into my lungs. I couldn't breathe. My skin was damp, burning and freezing all at once. Flashes of the dream—the memory—

still clung to me like an unescapable tar pulling me down until I suffocated.

I quickly moved to turn on the beside light and dared a glance at Serena. She hadn't moved. Her breathing came quick and shallow, her eyes wide as she stared at me in shock. Her arms were still above her head where I'd pinned them, as if she were afraid to move them.

My stomach twisted at the sight.

"Serena," I rasped, my voice wrecked. "I—I didn't—"

The words died on my tongue.

This is so fucked up. What can I say to make this better?

She swallowed, slowly lowering her arms to place her hands over the reddening skin of her throat.

I did that.

I wanted to be sick.

Another tremor ripped through me. I had fought my way out of hell, built my life into something untouchable, unstoppable. But in the end, the past had always been waiting in the dark, preparing for the perfect moment to drag me back.

And now, she'd seen it.

I raked a hand through my damp hair and forced myself off the bed. My legs weren't steady, like I'd just stepped out of the ring after a knockout fight, as I made my way across the room toward the wet bar. I grabbed the bottle of whiskey and poured, watching the amber liquid fill the tumbler. Then I picked up the glass, my fingers clenching it tighter than necessary, and took a long swig.

Behind me, Serena shifted, the rustle of sheets cutting through the heavy silence.

"Anton... what happened?" she asked, cautiously.

I didn't turn to look at her. I couldn't. Not yet. I also couldn't answer her at that moment. I needed a second to put the pieces together, to make sense of why the past had clawed its way out of the grave tonight of all nights. I thought about the little boy

I'd seen earlier in the alleyway. Perhaps that had been the trigger. I didn't know, but nothing else made sense.

I knocked back the rest of the whiskey in one swallow. It wasn't the good stuff I was used to, but it would still do the job. The burn grounded me to the present, but it didn't drown out the helplessness that had accompanied the nightmare.

It wasn't real.

But fuck, it had felt real.

I turned back to face Serena, keeping my expression unreadable. She was sitting up now, the sheets clutched to her naked chest, but her focus never wavered from me. Her brow was furrowed, lips parted slightly as she searched my face for something I wasn't sure I could give her.

"It was just a nightmare," I said, my voice rough. I exhaled sharply, rubbing my hand over my jaw as if the action would crush the tension. "Nothing to worry about. I'm sorry. It won't happen again."

She didn't blink, nor did she seem to like my answer. Her gaze was skeptical, and I should have known she wouldn't accept a quick dismissal.

"That wasn't just a nightmare, Anton. You pinned me to the bed like you thought I was…I don't know. An attacker? An enemy? What was that all about?" There was no mistaking the steel in her voice. She was already hardening herself against me —and rightly so.

"It doesn't matter. It's over." I looked away.

The silence stretched between us, thick and suffocating.

Serena inhaled slowly, as if deciding her next words carefully. When she spoke, her voice was softer, but the resolve remained.

"I don't know much about your past, Anton. In fact, I don't know much about *you*. Yes, we've slept together, but when you think about relationships in general, we're practically strangers." She hesitated, then added, "How do I know this won't happen again? Self-preservation matters, and if I'm expected to continue this arrangement, I deserve the truth about what happened tonight."

I clenched my jaw. There were a thousand ways to deflect, to bury this before it could surface, but I felt pinned down in a way I couldn't escape. It had nothing to do with the dream or the past—and everything to do with her.

Tonight, Serena had gotten a glimpse into my world in more ways than one—into the dark corners most people would run from. Instead of turning away, she'd met it head-on, even if she didn't yet know it all. The way she responded to the club, from the power balance between us, to the way I wielded control over her body. What we had was deeper than anything I'd ever felt before.

And we were just getting started.

Our time together was supposed to be temporary. Hell, right before we fell asleep, I'd told myself it would be thirty days with her and nothing more. But as I watched her now, absorbing everything I'd told her with understanding instead of fear or pity, I knew I wanted something beyond our agreement.

Now, I had a choice. I could let my past dictate my future, pushing her away to keep my secrets buried. Or I could give her just enough—enough to satisfy her worry and curiosity, and enough to make her stay. I didn't have to tell her everything. Not yet. All I knew was that I wasn't ready to let her walk out the door, and if I didn't give her something, that was exactly what she'd do.

I turned back to her. Her expression was patient, free of judgement, offering space for whatever answers I could give her.

For some reason, that made it harder to hold back.

I set the empty glass down, the clink of crystal against marble echoing through the room. Returning to the bed, I sat on the edge.

"I didn't have a normal childhood. I grew up in hell," I

began, my voice quieter now. "It was the kind of hell that eats you alive if you're not strong enough. It was survival of the richest *and* the fittest. My mother—" I let out a bitter breath. "She wasn't just an addict like I told you. She was a prostitute. And the man who ran the whore house where we lived didn't care much for rules. He took what he wanted and gave away what wasn't his to give."

Her eyes darkened, but she didn't speak, letting me continue.

"I was on my own. Unless I wanted to live on the streets, I had nowhere to go. My mother looked out for me sometimes, but not always. Half the time, I don't think she even remembered I existed. I learned the hard way how to survive in the kind of place I was living in. I got good at evading the johns who liked little boys and stayed under the radar." I looked down, flexing my hands as if trying to shake off invisible chains. "But eventually, they came for me, too. I was young—and they were bigger."

Serena inhaled sharply. I didn't elaborate. I didn't need to. It was better if I let her imagination draw its own conclusions. Speaking the details aloud wasn't something I was going to do. I'd already divulged too much as it was.

"The nightmare tonight was a memory," I continued, my voice hardening. "But that life is gone now. I don't think about it, and what happened here tonight has never happened before. That's why I'm not concerned about it happening again."

"How did you escape?" Serena asked tentatively.

"I took control of my destiny. I remember hearing one of the johns talking about hitting it big with a tech stock. I didn't know what he was talking about at the time, but I knew it meant money. And money was my key to getting out of hell. I already knew I was good with numbers and spotting trends." I paused, thinking back to my very first investment. Jerry could be counted on to be careless after drinking too much, and I used it as an opportunity to slowly swipe enough cash to get me started. "I made a plan, stole some money, and lied to open a bank account. Before I was seventeen years old, I'd turned a few hundred into a few thousand just by making smart predictions. From there, I built a life where the past could never touch me again."

I ended the story with a shrug and a tone of finality, hoping she would leave it there and not press for more details. I'd already given her more than I wanted to and wasn't willing to expand further. Giving her anything else would be too risky.

Serena watched me carefully, her expression unreadable. I expected pity, maybe even fear, but there was none. Just understanding.

"You were lucky," she finally said.

"Perhaps. I prefer to think I made my own luck. I have money and influence, and none of that came without effort. But sometimes, the past doesn't give a damn about how much wealth or power you have. That was evident tonight. For future, it's best if you don't come up behind me unexpectedly, especially when I'm sleeping. While I don't think it's going to be an issue, I don't want…I don't want to risk hurting you again."

Her eyes widened. "Is that why you reacted the way you did tonight? Because I curled up behind you?"

I inhaled deeply and exhaled through my nose. "It was a trigger."

She studied me for a long moment, allowing a beat of silence to passed between us as the truth settled in.

"Thank you for telling me, Anton. For trusting me."

I didn't respond. In truth, I didn't know how to.

So, I just stood there waiting for the horrors of the past to loosen its grip, grateful that Serena still wanted to stay in the same room with the man it had shaped.

CHAPTER THIRTY-THREE

Serena

When I entered the lobby of Anton's hotel in Lucca, my shoes echoed on the marble floors as I made my way to the concierge desk. I adjusted the purse slung over my shoulder, noting that it was dusted with specks of glass from my day in the studio. I absently brushed them away, distracted by the turn of events from the day, as well as what had happened over the weekend with Anton in Florence.

It had been a productive day in my workshop. The piece I had been working on for the gallery was coming together, the delicate curves finally taking form to my satisfaction. So lost in the craft, I'd worked straight through dinner and hadn't even noticed. If it hadn't been for my mother bringing me a porchetta panini, I would have skipped the meal altogether.

Just as I finished eating, my phone pinged with an email notification. It was from General Directorate of Archaeology informing me that there was another delay with the permits for the excavation in Rome. From that point on, any happiness I'd felt over the progress I'd made with the swan fell to the wayside.

At first, the bureaucratic red tape had seemed typical. There always seemed to be another obstacle to navigate. But now? Now, it felt intentional. The excuse for the delay didn't make sense. They were taking issue with the budget plan, citing logistical errors and reevaluations of excavation boundaries. However, nothing had changed. All we needed was a renewal for something that had already been approved. I knew what I was dealing with when it came to Italian institutions, but this felt like sabotage.

The thought left a sour taste in my mouth as I stepped up to the concierge desk. The man behind it recognized me and offered me a polite smile. Leading me to the private elevator, he pressed the button that would grant access to the penthouse.

"*Buonasera, Signorina*," he said smoothly, moving aside as the sleek doors slid open.

I nodded my thanks and stepped into the elevator. The moment the doors sealed shut, I leaned against the wall and sighed, my thoughts shifting away from problems in Rome and back to Anton. I thought about our time at the club, and then to the sexy interlude at the hotel. It was the most erotic experience I'd ever had. But mostly, I thought about the way things had shifted after his nightmare.

I recalled the way he had sat on the edge of the bed with his head and his hands. At that moment, I'd just wanted to take away his pain. I had put up a strong front, knowing he just needed me to listen and understand. But the reality was, his actions had terrified me.

The raw terror of waking up to Anton's arm pressing against my neck wasn't something I'd soon forget. The sheer weight of him had rendered me immobile, and for a split second, I couldn't breathe. But it wasn't just the pressure on my neck that had shaken me—it was the look in his eyes. He was wild. Unseeing.

It was as if he wasn't even in the room with me but trapped somewhere else.

Even after he let me go and realization dawned in his features, the fear of what had happened lingered in his expression. I'd seen fear before, but not like that. This was deep-seeded fear, clawing its way out of his past and into the present.

PTSD, maybe.

But he had brushed it off as if it were nothing. It was possible he had childhood trauma buried so deep he couldn't acknowledge it.

However, his actions afterward proved that it hadn't been nothing. He'd shut down, putting up walls that I'd never before seen from him. Our last night in Florence had been tense, filled with unspoken words and unanswered questions. We'd had sex, but it was far from the mind-blowing experience I'd had with him the night before. The act felt more like something we had to do rather than wanted to do.

Now that we were back in Lucca, and I was given a bit of time alone to think things through, I hoped that I could get him to open up a little more. We had planned to go for drinks at a neighborhood bar just down the street from his hotel, but I was beginning to think it was better for us to stay in. It would be more private. I didn't want this tension between us, but I wasn't sure if Anton was ready to be pushed.

The elevator opened, and I crossed the narrow hallway to knock on the door to Anton's penthouse suite. My pulse thrummed against my ribs, the emotions from the weekend pressing down on me as the questions I'd been holding in threatened to spill out before I even saw him.

The door swung open, and there he stood, looking slightly disheveled in the most devastating way. His slacks hung low on his hips, and his black dress shirt was unbuttoned at the top. He'd rolled his sleeves to his forearms, revealing ridges of toned muscles. Five o'clock shadow dusted his jaw, adding to the rugged edge that made him impossibly handsome. His hair was mussed, like he'd run his fingers through it too many times. And those onyx eyes, piercing and assessing, seemed to look straight through to my soul.

"Serena," he said, his voice low and unreadable. He was always so composed and in control.

I stepped inside, suddenly feeling unsteady now that I was here, but I pushed through it.

"I know we're supposed to go out," I began. "But I thought we could stay in and talk for a bit first. Maybe grab a drink a little later. I want to discuss what happened this past weekend."

I turned to face him as he shut the door, my throat tightening at the way his unmoving gaze locked on me. He appeared to be waiting, yet his expression gave nothing away.

"What's there to talk about?" he finally asked.

"I need to understand, Anton." My voice was softer now, but still firm. "You pinned me down, choking me in your sleep. And when I looked up at you, I saw something I've never seen before. It was like you weren't even there. Like you didn't know it was me. We can't just pretend that didn't happen."

His jaw clenched.

I took a step closer, placing my hand on his arm. "Do you know what it felt like to wake up like that? Unable to move?" My voice wavered, but I steadied it before continuing. "I should have expressed my concerns that night, but I played it off because my instinct was to make sure you were okay. The reality is, I was scared. The next day, I thought we'd talk about it more and my fears would ease. But you shut down and I didn't want to push you."

"And now it's okay to push?" he questioned, his tone cool and detached. His hands curled into fists at his sides, but his breathing was measured and controlled. That only made my frustration grow.

"I had a night alone to think about things." I bit down on my lower lip, then caught myself. I didn't want him to know I was nervous. "I can't continue this way without knowing if there's an underlying issue that might cause something like that to happen again."

His eyes softened, and for a moment, I thought he might finally open up—that he might give me the reassurance I needed. But then his expression hardened and his posture shifted, as if he were locking everything away behind an impenetrable wall.

"I already told you, Serena. It was nothing—and it's certainly nothing worth talking about. There are more important things we need to discuss than a stupid nightmare." His voice was even, firm, and completely dismissive of everything I had just said.

My heart sank at how easily he could brush it all aside.

"More important than this?" I stepped back, needing to create space. My voice was barely above a whisper, my chest tightening from the distance between us—not physically, but emotionally. His behavior shouldn't hurt me this badly. After all, we barely knew each other. But at the same time, it also felt like I'd known him all my life.

Again, he didn't answer me. Instead, he strode across the room to the desk, pulling open a drawer to retrieve a sleek black folder. When he turned back to me, his expression was hard once again. The conversation I had come here to have slipped through my fingers like sand.

And just like that, I knew.

He wasn't going to give me the answers I needed. Not tonight. Maybe not ever.

"You're concerned about your safety, and so am I," Anton said, tossing the folder on the desk. "However, I'm not whom you have to worry about."

"What's this?" I asked, suddenly confused.

Anton's expression shifted from unreadable to troubled in an instant. The gravity in his gaze sent a shiver down my spine.

Whatever was in that folder—whatever he had to say—it wasn't good.

He took a breath, exhaling slowly before speaking. "I think your father was poisoned."

I blinked, thinking I hadn't heard him right. "I'm sorry. What?"

"I had a medical examiner in the States review his records. Every sign and symptom point to arsenic," he said, his voice tight.

My stomach dropped. His words didn't make sense, seeming more suited for a twisted thriller rather than anything in real life. My breath hitched, my body tensing involuntarily. I stared at him, my heart hammering. The air in the room suddenly felt thick and suffocating. My head shook automatically, my mind rejecting what he was saying.

"No. That doesn't—he was sick. It was sudden, and he—"

"It wasn't natural," Anton interrupted, his voice firm but not unkind. "Do you know anyone who might have wanted your father dead?"

Is he suggesting murder?

The idea was absurd. Impossible.

A sharp pain clenched in my chest, like an invisible hands crushing me from both sides. I took a step back, shaking my head.

"My father was a good man. He didn't have enemies."

Anton's eyes held steady. "You said yourself that he had jealous peers."

"Yes, but that's all it was—petty jealousies and industry critics. That doesn't mean people wanted to *murder* him, Anton. The idea is crazy." My voice cracked, my throat tightening around the last word.

"I don't think it is," Anton insisted, handing me a piece of paper. "Or at least, I know enough to say poison is the most likely answer for his death."

I looked down at the document he'd given me, skimming quickly through the text. It was a medical report, detailing the symptoms of arsenic poisoning. Everything on here was nearly identical to what my father had experienced.

I squeezed my eyes shut, my mind racing.

Poison. Someone had done this to him. Someone had wanted him dead. No. That can't be right.

My chest rose and fell in shallow, uneven breaths. My father had always been careful, meticulous in everything he did. He wasn't a perfect man, but he was honest and good.

Who would want to hurt him? And why?

It didn't make sense.

"Why are you telling me this?" I asked, barely able to force out the question.

"Because I worry about your safety. There's more, princess."

Dread coiled in my stomach like a viper ready to strike. "What do you mean?"

He hesitated, then exhaled, his jaw tightening. "Your motel room in New York. When you were sick, Zeke and I went to get your things while you slept."

I nodded stiffly. "Yes, I remember."

"When we got there, someone had gotten into your room. The place was trashed—ransacked as if someone had been looking for something."

A chill ran down my spine, the hairs on my arms standing on end.

"What?" My voice was barely above a whisper.

He nodded. "Neither Zeke nor I thought it was random at the time—it was too vicious. They tore the place apart. But more, it felt...I can't explain it. It just felt personal. And then, after you mentioned seeing a crime scene at the motel, I looked more into it. What you'd heard was correct. Someone was, in fact, murdered. The body was found behind the building. The day

Zeke and I went there, it had been late at night but there was a sign stating that the staff would be back after lunch. It's safe to assume that the staff member who never returned from lunch is the same staff member who was found dead."

My heart pounded against my ribs, my thoughts spiraling.

Murder.

And who would break into my room?

What could they possibly have been searching for?

Was it all connected?

I was nobody of importance, and I certainly had nothing of value to take. I shook my head again, unable to believe the insanity of the situation.

"You knew this whole time and you never told me?" The realization cut through my confusion like a blade. When I spoke again, my voice carried a sharp edge, the accusation undeniable. "Did you call the police?"

Anton's jaw ticked for a moment before he admitted, "No, we didn't."

"Why the hell not?" My confusion deepened, frustration rising to the surface.

"I didn't know you at the time, Serena. You were just a stranger in my bed, and I am a very private person. I wanted to do some digging on my own first. Police involvement would have brought on a public scandal that I didn't want. I've told you enough about my past for you to understand why I wouldn't want that dragged into the spotlight. Also, I didn't want to scare you."

"Well, too late for that," I snapped. My arms crossed over my chest, my fingers digging into my sides in a desperate attempt to ground myself. My mind spun, everything unraveling too fast. "You had no right to keep this from me."

His gaze didn't waver. "I was only trying to protect you—to protect both of us."

I let out a short, bitter laugh, although there was no humor in it. "By keeping me in the dark? By deciding *for* me what I should and shouldn't know? This is serious. A member of the motel staff was murdered, Anton!"

He didn't reply, and the silence seemed to stretch on, thick and stifling.

"There's still more, Serena," he finally said.

I frowned as he reached for the folder on the desk, flipping it open and pulling out a photo. "This symbol. What does it mean?"

I looked down at the image. It was a rough sketch of a twisting, snake emblem.

"I don't know," I admitted. "I've seen it before in my father's journals. He began sketching it in the margins in the months right before he died, but I'm not sure what it means."

"This symbol was spray-painted on the back of your motel room door."

A cold dread settled in my bones.

"I don't—I don't understand," I stammered.

"There's also this." Anton's gaze darkened as he spread out a series of photographs, turning them toward me.

My stomach twisted, and my throat tightened.

Cade.

The pictures of him were taken from different angles, clear as day.

"Why do you have pictures of Cade?"

"Look at the back of his neck," Anton said, ignoring my question.

I swallowed, my pulse hammering in my ears as I studied the photos. The tattoo on Cade's skin sent ice through my veins. It was the same symbol as the one in my father's notes—the one Anton said was on my motel door. My breath hitched, the room tilting slightly. The implications clawed at my mind, demanding to be acknowledged, but I couldn't—I wouldn't. It had to be a coincidence.

My head jerked up, my voice barely above a whisper. "This tattoo wasn't there when we dated."

Anton's expression was grim. "I think it's all connected, Serena. I just don't know how. First there was the symbol at your motel, and then I saw it again in your father's journal—although I hadn't made the connection until recently. Now that I see the tattoo, I—"

"Wait. Stop. What do you mean you *saw* it in my father's journal? How would you have seen it there?"

"One of the books was in your motel room. I was looking through it, looking for clues about who you were."

I hadn't even realized it was missing, but now that I thought about it, it wasn't with my belongings that Anton had retrieved from the motel room.

"Where is the journal now?" I demanded.

"At my place in New York." He said it so flippantly, as if having a piece of my personal property was no big deal.

I thought about the journal, the intimate pieces of my father's mind recorded on those pages. A deep, burning anger surged inside me. My father's thoughts, his research, his private words —all violated. Knowing Anton had read through it without my permission felt like a betrayal.

"You had no right to read through my father's private notes —and you had no right to keep the journal. It doesn't belong to you."

"I hadn't planned on keeping it. I was going to give it back. I simply forgot to bring it to Italy with me."

"That doesn't make it better!" I snapped. My voice grew louder, my frustration boiling over. "And this conspiracy about my father being poisoned is just that—a conspiracy. I don't know what you're playing at. Nobody wanted to kill him."

But even as I said the words, doubt clawed at my mind, giving voice to a terrifying possibility.

What if Anton is right?

I glanced down, flipping through the remaining contents of the folder, stopping only when I saw a printout with my name at the top. I scanned down the page. Personal details about my life were everywhere—where I lived, where I went to school, how much money I had in my bank account.

It was a background check—conducted without my permission.

"What is this?" I whispered.

Anton's eyes flitted to the paper in my shaky hand.

"Fuck," he hissed.

I could only look at him, waiting for him to say more, but he remained silent with regret written all over his face.

"All that bullshit about wanting to get to know me was exactly that—bullshit. You already had everything you needed, didn't you? I don't care if you're some mega rich billionaire. You had no right to invade my privacy like this!"

The walls of the hotel suite felt like they were closing in around me as my pulse pounded in my ears. Anton was still watching me, his sharp gaze waiting for my next move, but I couldn't stay here. Not now. Not with all of this—poison, break-ins, murder, symbols, Cade, the assault on my privacy. Too much was swirling in my head like a hurricane I would never be able to outrun.

I stepped back from the desk so fast, I bumped into a chair. It made a loud scrape against the floor, but the sound barely registered as I turned and strode for the door.

"Serena, stop!" Anton's voice was tight, commanding.

I didn't. I couldn't. If I stayed, I would scream or cry or say something I couldn't take back. I needed to think. I needed space. I needed to find some rational explanation for all of this.

The moment I stepped into the hallway, I quickened my pace.

I barely heard Anton behind me, calling my name again. I didn't slow down. I reached the elevator, jabbing at the button repeatedly as if that would make it come faster. My chest was too tight, my thoughts spinning out of control.

The elevator dinged and the doors slid open. I stepped inside, pressing the button for the lobby. Just before the doors shut, I caught a glimpse of Anton stepping into the hall, pain and frustration etched across his face. He didn't try to stop me, and for that, I was grateful. He had no right to investigate my life like I was some puzzle he needed to solve. I had no idea what to do with the things he'd told me, but I knew I couldn't deal with them while under his watchful eye.

When I stepped outside, the crisp air bit at my arms. The temperature had dropped, making the evening cooler than normal for this time of year. I hadn't thought to grab a jacket, but I didn't care. I needed the walk to clear my mind. The streets of my neighborhood were familiar, giving me something to focus on besides the chaos Anton had just thrown into my lap.

However, the moment of peace was short-lived when the distant wail of sirens shattered the quiet. A fleet of fire trucks barreled down the street, their lights flashing against the darkening sky.

Then I saw it just up ahead. Thick plumes of smoke billowed into the sky, a dark stain against the horizon. My breath caught. It was coming from my mother's neighborhood. My stomach clenched, a deep, instinctual dread curling in my gut.

My feet moved before my brain could catch up, my heart hammering against my ribs as I increased my pace until I was in a full jog. The closer I got, the heavier the smoke became, the acrid scent burning my nose. People were gathering, murmuring, pointing.

And then I saw the house.

No.

Flames licked at the roof, curling around the windows like a hungry beast. Firefighters swarmed the scene, shouting orders, battling the inferno with powerful streams of water. But it wasn't enough. A strangled sound clawed its way out of my throat as I took off running.

My mother's house was burning.

CHAPTER THIRTY-FOUR

Anton

I paced the length of my hotel suite, jaw clenched, and my hands fisted at my sides. This wasn't how tonight was supposed to go. I shouldn't have let her leave. I should have made her stay—made her listen long enough for me to explain. What had started out as a fact-finding mission to protect myself had turned into genuine worry for Serena's safety. Now, I no longer cared about myself. It was all about her.

I exhaled sharply, running a hand through my hair. Her expression when she threw my concern back in my face before storming out flashed in my mind. Her leaving wouldn't have bothered me a month ago. She would have been just another woman, and I'd had plenty walk away before.

But everything had changed. Serena wasn't just another woman.

She'd gotten under my skin in more ways than I cared to admit. She had become my obsession, consuming my thoughts with an intensity I hadn't anticipated. She was fire and steel, sharp enough to cut when she felt threatened, yet soft in all the ways that mattered. I had made her feel threatened tonight, possibly shattering the fragile trust she'd placed in me.

I picked up the folder, flipping through it without really seeing it. Pages of information stared back at me—reports, photographs, timelines. My gaze landed on the serpent symbol. I traced the swirling lines with my finger as frustration coiled in my gut. Somehow, I knew everything led back to this. I just hadn't pieced together the connection.

I tossed the folder back onto the desk.

"Dammit!"

I began to pace again, the walls of the suite making me feel too confined.

Sirens blared in the distance, faint but insistent. A single instance wouldn't have caught my attention, but as I stood there, the sound repeated. More joined in. The sirens were different in Italy compared to New York City. Back home, they wailed with a high-pitched, undulating urgency. Here, they seemed to cut through the quiet streets like a relentless war cry.

I walked to the window, pushing aside the curtain to glance out. The street appeared quiet. Lights flickered against the darkened skyline, but nothing seemed out of place. But inside, my world turned to hell in the blink of an eye. Unease clawed at my chest, unsettling and persistent. I could still feel Serena's cutting words.

"All that bullshit about wanting to get to know me was exactly that—bullshit. You already had everything you needed, didn't you? I don't care if you're some mega rich billionaire. You had no right to invade my privacy like this!"

And then she'd run.

I hated seeing the icy betrayal in her ocean blue eyes when she looked at me, her words cold and heavy with feelings of betrayal. I may have deserved it, but I wasn't the enemy here.

While I had no proof that she was in imminent danger, something told me that Serena wasn't safe. Call it instinct or intuition, but my gut feelings were never wrong. I needed to protect her—to make her understand.

"To hell with this," I muttered to myself. I had to go after her.

I turned from the window and grabbed the suit jacket I'd left hanging over a chair. Pulling my phone from my pocket, I paused before dialing Zeke. As much as I was beginning to understand the need for constant security, I knew Serena didn't care much for his hovering so I pocketed the phone. If I wanted her full attention, I would need to do this alone.

The night air was cool as I stepped outside. I fastened the two buttons on my jacket as I began the walk down the quiet street toward Serena's mother's house. My frustration with the situation burned hotter with each step, fueling the restless energy inside me.

The sirens grew louder, an urgent wail cutting through the otherwise still night. I hadn't thought much of it when I'd first heard them from the hotel, but then I smelled the sharp, acrid bite of smoke curling through the air.

My pace quickened, the hairs on the back of my neck rising. Looking ahead, I noticed an orange glow in the sky. I began to jog when I realized it was coming from the direction of Serena's mothers house.

I turned the corner—and saw hell.

Flames clawed at the sky, devouring everything in their path. Serena's mother's house was an inferno, fire licking up the walls and spilling from the shattered windows like molten fury. The glass-blowing workshop beside it was barely visible through the churning smoke, the heat warping the air around it like a living thing.

For a moment, all I could do was stare, my mind struggling to process the scene before me. The workshop roof had already caved, fiery embers cascading through the air like vengeful stars. The fire crackled and roared like a beast devouring its last meal.

Then I heard her scream—a sound of pure, raw agony.

My gaze snapped away from the burning structures toward the chaos. I scanned the area until I found Serena. She was wild-eyed, straining against the grip of a fireman holding her back.

"No! Let me go!" she sobbed, her voice breaking. Her fists hammered against his chest as she fought to get free.

I was moving before I even realized it, instinctually surging forward. I shoved through the cluster of onlookers and emergency responders, reaching her within seconds.

"Serena!"

She didn't seem to hear me. She was lost in sheer panic as her entire world burned before her eyes. I grabbed her, wrenching her from the fireman's hold and pulling her against me. She thrashed at first, fists pounding against me just as they had against him, but I didn't let go.

"Serena, stop," I ordered, my voice rough. "I've got you."

As if she suddenly realized whose arms she was in, she stilled and sagged against me. Her fingers fisted in my jacket as broken sobs tore from her throat.

"My mother," she gasped. "She—she was inside. I saw her earlier. She brought my dinner to the workshop. She said she had a headache, and that she was going to lie down. She's in there!"

My spine stiffened, finally understanding the reason for her hysteria. If Sylvia Martinelli was truly inside…

I glanced back at the burned house, then turned to the fireman, my grip on Serena tightening. "Why are you just standing there? Her mother is in there!"

The firefighter shook his head, his face grim. "The roof is just too unstable. If we try to send anyone in now—"

A loud crack split the air, deafening over the roar of the flames. We all turned just in time to see part of the roof collapse, a fiery explosion of embers shooting skyward. The firemen scrambled back, barking frantic orders to one another.

Serena screamed, and I pulled her in closer, forcing her against my chest before she could try to run toward the destruction. Her nails dug into my arms as she choked out, "No, no, no!"

I gritted my teeth, my own heart hammering as I whispered, "Shh, princess. I've got you."

Her body shook, wracked by sobs as I stroked her hair. Flames licked at the night sky, casting an eerie glow over the frantic chaos. Firefighters barked orders to one another, their silhouettes a blur of motion as they fought to put out the fire. Smoke billowed thick and black, choking the air with the pungent scent of burning wood, plastic, and other things I couldn't name.

Serena sobbed against my chest, her fingers clutching desperately to my shirt.

"She was inside," she repeated. Her breath hitched, coming out in broken gasps. "She—she was inside."

I tightened my hold, needing to keep her anchored to me. Another loud crack, and we both flinched as the front part of the roof caved in, sending up a fresh shower of embers and debris. The firefighters closest to the house shouted, scrambling back. The inferno surged higher, the flames feeding on the oxygen created by the collapse.

Serena's strangled cry cut through the noise, raw and laced with a new kind of agony. "Oh, my God. What if this was me? What if I did this?"

"What do you mean?"

"I was working earlier today. I know I turned the needle valve off to close the fuel source, but I had to leave the blower running overnight to keep the burner tip cool. I think I cleared the area but now I'm not sure. I could have left flammable material or—"

"Stop." I seized her chin, forcing her to look at me. Her face was streaked with tears as her wide, devastated eyes locked onto mine. "Stop it right now. Don't do this to yourself. You don't know anything yet."

She let out another choked sob and collapsed against me, her strength giving out. My heart pounded against my ribs as I looked past her, back toward the fire. My mind scrambled for hope, for something to cling to.

Then I saw it.

The front door stood open. The fire hadn't fully consumed the entryway yet, leaving it eerily intact amid the destruction. My breath caught.

Why would the door be open?

Maybe there was a chance that Sylvia had made it out alive. I opened my mouth to tell Serena my thoughts, but the words never left me.

Because just beyond that open door, barely visible through the thick smoke, was a symbol spray-painted onto the far wall. It was a serpent—the familiar looping pattern the very same as the one I'd seen at the motel in New York.

"Holy shit," I whispered. Ice crawled through my veins.

This wasn't just an accident.

This was a message.

CHAPTER THIRTY-FIVE

Serena

The smoke was beginning to burn my throat, the harshness mixing with the salt of my tears as I clung to Anton. I forgot that I was supposed to be furious with him—that I'd stormed away from him just a short time ago. None of that mattered now. Not when my mother was likely inside the burning house.

And the idea that it might be my fault...

My mother. Oh, please, God. I can't lose her.

A fresh wave of grief crashed over me, tearing through my chest. I refused to believe there might be a world without her in it. The thought hit me like a physical blow, and I sucked in a strangled breath. I wanted to believe she'd made it out, but I knew it was highly unlikely. She never left the house at night. Never. But in the off chance that she had, she would have stayed close. The furthest she would have ventured was to a neighbor. If that were the case, she would know what was happening and she'd be here. But she wasn't.

I scanned the chaotic scene, searching again for any sign of her. Firefighters rushed back and forth, shouting commands, dragging hoses, and trying desperately to control the blaze. Red and orange flames licked the edged of the windows. The shutters had long since burned, exposing the exterior stucco walls to the intense heat. They cracked and crumbled, giving way to the vulnerable wood beneath that the fire was quick to devour.

Anton cursed under his breath, his hold on me tightening before his entire body went rigid.

"What?" My voice trembled, barely above a whisper.

His gaze was locked on the house. Something dark and dangerous flashed in his expression. Slowly, he lifted his hand, pointing toward the open front door.

"Serena," he said, his voice low, almost disbelieving. "Look. Inside the front door."

I followed his gaze. At first, all I saw was destruction. The door hung open, the flames kissing the frame. Smoke billowed out in thick plumes, swirling like ghostly fingers into the night sky.

And then I saw it.

A symbol, spray-painted in bold, black strokes on the wall opposite the entryway.

The snake.

The same one from my father's journal. The same one Anton had said was scrawled across my motel room door in New York. The same one that had been tattooed on Cade's neck.

The world tilted beneath me. I shook my head, unable to process what it could mean. Only one thing seemed certain.

This wasn't an accident.

My fingers clutched Anton's shoulders desperate for something—anything—to hold onto.

"I'm taking you back to New York," he said suddenly, his voice hard, leaving no room for argument.

I stiffened, blinking up at him through my tears. "What?"

"You're not safe here." His gaze never left the burning house, his jaw clenched tight. "This was no accident, Serena. I think someone did this."

My mind began to spin just as a sharp pop split the air.

No sooner did the sound register that my body jerked violently. Pain erupted in my shoulder, sharp and burning. A scream ripped from my throat, and my knees buckled.

"Serena!"

Anton's voice roared, but the pain swallowed everything. I couldn't think. My breath came in ragged gasps as heat seared through my body, my vision darkening at the edges. There was movement around me—Anton shifting, shouting—but I was barely seeing it. The world blurred into streaks of orange and black—fire and shadows.

"Someone help! She's been shot!"

My mind fought against the haze, confusion muddling my ability to think.

Shot? Who? Why?

I tried to speak, to force out words, but my lips wouldn't move. My body was no longer my own. It was nothing more than dead weight sinking into Anton's hold. The pain spread, radiating down my arm, into my chest and back. Something was terribly, terribly wrong.

Anton's right. I'm not safe.

He was still shouting, but the words were slipping away, fading into nothing. My vision swam, my mind feeling like the pulsing glow of dying embers. I was falling, sinking into the dark.

The last thing I felt was Anton's hand on my face.

Then, nothing at all.

CHAPTER THIRTY-SIX

Anton

The hospital room was too fucking quiet. Too sterile. The steady beep of the monitors was the only thing breaking the silence, a rhythmic pulse that was both reassuring and driving me insane at the same time.

Serena lay in the hospital bed, her dark lashes a stark contrast against pale cheeks. Her already slender frame looked thinner than usual, and I tried to ignore how frail she appeared. The painkillers had kept her under for most of the past two days, leaving her in a medicated haze. She hadn't been awake long enough to ask questions yet, and it had been a blessing. I wasn't ready to give her the answers she would surely seek. Because when that moment came, I'd have to tell her the truth.

Sylvia Martinelli was dead.

My jaw clenched, and I dragged a hand down my face. I had been by Serena's side since the moment she was admitted, refusing to leave even when the doctors told me she needed rest.

The bullet had gone clean through her shoulder—no major damage, no complications. She would make a full recovery. But knowing that didn't do a damn thing to settle the fury building inside me.

I picked up her hand, brushing my thumb gently over the top of it, careful not to disturb the IV. Someone had done this to her —to *my* princess. Someone had set fire to her world and then tried to end her life with a bullet. I'd spoken to the municipal police, and they claimed to have no leads on who pulled the trigger. That might've been true, but I didn't trust it. There were too many rumors about corruption within Italian law enforcement, and I couldn't take their word for it.

But it was of no concern to me. I'd already made a promise to myself to find the one responsible. I didn't care how far I had to go or what lines I had to cross. They'd made her a target, and now they were mine.

The door opened behind me, and I didn't need to turn to know it was Zeke.

"We need to move," he said without preamble. "It's not safe for you here. Paparazzi are swarming the place. Not sure if it was the police or the firemen, but someone talked and now the whole world knows you're here. I took the liberty of hiring a publicist. She's back in New York, managing the press by releasing regular statements. It will hold off the worst of things for a bit, but a publicist won't do anything to protect Serena. And if someone is after her, you could also have a target on your back."

Not taking my eyes off Serena's sleeping form, I said, "She's not strong enough to go anywhere yet."

"Boss, I can't stress this enough." Zeke stepped closer, his voice low. "I can't protect you here alone. I need more security. The best thing we can do is get you back to New York."

I considered his concern, already formulating a plan to address it, and looked back at Serena's sleeping form. Her features were drawn but peaceful under the haze of pain medication. When she eventually woke, she as in for a world of hurt that no medicine would be able to numb. Her mother was dead, and the one friend she'd mentioned had become estranged. As far as I knew, she had nobody to support and protect her. She was alone, but I wasn't going to let her stay that way.

I turned my attention back to Zeke.

"You're right. Security is better back home. So, we'll bring Serena back to New York with us. She'll be protected there," I said, my voice hardening as the realization of how far I'd go to keep her safe suddenly hit me. I couldn't stomach the thought of anyone trying to hurt her again. I didn't know when or how it happened, but I knew I'd do anything for her.

Zeke nodded once. "What do you propose?"

"The third-floor apartment. Club O," I said without hesitation.

His brow lifted slightly. "You sure?"

"It's the only option," I said flatly. "Nobody other than the members knows the club exists. It's the best-kept secret in New York, hidden in plain sight, and it's the one place no one would ever think to look. We know who's in that club every minute of the day. It's the safest place for her."

"You're probably right. I'll make the travel arrangements for us."

I shook my head. "She's still too weak to travel. She needs time before we can move her—a few days at least."

"Time is a luxury we don't have, but there are options." Zeke studied me for a beat, then continued. "I'll make a few calls, see about booking a private jet—medical-equipped. We can leave by tomorrow."

"Do it," I said with a nod. International travel wouldn't pose a problem. Thankfully, Serena's passport had been in the purse that she'd had with her the day the house burned down. She also had several duffle bags of personal effects in the backseat of her car, presumably bags that she'd never unpacked after leaving

Rome. Zeke had found them the day prior, when he'd gone back to the charred house to look for clues about the shooter.

After Zeke left, I turned my attention back to Serena. Her body was still, her breathing steady. She had no idea what was coming next, or that her entire world was about to change. I wasn't sure how she would handle the news when she woke up. I only hoped that she would trust me enough to manage things until she got better.

I reached for her hand again. It seemed so small in mine, delicate but not fragile—just like her. Serena Martinelli had more fire in her than most men I knew.

But even the strongest needed protecting sometimes.

"I'm bringing you home, princess," I said quietly. "And no one is going to hurt you again."

To be continued...

TAKE ME DARKLY

Dark. Addictive. Unforgiving.
Desire has never been more dangerous.

Anton
I brought Serena to New York to protect her.
She's grieving and fragile, clinging to the edges of a life that's slipping through her fingers.
Locked away in my private club, she tempts me like sin incarnate.
Keeping her safe means navigating a minefield.
The paparazzi want blood.
My empire is under pressure.

And someone still wants her dead.
I should be focused on protecting my interests.
But instead, I'm watching her learn the rules of my world—one secret, one punishment, one breathless surrender at a time.

Serena
They tried to burn me alive.
New York was supposed to be a place to disappear.
Instead, it's a cage—and the man holding the key is the only one I trust.
Anton Romano is irresistible and dangerously addictive.
Inside his club, survival demands I surrender to power, pleasure, and secrets I was never meant to touch.
He doesn't just protect me. He owns me.
But even here, I'm still being hunted.
And when they come for me again, not even Anton may be enough to stop them.

From *USA Today* bestselling author Dakota Willink comes Book 2 in the sinfully addictive Trustfall Trilogy, a seductive tale of obsession, secrets, and survival.

https://geni.us/TakeMeDarkly

TAKE ME UNDER MUSIC PLAYLIST
LISTEN ON SPOTIFY!

Thank you to the musical talents who influenced and inspired *Take Me Under*. Their creativity helped me bring Anton and Serena to life.

"The Elephant" by Lxandra
"Birds of a Feather" by Billie Eilish
"In the End" by Linkin Park
"Believer" by Imagine Dragons
"Love Again" by Dua Lipa
"Say It Right" Nelly Furtado
"Closer" by The Chainsmokers & Halsey
"Take Me Under" by Sakoya
"Breathe" by Tommee Profitt, Fleurie
"Sympathy for the Devil" by Rolling Stones
"Dark Horse" by Katy Perry
"Figure You Out" by VOILÀ
"Pleasure" by Two Feet

FOLLOW

SUBSCRIBE TO DAKOTA'S NEWSLETTER
My newsletter goes out once per week with the occasional sale notice in between. It's packed with new content, giveaways, sales on signed paperbacks, book boxes, and more from my online store. Don't miss out!
SUBSCRIBE HERE: https://dakotawillink.com/subscribe

BOOKS & BOXED WINE CONFESSIONS
Want fun stuff and sneak peek excerpts from Dakota? Join Books & Boxed Wine Confessions and get the inside scoop! Fans in this interactive reader Facebook group are the first to know the latest news!

JOIN HERE: https://www.facebook.com/groups/1635080436793794

MORE FROM DAKOTA WILLINK

THE STONE SAGA

It all began when I forgot my cellphone. He wasn't supposed to be there when I fell. I wasn't supposed to get lost in a sea of sapphire blue when he helped me up. And he wasn't supposed to be the billionaire investor... Alexander Stone.

Discover the dark billionaire romance series that started it all… It's complex, dirty, and wickedly hot.
Alexander Stone will ruin you—in all the best ways.
Welcome to The Shameless Billionaire Club.

THE SOUND OF SILENCE

There's a common expression I remind myself of every day: that which does not kill us, makes us stronger.
People think I live an idyllic life with my perfect husband, but they don't know what lies beneath the façade. Like the delicate petals of the daisies he loved to give, I was easily crushed—broken, just as he wanted me to be.
I've learned to accept what is, but I won't let it destroy me. Instead, I do the only thing I can to survive—I run.

***USA Today* Bestselling Author Dakota Willink delivers an emotionally-gripping, dark romantic suspense that is guaranteed to keep you on the edge of your seat!**

TRIGGER WARNING: This story contains situations of domestic violence and abuse. Some aspects may be sensitive for some readers.

FADE INTO YOU SERIES

He was a gorgeous troublemaker with a cocky attitude. She was the girl he shouldn't want. They only had one summer—and a promise to have no regrets.

What's your favorite trope? Second chance, secret baby, suspense, enemies to lovers, sports romance? *Untouched, Defined, Endurance* **will give you all that and more! Prepare to be left breathless!**

For more titles, please visit www.dakotawillink.com.

ABOUT THE AUTHOR

Dakota Willink is an award-winning *USA Today* Bestselling Author from New York. She loves writing about damaged heroes who fall in love with sassy and independent females. Her books are character-driven, emotional, and sexy, yet written with a flare that keeps them real. With a wide range of publications, Dakota's imagination is constantly spinning new ideas. Her work has been translated into five languages and she has sold over 1 million books worldwide.

Dakota often says she survived her first publishing with coffee and wine. She's an unabashed *Star Wars* fanatic and still dreams of getting her letter from Hogwarts one day. Her daily routines usually include rocking Lululemon yoga pants, putting on lipstick, and obsessing over Excel spreadsheets. Two spoiled Cavaliers are her furry writing companions who bring her regular smiles. She enjoys traveling with her husband and debating social and economic issues with her politically savvy Generation Z son and daughter.

Dakota's favorite book genres include contemporary or dark romance, political & psychological thrillers, and autobiographies.

AWARDS, ACCOLADES, AND OTHER PROJECTS

The Stone Saga is Dakota's first published book series. It has been recognized for various awards and bestseller lists, including *USA Today* and the *Readers' Favorite* 2017 Gold Medal in Romance, and has since been translated into multiple languages internationally.

The *Fade Into You* series (formally known as the *Cadence* duet) was a finalist in the *HEAR Now Festival Independent Audiobook Awards*.

In addition, Dakota has written under the alternate pen name, Marie Christy. Under this name, she has written and published a children's book for charity titled, *And I Smile*.

Also writing as Marie Christy, she was a contributor to the Blunder Woman Productions project, *Nevertheless We Persisted: Me Too*, a 2019 *Audie Award Finalist* and *Earphones Awards Winner*. This project inspired Dakota to write *The Sound of Silence*, a dark romantic suspense novel that tackles the realities of domestic abuse.

Dakota Willink is the founder of Dragonfly Ink Publishing, whose mission is to promote a common passion for reading by partnering with like-minded authors and industry professionals. Through this company, Dakota created the *Love & Lace INKorporated* Magazine and the *Leave Me Breathless World*, hosted ALLURE Audiobook Con, and sponsored various charity anthologies.